Stay Here With Me

Recipes for Romance: Book One

by

Suzie Peters

First Published in 2018
by GWL Publishing
an imprint of Great War Literature Publishing LLP

Produced in United Kingdom

ISBN 978-1-910603-51-2 Paperback Edition

GWL Publishing
Forum House
Sterling Road
Chichester PO19 7DN

www.gwlpublishing.co.uk

Dedication

For S.

Chapter One

Ali

My eyelids are starting to droop. But then, I've been working on the wording for this new mail shot for ages, and I'm getting nowhere with it. I check the time in the corner of my computer screen and decide, at just a few minutes before eleven-thirty pm, that I really should call it a night.

"Are you going to bed any time soon?"

My sister, Tess comes in from her bedroom, walks through the living room into the study area and leans over the back of my chair.

"Yes." I yawn, stretch, and look up at her. She's got shadows under her eyes. "I could ask the same question of you though."

"I've finally finished reading the last book I needed to get through. I've made my notes and, as a result have discovered another two books I really ought to read, so that went well. I was just going to get a glass of water and then I'm giving up – at least for today," she says, going back out into the hallway and through to the kitchen. "How's it going?" she calls.

"It's not." I reach out to switch off my computer, just as my e-mail pings, letting me know I've got a new message. "More junk," I murmur.

"Might not be," Tess says, coming back in and taking a sip from the tall glass of water she's brought with her. "Who knows, it could be Gordon Ramsay, asking you to come and re-design his restaurants for him."

I laugh. "And what would Gordon Ramsay need with a restaurant consultant? I doubt he needs help with his menu, or his decor, or staff management. You have seen those programmes he makes, haven't you?" Tess laughs with me. Still, I can't help it. I go to my mail app and check anyway. It won't be Gordon Ramsay, I know that much.

"Good God," I whisper.

"It's not him, is it?"

"No, of course it isn't. But it is an enquiry from my website." The first one for months.

Tess comes and looks over my shoulder again.

"So it is. Well, that's great," she says, her voice – though still quiet, as usual – full of enthusiasm.

"Before we get too excited, let's see what they want me to do."

I click on the message and wait for it to open, and together, we read:

Hi,

My brothers and I own an Italian restaurant in Hartford. We feel it's in need of a complete makeover, in terms of the menu, the layout of the kitchens and the design of the restaurant itself. I wonder if you could contact me by email, or on the number below to discuss the project and your availability.

I look forward to hearing from you.

Kind regards

Rob Moreno.

I look up at Tess.

"A complete makeover," I whisper. I know what this means. It means weeks of work for one thing. But it also means income. Quite significant income. Don't get me wrong, we're not poor. We're very far from poor. We've got money in the bank – Granny saw to that – but the idea of actually earning again, after the year I've had, feels good. It feels really good.

"It sounds like a big project," Tess says.

"It does. It's a shame he hasn't given me the name of the restaurant, or I could look up their reviews."

"You can ask him that when you get in touch. I take it you are going to get in touch?" she asks.

"Of course. Not now, obviously. It's far too late."

"I guess they've just closed for the evening and he thought he'd send the message before going home."

"Yes, probably. But I doubt he wants to hear back from me right now. Besides, I don't want a potential client thinking I'm still working at this time of day. He'll assume he can call me at midnight every night. No, I'll send him a message in the morning."

She leans over and gives me a hug. "I'm really pleased for you," she says.

"I haven't got it yet." I don't want to get ahead of myself.

"Even so, it shows you were right to get the website re-done."

Tess is right. It might have meant spending quite a bit of money to have the site re-designed, but it seems like it could just have been worth it.

"After what Liam did, I didn't have much choice, did I?"

"It wasn't Liam. It was Fiona."

"I know. But Fiona did what she did because of Liam." I don't cry about him anymore. I did that for the first few weeks after he broke up with me. After the tears, came the anger. Anger that he'd chosen another woman over me, that he'd been seeing her for most of the time we were together and that he'd got her pregnant, and decided to propose to her. I think I was entitled to be angry… bloody angry, actually. And at least the anger helped me to stop crying. Then, after the anger, came the shock. His fiancée, Fiona was one of those online bloggers. I'd never really seen the point of them, not until the night Tess pointed out the item Fiona had written about my company. What was really galling what that, when you searched online for my company, her blog posting came up ahead of my own website. And it was scathing. I can still remember the feeling of cold, abject horror I felt when I read her hurtful words. I contacted Liam by text and insisted he get her to remove the article, or I'd sue her for defamation. He was apologetic and promised he'd deal with it. Two weeks later, when it was still there, I got my father's solicitor to send a letter and she obeyed the demand to remove the posting. By then though, the damage was done. My business was all but dead.

That was when the self-pity started. I wallowed for a while, sitting in the flat, eating custard tarts and chocolate digestives by the packet, and watching episodes of Jeremy Kyle, just to remind myself that there were people out there with worse lives than mine.

Of course, one of the problems with programmes like that is that you get involved. You try and pretend you're not interested but, deep down, you desperately want to know whether the woman who claims she's always been faithful to her boyfriend and that he's just jealous and possessive, really has been cheating on him with his best friend. Normally, I'm the kind of person who flicks through the channels when the adverts come on, but I found myself watching avidly, in case I missed the next instalment of each story. And that's when I realised I had a problem. Not only was I interacting with the people on the TV programme, often shouting, commiserating, or even crying with them, I'd also started to yell abuse at the adverts as well. There was one in particular, that got shown in pretty much every ad break and became really annoying. It was for a company that handled personal injury claims. They made a big deal about all of their lawyers being personal injury specialists and, after the third time of hearing their slogan that particular morning, I found myself screaming at the screen that they wouldn't be much use if they were private fucking wealth lawyers, would they? It was a sobering moment, especially as I don't usually swear very much. It was almost as sobering as the moment, later that day, when Tess arrived back home at the same time as our online grocery delivery and, as she signed for it and began unpacking, she informed me that I hadn't actually ordered any food – not real food anyway. I'd ordered custard tarts, chocolate digestives – in both milk and plain flavours, in case I felt like a change – tea, coffee, bottled water, toilet rolls and bleach. And that was pretty much it.

By then, there was also the tiny matter that I was living in old leggings because I couldn't actually do up the zip on my jeans anymore. The way I saw it, I had a choice. I either consumed all the custard tarts I'd ordered, with a bleach chaser, or I snapped out of it.

I snapped out of it.

In fact, I decided to re-invent myself. I changed my website, updated my company logo, buried the TV remote down the back of the sofa, and threw out the custard tarts and digestives. I even ordered real food, and got it delivered the next day. We could eat properly again.

I changed my hairstyle and started going to the gym. I lost the pounds I'd gained and – most important of all – I learned to smile again.

Tess nudges me. "Stop thinking about him," she says.

"I wasn't," I lie. "Okay, I was, but not in the way you think. I'm over him now."

"Good, because he was never good enough for you."

"I know." I really do. She's right. Liam was only ever interested in Liam and I want a man who's interested in me. There's got to be one out there somewhere, hasn't there?

"It's going to mean you being away quite a lot, isn't it?" Tess says, nodding to the computer screen.

"Well, Hertford's only about an hour away – depending on the traffic."

"I think you might have to help this guy with his spelling," she says, pointing to the screen.

"Why?" I follow the direction of her finger.

"Because he can't spell Hertford, and he lives there – or at least works there."

I look more closely and she's absolutely right. He's spelt it with an 'a', instead of an 'e'.

"Well, he doesn't need to be able to spell, I guess." I cast an eye over the rest of the message. "He seems to have got everything else right." And then my gaze settles on the telephone number. "That's odd."

"What?"

"The phone number," I say.

"What about it."

"It's got too many digits. And it starts… Oh, my God." Realisation dawns on me.

"What's wrong?" Tess asks.

"It's not Hertford in Hertfordshire. It's Hartford in Connecticut."

"In America?" Her voice has dropped to a whisper.

"Yes."

"I—I suppose that would explain why he was getting in touch at this unholy hour of the night. What's the time difference?" she asks.

"Five hours, I think. So it's six-thirty pm there."

"I suppose you could maybe call him now then."

I look up at her. "I probably should. If I wait until tomorrow, I won't be able to call until the afternoon." I let out a long sigh. "The thing is, Tess, this changes everything."

"Why?" she asks.

How can she not understand? "Because if I take this job, I'll have to leave you on your own. I'll be gone for two or three months."

"During which time I'll be busy writing my dissertation." She moves around and perches on my desk. "I'll be okay," she says, trying to sound stronger than she is. "You've got to at least try and get this job, Ali."

"I can't."

"You must. I won't forgive myself if you turn it down because of me." I can hear the emotion in her voice and I swallow down my own. "You need this," she says.

"And you need me." She does. Tess has never been strong. We've been glued together since our parents died. The thought of breaking that bond for two or three months is almost unthinkable.

"We can text, and call, and Skype," she says. "And I'm twenty-one now. I need to try and stand on my own two feet at some time." I wish I could believe she meant that. "At least make the call," she adds. "See what this guy has to say for himself, find out how much they really want to do and if it's worth your while, then we'll decide from there." She holds out the telephone to me.

I take it, looking up into her eyes, and she smiles down at me. "Okay," I say, checking my computer screen and dialling the number before I can change my mind.

"Rosa's. How can I help you?" The voice on the end of the line is deep, soft, and obviously American, but sounds a little harassed.

"May I speak with Rob Moreno, please," I say in my best 'office' voice.

"This is Rob. What can I do for you?" He's polite, I'll give him that.

"My name's Alison Bishop. You sent me a message about upgrading your restaurant."

"Oh yes," he says, sounding surprised. "I didn't expect to hear back from you today."

"Well, I was working on something else when your message came in."

"I see. Um... Can you just give me a minute?" There's a pause.

"Yes, of course." I wait, listening to the noises in the background. He's covered the mouthpiece and all I can hear are muffled voices and the occasional clinking of a glass. Then, after a minute or so, the noise diminishes and then disappears altogether and I wonder if we've been cut off.

"Hi," he says. "I've just come back into the office. I can't hear myself think in the restaurant."

"Oh, I see."

"So, you got my message?"

"Yes. I just wanted to get a brief idea of what you were looking for. You... you do understand that I'm based in England, don't you?"

"Yeah. I chose your company intentionally. I wanted to get a European feel for this place."

"Your restaurant is Italian. Why didn't you look at Italian designers?"

"Because I came across your website, I went to your personal profile, and I liked what I saw."

I can feel myself blushing. He's flirting with me. I can't even remember the last time a man flirted with me, but I can remember that it feels good. Even so, I need to stop smiling and focus.

"What exactly is it you're looking for, Mr Moreno?" I ask, trying to sound as businesslike as possible.

"Call me Rob, please." He's not going to let me. "It's kinda hard to explain over the phone," he says. "I was hoping you'd be able to come over and take a look at the place, and that we could sit down together – you, me and my brothers – and discuss what you can do for us."

"You want me to fly to America?"

"Yeah."

"At who's expense?" I ask. It's not that I can't afford it, but I want to know the kind of people I'm dealing with.

"Well," he says, "how about we agree a compromise on that?"

"Such as?"

"You buy your ticket. There's a hotel just a couple of doors away from the restaurant; you can stay there. If we end up employing you, the air fare and hotel costs can be part of your fee."

"And if not?"

"Then I'll reimburse you."

That seems fair. Either way, I'm not out of pocket. After all, it's his choice to ask me over there.

"Okay," I say, looking up at Tess. She's nodding her head. "When do you want me to come over?"

"Is the end of this week too soon?" he asks.

I think about all the things I've got to organise. "No. I should be able to manage that."

"Great." He sounds really enthusiastic. "We'll look forward to meeting you."

We end the call and I hang up, and put the phone down carefully on my desk, unable to believe what's just happened.

"So, you're going then?" Tess asks.

"For a preliminary meeting, yes."

"And if they give you the job?"

"Then depending on the start date, I imagine I could well have to stay out there. There won't be any point in coming back here. I'll have to source suppliers and contractors." I look up at her. "Are you okay with that?"

She nods and leans forward, hugging me. "Yes. Like I said, you need this, Ali."

She's right. I do.

Sam

Jane's eyes fill with tears, but I'm not easily moved, and as much as I know this is for real, I just stand and look at her.

"I'm sorry, Sam," she whispers.

"I know you are."

"I don't know what else to say."

Neither do I, if I'm honest, so we stand and look at each other for an awkward moment before I realize that, as her boss – well, one of them – I should take the lead.

"I know it's not your fault, Jane." Well it is, but blaming her isn't gonna help. "But we had three customers send their steaks back tonight. Steaks you'd cooked."

"I know," she snivels. Why do women do that?

"You've been here for over two years now. I thought we were beyond the stage of me having to check your work, but I think the best thing is if we go back to that – at least for the time being." I pause. She's supposed to be in charge of her section, and this is a backward step for both of us – one which is going to take up a lot of my time, but needs must. "I want you to pass everything by me before you serve it. Okay?"

She nods and wipes her nose on the crumpled Kleenex in her hand.

"I'm really sorry, Sam."

"It's okay. Just try and get it right tomorrow."

She nods and sniffles again, then ducks past me and back into the kitchen.

"You could have been a bit kinder." I turn and come face-to-face with Rob, who's just come out of the office. He leans against the wall of the corridor that leads from the restaurant to the kitchens, the office and the entrance to my apartment.

"I *was* being kind, compared to how I might've been. And besides, I'm her boss, not her counsellor."

"Her boyfriend just left her for another woman," he says.

"And?" Ed had already given me this nugget of information earlier in the day, while suggesting I cut her some slack after I yelled at her for the second time in her shift.

Ed opens the door to the kitchen, letting it swing shut behind him, then leans on the wall beside it, opposite Rob. "I guess it went well with Jane," he says. "She just ran out the back door in tears."

"Why is this my fault?" I look from one of my brothers to the other. To be honest, it's kinda confusing, being as they're twins and – if it wasn't for the fact that Ed's got longer hair and is wearing chef's whites, while Rob's dressed all in black – they're pretty much identical.

"Because you've been on her case all evening," Rob says. "You, better than either of us, know how she must be feeling." That was a bit low. Okay, so we all know that my ex-wife cheated on me, but I don't need Rob, or anyone else reminding me.

"Thanks for that," I say, going to move past them toward the kitchen.

"Sorry," Rob murmurs. I ignore him and push through the double doors.

The whole room has been cleaned down now, the surfaces cleared and sparkling clean, and everyone's gone home for the night. Apart from Jane's mistakes, it was a good service – and by 'good', I mean 'busy'. I like it when it's busy, because then I don't have time to think. I don't like thinking these days, because all I tend to think about is Amber. I shake my head to banish the memories just as Rob and Ed come in behind me.

"I need to talk to you," Rob says and I turn to face him, glad of the intrusion for once.

While they may look the same – apart from the hair – my brothers couldn't be more different in their temperaments. Where Ed is shy, quiet and placid, Rob is playful, mischievous and downright annoying. Ed works with me in the kitchen, although we don't really do the same things. I'm in charge – and that makes Ed quite happy. He's a pastry chef – and that makes me completely delirious, because I'm really, really useless when it comes to pastry and desserts. And Ed is absolutely brilliant. He'd be even better, if he'd just have little bit more self-confidence, but then Rob says I've got enough for both of us. That's not true. I just tend to hide my professional insecurities better, especially in front of him. Rob works front of house, meeting and greeting the guests, showing them to their tables and making sure they're happy. And, if they should happen to be female, under thirty and vaguely attractive, it's highly unlikely that they'll leave without Rob picking up their phone number. He's the most outrageous flirt I've ever met – and I should know; I was married to the best. Fuck… that's Amber getting into my head again.

"What's up?" I ask, sitting up on one of the preparation surfaces.

Rob and Ed lean against the countertop opposite. "I've got something to tell you." Rob looks from me to Ed and back again. For once, I get the feeling even Ed doesn't know what's going on.

"What have you been up to?" I ask Rob.

He looks down at his own feet. "Earlier today, I—I contacted a restaurant consultant—"

"A what?" I interrupt him.

"A restaurant consultant. It's someone who comes into places like this and checks out what we could be doing better, then puts it right."

I can feel my anger starting to rise already.

"Okay," Ed says. "And?"

"And I asked her if she'd come visit us."

"Why?" I ask him.

"Because we need to update this place," he says, looking me in the eyes.

"We do?"

"Yeah. And you know it."

He's right. I do know, but that doesn't mean I'm gonna take this lying down. "And we need someone else to help with this, because…?"

"Because we're all too busy," he replies. "If we wait for the three of us to get around to it, we'll all be retired."

"What's she coming to look at?" Ed asks.

"Re-designing the outside of the restaurant, the restaurant itself…" He pauses. "Updating the kitchens and the menus."

"What?" I yell.

"Don't fly off the handle," he says.

"Why the fuck not?" I jump down from the countertop. I'm a couple of inches taller than both of them and I walk over, using my full height. "Where the hell do you get off making a decision like this without asking Ed and me?" I ask Rob.

"I haven't made a decision," he replies, holding his hands up in surrender to my foul temper. "I've just asked her to come over at the end of the week and take a look, then sit down with us and discuss what she can do to help."

"Come over?" I repeat. "Come over from where?"

"From England."

"England?" Even Ed's staring at him now. "Why England?"

Rob sighs. "Because I thought we could use a European angle."

I run my fingers through my short hair. "Our restaurant is Italian. We're Italian-American. So, if you really had to go down this route, then an Italian, or an American I could've understood. But someone from England?"

He smirks. "Funnily enough, she said that."

"Then maybe you should've damn well listened to her. She's making more sense than you are. How the fuck is some pompous English woman gonna have a clue about us and our market?"

"She's not pompous. She sounds really nice."

Light starts to dawn. "Oh Christ. Don't tell me, you saw her picture on her website and she's a beautiful brunette."

"No. She's a beautiful blonde, actually."

"Fucking hell, Rob." I raise my voice – again. "Did you have any other reason for choosing her, apart from her photograph giving you a hard-on?"

"Yeah," he says, sounding offended. "She has some really good testimonials on her website."

"All of which could be faked," I tell him, stating the obvious.

"I'm not an idiot." I'm tempted to question that. "I looked up the places who'd given her the reviews. And then I contacted them by email and asked for their real opinion."

"And?"

"And they all told me she's absolutely brilliant at what she does." I don't really have a reply to that. He obviously did his homework. "And her fees are more reasonable than any of the other consultants I looked at."

Speaking of money… "Who's paying for her to come over here?"

"She is."

Is she crazy? "Really? She's gonna pay to come over here, not knowing if she's gonna get the job?"

He looks at the floor again. "Well, I said if we didn't give her the job, I'd reimburse her."

"*You* will?" I ask.

"Yeah. *Me*, not the restaurant. I get that it's my idea. I get that I went ahead and did this without consulting you guys, so I'll pay for her flight, if we don't end up using her. If we do give her the job, we've agreed that she can add it to the fee."

It seems fair – although I don't want to admit it.

"When's she coming over, did you say?" Ed asks him.

"At the end of the week."

"You don't have a precise day, or time?" I say.

He shakes his head. "No. She's got things to arrange at her end."

"So all we know is that she's gonna be here sometime before the weekend."

"Yeah." Rob looks me in the eye.

I shrug. "Okay… well, on your head be it. I'll listen to what she has to say, but I just hope you're ready to pay the woman back, because she'd gonna have to be real impressive for me to let her have anything to do with this place."

Chapter Two

Ali

"If anything crops up, or even if you just want to talk, then call me. Don't worry about the time difference." I look into Tess's eyes to make sure she's listening and that she understands.

"I'm not going to wake you in the middle of the night, just for a chat," she says.

"I won't mind. I'd rather you did," I tell her. I'm still not sure this is a good idea, even though my bag is packed and the taxi is waiting downstairs to take me to the airport.

"I've written down all the numbers you'll need and stuck them on the fridge door," I repeat for about the tenth time and she rolls her eyes at me. The list of contacts I've left her with is huge – everything from the restaurant I'm going to be working in, to our doctor and dentist, and even a local handyman. Tess has never had to deal with any kind of emergency, so I figured I'd better try and cover all the angles.

"I'll be fine," she says, her voice wobbling just a little. "Now go." She gives me a last, tight hug, then steps back and opens the door, like she's dismissing me. I know this is her way of coping, and to prolong the 'goodbye' is only going to make it worse for both of us.

"I'll text you when I get there," I tell her, picking up my case.

"Try and enjoy yourself," she says as I pass her and go out through the door.

"I should be so lucky." I turn and smile at her, and she manages a smile back.

*

The taxi driver is quiet, thank goodness, because I'm not in the mood for making small-talk with a stranger. My head is too full of Tess and I'm still debating asking the man to turn around and take me back home. I've left her alone for a few days before – but if I get this job, it could take between two and three months. My visa doesn't permit me to stay any longer than that, anyway. I keep trying to tell myself that she'll manage, but that's never been Tess's strong point. And that's not surprising really, not after what she's been through.

There's a seven year age-gap between us, so we grew up almost as two only-children. I had my friends; Tess had hers. We didn't do 'sister' things together as children – it wasn't practical. When she was into dolls and dressing up, I was into make-up, boys and rock music. We were thrown together when I was fifteen though. I was spending the weekend with a friend of mine – Suzanna – because her mum was taking us to the Glastonbury Festival, and to say I was excited is the understatement of the century. Suzanna's mum was a bit of a hippy. Well, she still is, if the truth be told, but we had such a great time, despite the rain, the floods, the absolutely awful mud – that is, until two policemen arrived. How they found our tent among all the others, I'll never know, but they did. They woke us up and told us to get dressed, and took all three of us to their car where they sat me down, and told me that my parents had been killed. They were very kind, very gentle and sympathetic when they informed me that my whole world had changed forever. Suzanna's mum held me while I cried and cried. It was only later that I discovered the full story. My parents often lit candles in the evenings and it was thought that they'd gone to bed, having forgotten to blow one out – probably the really wide one with three wicks, which was on the table by the window. It seems they'd also left the window slightly open, because it was a warm night and they'd presumably opened it earlier, then closed the curtains and forgotten about it. They'd done that before, on several occasions, only to come downstairs in the morning to find the room a little damp and the window wide open. The curtain must have blown in the breeze, touched the flames of the candle, and caught fire – at least, that was the conclusion that was drawn at the inquest. My parents and Tess were all asleep upstairs and it was our neighbour from down the lane, Mr Bowen, returning from an evening out, who'd raised the alarm and called the fire brigade. My dad had managed to get into Tess's room and had dropped her from the window, into the arms of Mr Bowen, below. Despite Tess's screams that he should jump down, he'd then disappeared back into the house, saying he was going to get our mother. We never saw either of our parents again.

The police followed Suzanna's mum's car when she drove me to the hospital. Tess wasn't burned, but she was suffering from smoke inhalation and shock. Our grandmother was sitting at her bedside and seemed to have aged twenty years in an instant. She hugged me, while not letting go of Tess's hand, and I cried into her shoulder.

I can still remember turning around and looking down at Tess's slight eight year old frame lying in the bed, staring at the ceiling, her eyes blank, her lips closed. The hospital released her after a couple of days, but her eyes stayed blank and her lips stayed closed for nearly two years. The only noise she made was to scream. She screamed every night – the memories of the fire, of what had happened, haunting her.

We lived with granny from then on. We went to school, we came home and did our homework, we sat in front of the fire in the evenings, watching TV. At weekends, we walked granny's two dogs in the Surrey Hills where she lived. Granny chatted away to both of us, even though she didn't expect Tess to answer.

Granny took care of us in so many ways. She was there for us whenever we needed her, but she also handled all of our parents' affairs. Our mother was rich in her own right, and our father had worked in the City, although I'm not entirely sure what he did. As a result, they left several properties and quite a lot of money. Granny arranged for the sale of the land on which our burnt-out home had once stood. That brought in a tidy sum which, together with the cash they had in the bank and dad's investments, was held in trust until we reached the age of twenty-one. In addition, there was the flat in London – in which we now live, and a beautiful cottage on the Dorset coast. Granny put that in the hands of local agents and it has been rented out to various long-term tenants ever since, and gives us a regular income. She was a canny business woman, our grandmother, as a result of which, we're very comfortable indeed.

For a while, I honestly thought Tess might never speak again, but then, one day, in the summer holidays, two years after the fire, I made a cup of tea for all of us and brought it out into the garden, to find Tess talking to one of the dogs. Granny put her finger to her lips and together we just watched in stunned silence. I remember standing with tears rolling down my cheeks and Tess eventually noticed and came over, putting her arms around me and whispering, "Don't cry, Ali."

Over the following weeks and months, she slowly told us what she remembered of that night. Her most vivid memory was always of our father holding her close in his arms, kissing her forehead and whispering that she'd be safe, that she mustn't be scared, and that she had to trust him. She'd nodded and then he'd lowered her as far as he could out of the window, before dropping her into the arms of Mr Bowen. She remembered screaming for him and him calling that he'd come down when he'd got mummy. He'd shouted that he loved her, and told her to tell me he loved me too, and then he'd disappeared into the house. She remembered trying to struggle free of Mr Bowen, but that he'd held tightly onto her. And then the fire brigade had arrived.

They found mum and dad in their own bedroom, lying together on the bed, in each other's arms. At the inquest, the senior fire officer said our father didn't seem to have even tried to rescue our mother, or to have escaped himself, which confused a lot of people at the time. Not me though. You see, although I always hated the idea that he'd abandon Tess and me, there is a part of me that understood it. I think he already knew mummy was gone, before he even went to find Tess. That's why he told her he loved us like that. I'd always known how close our parents were, and the idea of him carrying on without her seems… well, impossible. I believe that, rather than leave her behind, he simply chose to lie down and die with her. Over the years, that belief has made it easier for us to bear their loss.

It's probably also given us a slightly unrealistic view of men and romance, but you can't have everything.

Looking down at the Atlantic, I'm a little less worried about Tess now. Well, I'm not, but my worries for her have been superseded by my concerns about the contract I may be about to take on. I've been doing this for nearly four years – well, three, I suppose. You can't count the last year of tears, anger, wallowing and re-building. So, that's three years. In that time, I've worked on maybe eight or ten projects – some big, some small – and they've all gone really well, so I should be feeling confident. But I'm not, for all sorts of reasons. I've never handled an overseas contract at all and I've always been recommended to each client by a previous one, so I've had a kind of introduction, rather than going in 'cold', as it were. Not knowing who I'm going to meet – that's part of what's scaring me the most. What if they're horrible to me? No, I'm being silly. That won't happen. They asked me to help them, and besides, Rob had a soft, gentle voice. I'm sure it'll be fine.

Some of those early clients were kind enough to give me testimonials that I used on my new website. After Fiona's blog-bashing, I needed all the help I could get. I take a deep breath and square my shoulders, recalling all the complimentary things that they said about my work. I need to pull myself together and remember that I'm really not bad at this, otherwise these Americans are never going to believe I can achieve anything for them and their restaurant.

Thinking about all of that is making me feel a little queasy, so I close my eyes and let my thoughts drift back…

Once Tess started talking, things got a bit easier. There was less tension, anyway, although her nightmares continued. They still do, occasionally. But granny and I were there for her, and between us, we made it through those first few years.

I stayed with her at granny's until I turned eighteen, and then I went to catering school. I moved into our father's old flat in North London, which wasn't far from where I was studying, and once I'd finished there, I managed to get a job working in a restaurant just around the corner. A couple of job changes later, and I was really doing well, working in a two-Michelin star restaurant in Central London, being yelled at by a better class of chef. A year or so later though, I'd got fed up with men shouting at me nearly all day and most of the night, assuming that their opinions, their ways of doing things were always right, and better than mine. I also got fed up with the patronising misogyny, with being given menial tasks and overlooked for promotions just because I had to tie my hair up before going into the kitchen, and because I occasionally had to take slightly longer toilet breaks, at a certain time of the month, every month, so at the age of twenty-four, I quit. If I'm being honest, there was another reason behind that decision. I was afraid. Suzanna was getting married, and she'd asked me to be a bridesmaid. I was going to be a bridesmaid. And I was still a virgin. A chef's hours are not entirely conducive to dating. When most people are sitting across a candlelit table, staring into the eyes of someone they love – or at least vaguely fancy – before falling into bed with them, chefs are still working. We get to collapse into bed, usually bone tired, sometime after midnight, six nights a week. The thought of having to actually do anything with another person before falling into a deep sleep is – frankly – ludicrous.

I have quite a lot of friends, a few of whom seemed to either be getting married or having kids at the time. The idea of attending another wedding – or Christening – in any capacity, and still being a virgin, didn't inspire me.

So, I decided to change my career, use some of my inheritance to take a couple of short courses at the local college, and started my own business, becoming a restaurant consultant. The hours were long, but they were more 'normal'; there was a lot less stress, and nobody shouted at me. I had it made.

And then, I met Liam.

For a while, everything seemed perfect. Okay, so the sex wasn't quite what I'd anticipated. Suzanna had been quite vivid in her descriptions. Her husband's French – they now live in Paris – and she'd regaled me with heady stories of steamy nights in his beautiful Montmartre apartment. I'd been to stay with them a couple of times and, based on the noises coming from their bedroom, I'd anticipated something spectacular, mind-blowing, life-altering even. In reality, it was just 'nice'. Such an inadequate word, but there really isn't another one that describes sex with Liam any better. It was 'nice'. But then our relationship was 'nice' too. It was kind of like walking along a quiet, pretty riverside path, in parallel lines, putting one foot in front of the other, always aware that someone else was walking beside you, but not always feeling the need to do anything about it. Every so often, we'd get together – always clumsily, and always in bed – we'd move around a bit, he'd come and sometimes I would too, and then we'd just go back to walking along the path again. I started to wonder if that's how it is for everyone; or whether maybe it's just the French who can make love like it really matters.

Despite the disappointing sex, for three years, being with Liam really was quite 'nice'. He moved in after a couple of months, but he wasn't at the flat the whole time. He worked for a football club, in the marketing department, and was never around at weekends and sometimes midweek as well, if they had matches. Even during the off-season, he'd have to travel a lot for meetings. I suppose he was with me three or four nights a week. Still, I was busy too, and he was very romantic and supportive. He bought me flowers and jewellery, paid me compliments, held my hand in public – he even held my handbag in public a couple of times. He accepted Tess moving into the flat when she started university in London about a year after we got together, and looked out for her – kind of like a big brother. He was there for both of us when granny died eighteen months ago. He came to the funeral and, while I held onto Tess as she sobbed into me, he held onto both of us. He brought us home again and helped me deal with granny's estate. I really thought I couldn't have found a better man than him. And then I found out it was all a big fat lie, and that Liam was a big fat fake. He wasn't travelling to football matches at all. He had another home – one that he owned – which he shared with another woman, living a different life. And the fact that he'd included Tess in his betrayal made it just a little bit harder to take. It felt like he was letting us both down.

I've found that one of the hardest things to forgive. He knew what had happened to her, he knew how vulnerable she is, and he let her trust him too.

*

There's an underground car park beneath the hotel. Rob sent me details of how to get here and I've followed them precisely – which meant driving past the restaurant, being as it's five doors down from the hotel. At first glance, all I can say is, it's going to be a learning curve.

The hotel is very comfortable. I've had a shower – which I needed – and I've changed into a dress, rather than jeans and a sweater. I feel as though I should at least try and create a good impression. I've booked a table at the restaurant for seven-thirty, but not in my own name. I know Rob's seen my photograph on the internet, but I look a little different since that was taken. My hair style is different, and it's slightly lighter – thanks to the Caribbean holiday that Tess and I took at Christmas; I'm tanned – also thanks to the holiday, and I've lost all the weight I gained during my wallowing season. If he does recognise me, then I'll have to come clean, but I'd rather do what I usually do, which is to have an unobtrusive meal in the restaurant, watch how they work, taste the food, get a feel for the place. And then, at the end of the evening, I'll tell him who I am, and arrange a time to meet him and his brothers tomorrow, so we can talk things through. It's not underhand, it's logical. I can't give them a fair opinion if they've put on a 'show' for me.

I stand outside the restaurant for a few minutes. It's got a fairly wide frontage, and I can see that, when it's warmer – rather than a chilly mid February evening – they could probably have seating outside. However, the decor out here is really out of date and a little brash for my tastes. There are three wide windows, onto which the Italian flag has been painted – one colour in each section – and over the top of this, lettering has been placed, explaining the type of dishes on offer. The rest of the frontage is made up of dark wood panelling, which has seen better days.

I open the door at seven-thirty on the dot and take a quick look around. It's a big place and there's a huge amount of potential here, which is currently being wasted, mainly because that wood panelling that I saw outside is continued in here, making it really dark, despite the wall and ceiling lights. A very good looking man, dressed entirely in black, approaches. His clothes fit him perfectly, showing off his muscular body, and he gives me the benefit of a broad, wide smile that reveals brilliant, white teeth. His eyes are brown, his hair is short and spiked. He exudes self-confidence. He's lovely to look at, and really not my type.

"Good evening," he says, and I know I'm speaking to Rob. His voice is deep, and soft, just as I remember it.

"Hello," I reply. "I've booked a table in the name of Suzanna Peterson." She's not Suzanna Peterson anymore. She's Suzanna Leclerc. But I use her name a lot.

He checks a book on a lectern. "You're dining alone?" he remarks. I nod my head. "Really? A beautiful lady like yourself?"

Oh, seriously? I smile. "Yes," I reply.

He picks up a menu and beckons me to follow him. We pass through the busy restaurant, and en route to my table, which is near the back, he nods to a few customers, and occasionally checks that they're happy. I like his style. He's friendly and attentive, and it feels genuine. The customers clearly like him too.

He holds the chair while I sit and remove my wrap, placing it on the seat beside me.

"Can I get you something from the bar?" he asks.

"Just a white wine. What would you recommend?" I look up at him, placing my hands on the table – more dark wood. This will all have to go.

He gives me the benefit of his smile again. It's a little contagious. "We have a really good Pinot Grigio delle Venezie," he replies. "Or you could try the Verdicchio dei Castelli di Jesi." His accent makes my smile broaden.

"Which is the dryer?" I ask him. I don't mind either and I know roughly what they'll both taste like, but I want to know if he does.

"Well," he says, looking into my eyes. "The Pinot Grigio has a hint of citrus and green apple, but the Verdicchio is more fruity, more mellow. I always think it tastes like pineapples and apricots, and at the every end, there's a flavour that's kinda like burnt almonds."

"It sounds as though you're recommending the Verdiccio," I say.

"It's one of my favourites," he replies.

"Okay, I'll take a glass."

"Excellent choice." He still hasn't taken his eyes from mine. "Ria will be your waitress for this evening," he says, "but if you need anything – anything at all – just ask for Roberto."

I nod and give him a final smile and he turns away toward the back of the restaurant, going down a short corridor and through some double doors, with round windows at head height. I try hard not to laugh. He was fun – flirty, but fun.

Sam

As if having Jane wandering around the place all week with a face like a slapped fish wasn't bad enough, after Rob's revelation that he'd invited an English woman over to take a look at the restaurant, there's been an awkward atmosphere between the two of us as well. Ed and I spent all of Wednesday and Thursday, between the lunchtime and evening services, clearing up the kitchens, giving them a thorough clean, just in case this woman decides she needs to inspect everything. She's English – she's gonna be picky. And I'm not having her find any fault in my kitchens.

I'm still not really talking to Rob. It feels like he blames me for the problems in the restaurant. After all, any establishment is only as good as the food it serves. And the food is only as good as the chef. And I'm the chef. What he doesn't realize is that I've been wanting to change the menu for ages – pretty much since the three of us took over this place. We've been stuck using dad's recipes for years, simply because we haven't had the time or the impetus to do anything about it.

It's not just that though. We might own this place jointly – and have the paperwork to prove it – but Rob and Ed have always kind of deferred to me. This is the first time either of them has done anything like this and I really resent the fact that Rob didn't come and talk to me about it first, especially as he seems to have done it in such a disorganized fashion. We don't even know when this damn woman is arriving. We've made it as far as Friday lunchtime unscathed, so I guess she may turn up sometime tonight. But then, she might not get here until tomorrow. Trust Rob to be too busy looking at her photograph that he forgot to get all the details.

I'm taking advantage of the quiet period before the evening service to have a final clear up. Call it paranoia – call it what you like – I like to keep a clean kitchen. I take pride in what I do. I always have done. And these days, that's about the only thing I've got to take pride in.

It wasn't always like that. A few years ago, I had a lot to be proud of, but then Amber came into my life and took away my pride, together with my self-respect, and while she was at it, she trampled my ego into the ground as well.

But that's Amber for you.

It's hard not to think about her when I'm working in here. I stop cleaning down the countertop and lean back against it for a moment, closing my eyes and remembering…

I still find it hard to believe it was only four years ago that I first met her. She'd come here for a meeting with Rob, but he was sick that day, so I saw her instead and I've often wondered how differently things would have turned out, if Rob had been here… if he'd seen her, and I'd stayed in the kitchen in blissful ignorance.

She worked for the wine supplier we used at the time and, as soon as she arrived, punctually at the appointed time, I couldn't take my eyes off her. She told me she represented the wine merchant and I discovered she had a deep, sexy voice that matched her perfect, hourglass figure, Titian-red hair, full lips, deep green eyes, and long, long legs. I already knew from Rob that she was new to the job and hadn't been here before, so I took her down to the cellar, but before I could even ask her name, she'd walked right over to me and placed one hand on my chest, and the other on my cock. Yeah, I was shocked, but I was also flattered. And hard. It was real clear what she wanted, and so did

I. She was wearing a tight business suit, with the highest heels I've ever seen and, without even thinking about it, I yanked up her skirt. She wasn't wearing panties, which kinda took my breath away for a couple of seconds – but it really was only a couple of seconds – before I pushed her back against the wall, putting one of my hands behind her head, while undoing my jeans with the other. I parted her feet with mine and was just about to push my dick inside her, when she stopped me and I thought she was gonna to say she didn't want to carry on – which, let's face it, would have made her the biggest cock tease of all time. But she didn't. Instead, she turned around so she was facing the wall, and told me to fuck her – hard. She stuck her ass out at me and I obliged, pinning her to the wall, with her hands above her head, and pounding into her. I can't deny the sex was amazing. Maybe it was more amazing because it was so impersonal. We'd barely spoken, and afterwards, she straightened her clothes and got on with the meeting, like nothing had happened. When she left, I still didn't even know her name.

Later that night, just after the restaurant had closed, I was on my own in the kitchen, finishing up. Ed had already gone upstairs and Rob was still in his sick bed, when there was a knock on the door. I opened it and she was standing there, wearing a coat and those same killer high heels. I didn't say a word, but stepped to one side and let her in. I closed the door and, when I turned around, she'd removed the coat and was standing, totally naked – except for the fuck-me heels – in the middle of the kitchen.

She sat up on the countertop, raising one foot up on the surface, exposing her naked wet pussy and, when I walked over, she grabbed me by the back of my neck, forcing me down, making it clear what she wanted – again. Although I really didn't like her pushing me around, she was the sexiest woman I'd ever seen, so I didn't argue. Well, who would, when faced with that? I licked and fingered her until she came, and then I fucked her on every surface in the room. Eventually, after more orgasms than I can remember, she put the coat back on and left. She hadn't said a word throughout the whole time she'd been there, and I'd found that one of the most erotic parts of the whole experience. It was like fucking a total stranger – a very willing, total stranger. When

I managed to stand properly, I noticed she'd left her business card on the surface by the back door. At least I knew her name now: Amber Ferguson.

She wasn't my first – obviously. My first was Ella, a kitchen hand who worked for my dad. I was eighteen, she was in her early twenties, I guess. I never actually knew her age. She took my virginity in the dry store cupboard, rolling a condom over my dick, then bending over, holding onto the shelving unit and telling me what to do. It didn't take me long to come that time, but we kept at it and I got better. According to Ella, I got a lot better, and we were always sneaking around the kitchen – usually quite late at night – fucking whenever and wherever we got the chance, for the next couple of years. We never actually dated at all. We never even saw each other outside the restaurant. We just had sex. And then one day she got another job. In Boston. She didn't look back and, if I'm being honest, neither did I. Ella was the one who gave me my taste for control and domination. Although she'd taken charge the first time, I took the lead from then on. I called the shots, and she so clearly loved it that way. Obviously, I did too, but the sneaking around was starting to grate a little. I wanted to have sex completely on my terms – and my way – not just when the circumstances suited. After Ella, there were a few dry months, and then I found someone else who liked the control thing too. She hung around for a few weeks, but then she wanted more – she wanted to date. I didn't. We broke up – not that we'd ever really been 'together' – not in the conventional sense, anyway. And so, the pattern was set. I'd meet someone, establish they were into the same kind of things as me, we'd have sex. My way. We'd have quite a lot of sex usually, and then they'd start talking about dinner, movies, spending the night together, why we never did anything but fuck, why everything *always* had to be on my terms – like they hadn't understood that from the start. And then we'd 'break up', because I didn't want a relationship. I didn't want to commit to anything more complicated than sex. Well, with my job it's kinda hard to commit to anything – hell, even drinking a cup of coffee while it's still hot can be a challenge.

Then Amber came along. In the cold light of day, the morning after I fucked her every which way around the kitchen, I realized how stupid I'd been – having unprotected sex with her, several times over – and I texted her number and asked if she was on birth control. She replied a day later, a very worrying day later, saying she was. I then asked if she was clean. I hadn't asked her that in my first message because I'd kinda hoped she'd come across with the information by herself. She didn't. She took forty-eight hours to confirm she was. I was more than relieved. I asked if she wanted to meet up again, but I didn't hear back from her until late the following week, when she arrived one night unannounced at the kitchen door for a repeat performance… and so it continued. Always on her terms. I should've seen the signs.

A couple of weeks after that, we had our first row. I know we were up in the apartment and that she'd only just arrived, but other than that, I can't even remember what it was about. That's the thing with rows – you rarely can. What I can remember is that we started off just disagreeing about something. That soon ramped up to yelling, and then she really turned up the heat. She was jabbing me in the chest with her finger, pushing me backwards and screaming abuse at me. And then, I fell onto the couch. I went to get up and continue the fight, but she gave me this look and, before I knew it, she'd hitched up her skirt and was straddling me, we both tried frantically to undo my jeans, but she slapped my hands away and did the job herself, before lowering her bare pussy onto my cock. She fucked me so hard I thought I was gonna die. Afterwards, she just got up, gave me a sexy smile and left. I've never really liked women going on top because it's hard to maintain control, but I liked it even less after that. What she did made me feel kinda used, but that was a scenario she set up on many, many occasions. Sometimes I'd let her, just for a quiet life, but other times I'd just stand up, with her impaled on me. She'd go completely crazy when I did that, like a child not getting their own way. Once, she bit my shoulder, real hard, and it was all I could do not to drop her. I really yelled at her after that – it was damn dangerous. One of us could've been hurt.

Yeah, I definitely should've seen the signs.

I didn't.

As time moved on, sex with Amber seemed to revolve around two things: the danger of being caught, or fighting – or both together. We fought a lot too, which meant we had a lot of sex. Sometimes it didn't even have to be us doing the fighting. She once came into the restaurant at the end of the lunchtime service and I was yelling at one of the junior chefs who worked here back then. In fairness, he had really screwed up. It was only when I'd finished balling him out that I turned and saw her standing just inside the door, her eyes on fire. I dragged her out the back door, but she turned the tables and pushed me up against the wall, undoing my jeans. We both realized that any of the kitchen staff – or Ed, or Rob – could've come out the back door at any time. The thing was, neither of us cared.

I don't know quite how or why, but we were married inside three months. Well, obviously I do know how. I asked her to marry me. I asked her to marry me while I was fucking her, which is hardly surprising, being as it's pretty much all we did. The position I had her in was a good one for me, although she was enjoying it too and had climaxed twice already. But, I think, for once I felt in control. Maybe that's why asked her – maybe I felt like things were changing; they were turning in my favor. I know I still saw her as a sexual challenge… one I was sure I could overcome. So, I proposed… just as I was about to come. She didn't actually say 'yes'. She just nodded her head, and then came again herself – really hard. I was twenty-six at the time and my brothers and I had just taken over the restaurant the previous year. What shocked the hell out of me was that, when we went to get the license, I discovered Amber was only just twenty. I thought she was around my age. She seemed so experienced. I guess that should have been a really big sign, but the thing was, I didn't want to see the signs, no matter how big they were. I didn't want to listen to advice either.

The advice came from Rob and Ed – but especially Rob. He never liked her, and neither did Ed, but with Rob it was different. A week before the wedding, he sat me down and really tried to convince me to call it off. He wouldn't tell me why at the time, but he was adamant I shouldn't marry her. I resented his attitude and we fell out about it for a while. It was only later, when I learnt what Amber's really like that I started to suspect that something might have happened between them… or at least that Amber might have wanted it to. I trust Rob and I know he'd never have done anything, which is why I've never mentioned it to him. To this day, he's got no idea that I even considered it.

The marriage was okay to start with. Amber was beautiful, there's no denying it. She had a fiery temper too, which was kind of matched by my own Italian temperament. We fought like cat and dog, but we also fucked like our lives depended on it. My parents had been similar, although my brothers and I weren't overly aware of the fucking part – obviously. We were aware that our parents fought each other and loved each other, probably in equal measure. So, I didn't think my relationship with Amber was that unusual. The fact that it revolved entirely around sex seemed completely normal to me. That was all I'd ever known.

For the first few months, it was a fairly heady combination of fighting and fucking. I liked the spontaneity, the unpredictability, but not the fact that she was now calling the shots an increasing amount of the time. So much for me taking control and overcoming the challenge… But then, as the months passed, and the arguments got worse, I began to realize that things *had* changed, just not in the way I'd hoped. She was intentionally instigating more physical, more vitriolic fights as a way of getting what she wanted – namely rougher sex than I felt even vaguely comfortable with. She'd also started demanding to be flogged, whipped, or even caned – and she'd bought the necessary equipment as well. I like control, I really do, but I'm not into that. When I refused – which I did, every time – she'd yell and scream and then, once she worked out she really wasn't gonna get her own way, because I'm a stubborn asshole, she'd go off and sulk silently and spectacularly around the apartment, sometimes for days… except, that is, for that one sobering time when she went too far… and so did I. We'd been fighting about her new demands for weeks, but that night she'd obviously decided to try a different tack. That night, when I got upstairs after work, rather than fighting with me, she just asked me outright to whip her, looking at me all doe-eyed and pleading, standing in the bedroom in lace topped stockings, high heels and nothing else, with a leather riding crop clasped in her hand. I said no… repeatedly. I saw the fury in her eyes right before she walked over and raised her arm, the riding crop high above her head. I don't know what she had in mind at that angle, but I caught her arm, grabbed the crop and threw it across the room, then I picked her up and walked her backwards to the wall, slamming her hard against it, and holding her there with one hand around her throat. The look in her eyes and the very slight smile on her face brought me back to my senses and I let her go in an instant. Her disappointment was made obvious by the abuse she hurled, right before she left, taking only her coat and her car keys. Where she went I have no idea; what she was doing and who she was doing it with became apparent later in our marriage. At the time, all I remember feeling was shame. I'd lost control, and I'd come really close to taking it too damn far.

By this stage, as far as I was concerned the whole thing was becoming quite stressful, and utterly exhausting. It certainly wasn't enjoyable, and I was starting to question whether it ever had been. There was no getting away from it, she wasn't the woman I thought she was, and she definitely wasn't the woman for me. But as far as I was concerned we were married… for better or for worse. I just kept hoping it would get better at some point, because I didn't see how it could get any worse.

Which just goes to show how wrong I was…

A couple of months after that incident, when we'd been married for around a year, she was promoted at work, and that meant she had to travel a lot more. I know it sounds bad, but I felt pleased when she went away. I enjoyed the peace and calm of her absence so much more than anything to do with her company.

Looking back, I realize that I should've seen the signs that she was cheating, but I'd missed all the others, so I guess I was just being consistent. Not only was she staying away from home more and more, but when she did come back, although we still had sex, she always insisted that we didn't face each other. She wanted to be on her knees on the bed, or facing the wall, or bent over in the shower. If she went on top – which I still hated – she faced away from me. Whatever we did,

I wasn't allowed to see her. It was another control issue that we fought over, but with hindsight, I should've realized she needed it to be that way because was thinking about someone else being inside her. She also stopped with her demands. At the time I felt relieved, I even thought – stupidly – that she might be coming around to my way of thinking, but afterwards of course, I worked out that another guy was fulfilling those needs for her.

Everything came to a head one morning a little under two years ago. She'd gone away on another of her business trips, but she'd slipped up. She'd left her phone behind. I was just getting ready to go down to work and it beeped. It took me a minute to find it, in the pocket of a jacket that she'd left hanging in the closet in our bedroom. I checked the screen, and saw the message was from her boss, a guy called Riley Fox. He said he'd got to the hotel early, he was waiting in their usual room, and that she'd better not be late, or he'd punish her – real bad. I stared at the phone for a while. Then I dropped it on the bed.

I think I was in shock. While I knew there were problems between us, I never thought she'd do that.

I sat down for a moment, and then it dawned on me to check the closet. Most of her clothes were still there – she'd only taken what she needed for the few days she was going to be away – but the riding crop, floggers, paddles and cane that she'd bought, and which I'd never used on her, were all gone.

Somehow – and I really don't know how – I managed to get through the following couple of days. I'm pretty sure I yelled at the kitchen staff a little more than normal, but whether anyone noticed, I have no idea. When Amber came home, I confronted her, showing her the phone and asking her what the hell was going on. She looked at me and told me it was just sex, like I was being naive even asking the question. Maybe I was. Let's face it, I'd missed some fairly obvious signs along the way. Not the least of which was that neither of us actually felt anything for each other.

I packed her bags that night. She told me she had nowhere to go and I told her to go find Riley Fox and tell him her troubles. She stood in the living room, her hands on her hips, and she tried to start a fight with me, but I knew where she expected that to lead and nipped it in the bud. I had no intention of having sex with her – ever again. Then she told me how long it had been going on for… that she'd first gone to him on the night she'd run out of the apartment, the night she'd tried to hit me with the riding crop and I'd pinned her to the wall. She told me he'd understood her needs, and wasn't afraid to give her what she wanted. They'd become lovers that night and he'd then deliberately promoted her at work, so they could spend more time together. He was a 'real' Dominant, or so she claimed, because he *always* gave her what she asked for, no matter how rough. That made me laugh, and I explained to her that, being rough with a woman does not make a guy a Dominant – it makes him an asshole. Then I told her that they were perfectly suited, being as Amber was hardly the ideal submissive. After all, the role of a sub isn't to ask or demand, like Amber always did, it's to obey, to please, oblige… submit. Amber never liked to lose an argument, and I can still remember her glare just before she delivered her coup de grâce, telling me that he was a better lover than me, how good his cock made her feel, and that he made her come harder than I ever could. Although I knew it was a heat of the moment argument thing, the dent to my ego was huge. It was bigger than huge.

Right before she left, I asked her if he'd used protection. She said he hadn't. I remember staring at her, just staring, not even arguing. I couldn't believe she'd take risks like that – with my health as well as her own.

I got tested the next day. It was clear, thank God.

So, that was the end of my brief marriage. Divorce is unheard of in our family and my parents all but disowned me. They wouldn't believe that Amber had done anything that couldn't be fixed, and assumed the fault had to be mine. That hurt. I let them know it hurt. The fallout was horrendous. Even now, they still barely speak to me.

The dent to my ego continued. I haven't slept with anyone since, and I haven't really wanted to. I also haven't really been aroused, which for me is pretty much unheard of. I wake up with a hard-on – sometimes, but not often – and it goes real quick. I'd like to say it doesn't bother me. But it does.

Of course, I've never told any of my family the detail. They know nothing of the precise nature of my marriage, or my difficulties since. I've also never told them that I didn't feel anything for Amber in the first place – they'd want to know why the hell I married her, and the truth is, I've got no idea, other than seeing her as a challenge, which isn't a great reason for committing your life to someone. There certainly wasn't any love between us, nor any romance. Not that I really know what romantic love is. It's not who I am. I'm not sure I'm even capable.

The evening service has been really busy – which I'm pleased about. My quiet contemplations this afternoon have left me feeling a bit low, to the point where I've started wondering if there's any hope for me at all...

"Sam?"

I look up. Rob has just come into the kitchen and, although I'm still madder than hell at him, I'm grateful for the interruption. I need something to pull me out of my self-pity, even if it is being angry with my brother.

"Yes, Roberto." I only ever use his full name when I'm pissed at him. He smiles. Annoying asshole.

"I've just met the woman of my dreams," he says.

"Again?" I've lost count of the number of times he's said this to either Ed or myself.

Ed comes over from the pastry section. "Does this mean I've got to stay with Sam tonight?" he asks. They moved into their own apartment just before I married Amber. Since she left, Ed sometimes stays with me when Rob's 'busy' at their place. Unless he's 'busy' himself, of course.

"Maybe," Rob replies, grinning. "She's beautiful."

"Another stunning brunette?" Ed asks.

"No, a stunning blonde, but I'll make an exception for her." Rob's always had a thing about raven-haired women.

"She must be beautiful," I say.

"She is. It's odd though, there's something vaguely familiar about her."

"You've haven't had her already, have you?" I ask him. Nothing would surprise me with Rob.

"No," he replies. "She smiled at me."

Ed and I both laugh. "Don't they normally smile at you afterwards?" Ed asks.

"Immediately afterwards – yeah, of course they do," Rob smirks. "Days, or weeks later… not so much."

"That's not surprising, considering you promise to call them, and never do."

"No, I don't," Rob defends himself. "I never promise to call. I'm always very clear that I'm not into commitment. Neither are they." It's true. We're talking about the kind of women who hand out their phone number to a waiter… commitment isn't too high up on their tick-list. "Besides," he adds, "I'd remember this one."

"You don't remember all of them?"

Rob rocks his head from side to side, like he's not sure, and again we all laugh. "To be fair," he says, calming down, "they probably don't remember me either – which is why they don't smile if they meet me again. I'm history…" He's not even remotely saddened by that thought.

"Okay," I say, taking the pan of sauce I'm stirring off the heat, "let's take a look at this rare specimen of beauty." Ed and I walk over toward the door. "What table is she sitting at?"

"Table ten," Rob replies.

"So we can see her from here, without having to go outside and stare at her. That's good. It's less obvious."

Rob gives us both a fake smile and leaves.

Ed stands by one round window and I take the other. As Rob moves out of the way, en route to the bar, we both get a full view of the woman seated at table ten. I've got no idea what Rob was talking about. She's not beautiful at all. She's way, way more than that. She's the most incredible creature I've ever seen. She's not even just 'blonde' either. She's got the lightest blonde hair, the ends of which are almost bleached, and it falls in soft curls over her shoulders. Even from here, I can see her eyes are pale blue and as clear as the brightest spring sky.

Her lips are full and pink, and I don't think she's wearing any lipstick – they're just naturally like that. Rob comes back again, carrying a glass of white wine which he puts down on the table in front of her, getting in the way of our view.

"He's right," Ed says beside me. "She is beautiful."

"Yeah," I reply absentmindedly, willing Rob to move. He does, just slightly and I can see her again. She's smiling up at him and I feel the weirdest sensation in my chest, like something heavy just landed on it. It's kinda hard to catch my breath for a moment, but when I do, I'm aware that I'm hard. I'm *really* hard. The stupid male pride part of me can't help but feel a little pleased with myself – just because I've got a hard-on, which, let's face it, is a biological reaction, and absolutely nothing to do with me, or my abilities. I focus on the woman again and see that she's laughing now. Rob's a lucky asshole. She's clearly interested and, for the first time ever, I'm really jealous of my brother and the way he always knows how to sweet talk women. Rob says something to her and she nods her head, and he walks away.

I should get back to work, but I'm kinda rooted to the spot, staring at her. It's hard to tear myself away. As Rob moves out of sight, she looks up the ceiling for a moment, then shakes her head from side to side. Well, I'll be damned. She's seen through him. That thought is just processing through my head when I realize she's looking right at me, and that a smile is forming on her perfect lips. I don't even know why, but my own mouth twitches upwards and I wonder for a moment what it would be like to kiss her. I've never been a great one for kissing – it borders on intimacy and romance as far as I'm concerned – but I'd really like to find out how those lips would feel on mine.

"Sam?" Jane's voice cuts into my thoughts. "Can you check this order for me?"

"Sure," I murmur. Ria's blocking my view now, presumably taking her order, and I turn away into the kitchen.

I need to focus, but all I can think about is a pair of pale blue eyes, and those perfect pink lips.

Chapter Three

Ali

Rob – or Roberto as he now keeps calling himself – brings over my wine. He's keeping up with the flirting, but despite that, I can see why their customers like this place. He seems to be at ease with all the female guests, very subtly making every single one of them feel like they're the most beautiful woman in the room, while with the men, he talks sport and business, acting like he's their friend – although I'm not sure it's that much of an act. He really does seem to be genuinely popular. He's good at what he does and is clearly an asset to the restaurant.

"You're not from around here, are you?" he says.

"No." I shake my head.

"I can't place your accent."

I'm not going to tell him I'm from England. It might give away who I really am. "Well, you'll have to guess," I say, laughing.

"Maybe we'll save that for later," he replies.

"Later?" I look up at him.

"Yeah… later," he murmurs, his voice deepening.

Well, if that wasn't a come-on, I don't know what it was. He moves away from the table and I can't help shaking my head, even though I'm still smiling, just a little. He's far too obvious. Definitely not my type.

I glance up towards the kitchen and notice two faces peeking out through the round windows in the swing doors. The man on the left is the spitting image of Rob. I'd go so far as to say they could be twins, except the man in the kitchen has longer hair. The man on the right though, is something else. I can feel a smile forming on my lips even as I look at him. He's a little taller than the other man and, while all three of the men are undeniably handsome, this one has something different about him. I feel a warmth stir inside me: a deep, satisfying glow, and my smile widens, like I have no control over my own facial muscles, just as he smiles back. It's not the smile that really catches my attention though, it's the way his eyes sparkle. I wonder, just for a moment, what it would feel like to have those dark brown pools boring into mine while *he* told me he wanted to save things for later.

He moves away from the door and back into the kitchen and I pull myself together, although my body is tingling all over, and it's all I can do not to shudder at the thought of what 'later' might entail with him...

Well, that was odd. Enjoyable, but odd.

The waitress, Ria brings my main course. I've ordered the gnocchi with spinach and mushroom cream sauce. It's good. It's really good. But it's nothing special. I finish the plate – because it really is delicious – and then Rob comes over, taking the dish away and asking if I enjoyed it.

"I did," I tell him. "It was lovely."

"Would you like dessert?" he asks.

I shake my head. "No, thanks."

"Coffee?" he offers.

I shake my head again. I'm too tired now. Eating has suddenly made me feel exhausted. "Just the check, please." I remembered at the last minute to say 'check' rather than 'bill', and he goes away, returning a few minutes later with the bill, on a small white plate. That needs to change too.

I pay in cash, including the tip and get up from my seat.

"You can't leave," Rob says. "I haven't guessed your accent yet."

"Well, I suppose it's time I came clean," I tell him, holding out my hand. "My accent is English, and my name's Alison Bishop."

His face pales, even as he shakes my hand. "Shit," he mutters under his breath. Then says, "I'm so sorry," out loud.

I smile at him. "Don't be. I've had a really nice evening." He gives me a look that says he appreciates me not mentioning his flirty behaviour. "And I really enjoyed the meal. Perhaps you could pass that onto whoever cooked it?"

"That would be Sam… my brother," he says.

"Well, tell him I really liked the sauce." It's true. I did.

"I will." He pauses for a moment. "Did you want to come and meet him and Ed?" he suggests.

I shake my head. "I'm sorry, but I only got here this evening, and I'm feeling a little jet-lagged. I was wondering if we could all get together tomorrow sometime. Maybe before you open up?"

He thinks for a moment. "Well, we could probably sit down with you for a couple of hours, around nine in the morning?"

"Don't you need to prepare for lunchtime service?" I ask him.

"We do, but we've got other people who can do most of that," he replies.

"Okay. I'll come back at nine then."

I go to move away, but he puts his hand on my arm. "Can I ask why you didn't just say who you were? Why did you book the table in a different name?"

I smile at him. "It's something I always do," I tell him. "I like to see how a restaurant really works, without having a display put on for my benefit."

He smirks and we both know we're thinking about his little flirtatious exhibition. He nods his head. "Okay, I guess that makes sense."

"If I'm going to help you – and your brothers – I need to see how you operate. The good and the bad."

"Was there a lot of 'bad'?" he asks, sounding worried.

"I'll tell you tomorrow." I smile, then I turn and leave.

Sam

Ria's given me the order for table ten. She wants the gnocchi. I like this recipe. It's simple, nothing special, but I know it tastes good.

I take a lot of care over her meal. I take care over every meal, obviously, but for some reason, I really want her to enjoy my food.

After it's been taken out, an order for eight covers comes in and we're slammed for nearly fifteen minutes. I've just passed the appetizers when Rob brings back the empty plate for table ten.

"What happened to Ria?" I ask him. Clearing tables isn't really Rob's job.

"Just helping out," he smirks.

"It's her job, not yours." My voice is a little gruff, but I don't want him to monopolize this particular customer.

"I know, I know."

"Is she having dessert?" Ed asks from the other side of the kitchen.

"No. She just wants the check."

Another strange sensation sweeps through my body. It's not jealousy this time, it's panic. I'm not used to this. It's really fucking weird.

"Did she book the table?" I ask Rob, trying to sound nonchalant.

"Yeah," he replies, a little confused.

I sigh out my relief. In that case we'll have some kind of contact detail for her. If people book online, we have an email; if they book over the phone, we take a cell number. Either way, I can contact her.

God, I'm starting to feel like Rob, chasing after female customers.

I look at him and, thinking about our different track records with women, I wonder if that's such a bad thing. He might sleep around, but he always leaves his women happy, they know where they stand, and he doesn't fuck things up anywhere near as spectacularly as me.

"I'd better get her check ready," he says, going back out front.

I go over to the door again and watch her. She's looking around the restaurant now, checking out the decor, I guess. It's a little old-fashioned. We haven't done anything with it since we took over from our parents. And I'm not sure they did anything with it since they bought the place in the 1980s. Still, the customers seem to like it. Our very healthy profits tell us that much. Rob reappears, standing beside her, and she pays in cash, then gets up. That strange feeling in my chest is back again. She's tall and slim, with really long legs. Rob says something and then, all of a sudden, she holds out her hand. Rob shakes hers and, from what I can see of his face, he's gone real pale. Whatever she just said, it shocked him. Maybe she just turned him down. He's not used to that, and the thought makes me smile. They talk for a little longer and then she leaves, giving him another smile.

I move away from the door, just as Rob starts to walk slowly towards it. He looks a little shocked still, although the color has at least returned to his cheeks.

"She turned you down then," I say to him as he walks in through the swing door.

He glances up at me. "Sorry?" he says

"The look on your face. I'm guessing she turned you down."

"No. I didn't even get to ask her."

"She's married?" Ed suggests.

"No," Rob replies. "She's the consultant. The woman from England. She's Alison Bishop."

Something snaps in my head. "What the fuck?" I yell.

"She's Alison Bishop," he repeats.

"I'm not fucking deaf, Rob," I say, lowering my voice a little. "Why didn't we know it was her? How did you manage to fuck this up quite so badly?"

"It's not my fault. She didn't use her own name when she booked the table," Rob says.

"What? She used a false name? Why did she feel the need to do that? Why couldn't she just be honest and tell us who she was?"

"Calm down, for Christ's sake, Sam." Ed moves closer.

"Why?" I turn to him. "Rob wants this woman to work for us, but she's already trying to deceive us. Typical damn woman, I suppose… incapable of telling the goddamn truth."

"Oh, grow up, Sam." Rob moves to stand in front of me. He has to look up a couple of inches, but he holds my gaze. "It was important for Alison to see us as we really are, not for us to put on a show for her. And I don't know what you're worried about. She told me to tell you she really liked the food. It's me who's just made an ass of myself, flirting with her for the whole time she was here. You agreed to hear her out and then make a judgement. She's coming round tomorrow morning at nine to have a talk with all three of us. So listen to what she has to say, and then we'll talk it through."

I glare at him, then turn away. If anything, I'm even madder with him now. Talking to me like that in front of the kitchen staff is never gonna go down well – no matter who does it – but what makes it worse is, he's right. I just completely overreacted, and I know why. Alison Bishop is beautiful. She's the first woman I've been interested in months. And I was *really* interested. And not just because looking at her got me bone hard. I liked her eyes, and her smile, and her lips… I especially liked her lips. Still, none of that of that matters now, because she's gonna come in here tomorrow and find fault in everything I do. She's gonna pick holes and criticize me. And I don't take well to criticism.

I can already feel a cold, hard chill running down my spine.

I got everyone to come in a little early today and I've given them all something to do, so by the time Alison arrives, the preparation for the Saturday lunchtime service is well underway. The three of us are sitting drinking coffee at a table in the front of the restaurant when she appears and knocks on the glass door. My breath hitches as I take in her tight jeans, which show off her long, slender legs, and her thin sweater reveals how cold it is outside. The problem is that now, as well as kissing her perfect lips, I also want to pinch those hardened nipples until she begs me to stop.

The door's locked, because we're not open, but Rob goes over straight away and lets her in. Ed and I get to our feet immediately, because that's what we were raised to do when a woman enters the room, and she comes over and holds out her hand to Ed as Rob makes the introductions. Then she turns to me and, as I take her hand, I feel her soft skin brush against mine and that crushing sensation in my chest is back again. Up close, she's so much more beautiful than she was through the kitchen window. Her skin is smooth and clear like the purest porcelain. And those lips that I so wanted to kiss last night are even more full and inviting. *Shit.* I seriously need to get my reactions in order and remember, she's the enemy.

"Hello, Sam," she says. Her voice is as alluring as the rest of her and, for a moment, I'm mesmerized. Damn her.

"Sam's the quiet one," Rob says, sarcastically and I find my voice.

"Unless I'm yelling at someone – like you," I say to him, then turn to her again. "Good morning," I say, formally. Her lips twitch, but I keep a straight face this time, remembering why she's here. Beautiful or not; alluring or not; she's still here to rip my work – and my world – to shreds.

"Let's sit," Rob says, then offers Alison a coffee, which she accepts and he tops up all our cups at the same time.

Once we're all seated, Rob turns to Alison, who's sitting to my right, at the circular table.

"What are your initial ideas?" he asks, getting straight down to business.

"Well…" She hesitates and I take the chance to say the thing that's been troubling me, perhaps more than anything, since Rob first came up with this dumb idea.

"If you're thinking about changing the name of the place, then you need to think again – or maybe just save us all some time and catch the next flight back to England." I know I'm being rude, but I don't care. I want her out of the restaurant – and out of my head – sooner, rather than later.

Her mouth opens just a little, but before she can say anything, Rob leaps down my throat.

"Sam, what's wrong with you?" he says.

"No," Alison interjects, putting her hand in the middle of the table, as though she's trying to take control. Seriously, sweetheart? You wanna try and control me? It's been tried before – it didn't work then either. She looks right at me. "I've got no intention of changing the name," she says quietly. "To do so would be counter-productive. You've already got a really good reputation locally. My body clock hasn't adjusted yet, so to me it's two in the afternoon, which means I've been up for a while, and I've spent that time checking you out online. You've never had a review of less than four stars – anywhere. I have to admit, reading what people have to say about this place, I'm a little puzzled as to why you asked for my help."

"So am I," I tell her. "But then that wasn't my idea. It was Rob's."

A look of confusion crosses her face and she turns to face my brother. "I was under the impression that I was working for all three of you – with everyone's agreement. But if that isn't the case, then it might be best if I followed Sam's advice and went home. It might save us all a great deal of time and trouble – and maybe a little embarrassment." She looks at me again, but I don't react.

"We don't want you to leave," Rob says quickly. *Speak for yourself.* "We asked you to come over because we need to modernize and update this place, and Sam has agreed to that, *haven't you*?" He emphasizes the last two words and gives me a look that tells me he's gonna hit me with something real heavy if I don't say yes. I give a single nod of my head, because I did agree to hear her out.

"Okay," Alison says. "Before I give you my feedback and views, can you give me some background on the restaurant?"

Rob starts the conversation, explaining that our parents came over here from Italy in the mid 1980s, choosing to settle in Hartford because our Uncle Giuseppe, my father's brother, had already come here a few years beforehand and had started a bakery – which is now run by his son, Fabio, but still supplies us with all our bread. Ed then takes over, telling her that our father is the youngest of nine children and, being fifteen years younger than Uncle Giuseppe, he just kind of followed him, unquestioningly.

"Nine children?" Alison stops him mid-flow.

"Yeah," Rob says, smiling.

"Your parents are Catholic?" she asks, smiling back.

"Well, *their* parents were. It's all kind of lapsed since then." He looks at me. My parents threw the religion in my face when I divorced Amber, after which I threw their hypocrisy in theirs. I've never practiced Catholicism any more than they have. It was a pointless argument on their part. None of that means a damn thing to me.

"I see." She smiles. "I bet parties back in Italy are fun."

"The parties are here now," I say, speaking for the first time since they started telling the story. "Pretty much the whole family lives in the US these days."

She nods her head, and Rob continues with the story.

"Papa's background was in cooking. He'd worked for a big hotel in Naples, which is quite near to where the family comes from. Our mother was a waitress in the same hotel. That's where they met. It transpired they came from the same village, although they didn't know each other. Mama's a little younger than papa, so they never mixed at home. They married after a whirlwind romance – or that's what they always told us, anyway. Then, a few years later, when Uncle Giuseppe suggested they come over here, papa decided to start his own restaurant and named it after his wife – our mother – Rosa."

"They retired about five years ago," I continue. "And they handed the restaurant over to the three of us."

"You must've been quite young at the time," she replies. I'm not sure if that's meant to be a compliment. I don't care either.

"I was twenty-five," I explain. "Ed and Rob were twenty-four."

"So you are twins then?" She looks from one to the other.

"Only so's you'd notice," Ed replies.

"That is quite young to take on a restaurant," she comments.

"We had no choice." My words come out harshly again and Rob gives me a look.

"Papa had a heart attack," he points out, before I can say anything else.

"I'm sorry," Alison replies. She means it too – it's obvious from her tone, and her eyes. "Is he okay?"

"Yeah," Ed says, smiling. "They moved to Florida and he's taken up golf. When he's not hitting a ball around the course, he spends his time fighting with our mom."

"Fighting?" Alison looks confused again – maybe even a little worried.

"It's what they do," I tell her. "They fight hard, they love hard." My voice fades. I'm thinking about Amber. I wish I hadn't. I didn't love her, hard, or otherwise. But I did fight her. And I fucked her – a lot. Don't get me wrong, I don't miss her. I just wish she hadn't happened.

"So," Alison says, looking around the interior of the restaurant, completely unaware of my discomfort. "What do you want to change?"

"You're the expert." I turn on her, raising my voice, and I know it's just because I was thinking about Amber. It's not Alison's fault, but I can't help it. "What do *you* think?"

Chapter Four

Ali

They're all really handsome when you get close to. Rob is definitely the ebullient, playful one – but then I think I learnt that last night. Ed is timid, quiet and thoughtful, probably a lot more sensible than his twin. And Sam is a complete bastard. He's rude, overbearing and incredibly arrogant. He might have soft brown eyes, a handsome face, with a square, rugged, stubbled jaw, and a sparkling smile that he uses far too infrequently, but none of that is ever going to make up for his attitude, or the way he speaks to me. Or, to be more precise, the way he shouts at me, being as that's what he just did, although I've got no idea why.

He's put the ball firmly in my court, asking what I think they need done here, so I'm going to damn well tell him, and if he doesn't like my reply, well I guess I'll be going home sooner than I expected. But at least I won't have to deal with him anymore.

"Okay," I say, still keeping my voice calm, even though his attitude is quite upsetting. It won't help if I get emotional. He'll just see that as a weakness and probably exploit it. He's that kind of man. He'd never hold a woman and comfort her, if she was crying. He'd look down his nose at her for letting her feelings get in the way. "I'll tell you what I think you need to change." I look at them in turn. "But I'm warning you in advance, I won't hold back. You've asked for my opinion and you're going to get it, so…" Rob and Ed nod, although Ed looks a little nervous. Sam just glares at me defiantly. "You've got a really nice place here," I start, "but it's dated. It needs bringing into the twenty-first century. You should be taking advantage of a lot more technology. I mean, for example, you're still taking orders on paper notepads, but you could be using hand-held devices or iPads. That would help with your inventory as well, enabling you to streamline your systems. There are so many things you could be doing differently, from the look of the place, to the menu, and just the way you give the customer their bill – sorry, check," I correct myself and pause for breath, but without giving them long enough to speak. "I can understand that this was your parents' set-up, but you need to move with the times." I turn to Sam. His eyes are like thunder, but I ignore that and carry on. "I haven't seen the kitchens yet but I can imagine they're probably the same as they were when your father installed them." No-one contradicts me. "The dish you made for me was well-cooked and it tasted great, but the menu is uninspiring. It's dull."

Sam stands and leans over the table.

"Who the fuck do you think you are?" he yells and I try really hard not to flinch.

"Sam. Sit down," Rob says, getting to his feet too. Ed pulls on Sam's sleeve, but he shakes him off.

"Well?" he says to me, as though neither of them are even in the room.

"I'm the woman who's just flown three thousand miles because you asked me to help you with this place. If you don't want to hear the truth, don't ask the question." My voice is calm, even though my hands are shaking underneath the table.

"I didn't ask you," he thunders.

"That's not true," I counter. "As far as I'm concerned, I was invited by all three of you. If you have a problem with me being here, you should take it up with Rob, not me."

He stalls for a moment and that seems to be one-nil to me. "What right have you got to pick holes in my cooking?" he asks.

"I wasn't, but nevertheless, I refer you to my earlier answer," I say. "You asked me to come."

"Yeah, to look at the restaurant, not the food."

"It's a package. A restaurant is only as good as its food."

He stops and stares at me, as though he recognises what I'm saying is true. "And its chef," he murmurs.

"Exactly," I say.

He shakes his head, like he's coming back to consciousness. "So, being as you're not a chef, I repeat, what right do you have to pick holes in my cooking?"

"And I repeat. I wasn't. I was picking holes – as you put it – in your menu."

He leans over a little further and lowers his voice to a barely audible whisper. "If you think you can do better, you go right ahead."

It's a challenge. And, coming from him, it's one I can't refuse. I laugh – trying not to sound nervous – and get to my feet. "Fine. Show me the way."

He smiles. It's the kind of smile that says he knows I'm going to screw this up, and he's going to be able to crow over me. Maybe I will. I don't know. It's been years since I cooked in a professional kitchen, but I know that if I don't accept his challenge, I might as well leave now. And besides, he reminds me of all those men who used to yell at me. And I'm done with being yelled at.

I follow him through to the kitchen, via the swing doors.

"I was right then," I say.

"What?" He flips around, glaring at me.

"This was your dad's kitchen."

He doesn't reply, but picks up a large serving spoon and hammers it on the nearest work surface. "Listen up," he calls. "This is Alison. She's just gonna cook something for me. Give her any assistance she asks for." He looks at me. "Obviously you might not know how the equipment works."

Oh, I'm really liking that patronising attitude. "Most of it looks vaguely familiar, but I might just need some help with ingredients."

"I'll help you." A young woman comes over.

"This is Jane," Sam says.

"Hello." I hold out my hand and she shakes it.

I turn back to Sam. "Give me half an hour."

He checks his watch and leaves the room. He's actually going to time me? Dear God, the man's impossible.

Jane is really helpful, once we get over the fact that we call some of the ingredients different things. She keeps telling me that, while Sam can be moody, he's a really good chef and he's taught her a lot. As I'm cooking, she asks a few questions, but I put that down to different teaching methods and her natural inquisitiveness, rather than her doubting what I'm doing. I was taught the French classical techniques, and from what she's told me, Sam came into the kitchen straight out of high school and learned his trade on the job. Sometimes that works better. In my experience, chefs with less formal training are more open to change. Having spent a short while with Sam, I'm wondering if he's the exception to that rule.

"That looks amazing," she says, as I plate up the dish I've cooked. "We don't serve anything like that."

"I know. That's why I'm here."

She shrugs. "Well, I hope he likes it."

I take off the dark blue apron she gave me earlier and she holds the door open for me as I carry the plate out to the restaurant. The brothers are all still sitting at the table and, as I approach, they notice me and get to their feet, which makes me smile a little. It's odd that Sam can be so gentlemanly in one way, and such an oafish, rude lout in others.

I lay the dish in the centre of the table and resume my seat.

"Wow," Ed says.

"Tell me what you've prepared." Sam's voice is calmer now.

I look at him, wanting to tell him it's fairly obvious, but I don't. "It's pan-fried cod, with tomatoes, capers and olives, and what I guess you'd call crispy zucchini spaghetti on top."

"Your presentation is very precise and modern," Ed says, still admiring the dish.

They all take a fork and taste each part of the dish, while I try to hide my smile. It's obvious they're from a culinary family. They all smell the food before tasting, and they sample each element individually, before trying a forkful of everything together.

"That is unbelievably good," Rob says, going back for another forkful.

"Thank you." I'm still looking at Sam, who's got a furrow on his brow.

"How did you make the zucchini spaghetti?" Ed asks.

I turn to him. "I hit a bit of a snag because you don't have a spiralizer, so I used a mandolin to julienne the courgette – sorry, zucchini – and then dried it thoroughly, seasoned it with salt and some chilli flakes, and then deep fried it."

"It's the chilli flakes," says Ed, nodding his head. "That's what I'm getting. I couldn't work out where that slight kick was coming from. It tastes really good."

Between the three of them, they clear the plate, although Sam still hasn't said anything. Once they've all laid their forks down, he leans back in his chair and looks at me for a long moment before he says, "Not bad. You over seasoned the sauce, because you didn't allow for the saltiness of the capers, but other than that, it was okay."

I stare at him, and then smile and shake my head. He doesn't seem to know what to make of my reaction and I wonder if he was expecting an argument. From him, that felt like a compliment, so I'm not going to bite – and besides I'm too tired to disagree.

Sam

I yell at people a lot. In my line of work it's almost expected, and most of the employees on the receiving end will either try and justify whatever it is I think they've done wrong, in which case, I'll put them in their place and we'll all move on, or they'll just accept my criticism and we'll all move on. Either way, the end result is the same – we all move on.

When I argue with Rob and Ed, they fight back a lot more, although Ed tends to be quieter about it than Rob. The thing with them is, they don't have to take my shit. And they don't. But none of us really bear grudges – not for long anyway – and once we've cleared the air, we just move on.

When I fought with my parents over Amber, that was totally different. I was raised not to answer back to my parents, so I didn't, other than to call them hypocrites over the religious thing, because that really pissed me off. Apart from that, I took their criticism and fumed. I let them know they were wrong about her, and that their accusations hurt, but I didn't fight back. Oh yeah, and then I punched a wall. That hurt too. It didn't help much either. We still haven't really moved on, but I hope we'll get there – maybe, one day.

Fighting with Amber was always highly charged. At the beginning, it always led to sex, but as time passed, that changed – mainly because it was sex we were arguing about – and we'd get real mad, swear and scream at each other, sometimes for hours, or even days at a time. It was rough, and often – especially near the end – there would be stony silences which went on, and on, before she'd cave in. It was always Amber who caved because, as I may have already mentioned, I'm a stubborn asshole. She'd come to me and find some way of getting around my foul mood and we'd end up naked, somewhere in the apartment. I don't recall either of us ever apologizing for the things we said and did to each other. We'd just fuck and move on.

Yelling at Alison was the strangest thing I've ever done. I mean, I've done some pretty odd things in my time, but that was *really* odd. I was mad at her, I'm not gonna deny that. She'd just criticized my food. She called it boring. The thing is, she wasn't criticizing my *cooking* and, if I'd been talking to pretty much anyone else, I'd probably have recognized that and discussed what they had to say, because I've known since before we took over this place that the menu is really dated. Instead, because it was her, and because just the thought of her has me more confused than I want to admit, I blew up at her. I had no real justification for saying what I did, other than the fact that, looking at her, thinking about how beautiful she is, and knowing what I want to do to her, but also knowing that she's come here to pick us to pieces, is really messing with my head. I'm a guy who likes control and yet it feels like she's taking that away from me, without even touching me. It's weird and I don't like it.

What was even more amazing though, was that she didn't really react to being yelled at. Women, in my experience, usually go one of two ways when I shout. They either shout back, or they cry. Personally, I've always felt that crying, in situations like that, is just using emotions to get your own way – so I'd far rather they shouted back at me. Alison didn't do either. She reasoned with me. What the hell is that about?

As for when she said that a restaurant is only as good as its food… well, I wondered for a minute if she'd been spying on me. Of course, I realized real fast that I don't often say that out loud. It sounds kinda arrogant. It's true, of course, but saying it aloud doesn't endear you to people. So, the fact that she said it must mean she feels the same way – and that's unusual. Most people don't share my feelings – about anything, let alone in my passion for food.

And then, as if that wasn't bad enough, she rose to my challenge and cooked the most amazing piece of fish I've ever eaten. Her own passion was there for all of us to see on the plate. I don't know that Ed and Rob noticed it, but it was there. I didn't tell her that, of course. I told her she'd over-seasoned the sauce, because I'm a sore loser, as well as a stubborn asshole.

"You want me to look at the outside as well?" Alison's talking to Rob.

"Yeah," he replies. "We want the whole place to have a new look." He's staring at me, like he expects me to argue. I'm not going to. The place is caught in a 1980s time warp.

"Okay," she says, starting to make notes. "So that's the front, the restaurant, including the rest rooms?" Rob nods. "The kitchens and the menu."

I sit forward in my chair, narrowly avoiding standing up this time. "No," I say sharply.

She turns to me slowly. "Do you have a problem?" she asks.

"Yeah, I do. You can do whatever you like to the front of the restaurant and out here." I look around the room. "But the I'll deal with the kitchens and menu."

Her eyes widen to a glare. "There's no point in hiring me to do half a job," she says, her voice still annoyingly quiet. She's not reacting at all. Why doesn't she just yell at me? She must want to by now. "If you just want to redecorate, then you can hire an interior designer, or buy some paint and do it yourselves. Either let me do my job, or let me go home."

I'm tempted to tell her to go home – life would probably be a lot easier – but Rob kicks me under the table, real hard.

"You're being stubborn," Ed says to me, his voice almost as calm as Alison's. Why is my stubbornness suddenly news to him? It's who I am. He knows that.

I take a breath and lean down to rub my leg where Rob just kicked it. It damn well hurts. I give him a stony glare, then look back at Alison.

"Okay," I say. "I won't interfere out here, but I insist on having total control of the menu, and we'll work together on the kitchens. That's my final offer."

She smiles and… *Oh, Fuck.* She's got such a sweet, sexy smile, I've completely forgotten what I was thinking…

"I'm not here to make, or receive offers," she says, and I try real hard to concentrate on her words, rather than all the things I could be doing to her mouth. "But I'll compromise with you." She holds out her hand to me and I take it. Although we've already shaken once, this time it feels like a bolt of electricity has shot through my whole body and I withdraw my hand quickly, like I've been burned.

I think, maybe, I have.

Chapter Five

Ali

Sam has got to be the most arrogant, difficult, stubborn, conceited man I've ever had the misfortune to have to deal with. Did I mention he's arrogant? If not, he is. He's really bloody arrogant.

Still, we've finally managed to put all the toys back into his pram, and have reached an agreement on the basic terms. Including the time it took for me to cook the fish, I've only been here just over an hour, which means we've got around fifty minutes for me to get some of the extra detail I'm going to need.

I turn the page on my notebook, and look up at them.

"I'm going to come up with three, maybe four designs for the restaurant," I tell them. "But in order to do that, I need a bit more background."

Rob nods his head. He's definitely the one I'd rather work with. Ed's fine. He's lovely, but he's too quiet and I doubt he could make a decision without deferring to one of his brothers. And as for Sam… well, we've already covered that.

"So, where exactly in Italy are your family from?" I ask. "I know you said it was a village near Naples, but where precisely?"

Sam shakes his head slowly. "You won't have heard of it," he says.

"Try me."

He sneers – he actually sneers – then rolls his eyes, and says, "It's a place called Positano."

A cold shadow passes over me and I can feel the stinging of tears behind my eyes. *I must not cry,* I chant inwardly, as I try to focus on my notepad and write down the single word, not that I need to. I'm not likely to forget it. I'm struggling to blink back my tears, as Rob leans forward and catches my eye.

"Is something wrong?" he asks.

"No. It's nothing."

"Have you heard of Positano?" Ed says.

I nod my head. "I've been there," I reply.

I manage to focus on their faces, and they're all clearly surprised. "Most people look at us blankly when we tell them where we're from," Sam says. His voice is so much softer. He actually sounds human and that makes me want to cry even more. "We've gotten used to saying that we're from near Naples, or Pompeii. Did you like it? Positano, I mean?"

"Oh, yes." Despite the tears that are still welling in my eyes, I can't help smiling. "I thought it was the most beautiful place in the world." Even I can hear my voice cracking and their faces are now filled with concern – even Sam's. "I—I went there with my parents when I was fifteen," I explain. "I've got nothing but good memories of it. Even though it was thirteen years ago now, I can still remember how breathtaking the village was. We had a suite in a hotel that overlooked the sea. The food was incredible." I look at Sam. "That's where I first got my taste for Italian cooking." He gives me a slight smile. "But I think I loved it most in the evening, when the whole village was lit up, and the lights reflected in the bay below." They're all staring at me now and I feel self-conscious. "Maybe we should get back to discussing your requirements," I say, wishing I'd never asked the question in the first place.

I'm just turning to another page in my book, when Sam leans over and says quietly, "We all love it too."

Despite seeing a slightly more human side to Sam, getting any kind of agreement out of him was like forcing blood from a stone, and it took the full two hours before we finally shook hands again. I told them I'd return on the Sunday morning and I'd have the contract ready for them to sign. Initially, Sam argued that Sunday was their one day off, but Rob told him to shut up.

I reassured him it would only take a few minutes to read through the paperwork and sign, and then he could get on with doing whatever he needed to. Frankly, I couldn't care less what he does, as long as he's not doing it with me.

Lying in my hotel room, I've made the necessary amendments to the basic contract and got the hotel to print it out for me; I've spoken to Tess, just before she went to bed, and I've had dinner and, for the first time since I got here, I feel really alone. Thoughts of that holiday in Positano keep floating around in my head. Tess and I travelled widely with our parents – although obviously I got more benefit from that than she did, being as I was around for longer, but that was our last holiday with them. We went in the May half-term, right at the end of that month, and it was the last weekend of June that they died. Now I'm on my own, I let those held-back tears fall, and I cry myself to sleep.

"We all need to sign?" Ed asks.

It's Sunday morning, and we're meeting, as agreed, for them to sign the contract. "Yes," I reply. I look at Sam. "I don't want there to be any confusion, or disagreements further down the line."

I've given them a copy each, and I've got one for myself.

"If you've got any questions…?" I say.

"It all looks fine," Rob replies, leafing through the pages. I'm not sure he's even reading it, but then he stops suddenly. "There are no prices in here though."

"No. You've given me your budget," I explain. "What I'll do is spend the next few days coming up with three completely different design ideas. One will be well under budget, one will be bang on the budget and I'll do one that's a little over, just in case you want to splash out." I smile at them. "Some people do." Rob nods. "At that stage, I'll cost everything up for you and give you a detailed breakdown, so you can drop things, or add them in, if you want. This contract is essentially an agreement between us, committing to working together, before we actually get started on anything. Otherwise, I could do all of that initial work and you could decide you didn't want to use me, and I'd have wasted a week of my time for nothing."

"Sounds reasonable," Ed says, nodding his head.

"I'll have to spend some time here with you" I add. "I'll need to see how you work behind the scenes, as it were, so I can get an idea of any layout changes that might be required. I'll try not to get in the way. And, Sam..." I look at him until he turns to me. "You'll need to start working on the menu over the next week. We'll need to be aware of any specialist equipment you might require as a result of the menu changes." He doesn't reply, or even acknowledge my suggestion. He just stares at me.

"I'm sure it'll be fine," Rob says.

I wish I had his confidence.

"So, they all signed?" Tess asks me.

"Yes. Eventually." It's the middle of Sunday afternoon for me, which makes it around eight pm for Tess. I've called her, because she sent me a text message and I got the feeling she might welcome the chat.

"What are they like?" she asks. We didn't get around to talking about the three brothers yesterday. She was tired and I was worried about her.

"Rob and Ed are really nice," I say.

"And the other one?"

"Sam?"

"Yes, Sam..."

"He's not so nice."

"Which one is he?" she asks.

"He's the chef."

"Will you have to work with him that much?"

"I hope not, although he's insisting on having total control of the menu and that we work together on the kitchens, so who knows?"

"Well, you're used to moody chefs," she replies, and I can detect what sounds like a smile in her voice. It's good to hear. At least she's not too down.

"I certainly am."

I've been at the restaurant every day this week. I spent Monday and Tuesday observing Rob and the waiting staff during the lunch and dinner services, making notes and rough sketches. They kept me fed and watered and I got the opportunity to try some more of Sam's cooking. He's very good and I made a point of asking whoever cleared my table to tell him how much I'd enjoyed each dish. When Rob isn't flirting, he's still just as much fun and we're getting along really well. He's still not my type, but I can see that we'd be friends – if I was going to be here long enough to make friends, that is.

Today is the first day I've spent in the kitchen. I've stuck myself in a corner, as far out of the way as possible, and watched everyone working. The room is basically one enormous rectangular space. It is big, but it's also chaotic. Ed has one area at the back for making desserts – but that's not ideal as the kitchen gets really hot, which isn't great for chocolate or pastry work. The walk-in fridges take up a vast amount of space along one wall, but I've looked inside and they're almost empty, while the other long wall is all for preparation. The centre of the room is taken up by ovens, griddles, fryers and broilers, but they're all free-standing. I don't particularly like that. It means they all have to be moved to keep the area properly clean. The first suggestion I'm going to make is that they invest in a modular unit that contains all of those features, but in one housing, fitted to the floor. I've taken measurements in the break between the lunch and dinner service, when the kitchen was empty, except for Sam and Ed, and I've worked out that we can put some partition walls in and create separate spaces for Ed, and for specialist catering. I'm also going to advise that they replace the walk-in fridges with two smaller ones. That will take up less space, so they can add some convection ovens along the side wall, and still have space for Ed's freezer and blast chiller.

Although I'm tucked away in the corner, I do have to ask quite a lot of questions and it soon becomes clear that Sam thinks of me as nothing short of a pain in the neck. He answered my first two queries reasonably politely; my third, he snapped at. Then I steeled myself and asked why the fridges were so empty. He looked at me and said, "Why do you think?"

"Well, I'm guessing you have daily deliveries?"

His look became a glare. "If you know the answer, why are you asking the goddamn question?" he yelled.

I didn't bother asking him anything after that, and went over to Ed. He was a lot more amenable. He was making raspberry granita and gave me some to try. It was delicious.

After those three days, I've been quite pleased to have some time to myself and I've spent it at the hotel, working up the designs, and doing the costings. I've arranged to meet Rob, Ed and Sam on Sunday morning again to show them what I've got. I hope they like something and I haven't just wasted a week of my life.

Sam

What an awful week.

To start off with, I struggled with getting the image of Alison sitting beside me with tears in her eyes out of my head. I know I said that I find crying women manipulative, but in reality, the only women I've ever been around who've cried have been the ones I've shouted at in the kitchen – the ones who chose not to fight back, but to cry instead. In most cases, I've known that they've cried in the hope that I'll go easier on them. That infuriates me, because nine times out of ten, those same women will also be the first to rant about equality. Don't get me wrong, despite my sexual preferences, I'm all for women's rights, but to me that means they get treated the same as a guy. I don't differentiate, but I've never had a guy break down in tears, or start telling me his personal problems by way of an excuse for fucking up. Equality means just that in my kitchen – everyone is the same, and I respect one thing: talent.

Apart from in the kitchen though, I can't think of another situation where a woman has cried in front of me. My mom never did. She's not that kind of woman. If she did cry, she kept it private, maybe between her and my dad, or as something that she did by herself. The other women in my life? Ella definitely didn't. She was too busy having a good time. And the rest? Well, I didn't really hang around long enough to find out, but none of them shed a tear that I was aware of. And Amber? Hell, no. She most definitely wasn't the crying type. So, when I saw Alison's eyes brimming over, I had no idea what to do. For once, I wasn't responsible for the situation, but that didn't make it any easier. Luckily, Rob stepped in first, because I had no idea how to react. I mean, my instinct – oddly – was to get up, pull her to her feet and hold her. I wanted to let her cry it out – whatever it was – on me. I sure as hell didn't want her to choose to do that with either of my brothers. But she held it together and the moment passed. And I think that's probably for the best.

No, I know it is, because what happened later in the week just confirmed that the two of us are about as incompatible as it gets. Although why I'm thinking about us in terms of compatibility is beyond me. Why I'm thinking in terms of 'us' is just as incomprehensible.

I hadn't realized Alison was going to be spending so much time at the restaurant, but it seemed to me that she was there every time I turned around. She wasn't, of course. For the first couple of days, she was front of house. I think it was just that I knew she was there. Well, it was that and the fact that, every time I cooked her something she insisted on sending back a report. I don't need her to tell me what she thinks of my damn cooking. I know I can cook.

As for Wednesday. That was pure, unadulterated torture. I don't really like having people in the kitchen at the best of times. Obviously the people who work with us have to be there, and that's fine. But when someone isn't working and they're just watching what we do, it feels like we're putting on a show. I'd decided on Tuesday that I could stop checking Jane's work again, and sure enough, on Wednesday lunchtime, someone sent back their steak because it was undercooked. They were quite right, it was. I was about to yell at Jane, when I caught sight of Alison out of the corner of my eye, and stopped myself. I've got no idea why. I mean, I've yelled at Alison, so why would it bother me to yell at someone else in front of her? But I didn't. I called Jane over and calmly explained what was wrong, then asked her to put it right and try a little harder next time. I think Jane thought there was something wrong with me. I know I did. The 'something wrong' was sitting in the corner of the room.

To make matters worse, Alison kept asking questions. To me, her tone seemed critical. So, when she got to her fourth question, which was about why the refrigerators are so empty, I yelled at her. Weird, considering that I'd held back with Jane, but there you go.

She went and spoke to Ed shortly after that. I ought to have felt relieved that she'd moved down to the far end of the kitchen, but the problem was, she'd left her scent behind and it was intoxicating. I heard her laughing with Ed and turned around to see them with their heads bent close together. He was offering her something to taste on a spoon and as her lips closed around it, my cock stiffened. He said something, and she laughed, then she glanced at me and her smile faded. This is great… She makes me hard. Ed makes her laugh. I make her sad.

It's going really fucking well.

I know I'm supposed to be working on the menus in my spare time, but I really don't get a lot of that – just an hour or so in the mornings and a couple of hours between services. It should be long enough for me to have put down some ideas, but I've been so distracted with having Alison here, that I haven't done a damn thing.

She arrives on Sunday morning and we all sit at a table in the restaurant. She's wearing jeans again today and, as she puts her briefcase down on the floor before taking her seat, I get a good view of her ass for the first time. Jeez. I thought every other part of her was perfect, but that ass is just too much.

"How's it gone with the menus?" she asks me, straightening the folder in front of her and looking at me.

Shit. She would lead with that, wouldn't she? I don't even get to find fault in what she's done before I have to admit I've done precisely fuck all.

"I haven't had time to look at them," I admit.

She stares at me and I feel like I'm in fourth grade all over again, and Mrs Radcliffe is telling me off for not handing in my homework. It was a fairly regular occurrence, but I always hated getting the 'look' and the 'lecture'.

"Well," she says, still with that quiet, tranquil voice. "It would have been useful to know what you had in mind, but I suppose we'll just have to work with what I've got and adapt the kitchen ideas as we go along."

Is that it? Is that the best she's got? I was expecting a roasting. I'm not sure whether to feel relieved, or disappointed.

She opens the folder and pulls out three separate sheets of paper, each of which has a hand-drawn illustration of the inside of the restaurant on it.

"These are just the rough sketches," she says, "to give you an idea of what I've got in mind."

These are rough? They're amazing. The three of us stand up, our heads together, and lean over the table, looking at her ideas and, without even consulting my brothers, I know we're all drawn to the same one. I move it to the center.

"Can you explain this one," I say to her.

"Sure," she replies, standing herself and moving to the side wall of the restaurant. We all turn and look at her. "The walls will all need to be stripped back and re-plastered," she says. "This paneling has to go." She's not wrong. Whatever we do, the damn paneling has to go. I hate it. "This wall will be painted in white," she adds. "And the photographs on the wall will be just dotted around." I glance back at the picture she's drawn and see that they are quite random. I like that. It's not too organized. She moves to the back of the restaurant now. "On this wall here," she says, "we'll create the the striped effect you can see in my illustration. That will involve one really large photograph that will be printed in long strips – a little like wallpaper – and laid over the white painted wall. The narrow gaps in between create that striped effect without detracting from the overall picture. It's hard to imagine, but it really does work."

She moves forward into the center of the room. "The bar will stay where it is, but again all the paneling along the front will go." *Hallelujah.*

"The tables will have white linen cloths, and the chairs will be high backed, soft gray leather. For the floor, we can use the existing wood, but strip it back, and re-stain it a much lighter color. The overall feel is simple and Mediterranean."

"And the outside?" I ask her.

She comes over to the table and picks out another piece of paper from her folder.

"To go with that interior, it's this one," she says, pushing the sheet forward. "The paneling goes, but other than that, all we're really going to do is strip off all that dark varnish and paint the woodwork in gray. The windows will be cleaned down, so people can actually see inside. Then we'll place a couple of small, trimmed bay trees by the door and you've got your outside look."

"What about the kitchen?" Ed asks.

She glances at me for a moment. Obviously, I haven't had time to think about this, because I haven't even looked at the menus yet. "Maybe we should leave that for another time," I say.

"Well, I've put down some basic ideas," she says, pulling out yet another drawing. I lean back over the table. Shit. She's done so much work. And I've done nothing. "I think the kitchen should be divided into three completely separate areas. It's going to mean putting up some walls, but they're just partitions, so it's nothing major. The main area will be for Sam. I get the impression he likes his space – and as much as possible, he likes it to himself." Great. She's seen right through me, like I'm fucking invisible. Maybe I am to her… "The next area is for Ed to prepare his desserts in a more temperature controlled environment," she continues, "and then the other is for the preparation of gluten-free items. I feel you should offer them on the menu," she adds, then glances at Ed, "and that you should maybe add a couple of dairy-free desserts too."

Ed nods his head.

"I couldn't agree more," Rob says. "We're constantly getting inquiries, especially for gluten-free, but we can't really provide anything now, because we don't have a separate preparation area." He twists the design around to get a better look. "This is all so good," he says.

I can't deny that. She's thought everything through – even down to the fact that we don't need to have those enormous walk-in refrigerators. We can easily just have two smaller ones – one for meat and one for everything else. The saving on space is huge and – again, she's right – that means we can get almost a whole wall of convection ovens in, so they'll be at eye level, rather than down on the floor. I've always wanted to do that. The idea for the central modular unit is going to really save time when it comes to cleaning too.

She's thought of everything.

Damn her. Again.

"What do you think, Sam?" Ed asks, his enthusiasm obvious.

I want to say that I love her ideas and that I can't wait to get started on all of it; that I think she's amazing to have done all that work; that I think she's amazing, period. But, I can't. I especially can't in front of my brothers.

I shrug. "It's hard to tell whether it's all gonna work out, until I've done the menus," I say.

"Well, if you'd done them already, like you were supposed to…" Rob replies. He's right, I know he is and I wish I hadn't brought it up now. But it was the only thing I could think of on the spur of the moment that wasn't complimentary.

"It's fine," Alison says, being really placatory again. "I deliberately made the kitchen designs adaptable. We can change things as we go, depending on what Sam comes up with."

Why the hell does she have to be so goddamn nice?

I really want to hate her, and a lot of the time, I do. She shows me up and makes me feel inadequate, but she somehow does it while being the most kind, warmhearted and beautiful person I've ever come across. At the moment, she's making it real hard to keep fighting the attraction.

Doesn't mean I'm not gonna keep trying though.

Chapter Six

Ali

I suppose a part of me didn't really expect Sam to get the menus ready. It was asking a lot, considering I'd taken up a chunk of his only day off last Sunday, and his hours are long and relentless. But that didn't alter the fact that he was supposed to do it, and he didn't. Fortunately, I kept the plans for the kitchen simple, and easily amended. And all of it seemed to go really well. They liked my minimalist design for the restaurant, which did surprise me a little, especially as they've got no idea what the photographs I've shown as being mounted and dotted around, and used on the back wall are going to be of. I'm going to try really hard not to tell them as well, because I'd like to surprise them with that when I unveil the finished product.

We all sit down again. "I've prepared the budgets and schedules," I tell them, pulling out the final documents from my folder.

I hand them around – one copy each again – and they start to read.

They don't get far before Rob queries the photography budget. I can't explain it fully without telling him what the photographs are going to be of.

"You're going to have to trust me on that one," I start to say.

"Oh, are we?" Sam replies, not letting me finish my sentence.

"I hadn't finished," I add. "I was going to say that, you're going to have to trust me, because I'm commissioning a photographer… well, two actually. One will take the photographs we're using in the re-design. The other is going to take some promotional and publicity shots. Please believe me, it'll be worth it in the end." Rob looks at me for a moment.

"Okay," he says. Sam goes to speak, but Rob cuts him off. "It's okay," he says to Sam. "If the photographs aren't exactly what you want, I'll pay for them to be re-done – personally."

Wow. He really is putting his faith in me.

"We'll remember you said that, little brother," Sam replies, grinning. God, he's so obnoxious sometimes.

While they're looking through the rest of the budget, I tell them that, as I'm now definitely going to be working with them for a while, I'd prefer it if they called me Ali, instead of Alison.

"Don't you like being called Alison?" Ed asks.

"It's okay, but I just prefer Ali. It's how I think of myself."

"Okay," Rob says. "Ali it is." He smiles at me.

They all finish looking at the budget and there's evidently nothing else they feel the need to query. Sam's the first one to turn over the page and get to the schedule.

"So," he says, reading it through, "you're gonna take two weeks to finalise the designs, source the suppliers and contractors, and then we'll have to close down for…" He pauses, then looks at me. "Three weeks?" He's incredulous.

"I know it's a long time. Well, it's a long time for you to be closed. And I understand that you'll have to give your staff time off, and time is money – and you're already spending a lot on the make-over – but I've checked your reservations and you've got nothing booked in after next weekend. And I've looked at it every way I can, trimmed the hours as much as possible, and I can't see how I can get a job of this size done any quicker. I've already spoken to a couple of contractors who've said they can start on the date we need, so I'm confident it won't overrun…"

"Oh, are you now?" Sam raises his voice.

"You surely didn't expect to be able to stay open?" I say.

"No of course I didn't," he replies impatiently. "But I didn't expect that we'd have to lose three weeks' takings either."

Rob turns to him. "We've gone for the lowest budget re-design," he says. "We can afford this."

"That's not the point."

"I understand that it's going to cost you money," I say, repeating my earlier comments.

"It's not just that," Sam replies, sarcastically. "In three weeks, who's to say what might happen to our regular customers. We've got some people who eat here several times a week – they don't book a table, but they're regulars. Hell, they even order the same thing when they come each time. If we're closed for that long, they're bound to find somewhere else to go, and then we've gotta work to get them back again."

He sounds like he's really worried, like the idea is affecting his confidence. "They come for your food, Sam," I say, putting my hand on his arm. He pulls away from me, but I ignore that and continue, "They're still going to come back. If anything – in my experience – they'll be even more keen to come back, because they'll want to see what you've done with the place."

"In your experience?"

"Yes. I have done this before, you know?"

"Sam," Rob says, trying to placate his brother. "We've got to trust Ali. She knows what she's doing."

"And closing down for three weeks is the way to go, is it?"

"Yes." I was feeling sympathetic towards him – just for a moment – but my sympathy is rapidly evaporating. He's being childish now. Surely he can't expect to stay open, or just close for the weekend. The amount of work they want done is significant. "We're going to be building walls through your kitchen," I tell him. "What do you want to do? Work around us?"

"Of course I fucking don't."

"Well then." I feel like that's the final word – it certainly should be.

"Well then what?"

"Oh, for heaven's sake, Sam. What's your problem?" I can't help it. I'd never normally speak to a client like that, but I've really had enough of his attitude.

"My problem?" he says, getting to his feet and looking down at me. His eyes are thunderous. "You really wanna know?"

"Yes!"

"My problem is *you*." He kicks his chair out of the way and walks off towards the back of the restaurant, his image blurring as tears form in my eyes.

"Sam!" Rob yells after him. "Get back here and apologise."

Sam ignores his brother and keeps walking, disappearing down the corridor and into the kitchen, through the swing doors on his right.

"I'm so sorry," Rob says to me, his voice much quieter, although his face shows how angry he is.

"It—it's fine," I mumble.

"No, it's not," Ed replies.

A tear drops onto my cheek and I quickly wipe it away with my sleeve. "It doesn't matter."

"Yeah, it does." Rob's talking again now as I start to pack away my papers. "You're not leaving are you?" There's a note of panic in his voice, and I turn to look at him.

"Leaving?"

"Yeah… going home."

"Back to England, you mean?"

He nods, then leans across and takes my hand. It feels like it should be intimate, and yet it isn't. It's just a friendly gesture. "Please don't," he says. "We really need you, even if Sam's too stubborn to admit it."

"I'm not leaving." I smile, even though the next tear is threatening to fall. "We've got a contract, and I don't back out on those."

I hear his sigh of relief. "Thank you," he says.

I finish packing away the papers and put the folder back into my briefcase before getting to my feet and pushing the chair back under the table.

"There is one thing though," I say, trying to sound as calm as I can manage.

"What's that?" Rob asks. He and Ed stood up at the same time as me and now they're standing in front of me, looking expectant – and maybe a little worried.

"I know all three of you signed the contract, but I'd really rather not work with Sam any more than I absolutely have to."

"That's fine," Rob replies. "Right now I can't say I wanna work with him much either. I've got no idea what's eating Sam," he says, "but between us, Ed and I will make sure he stays out of your way."

"Thank you." I go to leave but then turn back. "I'm not an overly emotional person – not as a rule. You can usually throw most things at me and I'll take them in my stride."

"Well, maybe we'll all just start showing things at Sam instead, and see how he likes it." I look at Rob for a moment and then we all burst out laughing. The release is so welcome, I could almost cry. Again.

Sam

Today is the second day of our closure and it's weird being at work on a Tuesday, with no-one else around. Well, I say no-one, but in reality, the place is heaving with people. There are workmen everywhere. Rob and Ed's apartment is about a block away and they're working out of there for the time being. Rob's checking out suppliers because he wants to stock some new wines, and didn't think he'd get any peace in the office, and Ed's coming up with new dessert ideas. I'm meant to be upstairs getting on with the main menus, but I'm down here right now, making sure that everything's going to plan.

I deliberately didn't come down here yesterday. Partly because they were gutting the place and removing all the furniture, and I didn't want to get in the way, but also because I needed to finalize the menus and write up the recipes. It took longer than I'd anticipated. Today, I'm gonna start the real work: testing them, tweaking them where necessary, and working on the accompaniments. These next couple of weeks are gonna be real busy.

I'm standing in the kitchen, leaning against the wall by the doors – although the doors have been removed so the workmen can get in and out more easily. It looks completely different. Most of the units have been taken out now and I'm already finding it hard to remember the things Amber and I did in here. I'm kinda grateful for that. It's good to walk into my own kitchen and not be faced with the mistakes of my past. Ali's done that. Well, I guess the workmen have, but it was at her instigation. *Ali*. The name suits her a lot better than Alison. It's more fun – and I think she's probably a fun person to be around, when she's not being yelled at by an asshole like me, that is.

She's ignoring me at the moment. I know she knows I'm here. She looked across earlier and our eyes met for a moment, before she turned away again. I also know she's ignoring me on purpose. I know this because Rob told me that she didn't want to work with me, and I can't say I blame her. I was horrible to her – again. Rob laid into me after she'd gone back to her hotel, but I already knew how mean I'd been, and that she hadn't deserved it at all. Hearing him say that she'd been crying, because of me, and that she didn't want to work with me any more than necessary was real sobering though. I didn't feel too good about myself then – I haven't done since. Not that there's anything I can do about it. She's right. It is best if we don't work together. She confuses me and I upset her. We're better off keeping our distance, and for the last two weeks, while she's been sourcing suppliers, we've done just that. She's worked out of the hotel, and I've been busy in the kitchen as usual, and that's made life a lot easier… for both of us, I imagine.

The problem is though, seeing her again, looking at her now, laughing and joking with the carpenters who are about to start building the walls to separate the different areas in the kitchen, I'd really like to join in. I'd like to get more involved, to show her I'm not always the way I seem to be. I want her to see my human side. I know it's still in there somewhere. It's gotta be… otherwise there really is no hope for me at all.

I take a step forward just as a big, tanned muscular guy comes over to Ali and starts asking her about something on the plan he's holding. She goes into the corner with him and he leans in – a lot closer than he really needs to. She points out a couple of things and he says something. She giggles, then rolls her eyes and shakes her head. I guess he's a bit like Rob. He knows how to flirt. I don't. I've never flirted in my life. I want to go over and tell him to back off, except I don't really know how to do that either – not without being really offensive anyway, and I'm not sure she'd appreciate that. Besides, for all I know she might like the guy.

God, I hope not.

I shake my head. I can't think like that. She's not right for me. And I'm most definitely not right for her.

I go back upstairs and, although I'm not really in the mood, I set about working on the new recipes. I've brought a lot of the pans upstairs from the restaurant kitchen and, with my notes spread out on the central island, I'm soon elbow deep in sauces and seasonings.

It's hard work. Not everything goes right first time and, being an impatient, short-tempered guy, I get easily frustrated. By early afternoon though, I've got two of the dishes absolutely how I want them.

Ed calls while I'm taking a coffee break and asks if he can come over tomorrow. He wants to run a few things by me. He says he's hit a couple of snags and needs some advice. He probably doesn't, but he lacks confidence in his own abilities, largely thanks to our dad. Ed and I agree a time, and that it might be wise to get together every couple of days to make sure we're both thinking along the same lines.

I've just settled down to working on the next recipe when I get a text message. It's from Ali. Rob told me he'd given her our cell numbers so she could stay in touch, in case there were any problems. I read the message through. It's addressed to all of us.

— Sorry to trouble you all. There's been a bit of a hitch in the kitchens. Would it be possible for you all to come in and meet me here at four o'clock this afternoon? Please let me know. Thank you. Ali.

She's so polite – even when she's texting. Four o'clock is just over an hour away. I can easily do that. After all, I've only gotta go downstairs.

I tap out a curt response.

— Fine. Sam.

A couple of minutes later, I get another message. I let out a sigh, hoping she's not gonna be one of those women who insist on texting every few minutes. I check my phone, but the message is from Ed, not Ali.

— Sam, being as Ali's asked us all to meet her, I'll come upstairs afterwards and we can discuss the things we talked about earlier, rather than doing it tomorrow, if that's okay with you? E

I type out my reply.

— Makes sense. See you later. S.

At just before four, I go downstairs, locking the door to the apartment behind me. I quite often don't, but with the back door being wide open a lot of the time, I decide it might be wise.

Rob and Ed aren't here yet and the workmen seem to have left already. Rather than going into the kitchen and finding myself alone with Ali, I decide to take a quick peek into the restaurant. I go along the corridor, past the open kitchen on my left, and the closed office door on my right, and out into the main restaurant. And I stand completely still, holding my breath.

This is amazing – already. The paneling has been stripped off, thank God, and although there's quite a lot of damage to the walls, the place is so much lighter and brighter without it. The bar has been covered with sheeting, and while the whole place looks like a construction site, I can see the progress. Why on earth did Ali say this would take three weeks? If they've been able to achieve this much in just a couple of days, why are they going to need so much longer to finish it off?

Rob and Ed come in through the front door and seem to have the same reaction as me.

"Wow," says Ed, standing on the spot, looking around.

"It's coming along, isn't it?" Ali's voice, from directly behind me, makes me spin around. She looks at me just for a second, then walks right past me like I don't exist, into the center of the room. "We're going to strip the floor tomorrow, and then the plasterers will be able to get to work. After that, things will really start to take shape."

"It looks so much lighter already," Rob says, voicing my earlier thoughts.

"Well, you did have a lot of dark wood in here," she says, smiling. Then she turns. "Shall we go through to the kitchen?" she suggests, still not looking at me, but clearly addressing her question in my direction.

"Okay," I answer, taking her lead.

We all follow her down the corridor and through the gap that used to be the door. I manage not to focus too much on her ass, encased in really tight jeans. It's hard, but so am I. Like me, she's just wearing a t-shirt on top, but then I've been cooking all day and I guess it gets quite hot in here when everyone's working. When she turns to face us, I can see her nipples are erect and yet again, I'm almost overwhelmed with a need to pinch them. Hard. Instead, I try to stifle the groan that nearly escapes my lips. Why does she keep doing this to me? More to the point, why do I keep letting her?

"The electrician came in today," she says, going over to the work bench that's been set up in the middle of the room. Some drawings are laid out in the center, not that she's really looking at them. I think she just wanted something to lean against, and there isn't anything else in here now. "He spent a couple of hours looking around the place, and then he told me the bad news." She looks from Ed, to Rob, and then to me. Then she looks away again, staring down at the floor between us. "The whole wiring system is antiquated and I'm afraid it's going to have to be replaced. I've sent everyone home early because we need to resolve this, and then we can get on."

Replaced? Did she really just say that? "You're telling us this now?" I say, raising my voice already. She looks up at me again and opens her mouth, but I don't let her speak. "Are you completely incompetent? You should have factored this in. Telling us now is no good, is it?" I wave my arm around at the shell that used to be our kitchen. "I guess you're telling us we need to find more cash – and that we're gonna need to be closed for even longer? For fuck's sake! What's wrong with you?"

Chapter Seven

Ali

I'm tempted to tell him that he is, but I decide not to lower myself to his level.

"Well?" he goads. "Care to explain why the hell we're only just hearing about this now?"

"You're not," I say quietly.

"Excuse me?" he bellows.

"Give it a rest, Sam," Rob puts in.

"It's fine," I say, even though I can feel a lump forming in my throat. I will not cry in front of this man. Ever. He's not worth it. Instead, I turn and lift up the plans that are lying on the work bench, pulling out my folder that I know is underneath. I open it and retrieve the budgeting document I originally gave them a couple of weeks ago. "It's all in there," I tell Sam, handing him a copy.

"What is?" he barks.

I snatch the document back and turn to the fifth page, before giving it back again. "Third paragraph down," I say. "I did point out that I'd had a look at your wiring myself and, although I'm not an expert, I thought it might need replacing. I allowed a contingency for it within the budget, and the schedule."

"So you don't need any extra money, or additional time?" Ed asks, looking at the document over Sam's shoulder.

"No."

"Then why the hell have you asked us to come down here?" Sam asks, his voice still a lot harsher than feels strictly necessary. "We're all busy, you know."

I cough, to clear that lump in my throat. It doesn't work. "I thought that, as the wiring is being re-done, it would give you the perfect opportunity to move things around out here. The plans as they are now, don't allow for that. I'd pretty much left everything where it was before, but the electrician said that, if you want to completely change the layout, now would be the time to do so, and he can accommodate that. It's entirely up to you, of course. It won't add to the cost – I've checked that with the electrician already. All you need to do is spend a little time down here, going over the plans, talking amongst yourselves, and working out if you're completely happy with where everything is going to be. If you are, then we can go ahead. If not, then you just need to let me know and we can all sit down with the contractor in the morning and discuss whatever you want to change." I turn to Sam. I can't look him in the eye, so I stare at his chest instead. I hadn't really noticed before how muscular he is and, just for a minute, I let my eyes wander down to the obvious six-pack that his tight t-shirt isn't concealing at all. "As... As you've always been keen to point out," I say to him, stammering a little, "this is your domain. I'm not trying to tread on anyone's toes. I just want what's best for you."

I take a glance up at his face. He's staring at me, his eyes boring into mine. I look away again and Ed steps forward.

"Thank you," he says. "We'll go over the plans and let you know later on. Is that okay?"

I nod my head. I'm feeling too emotional to say anything else.

Rob comes and stands beside his twin. "Why don't you go back to the hotel and we'll see you tomorrow."

Their voices are really soft and considerate, and that's almost my undoing.

"Thanks," I manage to say. "But I've got a meeting to get to anyway. I've just got a couple of things to do in the office first, then I'll be off." I don't look at any of them, but dart out across the hallway and into the office opposite, closing the door quickly and leaning back against it before I start to sob. Really sob.

Petra's waiting for me in the lobby of the hotel and we go through to the bar and order coffee. She's going to be doing the photography at the opening and taking some promotional shots as well. I arranged this meeting earlier in the week and, as much as I'd like to cancel it and go upstairs to my room so I can cry my eyes out a bit more, that's not really an option.

"I don't mean to intrude," she says, once the waiter's gone, "but are you okay?"

"No. But it's not your problem." I smile at her. She's got a kind, very pretty face, with pale olive skin, surrounded by thick curly black hair. Her dark grey eyes show her concern.

"I'm a good listener," she adds.

Tears start to well in my eyes again. "It's nothing. I'm probably just feeling homesick."

"You're from England, right?" she says.

The waiter brings our coffee and we thank him. "Yes," I tell her. "London."

"I've always wanted to go to London."

I don't know what to say to her. I am missing home, and Tess. But that's not the real reason I'm upset and, judging by the look on her face, I think she knows that.

I take a sip of coffee.

"I really am a good listener," she says again, watching me.

I smile. "It's nothing important. I'm just having a hard time on this job."

"Oh? Working with American contractors is different to British ones?"

"No. It's nothing like that. Working with American clients is proving challenging though."

"It's the owners who are difficult? I thought the couple who owned Rosa's were really friendly." She leans forward and picks up her cup.

I smile again. "They don't own it anymore. Where have you been for the last five years?"

"Busy," she smiles. "Why, what's happened in the last five years?"

"Mr and Mrs Moreno retired to Florida and their three sons now run the restaurant."

"Oh. I had no idea. I haven't eaten there for… well, years." She looks thoughtful for a moment, but then it passes and she focuses back on me. "So, why are they being difficult?"

"They're not. Well, not all of them. It's just one. Sam," I say, my voice dropping into a depressed note as I say his name.

"But the other two are okay?"

"Oh yes. They're lovely."

"What's Sam done to upset you?" she asks.

"I think he's just being himself." I look up at her. "Arrogant, self-opinionated, conceited."

"Oh… you mean he's being a guy," she says, grinning.

I laugh. "Yeah… pretty much." I sigh. "I know if I was at home I'd be able to handle it better, but being so far away and worrying about my sister just makes it all seem worse. I'm being pathetic."

"No you're not." She leans over and puts her hand gently on my arm. "Don't let him get to you," she says softly. "If he's anything like most men, he's not worth it."

"That's a bleak perspective," I reply.

"It's a realistic, hard-fought, bleak perspective," she says and we stare at each other for a moment in mutual understanding. "Now," she says, sitting back and squaring her shoulders resolutely, "let's get down to business."

Sam

"What the fuck is wrong with you?" Ed turns on me and I'm shocked into silence for a moment. This isn't like him. He's the placid one. He rarely swears, and if anyone was gonna go for me, I would have expected it to be Rob. "Ali's doing an amazing job, which we all agreed we needed help with, and all you're doing is being a pain in the ass."

I'm just about to yell back when Rob says, "Quiet!" He grabs Ed's arm, and puts his finger to his lips. We all stand for a moment.

We can hear the unmistakable sound of someone crying. It's Ali. And she's not just crying; she's sobbing her heart out.

I turn away and go over to the work bench, leaning down onto my elbows and putting my head in my hands. This is my fault. Again.

"Happy now?" Rob asks from behind me.

"No."

"You've made her cry again," Ed says.

"You think I don't know that?" I stand and turn around, facing them both. They look so disappointed. They're quite right to. *I'm* disappointed.

"Why do you keep doing this to her?" Rob asks.

I shrug. I'm not going to explain it to them. How can I, when I don't understand it myself? "I was never fully on board with this." I wave my hand around the room. It's a pathetic excuse and I know it.

"And that's a good enough reason for you to act the way you are?" Rob asks

I shrug again. I'm behaving like a petulant child.

"I can't talk to you when you're like this" Rob says. "You don't need me here, do you?" He looks at Ed, who shakes his head. "Good. I'm going home." He walks back out the door and Ed and I are left alone.

He looks at me for a long while. "Leave it," I tell him, quietly.

He shakes his head, but doesn't say anything, then comes over and we start looking at the plans. A few minutes later, we hear Ali leave, presumably for the meeting she told us about. Ed glances over at me, maybe expecting me to go out and apologize to her. I don't move, and he sighs deeply before shaking his head and returning his gaze to the plans.

It doesn't take us long to decide to leave everything exactly as Ali had already laid it out. Apart from the addition of the convection ovens and the new walls, she's avoided moving too much around from the way the kitchen used to be laid out, and it feels sensible to stick to that plan. We're used to things being where they were, and we'd probably get confused if the equipment was moved about too much.

"Do you want me to let her know?" Ed asks, pulling out his phone. "I can text her."

"It's probably for the best," I reply. "I'll see you upstairs."

"Okay. Put the coffee on," he calls from behind me.

"So you think I should experiment with different granita flavors?" Ed asks me.

"Definitely."

Ali's given him a real challenge with this dairy-free thing. Gluten-free isn't so hard, but a lot of Italian desserts feature cream in fairly large quantities, and although Ed's been trying a few substitutes, he's found the results aren't that impressive. He's already come up with an idea for a kind of semifreddo, which strictly speaking doesn't qualify for the name, being as it contains no cream, or eggs… but he says he thinks it'll work and I trust him. He's also worked out how to make a dairy-free gelato, using coconut or almond milk. He wants to start adding different flavors to that now as well.

"Was there anything else?" I ask him.

"About the recipes? No, I don't think so."

"Do you want another coffee?"

"Sure." He passes his cup across the island unit to me and I pour us both a cup from the machine. Before I've turned around I hear him let out a long breath and I know he's building up to asking me a question.

"What's wrong?" I ask him.

"Why are you being such an asshole around Ali?" he asks me outright.

I'm in the middle of stirring sugar into Ed's cup and I stop. "I don't know," I reply.

"Bullshit. You've gotta know why you're doing it." He takes the cup from my hand, looking up at me. "Why can't you accept that she's here to help, and that she's doing a really good job? She is, you know."

"Yeah, I know."

"Then why, Sam?"

"I don't know," I repeat. "I feel like such a shit for talking to her the way I do."

He puts his cup down and leans forward.

"Is it because you're attracted to her?" he asks.

"No," I say. "I'm not."

He smirks. "Are you blind? You have seen how good she looks, haven't you?"

I laugh, just slightly. "Okay, she's beautiful, and she's sexy, but that doesn't mean I'm interested in her."

"You keep telling yourself that, Sam. Who knows, you may even convince yourself one day."

"It's true," I say.

"Well, I'm not so sure it is." I shake my head at him. His eyes don't leave mine. "The thing is," he adds, "even if you're not – and I'm not saying I believe you – you need to remember she's a woman."

"I can hardly forget that, can I?" I point out.

"Well, evidently you can," he says. "What you're doing to her is all wrong. We don't treat women like that." He sighs. "Hell, Sam, you even treated Amber better than that."

"What are you talking about? I yelled at Amber all the time. We fought like cat and dog."

"Yeah, but Amber liked that. We all knew you two fought hard and we all knew why. It wasn't exactly a secret. We'd have had to be deaf and blind not to notice. That was who you were as a couple. From what I could see, it was pretty much all you were as a couple." I'm not sure I like the fact that we were that transparent, but I let it pass. "The thing is, when Amber cheated, you stayed calm. You were ruthlessly calm.

You weren't nasty. You just ended it. But with Ali, you're being so damn cruel. And it really isn't like you."

"Isn't it?"

"No, Sam. It isn't. Whatever it is you're fighting in your own head, stop taking it out on Ali. Try and think about what you're doing – because it's getting worse for her every time you do it. Treat her a bit more decently, because that's who you are, if you can try and remember back to the guy you used to be before Amber messed with your head. I know you never did long-term relationships with women before you got married, but you were always polite, you were always fair, and honest. And if you can't at least be those things with Ali – and yourself – then just walk away and leave her alone."

Ed's been gone for nearly an hour. I'm still sitting at the island unit. I've even still got my cold coffee cup clasped in my hand.

I'm not sure I agree with Ed's appraisal of my character, but he's right about one thing: I am attracted to Ali. Of course I am. Every man who sees her is attracted to her. I've wanted her since the first moment I saw her, like I've never wanted any woman before. And for the first time in my life, I don't just want her to give me control of her body, so I can fuck her – my way – until she's begging me to let her come… I want *her*. All of her. And I think that's part of the problem. This is all so alien to me. I've got no idea how to behave around her. I don't even know how to react to my own feelings. And the thing is, I can't. I can't react to them. Because I can't have her. I might be hurting her now, but if we got together, it would be like putting a delicate flower in the middle of a tempestuous storm. I'm the storm, and I know I'd break her. She'd fade to dust in the hands of someone like me. Even if I didn't mean to, I know I would destroy her.

I can't do that to her.

What's more, I won't.

Chapter Eight

Ali

I had a really nice time with Petra yesterday evening. After what happened with Sam, it was just what I needed. We turned coffee into dinner and, once the business part of the meeting was over with, we talked for hours – well I did. She was right; she is a good listener. We got along really well, which felt good, and I've left it that I'll call her next week to finalise the arrangements for the opening.

Ed sent me a text telling me that he and Sam have decided not to change the layout of the kitchen from the plans I'd had drawn up. He also asked if I was okay and said he could come and talk to me later, if I needed to. I was with Petra at the time, but texted back and thanked him for letting me know, and for being so kind. I told him I was fine. I wasn't. But I'm not sure Sam's brothers are the best people for me to talk to anyway.

Today, I've decided to try and have a better day. Even if only on the basis that it can't get any worse. Well, it can't, can it?

Sam seems to have taken to coming downstairs in the mornings. He did it yesterday and stood in the kitchen for a while, watching me. Today, he's back again. I decide that, rather than ignoring him again, I'll see if we can actually try and get along. Maybe if I involve him a little more, he won't be so hostile.

"Hi." I go over and stand in front of him. He's wearing jeans and another tight t-shirt and I can't help but take a quick look at him. I was quite right yesterday. He is very muscular. He's got really long legs too.

I hadn't noticed before   probably because he's been so busy being horrible.

"Good morning," he says, a little formally.

I decide not to be put off. "Did you want me to show you what we're doing?" I ask him.

"Okay." He shrugs.

I move away to where the walls are now being constructed, and he follows.

"This area here is going to be Ed's workspace," I say, pointing in to the room that Ed will occupy.

"Surely, it's not big enough," he says, looking down at me, his eyes turning dark already. "How do you expect to fit everything he needs into there?"

"We don't," I tell him, and move back a little, turning to my left. "This space here…" I indicate an area along the left hand wall. "This will house two convection ovens, a freezer and the blast chiller. The top of the partition wall will be made of glass, so Ed will be able to see what's going on in the ovens and there won't be a door, just an opening, so he won't have any trouble carrying things through."

"I see," he says. "And what about this space here?" He points to the area further down the left hand wall.

"There will be a housing for the two refrigerators, and then four more convection ovens for the main kitchen. You'll have further oven space in the modular unit," I explain, "but I think the convection ovens, being at eye-level, will be more useful."

He nods his head, then turns around. "I noticed we don't have as much storage as we used to."

"Well, putting in the additional rooms was always going to necessitate a compromise," I tell him. This feels like it's going well. He seems interested – even enthusiastic. And he's not shouting at me, for once.

"A compromise?" he replies.

"Yes. You've still got all the dry food storage you used to have, but we'll be creating a hanging wall for all the pans." I point to the wall opposite where the convection ovens will be housed. "I prefer to hang pans anyway," I explain. "It means you can see where things are and you know straight away when something hasn't been put back in the right place."

"Right." He moves over to the wall and looks up at it, even though there's nothing there.

"I noticed you use copper pans," I say, following him. "So, I've chosen the edging to match."

"Edging?" He looks down at me.

"Yes, around the ovens and the modular unit, we had the option of putting a decorative trim. It's not strictly necessary, but I thought it would look nicer. I've gone for the copper finish, to match your pans."

"Copper," he says, a little absentmindedly.

"Yes. Is that okay?" I hope we're not going to have an argument about the edging. It's so trivial.

He shrugs. "I'm not sure it matters," he says.

"Well, I just wanted to make the place look nice."

"You think that's important?" he says, and I hear that hard edge to his voice again.

"Not as important as the functionality, obviously," I reply.

"Good. I'm glad you worked that out."

"Please, Sam."

"What?" He bites my head off.

"Oh, just forget it. I was trying…" My voice cracks.

"Trying what?"

"Trying to be nice. I don't know why I bothered."

"Neither do I. I don't even know why you're showing me around. You've so clearly got everything under control, I'm not even sure why I'm here."

He glares at me, then storms out of the kitchen and I hear the key turn in the door up to his apartment.

I give up. I really do.

I've avoided Sam for the last couple of days and, although it's now Saturday, I'm still here. Sometimes I wonder why, given Sam's attitude, but I am still here.

I fully expected to have to work the weekends on this job. With such a tight schedule, there's no such thing as a day off. If we're going to get everything ready in time for the re-opening, then every hour of every day counts.

Tess either calls or texts each evening before she goes to bed. She seems okay. She's busy working on her dissertation. The deadline is looming and I think she's getting a little stressed. I haven't told her how bad things have been here with Sam. She doesn't need the additional worry and I'm fairly sure she'd tell me to come home, but that's not really an option. I couldn't do that to Rob and Ed, even if I did feel like I could go back on the contract – which I don't.

The thing is, if Sam wasn't such a horrible person, I still think I could really like him. I've thought that since the first time I saw him. He's the kind of man I've always dreamt of being with. There's no denying that he's good to look at. He's got beautiful eyes, and a lovely deep voice – when he's not shouting at me – and, although he doesn't smile as often as he should, when he does, it brightens the whole room. On a couple of occasions, I've overheard him talking to his brothers, or the workmen and I've discovered that he's not always arrogant, or obnoxious. He can be considerate, even kind. On top of all that, there's something else about him, although I'm not quite sure what it is. I've obviously worked out that he's strong-willed, maybe a little controlling, but he's also kind of mysterious, dark, and very, very sexy. He's the antithesis of Liam – who I've realised was never right for me – and, if it wasn't for the fact that Sam seems to despise me, I'd quite like to find out more.

Perhaps it's the fact that he despises me that upsets me so much. I guess I maybe want him to like me too, just a little bit. But that's never going to happen…

I've just finished lunch, which I've had to eat in the kitchen, because Rob's using the office for once to have a meeting with a potential new supplier, when I get a call from the refrigeration company. They're really apologetic, but the new units won't be with us until the end of next week. I tell them it'll be okay, as long as they absolutely guarantee delivery by next Friday. They assure me they won't let me down, and we hang up. I take a deep breath. I guess I should let someone know. The installation was planned for Wednesday afternoon. The electrician is going to be here all of next week, so it won't be a problem for him and I can speak to him later, but either Rob, Ed or Sam ought to know. If I don't tell them and they come down on Wednesday and find they don't have any fridges or freezers, they're going to think I'm not doing my job properly.

I obviously can't speak to Rob – he's in a meeting.

I decide to try Ed, so I look up his details and connect the call, but it goes straight to voicemail and I choose not to leave a message. I know he's busy working on recipes and that he's been having problems. I guess he's maybe turned his phone off and the last thing he needs is me causing more hassle.

This leaves me with no option other than to tell Sam. I have absolutely no doubt that he'll find some way to make this my fault and to blame me for being incompetent again, but that really isn't the case.

I take a deep breath and go out into the corridor. I know the door to his apartment is open, because Sam was down here earlier and didn't lock it when he went back up, so I go straight through and up the stairs that lie ahead of me. The stairway is steep and narrow and, at the top, there's another door. I knock, but there's no reply, so I push and it opens.

"Hello?" I call. Again, there's no response, so I go inside. I'm in a small entry way, which opens into a large living room, the walls of which are all exposed brick. There's a big L-shaped couch in the centre of the room, with a coffee table in front, and a TV set on the opposite wall, flanked by a couple of tall bookcases. On the other side of the room, over by the window, is a rectangular dining table, surrounded by eight chairs. To my left is a corridor with some doors leading off – bedrooms, I guess – and to the right is a wide opening into a huge kitchen. It's exactly the kind of kitchen I'd love. Almost everything in it seems to be made of either copper, or wood, with the exception of the stainless steel stove, in front of which Sam is standing, with his back to me.

"Hello?" I say again, and he turns, a wooden spoon in his hand. His eyes drop to my legs, for some reason, and then move slowly upward until he reaches my face. His expression changes and I flush, feeling guilty for invading his private space. "The door was open," I explain.

"It usually is," he replies.

I move forward into the kitchen, so we're separated by what some people might call an island unit, but I'd call it a really big butcher's block. It's basically a massive solid piece of wood, with some cupboard space beneath. I can see he's busy – much of the surface of the block is covered with various ingredients and pieces of paper, with notes scribbled on them. I can still see how beautiful the wood is though, and I run my hand along its worn surface.

"I—I came up to let you know that I've heard from the refrigeration company," I start to explain.

"And?" He's already turned back to the stove, and is stirring something in a pan.

I want to see what he's cooking and I move around the unit so I'm standing closer. He glances up at me. "And they're going to be late delivering the units," I tell him, leaning over slightly so I can smell whatever it is that's in his pan.

"Late?" he says.

"Yes." I stand upright again. I can't work out what he's making. I can't get close enough without really getting in his space, which I know will make him angry. "They should be here on Tuesday and being installed on Wednesday, but they can't deliver until Friday. I'm going to speak—"

"Friday?" He drops the spoon into the pan and turns to me. "Friday?"

"Yes, but it's fine—"

"Oh, is it?"

"Yes. I'll speak to the electrician." He folds his arms across his chest. "I'll speak to the electrician on Monday and we'll re-arrange the schedule to accommodate it."

He stares at me for a moment, then suddenly remembers the saucepan on the stove.

"Fuck it," he says. He yanks the pan off the heat and flicks off the gas, before moving the spoon around, lifting it up and staring at it. "Ruined," he mutters. "Completely fucking ruined."

"Sorry."

"Sorry?" He turns on me and, before I even have time to react, he hurls the pan. It lands in the sink which I hadn't realised was behind me and I jump at the violence of his reaction.

"Sam!" I raise my voice, shocked by his behaviour.

He runs his fingers through his hair. "What?" He glares at me.

"That was totally unnecessary."

"Was it? I've been working on that for hours. That's the fifth time I've tried to get it right and I really thought I had it that time… and now it's totally fucking ruined."

"And I said I'm sorry for distracting you."

He stops, just for a second, like he doesn't understand what I'm saying.

"I don't even get why you're here," he says eventually.

"I explained… about the refrigeration company."

"I know that. But why do you have to come up here and bother me with it? Why can't you just handle it yourself? What's the point in you even being here, if you're just gonna come running to me every time something goes wrong? "

It takes a moment – a moment in which all I do is stare at him – before I feel the familiar sting of tears in my eyes. Why do I let him do this to me? Well, for once, I'm not going to. I'm not going to let him see how vulnerable he makes me feel.

"What is your fucking problem?" I yell at him. His mouth drops open, probably because I just swore for the first time in front of him. I'm angry with myself for doing that, but I'm not going to show it, and I'm not going to give him a chance to interrupt, either. "I couldn't speak to Rob because he's in a meeting and I can't get a reply on Ed's phone. Trust me, Sam… I tried both of them before coming up here, because I'd rather speak to pretty much anyone before I have to speak to you. But I couldn't. I was only telling you that there's going to be a problem out of courtesy – something which you clearly lack. And, being as you still haven't worked it out, the point in me being here, is to give you and your brothers a better restaurant – which is what you asked me to do, and what I'm trying to do, despite your God-awful attitude towards me – which I don't think I deserve." I can feel my blood reaching boiling point as I glare at him. "Do you know what?" I shout. "I've really had enough of you. Just… Just get out." He stands his ground. "Didn't you hear me? I said get out. Now!"

Sam

I stare at her for a moment, unable to believe she really just said all that. I'm not denying it's true. I just can't believe she actually said it.

"Get out!" she yells again.

"Fine!" I yell back, and I turn and walk quickly around the island unit, through the living room and out the door, which I slam behind me.

I get halfway down the stairs before I stop in my tracks.

"What the fuck?" I say out loud, then turn and go back up the stairs, taking them two at a time. I crash back into the apartment, the door banging on the wall behind it. "This is *my* fucking apartment," I bellow. "If anyone's gonna leave, it's you."

She's still standing exactly where I left her, right by the sink. Her head is in her hands and her shoulders are shaking. Shit, she's crying.

She drops her hands and looks up at me, and I see there are tears streaming down her face, but before I can say a word, she runs toward the door.

"Ali?" I try to grab her arm as she moves past me, but she yanks it free.

"Leave me alone," she hisses, glaring into my eyes through her tears, and I release her. I hear her footsteps clattering down the stairs and I stand still, just for moment, thinking through what just happened.

She argued with me. She even swore at me. I was surprised by that. She threw me out of my apartment and, while that got me mad, as soon as I saw her crying, I knew I wanted to hold her. And I really mean that this time. I wanted her in my arms. No, I *needed* her in my arms, because for a moment then, *she'd* become the storm and, although I was in there with her, our emotions churning together, I knew she's not like Amber. She's nothing like Amber. She didn't belong in there, in that maelstrom with me, and I needed to catch her and calm her.

Fear suddenly grips me. I've known fear before. The night dad had his heart attack was real scary. Wondering whether Amber was on birth control, or whether her lover had used protection didn't make me feel too good either. But this fear is something else. What if Ali's gone? What if she's decided she can't handle this anymore and has gone back to the hotel to pack her bags?

I don't even think about it. I bolt out of the apartment and down the stairs, quickly checking the kitchen. She's not there. I run through to the restaurant. She's not in here either.

"You looking for Ali?" one of the workmen asks me. It's the muscular guy, the one she was laughing with the other day.

"Yeah."

"She just ran straight though here and out onto the street," he says, nodding toward the front door.

"Thanks."

I take off after her. "She looked real upset," he calls after me.

I know. I did that.

I stand out on the street, looking up and down. One advantage to being six foot four, is that you can see over a lot of people. But I can't see Ali. I can't see her anywhere.

I stand still, wondering what I should do. I'm assuming she's probably gone back to the hotel, but I don't know her room number. I could go there and ask. I could go up to her room and talk to her, although I'm not sure what I'd say. What are you supposed to say when you've done what I've done? I've got no idea. Sorry, I guess. Have I ever said sorry in my life? I might've done, once or twice, maybe. I turn, my hands clasped on the back of my head, my confusion almost overwhelming me now, and I stare up at the front of the restaurant, my mouth open. I hadn't seen this, and I let my hands drop to my sides again. All the dark wood has gone, as has the painting on the windows. I always hated that. A gray base coat has been applied to all the woodwork and I know that when it's finished it's gonna look absolutely amazing. It's much more tasteful, even now. What was there before was our parents' choice from thirty years ago. This is us, as we are now. Ali listened to us, watched us, got to know us, and she's making this place so much better. And she's not just making the restaurant better either, she's making us better too. We've stopped resting on our dad's laurels and we've finally started doing something for ourselves, instead of making excuses. So why can't I do that with her? Why can't I treat her better?

I feel my shoulders slump, just as the front door opens and Rob steps out, bringing a suited guy with him. They shake hands and Rob smiles.

"Thanks for coming over on a Saturday," he says, "and sorry again for all the mess."

"It's no problem," the guy replies. "It's really interesting to see what you're doing here. I'll definitely be coming along once you've re-opened, even if you don't give us the contract. I can't wait to see the finished product."

"Give me a call," Rob says. "I'll book you a table."

The guy nods and leaves. Then Rob turns to me.

"You okay?" he asks. "You look pale."

"I'm fine," I lie.

"And you're out here, because…?"

"I was just looking at the frontage."

He comes and stands beside me, looking up. "I know. It's gonna look so good, isn't it?"

"Yeah."

His phone beeps and he pulls it from his pocket, reading the message, before replacing it. Then he turns to me.

"Anything you wanna tell me?" he says.

"What about?"

"Ali."

"What about her?" I look down at him.

"The message was from her."

"What did she say?" I just want to know she's okay – and that she's not going home.

"That she's sorry she left early and she'll be back in the morning." I sigh out my relief and close my eyes. "Okay," he says. "Now I know this had something to do with you. What did you say to her this time?"

"Nothing I haven't said before – I don't think. I can't really remember now. She interrupted me making a sauce and I kinda lost it with her."

"Excellent. Way to go, Sam."

"I fucked up. I get it." And I don't need Rob to make me feel any worse than I already do.

"Do you? Do you really?" He stares at me. "We're going into the office," he says. "We're gonna talk, and you're not leaving until we've worked this out." And without waiting for an answer, he goes inside. I follow, just a couple of seconds behind him. We ignore the workmen, who all stop what they're doing and watch us pass through the restaurant, and then we go into the office and I close the door behind us.

He sits down behind the desk. This is his domain, after all, although he's sharing it with Ali at the moment. I sit opposite him and we just look at each other for a full minute, before he speaks.

"You seriously need to stop being a fucking idiot," he says. "Ali only wants what's best for us."

"I know. I've worked that out for myself. It's taken me a while, but I have worked it out."

"And have you worked out why you're being like this with her?" I don't reply and he continues, "You've gotta stop thinking that every woman you meet is gonna be like Amber, or you're gonna end up a really lonely, unhappy guy. Even more so than you are already."

"I don't think that." I really don't. Especially not after what just happened.

"Yeah you do," he persists. "That's why you haven't been with anyone since she left." I didn't realize he was aware of that.

"Well, I'm not even thinking about Ali like that," I lie, ignoring his comment.

"Yeah, you are. That's why you're being such a fucking idiot. She's got to you. I can see it; Ed can see it…"

"Have you guys spoken about this then?"

"Of course we have. We live together. You're being a nightmare to work with at the moment. Naturally, we're gonna talk about it." He pauses for a moment. "The problem is, Sam, that she's got to you, and you don't want to admit it. She may not be your usual type but you want to be with her, and the sooner you accept that, the better for everyone – especially her."

"My usual type?" What does he mean by that? He's the one that has a 'type', not me.

"Yeah. Before Amber, all the women you went with, they liked to be… how shall I put it? Dominated?" He looks at me. "They liked the way you did things." I lower my eyes and stare at the back of his desk. "I'm not judging, Sam," he says quietly. "We all have things we like doing, and things we don't like doing." He smirks. "Unless you're me, in which case you like doing pretty much everything."

"And everyone," I quip, looking up at him.

He smiles and shrugs. "Not quite everyone… The point is, as long as you do whatever you like to do with people who feel the same way, then that's fine." He pauses and sighs. "Of course, Amber didn't though, did she?" She's always been a bit of a sore point between us. We rarely talk about her because I'm fairly sure we both have things we'd rather not reveal. I don't reply. "She never wanted the same things as you," he continues, "and the best thing you two could have done for each other would have been to walk away."

"I should never have married her," I admit. "You were right about that."

"Yeah," he says. "But I don't get any pleasure from it, you know. Not this time."

"And what makes you think I could have something with Ali?" I ask him, my voice barely more than a whisper. "You've seen her. She's like an English rose. She's delicate, like porcelain. She's beautiful and kind and… romantic. I seriously doubt she'd be into the type of things I like to do, and I think five minutes with me would probably be the end of her." I stare at the wall behind him. I don't want to make eye contact. "You do realize I've never even been on a date, don't you? Not a proper one…"

"Yeah," he says, like I'm asking a really dumb question. "Sam, until you married Amber, we all lived in the same apartment, and had done since we were born. We all know pretty much everything about each other."

"Which means you should know that I'm almost certainly not the guy for Ali. Besides, what makes you think she'd be interested in me?"

"Oh, so many reasons," he says, smiling. "First, there was the fact that, despite my best attempts to flirt with her, she was no more than polite and friendly with both me and Ed, but she came alive when I introduced her to you."

"She did?"

"Well, you might have noticed it for yourself, if you hadn't been so determined to be such an asshole around her."

I don't have a reply for that.

"Then," he continues, "there's the way that, no matter how horrible you've been to her, she's sucked it up. Well, she has for the most part. You've made her cry, you've made her sad, you've made her every kind of crazy there is going, and she's taken it, and kept coming back."

I shake my head slowly. "I know," I murmur. "If I'd done any of that to Amber, she'd have turned on me and used any and every little failing of mine against me. She'd have started a big fight, based on all my shortcomings." Amber was good at that.

"Yeah. And then she'd have demanded you fuck her. Her way. Not yours. It was always about punishment with Amber."

"I know… But, well, even if you're right and Ali is interested in me, I still don't see how any of that helps. She's nothing like me and, like I say, I really doubt she'd be into the things I want to do."

"You don't know that. But has it occurred to you that you could try something different?" He holds my gaze.

"Who says I wanna be different?" The thought of giving up control terrifies me, but I'm not about to admit that to Rob.

"Well, you're not exactly doing great right now, are you?"

"I know, but I'm not sure I could handle a vanilla relationship. It sounds so… bland." And scary.

"You don't know if you don't try," he says. "And who says it has to be vanilla? Even if she isn't into the same things as you to start off with, she might get to like them, once she tries. And if she doesn't, you might find you can work something out that keeps you both happy, find some kind of middle ground. I'm not saying you've gotta stop being who you are, but let's face it, what you're doing now isn't working, man. You're just hurting both of you."

I let out a really long sigh. He has a point. Maybe I could try a compromise. I guess I don't have to start off as full-on as I normally would; I could try taking it slower, and as long as I kept within my boundaries, and wasn't giving up complete control, I might be able to handle it… "Okay, what do you suggest?"

"Well, you say she's romantic, and I think you're probably right. So why not try being romantic?"

"Me?" I scoff. Romance isn't exactly what I had in mind.

"Yeah. You. It's not that hard."

"What, you mean buy her flowers, or something? She'll see right through that, especially after the way I was with her today."

"No. Not flowers. You've gotta be yourself. You're not a flowers kind of guy. There's no point in trying to be something you're not."

"Well, I'm not romantic."

"Yeah. You are."

"Rob…" I glare at him.

"You are. In your own way. You've just never met someone you wanted to try being romantic with. It's basically just about putting her needs before yours; it's about caring, *and* showing it, making time, and taking time, and putting in a bit of effort. You can do that. You know you can. Look at how you are with Ed… If you stop being a jerk around her and start being the guy we all know you really are – when you're not yelling at people – then something will just happen."

"If it's meant to, you mean? Like fate?"

"I don't believe in fate. I mean that you'll see a situation and you'll decide you can act on it. You'll see something you can do that's kind, rather than mean. You've just gotta let yourself."

Rob's words have been ringing in my ears all evening. We haven't spoken like that since Amber left. It was Rob who sat down with me on the night I threw her out. He did his best to convince me that it wasn't my fault, that what she said and what she did wasn't a reflection on me, or my abilities – although I'm still not wholly convinced on that one – and then he got real drunk with me, because there's nothing worse in that situation than getting drunk by yourself.

He's right. I need to try and be different with Ali. She's different. I'm not sure if it's a 'different' we can make work, but I'd really like to try.

The only problems I've got now are, will she forgive me and let me try, and if she does, how will I even begin?

Chapter Nine

Ali

I've tried being kinder and more conciliatory with Sam. I've tried working with him, ignoring him, including him, and everything else I can think of. So, after yesterday, I've decided I'm going to just let it happen. If he wants to talk to me, fine. If not, fine. I'm not going to go out of my way to communicate with him, but I won't be impolite. I just can't handle another scene like yesterday's and, if I feel one brewing, I've decided I'm simply going to walk away. He can yell at himself, for all I care, but he's not yelling at me. Ever again.

I've got a lot to do in the office today. It's Sunday but the contractors are all still in, working hard. I need to look at the website. I decided to use the same designers who built my new site last year. They're based just outside London, but that doesn't matter. Rob said they wanted a European feel and I think we'll get that if we use a British based company for the design. I'm just applying his logic. They sent over the initial designs on Friday and I haven't had time to check them out. I've got to get back to them tomorrow, so I'll take some time today to sit down and go through them.

The boys don't even know I'm doing this. They think we're just revamping the old site and updating the photographs, but I decided we had the budget to completely change it, so we might as well.

The other thing they don't know about is that I've also been running an ad campaign in the local press, highlighting the re-opening date and, as we get nearer to it, I plan on ramping this up.

I sit down at the desk and open up my laptop. The designs look really good. I'm pleased with what they've done and I'm happy for them to go ahead. Because it's a surprise for the boys, I'm making the decision by myself, and if Sam doesn't like it, he can whistle.

The senior designer has sent in a separate email, asking for the copy for the menus and biographies for all three brothers. And she also wants photographs of them. I should have thought of this. I've arranged for Petra to come in for the opening to take pictures then, and she's coming in the weekend after the opening to do some pictures of Sam and Ed, being as it's going to be hard to get those on the night – but I should probably have asked her if she could come in beforehand to take some headshots for the website. After our conversation the other evening, I know she's not available over the next couple of days. She told me she was booked up with a wedding shoot, which was going to take the whole weekend, from Friday to Monday. And she wasn't looking forward to it, because the bride was being difficult. I've brought my own camera though, so I guess I could do it myself… providing I can get them to agree, that is.

I pick up my phone from the desk and tap out a message to all three of them. I've set up a message group now. It makes things easier.

— Good morning. Sorry to trouble you on a Sunday. I need a couple of things. Rob, if possible, could you let me have biographies for all three of you, about 150-200 words each. Sam, I need the menus as soon as they're available. And I need all three of you here tomorrow morning for me to take some photographs. If Sam and Ed can wear their whites and Rob can be in his usual restaurant attire, that would be great. Shall we say 10am? Thanks, Ali.

I've found it's best not to give them too many options.

Rob's reply comes through straight away. He says he'll get onto the biographies, and have them with me before the end of the day. He's intrigued by the photography and wants to know what it's for, but says he and Ed will be here.

Sam, on the other hand, still hasn't replied by early afternoon.

I'm starting to wonder whether I'm going to have to go upstairs again. Maybe he's turned his phone off, so he can concentrate on cooking. The thought of another scene with him fills me with dread, but I need an answer on the menus. I'm just wondering if I should send the message again, or maybe call him, or Rob, when there's a knock on the door.

"Yes?" I call out.

The door opens and Sam comes in.

It seems to me that – outside the kitchen – he must only wear jeans and tight t-shirts, because that's what he's wearing again. He has to know how good he looks, surely? That's got to be the reason he dresses like this – because he knows his physique is shown off to its best.

"I'm sorry I didn't get back to you sooner," he says. His voice is soft – deep, but soft. "I had a couple of things I needed to adjust. I've changed some of the ingredients since I wrote this, so I had to amend the descriptions on the menus."

"Oh. Okay." I'm a bit taken aback. He's being so polite. I'm almost tempted to ask if Rob and Ed aren't the only twins in the family and the man before me is actually Sam's twin – the nicer one.

He's got his laptop tucked under his arm and puts it down on the desk in front of him, opening it and turning it around to face me.

"Why don't you take a look," he says, "while I go and get us both a coffee?"

"Where from?" There are no coffee machines down here anymore. A new one is being fitted next week.

"I'll run upstairs and make one," he replies.

"Oh. That'd be lovely. Thank you."

"How do you take it?" he asks.

"White, no sugar."

"Okay. Back in a minute."

I stare at him. Actually, I stare at the space he was standing in, long after he's departed it. Can this really be the same man who threw a saucepan at me yesterday, and then yelled at me to get out of his apartment? The same man who's called my abilities into question at every opportunity, who's doubted everything I've said, and insulted me more times and in more ways than I care to remember? I guess it has to be. But what on earth is going on here, I have no idea.

I force myself to focus on his laptop screen and start reading through the menu, and I've only gone through the appetisers when my stomach starts to grumble. I haven't had lunch yet and I didn't think I was that hungry, until I started reading all the delicious things Sam's planning.

"What do you think?" The sound of his voice makes me jump and I look up. He's holding out a mug of coffee to me and I take it.

"Thank you," I say. "The menu looks delicious. I'm really impressed."

"So, not dull then."

I look up again, half expecting to see a scowl, but he's smiling at me. "No, not dull at all." I smile back. Wow. He's even got a sense of humour now?

I turn the computer back around to him. "I'll email it to you," he says. "So you've got a copy."

"Thank you."

My phone beeps and I pick it up, expecting it to be Rob. It isn't. It's Tess.

—Just having dinner by myself. Didn't bother with take-away. Sunday nights aren't the same without you. Miss you lots. T xx

Reading her words brings tears to my eyes and I dwell on the last sentence. I miss her too. I've been here for a month now and I really do miss her. A lot. I miss the same things she does. Our little routines, the things we do together. God, I'd really just like to curl up and cry right now.

Sam

I'd been wondering how to take Rob's advice. All night – well most of it – I'd been thinking about when such an opportunity might present itself, imagining scenarios and how I could react to them. I never expected something to happen the very next morning.

Getting Ali's message about the menu gave me my first chance to show her I can be a nice guy. Okay, so all I did was bring the menu down and offer her a coffee. Not exactly ground-breaking stuff. But, a couple of days ago, I'd probably have told her she had to wait until it was ready and to stop hassling me. This feels like progress. We even shared a little joke – I asked her if the menu was dull, reminding her what she'd said about the old one, and she'd smiled at me. She actually smiled at me. And I have no idea why that's got me so fired up, but it has.

I'm watching her read a message on her phone and I feel more drawn to her than ever. She's biting her bottom lip as she's reading and I'm finding it hard not to walk around the desk and bite it myself. Feeling the way I do right now, I'm wondering why I ever bothered to fight this. I should have acted sooner, instead of wasting so much time being a jerk.

She looks up and I'd swear to God my heart stops beating. There are tears in her eyes.

"What's wrong?" I ask. I don't think it's anything I did, is it? Did I do anything?

"It's nothing."

"It's clearly something, Ali."

She looks at me, like she's really confused. I guess she would be. She's got no idea why I'm suddenly being so much nicer to her.

"Okay, it is something," she admits. "I'm… I'm feeling a bit homesick, that's all."

And I'm suddenly reminded that she's miles from home. That, one day, she'll go back there, and I'll be on my own again. What's wrong with me? We haven't even started anything yet and I'm already worrying about it ending. I shake my head. I can't think about that. Not yet, anyway.

"Homesick?" I clarify, buying myself some time while I get my thoughts in order.

"Yes."

And then an even worse thought strikes me. Is she missing home? Or is she missing *someone* at home? I don't know why, but I've never even considered that she might have boyfriend. She's not married, or engaged. I know this, because I checked her ring finger ages ago, but that doesn't mean she's not in a relationship. Ali's a 'relationship' kind of person.

"It's just silly things," she says, her voice cutting into my worrying thoughts. "Sunday nights have always been the night my sister and I would spend together." She makes eye contact with me and my breath catches in my throat. "That goes back to when I was training to be a chef," she says.

"You were a chef?" I interrupt.

"Yes."

Her eyes are filled with anxiety, like she expects me to shout at her for not telling us this earlier. I don't. I'm too busy feeling ashamed of myself for assuming she knew nothing, and I knew it all. "Sorry, I interrupted you," I say.

She looks surprised, but continues, "We didn't live together then. Tess lived with our grandmother and I lived in London, but I always went home on Sundays and Tess and I would make a point of spending the evenings together, before I went back to the city. And then, when she started Uni and moved in with me, the tradition kind of continued."

"Were you still a chef by then?" I ask. "Did you stick to Sundays because that was your day off?"

"No, I'd already started my company by that stage." She shrugs. "I know we could've changed the night, but Sundays just became our night."

"And what do these Sunday night traditions consist of?" I ask her. I'm surprised that I'm genuinely interested in hearing about her life. That's never happened to me before. I didn't even know how old most of my previous sexual partners were, let alone anything about their backgrounds.

"Oh, nothing special," she says, smiling. "We'll normally just get a takeaway and sit in front of the TV watching a box-set."

"And what reminded you of that?" I ask her.

"The message was from Tess," she explains. "She was just saying that she misses me." Her voice cracks on the last three words, but she attempts a smile.

I'm about to get up and go to her, when the phone rings on the desk.

"Excuse me," she says and picks up the handset. "Rosa's. How can I help you?" God, she sounds so businesslike, so professional. And certainly not like she's in tears – which she is. And I want to hold her more than ever.

She opens a file on the desk, confirming the specifications of something, and I stand. She looks up at me, and I point upwards, indicating that I'm going back upstairs. Nodding, she gives me another smile, then holds up her cup and mouths 'thank you' to me.

"You're welcome," I whisper and then turn and leave.

Back in the apartment upstairs, I sit down on a stool in the kitchen and wonder what I can do to cheer up Ali. It really bothered me seeing her so upset. It also bothered me that she's gonna go back to England at some point, but I'll cross that bridge when I get to it. At the moment, that bridge is far off in the distance still, and I've got a long way to go to even get to it.

I need to think of something I can do to make her feel better, even though she's miles from home and missing her sister – evidently. She didn't mention a boyfriend at all, and while I know that doesn't mean I'm in the clear, I feel relieved that it's her sister she's pining for, and not some British hunk. I look around. I love this room. It's my favorite part of the apartment – except for my bedroom. I remodeled the whole place after Amber left, to try and banish the memories of her. It worked. I can't picture her – or us – here at all anymore.

In the kitchen, probably my favorite thing is the island unit. I run my hand along its wooden surface. I guess you'd really call it a butcher's block. That's what the top of it is. It's great for preparation, even if it does take little bit of looking after.

Suddenly, I realize exactly what I can do for Ali. I'm being dumb… Of course. I can do the thing I do best. And I'm not talking about yelling. I'm talking about cooking.

A couple of hours later, I've finished all the preparation, tidied the apartment and showered. I've changed into a clean t-shirt and jeans. I know Ali usually goes back to the hotel at around six, so at five o'clock, I text her and ask if she'll come up here before she leaves.

She replies straight away, saying yes.

And as soon as I receive that, my stomach flips into nervousness. I know why. I'm fairly sure I'm gonna screw this up. Not the cooking bit, obviously. I'm fairly confident with that. It's everything else I'm panicking about. I'd intended this as something to cheer her up, but in my own head, I've turned it into a date. And I don't date.

I check over everything – twice. I pace around a bit, put on some music and then decide that's not really me, so I turn it off again. The silence drags, and then, at just before six, there's a timid knock on the door. I go over and open it, rather than calling for her to come in.

She's standing there, with her coat over her arm and her purse in her hand.

"Hi," she says.

"Come in." We speak at the same time and, smiling at me, she enters the apartment. I close the door and we both stand there, a little awkwardly.

"Is everything okay?" she asks.

"Yeah. I was just wondering if you had any plans for this evening."

She's shocked. Her eyes widen. "Um… not really. I was just going to go back to the hotel. Why? What did you need?" she asks. She obviously thinks this is something to do with work.

"I don't need anything," I reply, although that's not strictly true. I need her. "But I think you do."

She looks up at me, her confusion obvious and, without touching her, I take her coat from her and hang it on one of the hooks by the door, then lead her into the living room. She follows, bemused.

"Take a seat," I say. "Would you like a glass of wine?"

"Um… okay." She's still really puzzled and I don't blame her. I'm not entirely sure what's going on, and I planned this.

I go into the kitchen and pour us both a large glass of chilled Pinot Grigio, bringing hers back to her in the living room. Then I turn on the TV, and hand her the remote. I've already set it up so all she's got to do is make her selection.

"Choose a box set," I tell her. "Anything you want… within reason."

She looks up at me, the remote in one hand, her wine in the other, her mouth open and kissably perfect.

"A box set?" she repeats.

"Yeah. Anything you want."

Her eyes start to glisten and I wonder if she's gonna cry. I'm not sure I can handle that. It wasn't part of the plan.

"I've got something I need to do in the kitchen," I say, pointing toward the room, even though she knows where it is and can see me from where she's sitting. "I'll be back soon, but call me if you need anything."

I make my escape as quickly as is decent and take a large gulp of wine. I need to calm down and steady my nerves before I blow this completely.

The fish is prepared, the batter is made, the potatoes are cut. The only thing I have left to do is cook it all. I wait while the fryer gets up to temperature, watching her out of the corner of my eye. She's flicking through the options, reading the write-ups. I guess some of the shows may not be familiar to her. Not everything gets shown in England. Every so often, she pulls a face, or shakes her head and moves forward.

It takes a while to cook everything. To get really good fries – well, chips, as Ali would call them – you have to double-fry them. So, I cook them once, then put them to one side and cook the battered fish, before putting that in the oven to keep warm, and re-cooking the chips again. If I could make this downstairs in the main kitchen, it would be much quicker. There are more fryers, for one thing – or there will be once it's finished. Also, this is not a dish I'm used to making and, although I had a fairly good idea of what to do, I had to look it up on on the Internet, just to be sure. It's not exactly an Italian classic.

Once I've served it up onto warmed plates and added a slice of lemon and some parsley, I carry the two dishes through to the living room and hand Ali hers.

"The plate isn't too hot, I don't think."

She takes it from me, then looks up into my face, confused once more.

I put my plate and the cutlery down on the table and go back into the kitchen for my wine, returning to sit on the other part of the L-shaped couch from her. We're kind of facing each other now and she's still staring at me, holding her plate.

"Fish and chips?" she says.

"You said takeaway," I reply. I hope I've done the right thing here.

"You… you made me fish and chips?"

"Yes." I reach forward to pick up my meal, just as she starts to let her plate fall and I grab it from her.

She's kind of crumpled up in tears. Oh fuck. I've really screwed up. Spectacularly.

"Ali?" I say, putting her plate down beside mine. "What did I do wrong?"

She looks up at me, shaking her head. I move closer to her, pulling a Kleenex from the box on the table and handing it to her. She takes it and wipes her face.

"Ali?" I repeat.

"You didn't do anything wrong," she whispers. Her voice sounds a little deeper, kind of thick with something. Emotion, I guess. I don't know what to do, but it seems I don't have to.

She leans over and, very gently, kisses my cheek. "Thank you," she says, sitting back again. "This is – without a doubt – the nicest thing anyone has ever done for me."

"I didn't get it wrong then?"

"No, Sam." She smiles over at me. Christ, that's a beautiful smile.

It takes me a moment just to recover from the sight of that, and from the kiss. I wasn't expecting that and her lips felt so soft against my skin…

"I suppose we'd better eat," she murmurs.

"Um… yes." I pull myself together and reach over to hand her the plate again.

"There's nothing worse than soggy fish and chips," she adds, her smile broadening.

"Nothing?" I turn to her.

"Well, maybe a few things." Her eyes twinkle and I wonder… Did we just flirt?

"What did you choose?" I ask her as we start to eat, trying not to think too hard about that.

"Sorry?" She's so engrossed in eating, she's not sure what I'm talking about.

"To watch?" I nod toward the television.

"Oh. Sorry. I was enjoying this so much, I'd forgotten all about that."

"It's okay then?"

"It's a lot better than okay. You make really good chips," she says, picking one up and putting it in her mouth. Whenever she does something like that – like when Ed put that spoon in her mouth – my cock instantly comes to life. There's something about her lips that turns me on. "They're fantastic."

"Yes, they are." I'm still staring at her lips, not eating a thing, and she looks at me. She sees that I'm staring and she blushes.

"Are we both talking about the chips?" she asks.

"No."

"What are you talking about then?"

How do I tell her? I can't. "That would be telling," I tease.

Her eyes widen and twinkle again. If this is flirting, I really like it. Well, I like it with Ali, anyway.

She picks up another chip, pausing with it just touching her lips. Fuck, that's erotic.

"You're not going to tell me?" she says, looking at me.

"No."

"Not even if I beg?"

Oh seriously… fuck. An image flashes through my head. Ali, kneeling before me, her hands bound, her eyes locked on mine, her mouth open, waiting… Shit.

"No," I manage to say. She stares into my eyes and I wonder what she's going to do or say next. It's unnerving and kind of thrilling at the same time.

"*Breaking Bad*," she says, all of a sudden.

"Sorry?"

"I chose *Breaking Bad*."

"Oh." That was a change of topic. "Um… Any reason?"

"No," she says, eating the chip. "I've never seen it before and I've heard good things about it."

"You've never seen it?"

"No. Tess is a lot younger than me. We tend to watch things like *Sex and the City* or *Friends*. And I've seen every episode of *Friends*," she says, "several times. It's one of Tess's favorites."

"*Breaking Bad* it is then." I grab the remote and press play.

After three episodes, Ali yawns and I realize that it's getting late.

"Do you want me to walk you back to your hotel?" I ask her. "You don't have to leave, if you don't want to." I guess that might have sounded like I was kicking her out. "I mean, you can stay as long as you like, but you seem tired."

"I am tired," she says. "I still can't seem to get my head around the time difference."

"Well, I'll take you back, if you want?"

"I can get myself there," she says. "It's not exactly far away."

"Yeah, and it's dark and you're not going by yourself." I want to take care of her. Always. And, no, I have absolutely no idea where that thought came from, but I'm not gonna fight it. Not any more.

She looks over at me, a smile forming on her lips. "Thank you," she says.

"You're welcome."

We both get up and I grab her coat from the hook and help her into it, before shrugging on my leather jacket and picking up my keys from the bowl on the shelf by the door.

"Ready?" I say.

"Yes."

She walks ahead of me down the stairs and out through the restaurant. It's chilly outside – it's the middle of March, but it's been unusually mild for the last ten days and I think we've gotten used to that. We turn to our left and walk along to the hotel. It's literally just a few doors down and it doesn't take more than two or three minutes to get there. As we walk, she turns to me.

"Thank you," she says again.

"For?"

"For tonight. For all of it." Her voice cracks again.

"I enjoyed it," I tell her. It's true. I really did. I feel like I owe her more of an explanation though. "I wanted to do something for you," I say, feeling embarrassed, but determined to go on. "I didn't like the idea of you being homesick... and I wanted to apologize for being so horrible to you since you got here. I know a plate of fish and chips doesn't really make up for all the things I've said and done to you, but it's a start." That's the longest speech I've ever made to a woman in my life and I'm holding my breath now, hoping she doesn't laugh at me.

We've reached the hotel. The lights from inside are shining on her hair and face, giving her a kind of glow. God, she's beautiful...

"You made it seem a little more like home," she whispers.

I don't know what to say, because the immediate thought that's just gone through my head is that I want this to be her home... here, with me. I can't say that though.

"I'm pleased," comes out of my mouth instead.

"And thank you for the apology."

"It feels inadequate."

She puts her hand on my bicep. "It's not," she says, "and I appreciate it. You went to a lot of effort."

"Well, I have been spectacularly horrible."

Her hand is still resting on my arm and instinctively I flex the muscle. She gasps, just slightly.

"You're really not going to tell me, are you?" she asks.

"Tell you what?"

"What you were talking about, when I was saying that the chips were fantastic, and you were looking at me."

I smile. "No."

"Are you always this much of a tease?" she asks, and I think she just moved a little closer. Or was that me?

"Sometimes." I grin at her.

"What would I have to do to get you to tell me?" she whispers. She really did move closer that time and her eyes just lit up. She's flirting. She's really flirting. Fuck, I like this.

I lean down, my lips right next to her ear, so I know she'll hear me. "I can think of a hundred things," I murmur, "but I doubt you'd be willing to do any of them."

I hear the sharp intake of breath, and I wonder if I've gone too far, if I've shocked her. But then her grip tightens on my arm, and I make out an almost imperceptible moan, followed by a sigh, and a shudder ripples through her body. Was that what I think it was? I mean… was that for real?

She leans back, just a fraction and looks up again. Her eyes lock with mine. This is hot. Really, seriously hot.

"Well," she whispers. "If you don't ask, you'll never know."

She lets her hand fall from my arm, gives me a long, slow, sexy smile and then turns away and walks into the hotel.

And I'm left standing on the sidewalk like a dumb teenager who just screwed up his first kiss on his first date – which, I guess I pretty much just did. Except I'm not a teenager. And I want more than a kiss. A lot more.

Chapter Ten

Ali

I close my hotel room door behind me and lean back against it.

Did I really just do that? Did I really just suggest that he could ask me to do those things he thinks I'd be unwilling to try? I don't even know what they are. But that feeling when he whispered those words into my ear, the way his voice resonated through my body, was the hottest, most erotic thing I've ever experienced. My pussy clenched, my body spasmed. I know I moaned, and I think I sighed. I definitely felt a shudder rock through me. It was like a sudden, fast orgasm. It was so intense. And all he did was whisper in my ear. What could he do to me if he actually touched me? Judging from his words, I'm seriously wondering. What would he *want* to do? All I hope is that he wants to find out as much as I do.

This new side to Sam, this kinder, gentler side, is a revelation, and I like it. But what I'm enjoying even more is the sexy, romantic side to him. I never thought he'd be like that – not with me, anyway – and the thought of things going further between us, of him fulfilling those whispered words… God, I can feel myself shuddering again at the thought.

I get into the office early. We've got to take the photographs this morning, but first I want to have a look at the biographies that I know Rob's sent through. I sit at the desk and open up his message, reading through each one in turn.

It seems that all three brothers trained as chefs under the guidance of their father, starting at the age of eighteen. Rob, however, gave up after a couple of years and went to college to study business management. Ed started off training in the main kitchen, but then discovered early on that he had a talent for pastry cooking and has made that his specialism, perfecting his art over the years. Sam is equally talented – taking over as head chef within a few years of first stepping into the kitchen. It's interesting. I would have said, of all three brothers, Rob was the one with the biggest ego, but he's played down his own role and enlarged those of his brothers. He clearly thinks highly of them, and their abilities. He's focused on their professional skills and qualifications, but hasn't said anything about their hobbies or personal lives. I'll see if I can get him to add that, or at least give me some details so I can put them in later on and send them off to the design company, with the photographs.

Ed and Rob are with me in the restaurant. I've managed to clear us a space and get the workmen to move to one side, and find a patch of wall that we can take the photographs against. Ed is standing in front of it, looking awkward; Rob is to my right, and Sam hasn't come down yet. Part of me is relieved about that. I lay in bed last night, worrying that he'd have been aware of my reaction – my moan and sigh, the shudder I gave off, as well as the way I had to grip his arm just to stay upright – it must have been obvious to him. If it was, the idea of seeing him today, knowing that he'll have been conscious of how he made me feel, is making me nervous.

"Why are we doing this?" Ed asks, straightening his white chef's jacket.

"You're going to have biographies on the website," I explain, checking the camera. "It'll be good to have pictures of the three of you as well."

"Why?" The voice behind me makes me jump. It also makes every nerve in my body shiver. Oh, God… he's doing it again. I turn and Sam smiles at me.

"B—Because you're the restaurant's USP," I explain, frustrated that he's also making me stutter now. "All three of you."

"What do you mean?" Ed asks.

I turn back to him, acutely aware that Sam has moved closer. He's right behind me now, and I can feel the heat radiating from his body into mine.

"Y—You're the unique selling point," I say, stammering again as I look through the viewfinder. My hands are shaking and at this rate I'm never going to get a decent shot. I lower the camera again, pretending to adjust the settings.

"In what way?" Rob asks.

"Not many restaurants have three handsome Italian brothers as their owners. You should take advantage of that," I reply, not taking my eyes from the camera.

When they don't reply, I look up. Ed's blushing, and I hear Rob scoffing to my right.

"What?" I say, looking from one to the other. "Come on. You guys know you're handsome, right? You must get told that all the time."

Ed shrugs and then I'm aware of a warm sensation on my neck. I've tied my hair up to keep it out of the way of the camera, and I can feel Sam's breath on my skin as he leans forward.

"Not by anyone who matters," he whispers.

I feel that shudder again and take a deep breath to try and control it, even though my thighs are trembling too. Sam moves away a little and leans against the wall a few feet away. I glance across at him and he's staring at me, his eyes dark and intense, his lips curling up just a fraction. He knows exactly what he's doing to me and, for some reason, rather than making me feel embarrassed, that knowledge turns me on even more.

I try and concentrate, and ignore his implication that I matter, and remember that I need to ask them about their hobbies for the biographies.

Ed looks at me as I take a series of photographs of him.

"When do we have time for hobbies?" he asks, smiling.

He has a point. I remember when I worked in kitchens, all I ever wanted to do was sleep.

"I knew you were going to ask that," Rob adds, "but there really isn't anything." I glance at him and he's got the most wicked smile on his face. "Nothing printable anyway."

I can feel myself blushing.

"Okay," I say quietly. "Maybe we'll just go with the biographies as they are then."

I look across at Sam. He's still staring at me, but pushes himself off the wall and comes closer again. "I think that's probably just as well," he says. His voice is low, soft and really sexy.

"Especially in Sam's case," Rob adds. "If I told you what he's really like, I'd probably scare you off."

"I'm not that easily scared." I murmur out my reply, still holding Sam's gaze.

His eyes widen and I know I'm not imagining the tension between us. It's nothing like the tension that's been there for the last few weeks, though. This is sexual. Pure and simple. I ache for him.

"Sorry, Ali." I jump at the sound of my own name. Chad, one of the carpenters, is standing off to one side, looking at me. "Are you gonna be much longer?" he asks.

"Um… no," I reply, feeling flustered. "Just give me another ten minutes." I turn back to Ed. "I'm finished with you now," I tell him and he moves out of the way.

"Who's next?" Rob asks.

I turn towards him. "It'd better be Sam," I reply. "I've got everything set up to compensate for the whiteness of the jacket. Then I can adjust it for the black shirt that you're wearing." Rob nods and looks over my shoulder at Sam.

"You're up then." He smirks.

"Where do you want me?" Sam asks, his voice the barest whisper, tracing across my skin.

"Um…" I turn to face him. His eyes spark into mine, turning my insides to liquid – hot, molten liquid. I so want to say anywhere he damn well likes, but I manage to mutter out, "Can you stand where Ed was?"

"Sure." He moves away and I'm not sure whether to feel disappointed or relieved.

I've sent the best of the pictures and the biographies off to the designers. I have to say, they all look really handsome, but there was something about Sam's eyes in his photographs; something intense, passionate and demanding. How he did that, just with his eyes, I don't know, but it was definitely there.

Just after lunch, the modular kitchen unit is delivered and the fitters install it. This is the biggest single expense of the whole re-fit and I'm determined to oversee it, even though I'm sure these guys know what they're doing. Surprisingly, Sam's down here too. I expected him to go back up to the apartment after the photographs were done, but when I came back out of the office after sending my email, he was in the kitchen, laughing with the workmen and he's been here ever since, helping out. The sound of his voice, and especially his deep laugh sets my nerves on edge in a very good way and, by the middle of the afternoon, I'm a mass of sexual tension.

The fitters leave late in the day, their job done.

"It looks amazing," Sam says, suddenly standing next to me. "I see what you mean about the edging."

Thin copper trim runs all around the top and bottom of the unit. "It's not a big deal, but it just makes it look so much nicer."

"Yeah, it does."

"I wish we could turn it on," I say, running my hands over its sleek contours. I'm like a kid with a new toy. "But the power and gas need reconnecting."

"When's that gonna be done?" he asks. He's not being demanding, or even difficult. He's just asking the question.

"Tomorrow morning."

"Well, I guess you'll just have to wait," he says. I look up and he's smiling down at me with a dark, fiery look in his eyes.

"I'm not very good at waiting. I want to play…" I realise that he might take that the wrong way, but I'm not sure I care. The innuendos between us have been fun so far and I'd like them to continue. Flirting with him is so much nicer than fighting.

"You want to play?" he repeats, his voice dropping to a whisper.

"Yes. I like playing." I stare into his eyes. They darken further still, and his mouth opens just a fraction.

"Do you now?" he says.

I nod my head. God, I'm so turned on right now, I think I'd be willing to do anything, no matter how much he might doubt that. My breathing quickens and I lick my lips. He stares.

"I'll have to bear that in mind," he murmurs.

"Will you?"

"Yeah. Although I'm not sure we're talking about the same kind of games…" He leaves his sentence – and me – hanging.

"I—I think we might be," I whisper.

He moves closer, leaning in, so his mouth is right next to my ear. My hair isn't in the way now – unlike last night – and I can feel his breath against my earlobe. "You think you'd like my kind of games, do you, Ali?" His voice caresses my skin and I shudder again. Just like outside the hotel, the tiniest moan escaping my lips, my pussy tingles in anticipation and I let out a sigh. How does he do that?

"Ali?" Rob's voice makes me leap in the air – well almost. "There's someone called Petra Miller on the phone for you. She said she's returning your call from this morning." I turn to see him standing by the door, and he looks from me to Sam and back again. "Sorry," he adds, "did I interrupt something?"

"No," I say quickly. "I—I'd better take her call."

I reluctantly move away from Sam, toward the door, where Rob's still standing. "Who is she?" he asks.

"She's the photographer who's going to be covering the opening and doing the promotional pictures."

He nods his head. "She's got a real sexy voice," he remarks, grinning.

I turn and look back at Sam. "Hmm… She's not the only one," I murmur, just loud enough for him to hear. His lips twitch upward and I smile at him.

I want him so much. I don't think I've ever wanted anything, or anyone more.

Today hasn't been as good as yesterday. I know why. Sam's been upstairs, and I've missed him. That's pathetic, isn't it? I know it is. He's not mine to miss, and yet I do.

I know he's completed all the elements of the recipes for the main menu, but we decided in a very brief discussion between all four of us a couple of days ago, that there should be some seasonal specials as well, so those are what he's working on now.

It's just gone five and all the workmen have gone for the day. The power and gas have been reconnected and I'm standing in the kitchen all by myself. It's really taking shape now. The walls are in – minus the glass, which is being fitted tomorrow – the convection ovens are going in the following day. That means the fridges and freezers can all be fitted on Friday as planned. That will leave us the weekend and Monday to complete all the finishing touches, before Sam and Ed move back in on Tuesday. I've allowed a few days before opening for them and their team to get back in here and get used to the new equipment, before they actually have to serve any food to paying customers. We don't want any disasters on opening night. And, while they're doing that, the workmen will be completing the restaurant and the restrooms. Even allowing for the odd hiccup, we're right on schedule…

I lean against the modular unit. It's very impressive. There are six gas burners on each side, two broilers, a griddle and four fryers. I turn on the broiler beside me and it fires into life – literally. The heat is instant and tremendous. I leave it running for a moment and check out the gas burners and the griddle. Everything works just fine and I stand, admiring the whole thing in action. I must own up to feeling a little sad that I won't get to cook on it. I sigh and go around switching everything off again, before looking around and admitting to myself that what we've all managed to achieve here is pretty special.

"Ali?" I turn and come face to face with Sam.

"Yes?" I can feel that nervous tension in the pit of my stomach again. He's standing in the doorway, holding a saucepan, with a wooden spoon resting inside it.

He moves toward me, slowly. I feel like the prey, waiting for the predator to pounce – and yet it's so exciting I can barely breathe. I'm not scared of him at all. Not any more.

He stands right in front of me, with my back to the broiler and I know the rise in my temperature isn't just the residual heat from the equipment.

"I wondered if you'd like to try something," he offers and I wonder what he's suggesting, until he nods towards the saucepan in his hand.

"What is it?"

"Something new," he teases, smiling.

"You're not going to tell me, are you?" I smile back.

"Not until you've tried it," he says. "You've gotta try first."

"That's a rule with you, is it?" I ask.

"Yes. It's one of many," he replies mysteriously. I can feel myself leaning into him. "So? Wanna try?"

"Yes." I don't hesitate and his eyes sparkle.

He takes the spoon from the pan and blows gently across the surface before moving it towards my mouth. I open up for him and he inches it closer, tipping the creamy liquid onto my tongue. He studies my lips and I wish he'd just kiss me and let me taste him.

He slowly pulls the spoon back and I let the sauce swirl around my mouth. It's heavenly. I close my eyes for a moment, savouring the creamy, slightly salty flavours and then lean back, resting my hands behind me.

It takes a moment before I feel the pain, and then I jump forward, letting out a yelp and shaking my hands, unable to believe I just did something quite that stupid. My brain seems to shut down and I can't think what to do as the agonising throb takes over.

"Come here," Sam barks, putting the pan down and grabbing my arm. He pulls me to the sink and turns on the cold tap. "Put your hands under there and don't move them," he says. He holds my hands in the stream of chilled water for a moment, then turns toward the back of the kitchen. "Shit." He turns back to me. "No fucking freezers," he snaps. "Stay there. Don't move." I nod my head. Tears are now streaming down my cheeks and he hesitates for a moment. "You'll be okay," he says, his voice much softer.

I nod again.

He turns and runs from the room. Alone, I realise that I'm not just crying because of the pain, but because I feel humiliated. If I hadn't been so busy flirting and looking into his eyes, I'd have remembered that I'd just turned off the broiler, and that it would still be boiling hot. It was a really dumb thing to do – even by my standards.

He's back within moments.

"This'll work better," he says. He's holding a towel with some ice inside it. He comes over to me, putting the towel down beside me, and turns off the taps. Then he takes my hands in his, looking down at them, and murmurs, "Fuck," under his breath. God, he swears a lot. "You'll be fine," he says a little louder, looking into my eyes. He smiles, then places my hands inside the towel, not right next to the ice, but wrapped up between the towel. He holds onto the outside, keeping the ice packed against me.

"It's cold," I say to him, although he must be able to feel it too.

"I know," he replies. "It's meant to be. We need to cool the burn. Come with me," he adds and takes me out of the kitchen and up the stairs to his apartment. His freezer door is wide open.

"You'd better close that," I say to him.

"Yeah." He goes over and slams the freezer door shut and then pulls out a seat at his butcher's block. "Come sit down," he says. I do as he commands and he sits beside me, holding the ice pack against my hands again. He must be getting cold doing that.

"This is freezing, Sam." I can feel my teeth chattering.

"I know it is." His voice is so soft, I look up at him. He's studying my face now, and I feel tears forming in my eyes again.

"It hurts," I whimper.

He seems uncertain, like he doesn't know what to do. "It'll be okay," he says eventually. He looks around for a moment, then turns back to me. "Where did you train?" he asks.

"Train as what?" I ask. It seems like such a random question.

"A chef." He smiles at me again.

"Oh, in London. I went to a cookery school there. I have to say though, I learned more on the job than I did at school."

"And what's your favourite cuisine?" he asks.

"This is going to sound corny, but it's Italian. And I'm not just saying that."

"Glad to hear it." His smile broadens. "And where did you work?"

I tell him about the different restaurants I worked at – and why I left them. He smirks but doesn't comment when I tell him about the loud, bad tempered chefs who drove me out of the industry.

"And… and you live with your sister?" he continues. He faltered just a little when he asked that and I wonder if he's fishing.

I nod. "Yes. Tess has lived with me for the last three years. She's at university in London. We get on well."

"Is it just the two of you?" he repeats. He is fishing.

"Yes." I look at him closely. It seems important to me that he should know I'm single. "We share a flat – I guess you'd call it an apartment – in North London."

"So, you're not with anyone?" he says, tilting his head to one side. He must've got bored fishing.

I blush. "No," I whisper.

He nods slowly. "Good," he says simply.

We stare at each other for what feels like forever, my body tingling with anticipation, but then he looks away and checks his watch. "It's been forty-five minutes," he says.

"Really?" I swallow down the tension, and realise he's been distracting me. Very well. "I can't feel my hands anymore."

"Well, that's probably just as well. They're gonna hurt like a bitch."

He unwraps the towel and turns my hands so he can see them.

"Okay," he says, like he's talking to himself. "Not too bad."

"Not too bad?" I repeat.

"Well, I've seen worse," he comments. "Are you okay for a minute? I just need to get the first-aid kit."

I nod and he gets up and goes into the living room, then toward the front door, returning a moment later, carrying a large red box.

"That's a serious first-aid kit," I say, managing a smile.

"It's not mine," he replies. "It belongs in the kitchen downstairs. It got put up here when the work began."

"Oh, I see."

"Still," he says, laying it on the block and opening it, "that works well for us, because I know we're gonna find just what we need in here."

He pulls out a tube of ointment and several bandages, then sits down again and, taking one hand at a time, he gently applies the burn ointment before wrapping each of my hands in a bandage. His touch is delicate and careful. The burns don't hurt as much as I thought they would – although I wonder if that's because my hands are still numb.

"It's only really bad over the heel of your hand," he says, pointing to the bottom of his own palm, just above his wrist, to demonstrate. "How does that feel?"

I look down at my bandaged hands. My fingers are still completely free and I really can't feel anything. "I can't feel a thing," I tell him.

"The cream contains a mild anaesthetic," he explains, putting everything away. "I've got some painkillers in the bathroom. I'll give you some later. You're gonna need them."

He closes the first-aid kit and goes to get up, but I touch his arm with my fingers, wary of my burned palms.

"Thank you," I say, feeling the tears well up again. "I don't know what I'd have done if you hadn't been here."

"You don't have to thank me, Ali." He stands, then leans over me. "I'll always be here."

Sam

She stares at me for a minute, then thanks me again, and goes to get up.

"Where are you going?" I ask her, panic rising inside me.

"I should be getting back to the hotel," she replies.

"I don't think so." She's gotta be kidding. Apart from the fact that she's just burned her hands – badly – I want her to stay. I thought we were getting somewhere. Okay, so it was just conversation, but it was something. "I'll make us some dinner," I tell her.

"You don't have to do that. You've done enough for me already."

"Don't argue with me." Was that too strong? I need to calm down; stop panicking.

She looks up at me, uncertainty filling her eyes. Yeah, it was too strong. "I don't want to be any trouble," she mumbles.

I make a conscious effort to soften my voice, bury the panic, and smile. "Then stop arguing with me, and go sit down on the couch."

"Let me at least help with the dinner." She's agreeing to stay, and she's smiling again, and that feels a whole lot better.

"With those hands?" I nod toward her bandages.

"Hmm. Fair point."

"Come on." If she won't go into the living room of her own free will, then I'll take her there. I can hardly hold her hand, so I just lead her and she follows. Thank God. "Sit down and rest," I tell her, and she does, sitting back into the corner of the couch. "You've had a shock. I'll make us something to eat." I grab the remote and flick the TV on. "Why don't you watch some more Breaking Bad. It'll take your mind off things."

"You're sure?" she asks.

"I'm positive. Besides, I need to check on your hands again later. If they're looking any worse, I'll take you to the ER, and if not, I'll re-dress them and take you back to your hotel."

She leans forward, her fingers touching mine. Although I get that same electric shock sensation, I don't pull away this time. "There's no need for all this," she says. "I'd be perfectly okay by myself."

Entwining our fingers, I lean down, putting my mouth beside her ear again. I like the effect that seems to have on her. "I know," I whisper. "The thing is, I don't want you to be by yourself." She gasps, and I stand up straight. Her eyes are wide, staring up at me. She looks confused. She also looks a bit shocked. Not the reaction I'd hoped for… "I'll go cook," I say, and I reluctantly pull my hand from hers.

Out in the kitchen, I stand for a moment by the butcher's block. Did I really just say that to her? The implication is obvious. In saying I don't want her to be by herself, I'm implying I want her to be with me. I don't say things like that. It's not my style. But then, I don't do a lot of the things I've been doing these last few days. I turn and look at her. She's watching TV, fixated, and the thing is, I'd really like to just go sit with her, maybe hold her in my arms, let her rest on me, and keep her safe. I do want her to be with me. Always. And I guess there's nothing wrong in saying that, especially as I now know exactly how I feel about her. I've suspected it for a while now, but I worked it out for sure while I was running up the stairs to get the ice. Seeing her in pain like that hurt me. And I'm not talking about a wounded ego and damaged pride, like I felt when Amber left. This felt like a tear in my chest – a physical wound. I've never experienced anything like it. I'm not sure I want to again. But those few moments of agony made me realize that my feelings for her run a lot deeper than I've been prepared to admit. A *lot* deeper. They run right through my core. For the first time in my life, I've let a woman get inside me, and even though it scares the hell out of me, that's exactly where I want her to be, because I've fallen in love with her. I'm not gonna tell her that. Of course I'm not. I don't know how to for one thing, and besides, it's way too soon. But that doesn't make it any less true, or any less real.

Realizing how I feel about her made it all the more important that I find out whether there's anyone in her life. I didn't think there was. She's been flirting with me for the last couple of days, and I don't think she'd have done that if she had a guy at home. She's not that kind of person. So, I fished a little. Like most of this, it's not something I've done before, and I quickly got bored. I wanted to know. So I asked. She's single. I don't think I've ever felt so relieved in my life.

It's odd. Part of me had expected love – real love – to be something melodramatic, painful, tortuous. And I guess seeing her hurting was all of those things, but as for the feeling of being in love itself, it's nothing like that. It's beautiful – like Ali. Everything suddenly seems just a little bit better, just a little bit brighter, lighter, more colorful. Although I don't have the slightest clue what I'm doing, I like this feeling, and I *really* love her.

I set about making a quick pasta dish, boiling some water and throwing a few ingredients into a blender. I can do this with my eyes closed, but I don't because I want to keep watching Ali.

The meal takes around fifteen minutes to prepare. I've cheated and used dried pasta. Normally, I'd make it, but I'd rather spend the time with Ali, instead of up to my elbows in flour. I dish everything up and carry the bowls through, and I stop dead as I come level with the couch. She's kicked off her shoes and is lying out on the couch. She looks so comfortable and so at home, it makes my heart skip a beat.

She notices me and quickly lowers her feet to the floor, sitting up a little.

"Sorry," she says.

"It's fine." I come around and hand her a bowl. "Put your feet up again."

"I came over all tired," she explains, raising her legs back onto the couch.

"That'll be the shock." I put my bowl down and go out to the kitchen, bringing back a couple of glasses of iced San Pellegrino. "No wine for you tonight," I tell her, setting them down on the table. "It's not good for shock."

"You can drink, if you want," she says.

"I'm okay with water."

I sit down on the other part of the couch and grab my bowl.

"This tastes incredible," she says. "What's in it?"

"It's just penne, with peas, bacon and pesto."

"You made the pesto?" she asks. "I heard a blender."

"Of course I made the pesto." She glances up at me, a slightly worried look in her eye again. "Hello? Off duty chef here…" I point to my chest. "As if I'd use pesto from a jar…" I smile at her, trying to get her to relax and get used to the idea that I'm not gonna yell at her again. Ever.

She nods, and her shoulders sag a little, with relief I guess, and I regret every single time I shouted at her. Did I really make her feel like that? I guess I must've done. What a waste of time. I could've been enjoying times like these; times better than these. Instead of which, I was too busy being a jerk to make the most of what was staring me in the face.

She starts really yawning halfway through the second episode.

"You're tired," I say. "Let me take a look at your hands and I'll walk you back to the hotel." I get up and kneel down in front of her as I'm talking. She doesn't reply, but looks up into my eyes. She looks so helpless, I just want to keep her here and hold her for a while – I think forever might be long enough.

She offers up her left hand and, coming to my senses, I take it and carefully undo the bandage. Her skin has blistered, but the burn is much less severe than it might have been.

"I'll just get some more ointment," I tell her, and I go out to the first-aid kit and grab the ointment and some more bandages. I'm gonna have to re-stock this before we open the restaurant again.

Going back to her, I re-dress both her hands, taking care not to hurt her.

"You've got a very light touch," she murmurs. She sounds sleepy, almost drunk. It's really sexy.

I want to flirt with her, but she's not well. It feels wrong. "Next time you see me cracking a lobster, I'll remind you that you said that," I say, and I grab her trainers, untying them and slipping them onto her feet.

She pulls away. "You don't have to do that," she says. "I can still use my fingers."

"I know." I lean closer. "Just let me help, will you?"

She looks at me with that confused, slightly lost look again. "Okay," she whispers.

I finish tying her shoes and help her to her feet. Our bodies are almost touching and she looks up at me. "Thank you," she whispers.

"You're welcome." I want to lean down and kiss her. I want to hold her. I want her to stay.

Forever.

Before we leave, I grab some painkillers from the bathroom cabinet and give them to her, then we go downstairs and into the office, where we pick up her coat and purse, before heading out into the street.

"I can't believe how tired I am," she says as we start walking.

"If you need some time out tomorrow, just call, or text," I tell her.

"I'll be fine," she replies. "As long as I can get some sleep."

"Take the painkillers before you go to bed and I'm sure you won't have any trouble." She nods her head a little absently. "I'll see you up to your room," I say, being as we're almost at the hotel already.

"Thank you," she murmurs.

I look down at her. "You mean you're not gonna fight me on this one?"

"I'm too tired to fight," she replies. I open the door to the hotel and we pass through and make our way to the elevators.

"Good."

"Good?" she queries, just as the doors open and I realize that came out wrong.

"I don't mean 'good' that you're tired, but I don't want you to fight with me. I want you to let me take care of you."

She turns and stares at me, then she swallows hard. "You have been," she murmurs. "Perfectly."

"Perfectly?"

She nods her head.

"What floor?" I ask her.

"Third, please." I press the button and the doors close. It's a confined space and she's still staring at me, her beautiful blue eyes fixed on mine. "Thank you for everything you've done," she says. "I really am grateful."

Looking into those eyes, there's nothing I'd like more than to take her to bed, but I know that if I make a move, if I even suggest it and she says yes, I'll always wonder whether she did so out of gratitude. I don't want that. I want her to come to bed with me because she wants me as much as I want her. Of course, I could make a move, or suggest it, and she could say no – and that'd be even worse. I realize I'm just staring at her. “You don’t have to be grateful,” I say. “I told you. I want to take care of you.”

She moves a little closer. “I think I’d like that,” she whispers.

My breath catches, but right at that moment, the doors open and a couple are standing there waiting for us to exit. The moment’s lost. So am I. Completely.

I left her at her hotel door. It’s room number 315, and I told her that now I know that, if she finds she needs anything during the night, I want her to call me on my cell and I’ll come over and help her. She agreed, no arguments – again.

We didn’t say much more after that. She was too tired. Now, in the silence of my apartment, with a glass of Barolo in my hand, I’ve had some time to think. Being with her is like being in the safest, warmest, calmest place I can imagine. She makes me feel comfortable with myself, and I know I’ve never really felt that before. I want more of it. The only problem is that her reactions have been a little mixed. Sometimes, I think she wants me as much as I want her; and other times, she looks so lost and so confused, I’m not sure if she knows what she wants herself. I think she’s finding my words a bit puzzling, given the change in my attitude toward her, so I need to maybe *show* her how I feel as well. I’ve got no idea how to do that, but I guess if we were doing things her way, the best course would probably be to kiss her. The problem is, it’s not something I’m really experienced at.

I suppose the first thing I need to do is to find some way of getting her on her own again, because I don’t want to do this in front of all the workmen and my brothers. I want it to be just the two of us. And then I just have to hope I haven’t misread everything, because I don’t want to get this wrong. I really don’t.

Chapter Eleven

Ali

I wake to the sound of my alarm clock, surprised that I've slept all night. I fully expected the pain in my hands to keep me awake, but I took the painkillers as Sam suggested and fell asleep pretty much as soon as my head hit the pillow.

I go into the bathroom and it's only when I try to wash my hands that I realise my next problem. How am I going to shower and wash my hair? I stare down at the bandages and then look at the shower cubicle, like I'm expecting some kind of divine, providential answer to appear before me. It doesn't. I wander back out into the bedroom. I've already caught sight of my reflection in two mirrors and I know I can't possibly go to the restaurant looking like this. I could tie my hair up, I suppose, but I still need to be able to wash, without getting my hands wet. Some hope.

I sit on the bed and look at my hands and, although I know it's pathetic, I can feel tears welling in my eyes. I'm never like this normally and I know if I was at home, I'd just find a way of coping with it.

I'm just about to actually start crying when my phone rings. It might be Tess, so I'd better answer. I guess I could cry at her… except she'll worry.

I answer without checking the screen.

"Hello?"

"I was going to ask if you're okay, but I can tell you're not."

It's Sam.

"No, I'm not," I whimper.

"What's wrong?" he asks.

"I'm being pathetic." Tears start falling down my cheeks and there's nothing I can do to stop them. "I—I've just realised I can't get my hands wet, which means I can't shower, or wash my hair."

"Okay," he says, like he doesn't really understand how this is a problem. "Can I come and help?"

"You want to shower with me?" Is that what he's suggesting? He's got my emotions all over the place; I have no idea what he wants from me… but he wants to shower with me? Is that even vaguely normal?

"Yes, I'd love to shower with you, but maybe not today. I'll be there in five minutes. Just let me in and I'll help you."

"But…" I realise I'm talking to myself. He's hung up already.

I look around the room. He's on his way here. And he's just said he wants to shower with me – maybe not today, but he definitely wants to shower with me. Does that mean he wants to do other things with me too? My stomach churns and everything south of my waist heats up at the thought of being naked with him, even though he got me kind of nervous yesterday when he snapped at me to sit down. I'm fairly sure he didn't mean it to come out as an order, and he quickly softened again, and even said he wanted to take care of me, but for a brief moment, I was reminded me of how he used to be. I'm still thinking about that when he knocks on the door and I go over and answer it, to find him standing there in jeans and a tight t-shirt – again. He looks so good. His hair is damp – he's obviously just showered himself – and he smells utterly gorgeous.

"Good morning," he says. His eyes drop downwards and I remember that I'm just wearing short pyjama bottoms and a skimpy top.

"Um… sorry." I try to cover up – although I don't know how I expect that to be possible with just my bandaged hands.

He comes in, smiling, and closes the door. "Don't apologise," he says. I can feel myself blushing and start to wish I'd never answered the damn phone in the first place. Except if I hadn't, I'd still be sitting on the bed, staring at my own hands and crying my eyes out… "Now, about this shower," he says.

"W—What about it?" I sound nervous, even to my own ears.

"Don't panic." He looks into my eyes, moving a little closer. "I know I said I wanted to shower with you – and I do – but I think we should build up to that, don't you?" I stare up at him, unable to move. God, his eyes are hypnotically sexy. "We need to be more practical today," he continues and pulls something from his back pocket. "I brought you gloves."

He shakes out a pair of plastic disposable gloves – the kind they use in kitchens when preparing fish.

He reaches into his front pocket. "And I figured the water might still get inside, so…" He shows me a couple of elastic bands. "I picked these up from the office. You can put them around your wrists once you've put the gloves on." He hands them to me. "Do you need me to help you put them on?" he asks.

I stare at him. "I don't know," I whisper, my mind still contemplating what might be involved in building up to taking a shower together.

"Well, try one and see how you get along by yourself."

I'm still staring at him. He waves a hand in front of my face.

"Are you okay?" he asks.

I snap out of my trance. "Yes," I reply.

"Try a glove." He nods to my hands. I obey him and pull a glove on over my bandaged hand, then snap the elastic band over the top, settling it around my wrist. "It's not too tight, is it?" he asks, putting his finger inside the band and trying it for himself.

"No," I whisper.

"Even so, I think you should be as quick as you can. You don't want to cut off the circulation."

"No."

"Are you sure you're okay?"

"Um… yes."

"Only you don't sound too sure."

"Sorry." He's got me so distracted, I can't even think straight, let alone string a sentence together.

"Don't keep apologising," he says. "Are you gonna be able to manage without me?"

No.

"I can stay if you need me to," he offers.

"Can you?" There, I've said it.

"Sure." He smiles. "Go shower. I'll wait out here."

"Okay." I pull on the other glove and elastic band and go into the bathroom.

I put on one of the hotel robes and wrap my hair in a towel before coming back out into the bedroom. He's sitting in the chair by the window and gets up the moment he sees me.

"How did it go?" he asks, looking me up and down.

"It worked well. I've left the gloves in there for tomorrow."

"We've got boxes and boxes of them," he says. "You can bring some back later."

"Oh, thanks."

"Now, do you need me to help with your hair, or anything?" he offers.

"No, I can just let it dry naturally."

He stares for a moment. "Can you dress?" His voice is quiet, like he's struggling to speak.

"I think so."

He must be wondering why I asked him to stay.

"I feel like I've wasted your time," I say. "I wasn't sure I'd be able to manage by myself."

"It's fine. I didn't mind. I've been thinking up recipes."

"Well, I'd better let you get back to work, before you forget them."

He moves closer. "I won't forget them," he says, then steps nearer still, so we're almost touching and he leans down, his mouth next to my ear. "I won't forget anything about this morning," he says. "Not a damn thing."

My head tips back, involuntarily, and I sigh out the tiny bolt of pleasure that grips my body. It's over in an instant, but I can't deny it happened.

He leans back and looks down at me, taking a half step back.

"I'll see you later," he says, and his tone makes me wonder if he's got something planned. He moves past me to the door. As he's about to leave I call out his name, and he turns.

"Thank you," I say. "Thank you for coming and helping."

"Anytime." He grins at me, and leaves.

It's all I can do to remain upright. He's got me about as horny as I can ever remember being, just with his words and his looks. I'm desperate – absolutely desperate – to discover what he could do to me with the rest of his body. And I'm even more keen to know what it is that he thinks I'd be unwilling to try.

By mid-morning, I'm almost at my wit's end. I can't focus on anything. I can't concentrate, or think straight. I just want him. My whole body feels like a mass of nerves, all tingling, all aching for his touch. The tension inside me has got me almost at breaking point.

I'm working in the office – or trying to – when there's a knock at the door.

"Come in," I call and Sam appears.

My whole body trembles at the sight of him. He must've noticed. His eyes have just widened and his lips have parted.

"Can you come upstairs?" he asks.

"Um… sure." *Please say you've decided you want to start working up towards that shower…*

"I've got some new dishes I want you to try." I can almost feel my disappointment.

"Okay."

"And I think I should probably change the dressings on your hands," he adds.

He's going to touch me. Thank God for that. Even if it is just my hands – right now, I don't care.

*

"Okay," I say, mulling it over in my head, "I'm normally really good with ingredients, but I can't place it. It tastes like liquorice but it can't be…"

"Why not?" He looks down at me, smirking.

"It's liquorice?" I take another bite of the salmon. "Where? In the sauce?"

"No, in the crust." There's a thin crust on one side of the salmon.

"I thought that was just herbs," I say.

He smiles. "No, it's black garlic, liquorice, and herbs."

"It's really subtle."

"Well, it's liquorice. It needs to be subtle."

"It tastes amazing," I say to him.

"Thanks." He almost seems embarrassed.

"I like them all."

He's created four new dishes for the seasonal menu and they're all incredible.

"You're really talented, Sam."

He blushes, but doesn't reply and I wonder how often anyone really compliments him.

"We'd better look at your hands," he says, changing the subject.

"Okay."

We sit at the butcher's block and he carefully undoes the bandages before inspecting the burns.

"They're looking a little better," he says. He's already put the ointment and some fresh bandages on the work surface and he gets up and brings them over, reapplying the ointment with the gentlest of touches. "Your knowledge of ingredients is really good," he mutters, focusing on what he's doing.

"Thank you."

"Do you miss it?" he asks as he starts to bandage my hands again, first one and then the other.

"Miss what?"

"Working in a kitchen," he clarifies.

"I miss the atmosphere, and the buzz I used to get from it, but I don't miss the hours, or the stress."

"I don't mind the stress so much, but the hours can be tough," he says after a pause. "There's not much time for a social life. People outside the business can find it hard to accommodate."

He finishes my hands, still holding onto them, inspecting the bandages, although they seem fine to me. I study his face, his strong stubbled jaw, his full lips, his high cheekbones. I feel myself leaning closer to him, just as he looks up and our eyes lock. He shifts in his seat and moves toward me. Our lips are almost touching and I know he's going to kiss me. I close my eyes and tilt my head, leaning just a little more… and nothing happens. I wait for a second, then open my eyes again. He's pulled back and is sitting upright again, and although he's still looking at me, his expression is completely different, like he's got no idea what's going on.

Shit. I got that so wrong. I'm mortified, embarrassed, and really disappointed.

"I—I'd better be going," I say, jumping off the stool. "Thanks for everything."

"Wait," he calls, but I can already feel the tears stinging my eyes. I'm not going to let him see how much I wanted that kiss. How much I wanted him. How could I have misread that so badly? I get to the door and run down the stairs and into the office, collapsing into the chair, my head in my bandaged hands. How am I ever going to look him in the eye again?

I hear the door open and close, and look up. He's standing on the other side of the desk, looking at me.

"I'm sorry," he says quietly.

"It's fine. You didn't want to kiss me. I misunderstood. It's me who should be saying sorry."

He tilts his head to one side, then walks around the desk.

"I did want to kiss you," he says, standing over me.

"Then why didn't you?" I'm confused now. Very confused.

"Because it's not something I'm used to."

I get up but he doesn't move back and our bodies are almost touching. He looks down into my eyes. It's unnerving. "H—How can someone like you not be used to kissing? That doesn't make sense."

"Someone like me?" He sounds more puzzled than I feel.

"Someone as handsome as you. Someone as sexy as you," I start to clarify.

"I've never been intimate in that way with anyone before," he says.

Is he serious? I choke, then cough for a moment.

"Are you okay?" he asks.

I nod. "Yes, thank you. I'm completely bewildered, but I'm okay."

"What are you bewildered about?"

"You."

"In what way?"

"You've... you've made all kinds of suggestive remarks. You've implied that you want to do things with me – or to me – that I might not be willing to do, and yet... you're a virgin?"

He stares at me, and then shakes his head. "No, Ali. I'm not a virgin."

"But you just said..."

"I said I wasn't intimate *in that way*. I didn't say I don't have sex. I've never been into kissing – at least not in the way I want to kiss you. I've never been into a lot of things that you'd probably consider normal."

"God, now I'm really confused."

"I know you are."

"Are you trying to tell me you've never... how do you put it over here...? You've never made out?"

He smiles. "No, I've never made out."

"I see... Well, actually I don't see at all."

"No, I didn't think you would."

I take a deep breath. I need to try and work out what he's saying, without dying of embarrassment first, especially as it seems I don't understand very much at all. Suddenly a thought occurs. "Okay... I believe you use some kind of baseball metaphor for sex over here, so why don't we use that and you can explain to me what you mean by not being intimate and yet not being a virgin."

"Do you have baseball in the UK? Do you even understand the metaphors?" he asks.

"No, but I've heard of them, and I'm just hoping it might make this less humiliating."

He smiles and shrugs. "If you think it'll help, then I'll explain the baseball thing."

"Okay."

"First base," he says slowly, "means French kissing."

"So tongues definitely have to be involved?"

He stares at me, deep into my eyes. "Yes. There have to be tongues."

I nod slowly. This was supposed to help, but it's actually starting to turn me on, and now I'm not sure it was such a good idea. "And second base?"

"Touching, kissing or licking anything above the waist." Oh, God. His voice is making me tingle. Or is that his words? I have to try and stay focused.

"And, I'm guessing third base is anything below the waist?" I manage to ask.

"Correct."

"And a home run is…?"

"Sex." The way he says the word 'sex' makes my whole body shiver.

"So… so, you just skip first base then, do you?" I stutter out my question.

"No."

Seriously? "Sam, you've got me so confused now."

"I skip first, second and third bases and just go straight for the home run."

Everything below my waist just turned to liquid. "Oh," I whisper.

"Which is why I don't know how to kiss you," he says.

"You really want to kiss me?" I'm surprised.

"Yes," he murmurs. "More than anything."

"Anything?" Is teasing really a good way to ease all this tension? I'm not so sure…

"Okay, maybe not more than anything," he replies, moving closer, "but we need to start somewhere."

"We do?"

"Yeah, we do."

He leans down and I can't take my eyes from his lips.

"Ali?" Rob barges in behind us and Sam jumps back like someone scalded him.

"What?" I turn to Rob.

"There's a delivery," he says, looking from me to Sam and back again.

"Can't you deal with it?" I ask him.

"No. They want you to check it before they go."

"Oh, fuck this," Sam says and storms off, without saying a word to me, or even looking in my direction.

"What's wrong?" Rob says, looking at his brother.

"Nothing." Sam pushes past him and out of the door.

"Has he upset you again?" Rob asks me. "I thought you guys were getting past all that."

"We were," I say to him. "Well, we were trying to." I walk around the desk and he suddenly sees the light.

"Oh, sorry. I interrupted something?"

"Yes."

"I didn't realise."

We go out into the restaurant.

"I'm really sorry, Ali," Rob repeats.

"You weren't to know," I reply. But I'm suddenly scared that Rob's interruption might have ruined everything, just when we were so close to getting it right.

Sam

I'm so angry. No, angry's not the right word. I'm disappointed and really frustrated. I wanted to kiss Ali so much, and it's gone wrong –

twice. I'll admit the first time was my fault entirely. I got cold feet. We were sitting in my kitchen and I was sure the moment was right. I leant in. She leant in. She closed her eyes. It was perfect, until I remembered for some obscure reason that I'd never actually done that before, and my nerves got the better of me.

I know it sounds odd that a thirty year old guy, who's been married and had sex with a fair few women has never kissed any of them, but that's just the way it's worked out. Before Amber, it never felt right. It felt too romantic, too intimate and all wrong for the kind of relationships I had. With Amber, I'll admit we kissed, but it wasn't conventional. We never kissed before we were married, but afterwards, I thought maybe we ought to, what with her being my wife and everything, but whenever I tried, she would bite me, sometimes until she made my lips bleed, because she knew it would piss me off. She thought that would make me fuck her harder. It didn't. It just pissed me off. But it was part of what she did. I didn't like it. The only way I could control it was to stop even trying to kiss her. But I want to kiss Ali properly and, when I saw her sitting there with her eyes closed, waiting for me to close the gap, I was suddenly really scared I'd get it wrong and ruin everything. When she opened her eyes again, she looked so crushed, so disappointed. And then she ran, and I felt like such a jerk – again – because I realized real fast that Ali wasn't gonna be critical about it, even if I did screw it up. I knew if it went wrong, I could just explain it to her and she'd understand. Because that's the kind of person she is. So, I followed her straight downstairs.

She was upset, which was understandable. She thought I was going to kiss her and I didn't. She thought that meant I wasn't interested. I owed her an explanation and that confused the hell out of her. I'm not surprised she looked so puzzled. Her assumption that I must be a virgin came a bit out of left field, but I guess that's understandable too. Most people work up to sex, starting with kissing. Even I know that. That's why I wanted to kiss her. That's why I told her we need to work up to having a shower together at her hotel room this morning. She had me wired as hell, in her sexy pajamas, and I know I could've done something while we were alone in her hotel room. But the thing is, she'd been crying, and it didn't feel right. Even so, I'm not like most people. This is new to me, and I think she's beginning to work that out now, especially after we did the whole baseball metaphor thing. That was less embarrassing than I'd thought, and she even seemed a little turned on by the idea of skipping to a home run. That feels promising for the future… although how we're ever gonna have a future if Rob keeps interrupting, is beyond me. He wasn't to know, but that doesn't make it any less frustrating.

I sit at the island unit and go over the recipes I was working on earlier, making a few amendments. I think I'll stay up here for a while, get my head together and go down later. At the moment, my instincts are telling me that I should invite Ali to come up here after work. Maybe I'll see if she wants to stay for dinner again. We need to work this out. We've taken it too far to turn back now.

I go down at around three o'clock. The whole place is alive with workmen. It's not long until Ed and I can move back into the main kitchens now. Ali's allowed several days before the opening for us to practice using the kitchens and I need to train everyone on the new equipment and get them up to speed with the new menu and recipes. It's going to be hard work, but I'm looking forward to it.

I go into the office, but Ali isn't there. She wasn't in the kitchen, so I guess she must be out front.

I walk through, my hands in my pockets, and see that there are fewer people in here. Rob's over by the bar, talking to one of the carpenters. The walls are covered with sheeting to protect them from dust, so it all looks a bit spartan in here.

"Where's Ali?" I ask him.

"She's left," he says.

"What do you mean, 'left'?"

I feel myself panic.

"She's gone back to the hotel."

"It's early." I'm confused and I can't think of anything else to say.

"Yeah." He comes over and pulls me into the back corner of the restaurant. "I'm sorry about earlier," he says. "I didn't mean to interrupt. I didn't know you were in there with Ali. Come to that, I didn't know you two were… together."

"We're not. Not yet."

"I know… and if I keep interrupting you, you never will be."

"Precisely."

"Just thought I'd say it before you did."

He smirks. I know he means well, but I'm more interested in why Ali left without saying goodbye. Did I offend her when I stormed off? Is she worried about our conversation earlier? Does she think that's all I want from her? A home run…?

"I'll be back in a minute," I tell him and, without waiting for a reply, I walk straight out the door. Once I'm on the street, I start running to the hotel.

I knock on her door and wait. She takes a while but eventually she answers. She looks pale.

"Shit. Are you okay?"

She touches the side of her head. "I've just got a headache, that's all. Is something wrong?"

"No. I was just worried. You didn't say goodbye and… well, after what we talked about…" I can't finish my sentence.

"Sorry," she says, swaying slightly. "I just felt so rough, I had to come back here."

"It's okay." I guide her back into the room and take her over to the bed. "Do you still have painkillers?"

"I've already taken some," she murmurs. I lie her down and pull the cover over her, even though she's still fully clothed, then I go over and close the drapes, so the room's in near darkness.

"Where's your phone?" I ask her.

"In my bag." I search around and find it on the dresser, opening it and delving inside.

"I'll put it beside the bed," I tell her. "If you feel worse, or you need me, call. I'll be here in five minutes."

"Thank you," she whispers.

"I can stay," I say, "but I think you're better off sleeping."

"Yes." Her voice drifts off.

I lean over and very gently kiss her forehead. Not exactly what I had in mind for our first kiss, but I don't care. "Call me," I say. "Whatever the time; whatever you need. Call me."

"Thank you."

We're really on the last stretch now. We're back in the kitchens and I don't think I've ever been so busy, or so tired. We've hit a few hitches with the recipes. The new equipment takes some getting used to and certain things that worked perfectly well upstairs don't seem to be as feasible down here.

Ali came back to work the day after her headache, although she was a little subdued. She said it was just because she wasn't feeling well, and by the following day she was her normal self. I was worried about her. Very worried. I checked up on her regularly, made sure she had whatever she needed. I'm not used to that, but it felt good. Not that she was ill, but that she was letting me care for her.

My love for her is everything. She's the first thing I think about in the morning and the last thing on my mind when I finally drift off to sleep at night, wishing more than anything that she was with me. When I'm working, I just about manage to concentrate on what I'm doing, but I imagine the meals I'm cooking are for her, that I'm creating them for her enjoyment alone. Everything I do now is for her.

We've seen a lot of each other, but we haven't had any time alone since those few minutes in the office. I'm even starting to wonder if that ever happened. I know it did because I can remember every second of the conversation, but it feels like a different life, a different time. That's not to say I'm giving up on us being together. I'm not. I'll never give up on that. I think she feels the same too. It's just we're both so damned busy that being together is starting to feel unattainable. Every so often, we catch each other's eye and she gives me a look. It's a really nice look. I'm not entirely sure what it means, but I like it.

Ali's hands have steadily improved and, although to start with, I still changed her dressings, it was done in the main kitchen, or the office, and always with someone else present for some reason. Now they've improved so much, she's just got a band-aid on her left hand and the right one is almost back to normal. She heals well – but then she seems to do everything well.

Not being alone with her is tough, but even the evenings are taken up. For me, the time is spent perfecting the dishes in the kitchen – making small amendments and ensuring everything works perfectly – and then I'm trying to help Ed as well. He's had a few crises of confidence, and has turned to me, which has meant I've had to be there for him. As for Ali… she's spending most of her time with Rob, training the restaurant staff, going over the menus with them and making sure they know how to use the new iPads, which we bought for taking orders. She's also been working late in the office. Regardless of what we're both doing, because we see still each other all the time, it feels like we're together – and yet at the same time, we're miles apart. Every night since the episode in the office, I've climbed into bed in the early hours, ruing another lost chance, another wasted day, and hoping that tomorrow will bring me better chances. So far, it's been a forlorn hope.

Despite the craziness of these last few days before the opening, Ali has revealed a couple of things to us. Firstly, yesterday, she called us into the office late in the afternoon and showed us our new website. None of us even knew this was happening. We thought she was just revamping the old one and changing the pictures and some of the text. Instead, we've got an amazing and very stylish-looking site. She's put in so much work. Work none of us were even aware she was doing. Rob put our last one together, so I think he was probably more impressed than any of us. He knows what went into it. He asked her how long it had taken and where she'd found the time, and she explained that she used a company in London for the design, and that she had nothing else to do with her evenings when she first got here, which gave her the time to work on the content. That made me feel a little sad. She could've been spending those evenings with me. We wasted all that time, because I was too busy being a stubborn idiot to see what was right under my nose.

She also explained that she'd been running an ad campaign. Again, we didn't know she'd been doing this either. She laughed at that point and asked if any of us had actually bothered to read the contract, and for a moment I was reminded of how much I argued with her over it. Fool that I am. She explained that there was a budget allocated for an ad campaign and that she's been controlling that and ramping it up as the opening approaches. She's so damn impressive, it takes my breath away sometimes… well, all the time, really.

Finally, this afternoon – two days before the opening – she asked us all to go out into the restaurant. I was busy at the time, so she said we could do it later and we've arranged to meet her out there at seven this evening. I know that's late, but my day has been horrendous. I apologized to her for keeping her late and she said it's fine, adding that it's not late by recent standards and she'd rather do this when the contractors have left anyway. I don't know what she wants to tell us, but I'm looking forward to just spending a bit of time with her – even if Ed and Rob are there too.

Having been in the bright lights of the kitchen all day, it's quite dark in the restaurant – the only source of light coming from the street lamps outside.

"Can we turn the lights on?" I ask.

"In a minute," Ali says. "Just walk to the front by the window, and turn around," she adds, although she stays back by the corridor that leads to the kitchen. "The tables and chairs are in situ, so watch yourselves." We pick our way between the tables.

"This feels very mysterious," Rob says.

Ali doesn't reply.

"Okay. We're here," I tell her once we've reached the front of the restaurant and turned back to face her again.

"Right," she says and, after just a moment's pause, she flicks on the lights.

I hear both Ed and Rob suck in a breath and I'm fairly sure I just did the same thing.

We've all walked through here multiple times over the last few weeks, when the place has been shrouded in dust sheets, filled with workmen and their tools, a shell of its former self. Now, the transformation is complete. And it's breathtaking – literally. We all look around slowly, taking in the modifications. The bar is where it always was, but the panelling on the front has disappeared, and has been replaced by a curved perspex sheet, behind which soft white light gives a romantic hue to the whole restaurant. The only other light source comes from down-lighters in the ceiling. Otherwise, there are candles on the tables, as yet unlit, but I can imagine how the place will look when they are. The left hand wall features the various pictures we saw in Ali's drawing. All different sizes, they're encased in plain gray frames and scattered over the wide expanse of white wall. The tables, surrounded by gray leather chairs, are covered with white linen cloths, and have been laid with silver cutlery and long-stemmed wine glasses, and each table has a single white rose, placed in a vase in the center. However, the thing that really draws our eye is the back wall. Here, a huge photograph fills the wide expanse, interrupted every so often, and at irregular intervals, by a narrow white vertical stripe. The effect is stunning – as is the photograph. It's of Positano, in the early evening, the lights of the hillside village sparkling and reflecting in the bay below.

Ali is standing by the corridor, her thumbnail in her mouth. She looks worried, and doubtful, as though she thinks we might not like it.

"Look," Ed says. He's wandered over to the left-hand wall and is gazing at one of the photographs hanging there.

"What?" Rob follows him. "Oh my God… Sam, come see this."

I drag my eyes away from Ali, who's staring at me, and join them. The photograph is long and slim. It's a close-up of a building. A familiar building. The walls are terra-cotta colored, the windows high and narrow, the door is red, although the paint is flaking, with three steps leading up to it, steps that are covered with pots of flowers and herbs.

"It's Papa's house," I whisper and I turn to Ali, confused. "How did you know?"

She moves forward, just a couple of paces and stops, her hands in her pockets. I've never seen her look this shy, or this beautiful.

"I didn't," she replies. "I hired a local photographer, in Positano. I got him to ask around and find out where your parents were born." She points to another photograph, further along the wall. "That's your mothers's house," she says and we all move along. She's right. It is.

"They're all Positano," Rob mutters, studying each picture. Some are wider shots, scenics taken at different times of day, showing the village in all its glory. Others are of individual buildings, and the small ones show details – little things like ornate railings and windows, or doors. They're beautiful.

"Yes, they are." Ali's biting her bottom lip now. God, she's so nervous. Did she honestly think we wouldn't like this… wouldn't *love* this?

I move over toward her.

"Thank you." It's all I can think of to say. It's all my voice will let me say.

"Is it okay?" She looks up into my eyes.

I nod my head and move closer, so our bodies are almost touching. I lean closer. I want to kiss her – not to thank her, but because I love her. I've loved her for a long time now, longer than I've been willing to admit, but I love her more than ever for giving us this. I don't care that Rob and Ed are standing right behind me. I don't care that I've never done this before and messing it up in front of them will be ten times worse than doing so in private. I tilt my head. She does too, her eyes still fixed on mine.

"You commissioned all this photography?" Ed asks. He's almost beside us, moving closer. Ali pulls back, startled. *Damn.*

"Um… yes," she replies and, with a quick, nervous glance at me, she turns away. I want to pull her back. I want to take her in my arms and kiss her. But I don't. I can wait a little longer. "That's why the photography budget was so high," she explains. Rob's come over too.

"Why didn't you explain that at the time?" he asks.

"I wanted to surprise you," she says.

"You've certainly done that," Ed replies.

"Good surprise?" she asks, like she's still not sure.

"Very good," I say, before the other two can answer. She smiles up at me – a smile that makes my heart beat a little faster. I worked out a while ago that she was making the place so much better – I even worked out that she was making us better. What I didn't realize was just how much better, or that she'd put so much into it. So much of herself too.

There was something that happened to her when we talked about Positano. She got upset. She's got memories of the place, and although she said they were good memories, something about it made her cry. And yet, she put all that to one side to give us this – a piece of the place we all call 'home'. It isn't our home. We were all born here, in Hartford, but Positano was home to our parents, and they always call it 'home', even to this day – and so we do too.

I turn away for a moment, because I'm really struggling to come to terms with the fact that I wasted so much time being mean to her. I'm struggling even more with the fact that she actually seems to want to have some kind of relationship with me. I don't feel like I deserve her. Not in the slightest.

"Shit, shit, shit." Ed doesn't swear very often, unlike Rob and me, so I know something's wrong straight away.

"What's happened?" I go over to him in his new area and give him a pat on the back.

"It's the panna cotta… they're not quite set enough."

"You've got time. We're only half an hour into service. No-one's gonna be ordering dessert for a while yet. Put them in the blast chiller." I put my hands on his shoulders and turn him around to face me. "And calm down."

He nods, giving me a vague smile, then gets back to work. Opening night has come round real fast and he's not the only one who's nervous. So far, we've had three dropped plates – luckily all empty – and one burnt salmon, and we've only been open for thirty minutes. I'm trying to imbue an atmosphere of calm into the place but the nerves in here are ridiculous.

I walk back into the main kitchen. Everyone looks so on edge. "Come on, guys," I call out, trying to sound reassuring, "we've practiced this. It's what we do." They turn to look at me, seemingly shocked. That's probably because I'm not known for giving pep talks at the best of times, but there's no point in me yelling at them. They're nervous enough already.

I check the appetizers for table four and let them go, then get back to preparing main courses for tables seven and twelve. At the moment, I'm checking absolutely everything – nothing's leaving this kitchen without me casting an eye over it.

Rob comes in, looking worn out, but happy. "It's crazy out there," he says. "We've already taken bookings for well into next month."

"Already?" I look up at him. "They can hardly have tasted the food yet."

"A lot of them haven't. They just love the way the place looks, and feels."

I smile. Ali did it. She really did it.

He grabs some more ice from the deep freeze and disappears again.

The next couple of hours are insane, but good. I like it when the kitchens are busy. Like I said, it's what we do.

Not long after nine-thirty, Ali comes in. I've gotten so used to seeing her in jeans, it takes me by surprise to see her in a dress. It's a great dress, too. It's deep red, knee length, with a soft, kind of floaty skirt, and fitted bodice. It's very sophisticated and stylish. She's wearing high-heeled pumps too, which make her legs seem even longer than usual. She's put her hair up and she's smiling, and a little flushed. She looks real sexy – *real* sexy.

"You okay?" I ask her.

She nods. "Yes. I just wondered if you had a few moments."

I glance around. "A few – no more than that. Why?"

"I thought you might like to see something… you and Ed."

She calls him over and, after checking something in the oven, he joins us.

"Come with me." She takes my hand, but lets Ed just follow, and leads us down the corridor to the end, so we're standing on the threshold of the restaurant.

It's noisy, full to bursting, with smiling diners, eating, drinking, talking, laughing. The candlelight makes the whole place glow and it's perfect. It's exactly what we wanted it to be.

Ali lets go of my hand and I'm aware that she's taken a step back and, just at that moment, a man sitting nearby notices us, gets to his feet and starts to clap. Within seconds, the whole restaurant follows suit, everyone applauding loudly. A couple of regulars come over and shake my hand – and Ed's – congratulating us on the food, the decor, the ambience. We thank them all, and I have to admit that all my fears about people not wanting to come back here after we'd been closed for so long seem to have been unfounded. I've never been praised like this before – just for doing my job – but I feel Ali should be taking the credit, not us. She came up with the ideas, she created this, and she made us do the work to get it to where it is. I turn around, but she's disappeared.

"Look at that," Ed says, smirking.

"What?" I turn back and look toward where he's nodding. Over by the bar, Rob's standing talking to a woman, who's holding a very professional-looking camera. He's facing us, and – I've gotta say – he looks completely besotted. But we can also see her in the mirror behind the bar and the reason for his devotion becomes immediately obvious. She's very beautiful – and just his type. Long, curly dark hair, almost black, I'd say, with sultry pouting lips, light olive skin, sparkling eyes and the kind of curves Rob would probably die for… yeah, she's just his type. I grin at Ed.

"Poor woman," I mutter.

He nods and, having thanked the last few customers for their compliments, we make our way back to the kitchen. There's no sign of Ali and, with new orders having come in, I don't have time to find her.

It's gone midnight by the time we've cleaned down and cleared away. It was a truly fantastic night and Rob's told us that we're actually booked solid for the next two months now. He's even got a waiting list for cancellations. We've never had that before.

Ali materialized again about half an hour after abandoning us in the restaurant. She'd been in the office, evidently, and then went back into the restaurant, and now the four of us are sitting around one of the tables, Ed and I have taken off our whites, and Rob's just cracked open a bottle of champagne.

He pours it into four long flutes, handing them out.

"To Ali," he says, looking at her. We raise our glasses.

"Hmm… To Ali, who wouldn't take any credit," I say, leaning into her. She's sitting next to me and it feels good to be this close to her after so long spent apart.

"Of course I wasn't going to take the credit," she says, sipping her champagne and putting the glass down on the table.

"Why not?" I ask. "You did all the work." I wave my arm around the restaurant. "You made this happen."

"No." She shakes her head. "I helped *you* make it happen." She takes another sip, keeping hold of her glass this time and, when I glance at her hands, it looks to me as though they're shaking. "Besides," she adds, "my work here is almost done." Her voice drops to a cracked whisper. "I'll be gone soon and you'll need to carry on without me." She looks up and swallows hard. "So, you'd better get used to it." She smiles, but her eyes are glistening, and my heart starts to ache. She's going home. Of course she is. She was never gonna be here forever. Her contract was always limited. But… we haven't even kissed. I haven't told her that I'm in love with her. She can't go home – not yet. She can't go home at all. The ache in my chest intensifies to a crushing pain.

"Rob…" She continues speaking, even though I feel like my heart is breaking. "I'll need to sit down with you on Monday and go through the advertising campaign."

"Okay," he says.

"And I've arranged for Petra to come in again next Sunday."

"*Next* Sunday?" Rob queries.

"Yes. I figured you'd all be too tired to have your photographs taken tomorrow, but we're going to need some publicity shots of the three of you. I'll speak to her before next weekend and make sure she's up to speed."

"You'll still be here though, right?" I ask.

"Yes, I'll be here, but I only allowed for her taking pictures of you and Ed. I just need to make sure she's okay with Rob being included, in terms of her schedule for the day."

"So, you're not going home yet?" I turn toward her. "You're staying?" I feel like I'm repeating myself.

She looks up at me. "For a little while, yes." She shakes her head slowly. "Didn't you read the contract at all?"

I shrug. "No. I think at the time I was probably too busy being an asshole to bother."

She smiles, that real sexy smile. "Hmm... Well, in the contract it says that I'll be here for two to three weeks after opening night, just to make sure everything runs smoothly, and to deal with things like this photography shoot." Her eyes lock with mine. "I know how difficult you chefs can be," she adds.

"Yeah. I'm glad you learned that one. At least you're not bringing that photographer in while we're trying to work. She'd get in the way."

"She can get in my way anytime she likes," Rob interjects and Ali laughs.

"Ah, but Sam's different," she says, turning back to me. "I'd never bring someone into your kitchen who didn't belong there. I learned very early on that you don't appreciate outsiders."

"Only certain outsiders," I whisper, leaning into her again.

I'm aware of Rob nudging Ed and the two of them get up. They're not being exactly subtle, but I really don't care anymore. I only care about the fact that a moment ago, my world was falling apart and now I feel like I've got another chance.

"We'll be going," Rob says.

"You haven't finished your drinks." Ali nods toward their half-empty glasses.

"We're tired," Ed replies. "It's been a busy day."

"It certainly has," Ali says.

Rob comes around to our side of the table and leans down, kissing Ali on the cheek. "Thank you – for everything."

She blushes. "You're welcome," she says.

Ed copies Rob's actions and the two of them leave, telling me they'll see me on Monday morning.

Once the door has closed, I turn properly in my seat, so I'm facing Ali.

"It's late," she says. "I suppose I'd better get my things from the office and head back to the hotel."

"Please don't." I reach out and take one of her hands in mine. "Please don't go." I sound desperate – but that's because I am. "I know you're tired, but please… come upstairs for a while. Stay. Please."

I lean in a little closer, gazing deep into her eyes. I'm fairly certain that neither of us blinks. *Please say yes. Please.*

"Yes," she whispers.

Chapter Twelve

Ali

I knew. I knew the moment the moment he asked me that I'd say yes. So why delay in answering him? He asked me to stay, and he said it in such a way that I don't think he was talking about stopping for coffee. I think he meant a lot more than that, and it dawned on me that I'll be leaving in a couple of weeks, and we might never see each other again. I know that staying, that letting anything happen between us, means I'm just setting myself up for a broken heart, but I can't deny myself the chance of finding out what it would be like to be with him. I need to know what he feels like; I need to see if his touch can make me feel as alive as his words and I want to discover whether there really are things I'm not willing to try – because when I'm with him, it really doesn't feel like it.

He smiles and stands, offering his hand and I take it and let him pull me to my feet.

"Wait here," he murmurs, going to the front of the restaurant and locking the door. He returns and takes my hand again, leading me to the corridor, where he flicks off the lights, before opening the door that leads up to his apartment. The nervous tension in my stomach is almost overwhelming, but I follow and, as we reach the top of the stairs, he turns on the lights up here, and a soft glow from the side lamps fills the room.

"Take a seat," he murmurs, "I'll get some coffee."

I turn and stare at him. Did he really just invite me for coffee? Did I read that all wrong? He smiles and his eyes lock with mine again and I know I didn't.

"Do you mind if I take my shoes off?" I ask. "They're killing me."

"Make yourself at home," he says, going over to the kitchen.

I kick off my shoes, leaving them in the hallway and, going over to the sofa, I sit and lean back into the soft cushions, letting my hair down, shaking it around my shoulders, and relaxing for the first time since about five o'clock this evening. It's been one hell of an evening too.

"Everything went well, don't you think?" I call out to him.

"Yeah. It went really well. We had a few hiccups in the kitchen, but nothing we couldn't handle."

"There were always going to be teething troubles. That's one of the reasons I'm staying on. Normally when I've worked for restaurants at home, I just stay on the end of the phone, and pop back to see them a few times in the weeks after they re-open, but that's not practical in this instance, so I factored in a longer stay."

There's a moment's pause and then I feel his breath on my ear. "I'm real glad you did," he whispers from behind me.

I tilt my head back and look up. He's leaning over, our lips almost touching, and he smiles down at me, before going back to the kitchen.

He re-appears just a couple of minutes later, carrying two cups of coffee, which he places on the table in front of us, before sitting down beside me, much closer than he has done before when I've been here.

"I'm even too tired to watch more Breaking Bad," I say, looking up at him.

He leans closer. "Good. I really don't wanna watch TV with you." His voice seems a little deeper than usual.

I swallow. "What do you want to do with me?"

"Well, to start off with, I want to kiss you." He moves nearer still. "I've wanted to kiss you for days." He's staring at my lips, and then into my eyes, before dropping his gaze back to my lips again. "Actually," he says suddenly, "that's not strictly true. I've wanted to kiss you since the first time I saw you sitting in the restaurant – when you turned up unannounced."

I'm surprised and I can't disguise it. "Is that why you were so horrible to me? Because you were desperate to kiss me?"

He shrugs. "I did explain… I've never done this before. I guess I'm not very good at this kind of thing." He's so unsure of himself.

I put my hand gently on his cheek and he closes his eyes, leaning into my touch. "No," I say softly, "you're very good at it."

He opens his eyes again and leans closer, his lips brushing against mine. He pauses, like he doesn't know what to do, and I let him. I guess he needs to find his own way around this. He leans back, and then tries again, covering my mouth with his. I feel his tongue sweep across my lips and gasp at the gentleness of the contact, opening to him. His hand comes up, cupping my face and I feel him change position, kneeling on the couch and pushing me down and back into the corner, so he's leaning over me as he delves inside my mouth, searching. God, the intensity… In an instant, I'm breathless, panting for him. He changes the angle of his head, taking me deeper and, instinctively, I part my legs, so he can kneel between them, moving closer. This is so much more than I'd expected from him… it's almost too much. My whole body aches and throbs to feel his touch. He's so forceful and passionate. I arch my back up, pushing my breasts into his chest and he groans deeply into my mouth. The sound echoes through me, and I feel the dampness between my legs. I'm wet for him already.

He pulls back, looking down at me, and I heave in a breath.

"I've never been kissed like that before," I whisper, trying to excuse my slightly wanton behaviour.

"Is that good or bad?" he asks, still uncertain of himself.

"Oh, it's good." I reassure him. "It's very good." I look up into his eyes and he smiles.

"I didn't mean to be horrible to you, and I'm sorry I was such a jerk," he says, like he thinks he still owes me an explanation for something I feel like we discussed a lifetime ago – although it was probably only ten minutes. "I'll admit I resented you."

"You did?"

"Yes. I don't anymore though."

"I'm glad to hear it."

"I appreciate everything you've done for us, Ali," he adds, one hand still cupped around my face, the other resting behind my head, his lips maybe an inch or two from mine and his eyes gazing at me. "You're kind and thoughtful, and so tolerant – especially of me. I'm sure I've pushed you to your limits sometimes."

"Sometimes." I can't lie to him.

"Then I'm sorry." He seems so genuine.

"It's alright," I say.

He leans closer, his lips almost upon me. "No, it's not. But it will be."

And he kisses me, even harder than before, and within seconds, he's ignited the fire again. I'm burning for him. I'm desperate, needy. I want him so much. I rest my hands on his huge biceps, and part my legs even wider, the skirt of my dress hitching up a little. He must know what I want, and he nestles into the cradle of my thighs, resting against me. For the first time, I can feel his arousal. He's bone hard. And enormous.

I break the kiss and pull back, leaning into the cushion behind me.

"What's wrong?" he asks.

"You're… you're very hard," I murmur.

"Yes," he replies. "There's not a lot I can do about that. You're very sexy."

I look into his eyes. "You're very sexy too," I reply.

He kneels up, staring down at me. "Do you wanna sit here and drink coffee, or do you wanna come to bed with me?" he asks.

Hearing him say those words has me feeling suddenly overwhelmed and I pull my legs right up, twist around and sit up, right on the edge of the couch. "Ali?" I can hear something bordering on fear in his voice.

"Sorry," I murmur, and he shifts, sitting down beside me, obviously confused, which isn't surprising.

"Is something wrong?" he asks.

"I don't know." I look at him and he's so concerned it makes my heart contract.

"We can just sit and drink coffee. We don't have to go to bed, if you don't want to," he says.

"I do," I reply. "I do want to. I'm just not sure you do."

He frowns, tilting his head to one side. "What makes you say that?"

I take a deep breath and turn to face him. "What do you want from me?" I ask him.

"I want to take you to bed," he replies.

"And?"

"And I want to make love to you. Isn't that what you want too?"

I nod. "Is that enough though."

Again, he frowns. "I don't understand, Ali. What are you trying to say?"

"You said to me a while ago, that I wouldn't be willing to do the things you wanted. I didn't really understand what that meant. What do you want from me, Sam?" I repeat the question.

"Do you trust me?" he asks, not really answering me.

"Yes." I don't even hesitate.

He smiles again. "Good." He moves closer, his eyes boring into mine. "You've got nothing to be scared of. I promise. We can just make love."

Just? "There are alternatives?"

He chuckles lightly. "Oh yeah," he says. "There are lots of alternatives."

"In which case, will making love be enough? For you, I mean..."

He shrugs. "I don't know," he says with chilling sincerity, while getting up and holding out his hand. "Why don't we try it and see?"

I take his hand and let him pull me to my feet.

I'm confused again now. He said he wasn't a virgin... "Are you saying you've never done it before?"

He bends over, his mouth right next to my ear again. "Not in the way that you mean, no."

I lean back. I can feel how wet I am for him; my body's tingling with anticipation. "What does that mean?"

"It means I want to take you to bed and make love to you – your way."

"My way?"

"Yes. And then maybe – if that goes okay – we can try a few things my way."

"Your way?"

"Yeah – my way." His voice drops, to a deep, gravelly tone and he stares at me, not moving. He's waiting. I nod my head and he leads me down the corridor, flicking off the lights as we pass. We enter the second door on the right.

"Lights on, or off?" he asks.

"You choose."

"We're doing this your way," he says. "Remember?"

"On," I reply. I want to see him.

He smiles "Okay." He turns and switches on the lights. Two lamps on either side of the bed spark into life, revealing an enormous iron bedstead, covered with a pale grey duvet and, at the foot end, a dark grey throw. There's a big chest of drawers and a wardrobe, and two bedside tables, and that's it. A door in the corner is open and seems to lead to an ensuite bathroom.

He turns to me and, still holding my hand, leads me over to the bed. Although I want him, I feel nervous. How fast is he going to want to take this? He's made it clear he's not a great one for foreplay. He must sense my anxiety.

"It'll be alright," he whispers, leaning down and kissing me gently.

I decide honesty is the best policy. "Except you're someone who goes straight for a home run."

His smile widens. "Not with you, Ali. I told you, we're doing this your way."

I nod, relaxing slightly, then wonder… do I even have a 'way'?

He kisses me again – harder this time, his tongue finding mine. I feel his hands come around the back of my dress, lowering the zip to just below my waist and he pulls it from my shoulders, letting it fall to the floor. Then he unfastens my bra, and releases me, dropping the white lace garment at my feet. He breaks the kiss and looks down at me.

"Fuck, Ali," he murmurs. "You're so beautiful." He leans down, squeezing my left breast in his hand, and captures my nipple between his teeth, nipping gently and I feel a bolt of pleasure charge directly to my pussy. I moan, loudly, my head rocking back. "Slow, baby," he whispers, changing sides and repeating the process with my right breast. The same thing happens again and I gasp. "Shh," he says, standing upright and kissing me again. My brain might have been anxious, might have thought I needed him to go slow, but my body wants him to take me. Now.

He kneels down on one knee and, with his thumbs in the top of my knickers, slowly pulls them down. Then he takes my hand. "Step out," he says, and I do. Something about his voice and the way he behaves, the way he talks, makes me follow his instructions. I want him so much, but he doesn't touch me. Instead, he stands again and turns us, my back toward the bed. "Sit," he says, and I do, looking up at him. His eyes rake up my naked body. "Now lie back." His voice is gentle, but kind of strangled, like he's struggling to get the words out. Again, I do as he says, lying back. He leans down, puts his hands on my knees and brings them up, so they're bent almost up to my chest, then parts them, really wide. I'm exposed to him and he runs a single finger from my clitoris down to my entrance. I groan and shiver.

"You're wet," he whispers, his eyes devouring me.

He kneels on the floor again, then pulls me toward him and leans forward, and I feel his fingers parting me, his tongue sliding up from my entrance to my clitoris, taking the same journey as his finger, but in reverse. Then he starts to flick the very tip over me. Within seconds, I feel a quivering deep inside me and instinctively raise my hips toward him. He places a hand on my mound, pushing me firmly back into the mattress and holding me there, keeping me still, while his tongue works me harder, pushing me closer. His other hand moves down, and I feel him gently insert a finger inside me, and that quivering turns into an explosion. He keeps up the motions of his tongue and his finger as I moan and scream, my head thrashing from side to side. I'm bucking into him, while he holds me down. It's relentless, overwhelming, like nothing I've ever felt before.

Eventually, the feelings subside, my breathing starts to return to normal and I open my eyes. Sam's staring up at me. A smile on his glistening lips.

"That was… incredible," I whisper. "Are you sure you've never done that before?"

"I've done that before – once – it wasn't like this." He's very mysterious, and that's very arousing.

He stands, still looking at me, and pulls his t-shirt over his head, dropping it to the floor. I raise my head off the bed slightly, taking in the view. I knew he'd look good – his tight t-shirts revealed that much – but his body is so hard, so toned. He's like something out of a magazine – the type women drool over. He puts his hand on the buckle of his belt, then pauses.

"Do I need a condom?" he asks.

I shake my head. "I'm on the pill."

"I'm clean," he says.

"Oh… so am I." I never thought that would be an issue, until Liam announced I wasn't the only woman he was sleeping with, and that she was pregnant by him. Their sex was obviously unprotected. Needless to say, I got tested. Thankfully, it was fine.

Sam nods, then undoes his belt, and the button behind it, lowering the zipper of his jeans. It's like he's performing a slow, sexy striptease for me and I'm beyond turned on by the display. Putting his thumbs inside the tops of his jeans and the trunks beneath them, he lowers them both at the same time, steps out, and stands back up again. And I see him for the first time. I gasp and snap my legs together, sitting up, pulling my knees in to my chest, then wrapping my arms around them, protectively.

"What's wrong?" he moves closer, putting one knee on the bed.

"You need to ask?" I stare at his erection. It's huge. I don't even want to hazard a guess at how long it is, but the thing that scares me the most – more so even than the enormous length of it – is the girth. There's no way I'm letting him anywhere near me with that thing.

"You look so scared," he says.

"That's because I am."

He moves forward, raising the other knee onto the bed and crawling toward me. "You don't need to be. I won't hurt you."

"You might not, but I have a feeling that will."

"Well, this is mine and I won't let it hurt you," he says, smiling a little wider. "You said you trusted me."

"I do."

"Okay then." He thinks that's all there is to it? Evidently he does. He takes my hands, moving them away from my legs and lowers me back down onto the mattress. "Spread your legs, baby," he whispers. I look up at his face. His eyes are locked with mine and, like a lamb to the slaughter, I part my legs for him. "Good girl," he says. He leans over me, one hand by my head, the other holding onto his erection. "I will not hurt you," he says, emphasising each word.

I nod my head and feel him lower himself, the head of his arousal gently rubbing against my entrance.

"You're really wet now," he says.

"Well, you did just make me come."

"I noticed." He smiles broadly, then pushes into me and I wince as I feel the stretch. "Relax, Ali," he whispers, adjusting his position and bringing his other hand up by my head now. I'm trapped by him, surrounded by him. It feels intoxicating and I struggle to take a breath, and make a conscious effort to calm my nerves. He waits, then pushes a little further. It doesn't hurt this time. In fact, it feels sublime. The stretch is still there, but it's so good, so fulfilling. "Better?" he asks.

"Hmm… yes."

"Okay." He moves deeper still and I let out a moan, bringing my legs up.

"More," I whisper, staring into his eyes.

"More?" he queries.

"Yes." I grind out the word. I want to feel all of him. Now.

"You want all of it?"

"Yes."

"You got it," he says and, in one move, he slams into me.

"Oh… Yes!" I scream, clutching at the duvet with my balled fists. "Yes. That feels so good."

He doesn't wait, not even for a second. He starts to move, slowly at first, pulling all the way out of me each time, so with every stroke I get that glorious feeling of being penetrated afresh. His eyes never leave mine.

"Lift your legs up," he urges and I do as he says, raising them higher. The sensation of being full of him is shattering, consuming. He increases the pace, and the depth, taking me harder. I bring my hands up and hold onto his biceps, trying to ground myself, as the first wave of my orgasm crashes over me. I scream out his name, my whole body shuddering and trembling beneath his as I try and keep control, but it goes on and on, claiming me.

As I start to calm, I let my hands drop down beside my head, then feel his own, clasping them, entwining our fingers and pinning me down, holding me in place as he takes the pace up another notch, pounding hard into me. He's still staring at me. Occasionally his eyes drop to my lips, or to my breasts, and then he leans down clamping my right nipple between his teeth, nipping hard on my flesh. I can't take it. The sensations of being overpowered by him, consumed by his obvious need, and devoured by his expert abilities overwhelm me and I climax hard again, losing control completely this time, and thrashing against his body, which seems to push him over the edge. He stills, then plunges deep into me, with a loud groan, and I feel him expand, stretching me still further, just as he explodes. He throws back his head and yells my name over and over at the top of his voice, his whole body convulsing.

Eventually, he releases my hands and lowers himself to his elbows, before turning us onto our sides.

"You okay?" he asks, his voice filled with concern.

"Oh, God, yes," I pant unable to wipe the smile from my face.

He laughs. "So, not as hard to take as you thought then?"

"No." He's still inside me, and as he seems to be hard, I move against him.

"You want more?" he asks. I nod my head. I want so much more. "You wanna try it my way?" I nod my head again, really fast. I'm desperate to know what 'his way' involves. He pulls out of me, then twists and switches off the lights. I feel lost and empty without him. The disappointment is palpable. What's wrong? "We'll do that in the morning," he says. The moon is bright and the curtains are open. I can see he's smiling, and staring at me, but there's no clue as to the sudden change in him. What did I do?

"Why not now?" I whisper.

"Two reasons," he replies. "Firstly, it's nearly two in the morning."

"It is?" I'm surprised. We came upstairs at about twelve thirty. It doesn't feel like an hour and a half has passed, but it clearly has. "And the second reason?"

"Thats's not how it works."

"What does that mean?"

Even in the moonlight I can see his smirk. "You'll find out in the morning."

"Tease." He smiles. Is that what this is about? He wants to tease me? To make me wait?

"Maybe. But this way you'll stay the night, even if only because you really wanna find out what I'm gonna do to you." He looks at me. "You do, don't you?"

"I'd have stayed the night anyway – assuming you wanted me to." He doubted I'd want to stay? He seems less secure in himself than I would have expected and I wonder if my admission will change his mind and he'll stop teasing.

He runs his finger down my cheek, really gently. "I want you to stay." His voice is soft, sincere.

He doesn't take his eyes from mine. He's still waiting for my reply. "Yes, you're right," I say eventually. "I want to know what you're going to do." Preferably now.

"I thought you might." He plants a chaste kiss on my lips and turns me over, so my back is to his front, then he pulls me into his arms, holding me tight. "Sleep, baby," he murmurs.

"Tease," I repeat, snuggling back into him, his erection pressing into me, temptingly.

"Trust me, you don't know the half of it," he whispers in my ear.

I wake with a start. Where am I? I'm being held down by something, my movements restricted. I twist and realise I'm still clasped in Sam's strong arms. His hand is clasped over my breast and his erection digs into my behind, and I'm instantly reminded of last night. He made me come so hard, harder than I ever have before and I know I want more.

I want to try things his way and he teased that we could do that this morning. I want to know what more he's going to do. I want to feel him again, and – more than anything – I want to tell him I've fallen deeply in love with him. I have no idea when that happened, but as I was falling asleep last night, I suddenly knew, without a doubt, that I love him.

Of course, even in this short space of time, I've realised there could be a few roadblocks to our eventual happiness, such as the fact that we've only just started seeing each other properly, that we live on separate continents, that I'll be going home soon, and that he might wake up any minute now and decide last night was a huge mistake and he never wants to see me again. Apart from that, I can't see any reason not to tell him that I'm head over heels in love with him. I let out a deep breath.

He stirs behind me.

"Good morning," he murmurs, somehow aware that I'm awake.

"Good morning."

"I just need the bathroom," he says. And he gets up and goes over to the room in the corner, closing the door behind him.

I lie on my back, almost twitching with nerves, half expecting him to come back and admit that last night should never have happened.

He doesn't take long, reappearing in a matter of minutes and coming over to the bed, getting back under the covers and propping himself up on one elbow. He looks down at me, an intense, slightly dark expression on his face. It makes me shiver, but in a good way. It heralds something deeply pleasurable.

"You okay?" he asks.

"Yes," I whisper

"Not sore?"

"No."

He leans closer. "Yet," he murmurs and my breath catches in my throat.

His eyes are on fire now and I know that he doesn't regret last night any more than I do. I also know that whatever happens next, my life is unlikely to ever be the same again.

Sam

I come to slowly and I realize Ali's already awake. Don't ask me how I know, but I do, and I lie as still as I can, enjoying the feeling of her soft skin against mine, my hard cock pressing into her ass, my hand resting on her perfect breast. She feels so damn good in my arms – even better than I'd expected. It's odd; I've never wanted to sleep with anyone in this way before – cuddled up and not wanting to let go, all night long – but this feels right. It feels as though we belong like this, and even if we hadn't made love last night, I'd still want to hold her, I'd still want to fall asleep with her, and I'd still want to wake up with her right by my side.

I don't want this to end. I know she lives in England and I live here, and she's only got another couple of weeks before she has to leave, but we can work that out. As long as she enjoys being with me, as much as I enjoy being with her, then we'll be okay. I know we will.

Of course, we haven't tried doing anything my way yet, and I guess there's a chance she might not like the things I do, and if that's the case... well, I'll still find a way to work it out. Because, after last night, I know I'd rather give up my lifestyle... I'd rather give up who I am, than even think about giving up Ali.

I've gotta admit, I had no idea making love could be like that. I've never come so hard in my life for one thing, but more importantly, I've never enjoyed making a woman come more. Although she doesn't know it, and I'll probably never tell her, she laid all my ghosts to rest last night. All of Amber's bitter insults were forgotten as I pleasured Ali, and she didn't hold back in letting me know how good it felt. My ego needed that, as did the rest of me. Ali's responsiveness, her enthusiasm and willingness took my breath away. She seemed to like being held down, and when I suggested trying things my way, she was definitely keen – positively impatient, in fact. She obviously wanted to go again last night, and so did I, but making her wait is fun. It's also part of showing her how things work in my world. Plus it will make it so much better... for both of us.

She takes a deep breath and I decide to let her know I'm awake too, shifting just slightly closer.

"Good morning," I whisper.

"Good morning." Her voice is low and sexy.

We're doing things my way this morning, so before she can turn over and try anything that might distract me, I get up, telling her that I need the bathroom. With the door closed, I think through what I've got planned. It's Sunday, which means we've got the whole day to ourselves, and I plan to take advantage of that. I want to take my time, introduce her to my world, maybe test her limits, just a little. I want to show her and teach her, but not explain to her – it'll make it less fun – and I want her to try and pick things up by herself, learn as we go along, react to what I'm doing, so she understands it better, and so I can understand her better too. But she's new to all this, so I'm going to have to go slow, and careful, be gentle with her, keep that enthusiasm building and not scare her off. I've never had to do anything like this before; I've always been with like-minded women, who knew the score – well, except for Amber, who scored off of me… But I want to try and make this work. I want her to see how good this can be.

I come back into the bedroom. She's lying on her back and looks over at me as I get under the covers, raising myself up on one elbow and looking down at her. She seems nervous, but as I move closer, her eyes spark and her expression changes to one of lustful expectation. In a way, that's good – I don't want her scared. But I also don't want her jumping on me and trying to call the shots. She doesn't know how this works yet, so I need to nip any ideas she might have in the bud and let her know who's in charge.

"You okay?" I ask her.

She nods slightly and whispers, "Yes." That's real sexy.

"Not sore?" I need to know she's going to be physically capable of doing the things I've got in mind for her.

"No." *Good.*

I lean in closer, so our lips are almost touching. "Yet," I murmur. *That's a clue, babe. A fucking big clue.* She sucks in a sharp breath and it catches in her throat so she almost chokes. God, that's hot. I could take her now…

"Breakfast," I say, keeping my voice as normal as possible.

"Um… sorry?" She didn't expect that.

"Let's have breakfast." I pull the covers from her. "C'mon." I get up and hold out my hand.

"But I've got nothing to wear…"

"Good. I don't want you to wear anything." I keep my hand in place, looking at her. She's shy. It's cute. "Take my hand," I instruct her. She looks from my hand, to my face and back again, then does as I say. *Good girl.*

I lead her along the corridor, through the living room and into the kitchen, where I sit her down on one of the stools and set about making us breakfast. I keep it simple because I don't want this to take too long. I'm nearly as impatient as she is; I'm just hiding it better.

"Scrambled eggs okay?" That's not a question I'm used to asking. The women I've been with in the past didn't get to stay for breakfast. We'd have parted company the night before, once we'd finished whatever we were doing. It's unusual – unheard of – for me to spend the whole night with someone, other than Amber of course… but I'm not going to think about her.

"Scrambled eggs are fine." This is going well. She's sitting watching me intently.

"Good," I reply, giving her a slight smile.

I get on with preparing them, and put on the coffee at the same time.

I'm whisking the eggs when I become aware of Ali moving behind me. Her breath on my back is the first giveaway that she's closer than she should be, but then I feel her hands on my shoulders. I put down the bowl and twist to face her, capturing her hands in mine.

"What's wrong?" she asks.

"Nothing's wrong."

"Then why don't you want me to touch you? It was okay last night, so what's changed?" There are tears in her eyes. I need to explain – at least in part.

"Don't," I tell her, releasing one of her hands and touching her cheek with my fingertips. She needs to know I don't regret any of what we've done so far, and that I want more. But this is my way. This is who I am. "Don't get upset."

"But why can't I touch you?" she asks, her voice cracking with emotion. This clearly matters to her and, although I don't want her to cry, the thought that she's that affected by the situation feels reassuring. It means I'm not the only one who cares.

"Because we're doing things my way today, remember?"

"And that means I can't touch you?" She's confused now.

"Not necessarily." I lean down and kiss her forehead. "But – for now – it means, you wait."

"I wait?" She stares up into my eyes, hers shimmering. The sadness has gone now though. Instead, she looks intrigued and just a little bit turned on. That's a good combination.

"Yeah. You wait. Go sit down." I nod toward the seat and she hesitates for just a moment before going back and sitting down again.

It takes about ten minutes to prepare the breakfast and by then the sexual tension in the room has risen to boiling point. I can feel her eyes on me, watching my every move, but I know she's not wary any longer. I don't think she's even confused. She's waiting. She's waiting to see what I'm going to do next. That thought makes me smile.

After I've served the food, I bring it over, with the coffee, and sit beside her. She looks beautiful, stark naked sitting at my butcher's block, her breasts pert, her nipples hard, her breathing a little faster than usual. As I pick up my fork, I reach over and, with one hand on her knee, I pull her legs wide apart, exposing her shaved pussy to my view. She looks incredible now. So sexy. So ready. So mine. She gasps and looks up at me.

"Eat," I say.

She pauses, again just for a moment, and then picks up her fork and starts to eat.

I smile at her, and she smiles back. This feels good.

We talk about the opening, and about how well everything went last night. It's an easy conversation between two naked, very aroused people.

I guess we're about halfway through the meal, when I notice that she's slowly started to move her legs back together again. I'm not sure whether it's deliberate; it's hard to tell, but she just adjusts her position while we're talking and, as a result, her legs close slightly, and then a little more, until they're almost back where they started. I reach over and pull them apart again, putting them back where I want them.

"Leave your legs where they are," I tell her, taking another forkful of eggs.

"Why?" she asks.

"I can give you three reasons." I smile, but try not to smirk.

"I can't even think of one – it's not like you're doing anything."

I shake my head slowly. "You think? Well, that's reason number one. I *am* doing something. I'm looking at you." I lean in real close and lower my voice to a whisper. "And I really like what I see."

"Oh."

"The second reason," I continue, sitting up straight again, "is that I put your legs in that position."

"And… and that means I have to leave them there?"

I stare at her. "Yes."

Her mouth drops open, but she doesn't say a word.

"And the third reason," I add, not taking my eyes from hers, "is that you calling the shots isn't how this works."

She tilts her head to one side. "What does that mean?" she asks. "You said something like that last night too."

"It'll make sense soon enough." I put down my fork and turn around, twisting her as well, so we're facing each other. She lets her eyes drop to my erection and lets out a tiny sigh. "I want you to try and figure this out for yourself," I tell her. "I don't want to explain it to you."

"Why not?" She's confused again.

I lean forward, resting my forehead against hers. "Because it'll be so much more fun this way."

"For whom?"

"For both of us… but mainly you. I want you to discover my tastes, not have them spelled out to you."

She gasps again. "Your tastes?"

"Yes. My tastes. Although, in time, I hope they'll become your tastes too."

We're nearly finished, but I think her needs right now are for a lot more than food. The tension is pouring off of her.

"Are you done?" I ask.

She looks at her plate. "I guess so."

I pull her to her feet. "Do you need some relief?" I ask her.

"God, yes." Her reply is instant and eager, and I almost laugh out loud. And that would never do.

"Come with me," I whisper.

We leave the dishes and I take her back to the bedroom, closing the door and leading her over to the end of the bed.

"Do you want to take a shower?" I suggest.

"Now?" Her frustration is obvious and I half expect her to stamp her foot and demand that I fuck her.

"With me," I add. Her eyes light up and she nods her head.

I steer her into the bathroom and straight to the large shower cubicle, closing the door and turning on the water, without saying a word.

I stand her under the cascading spray and reach behind her for the soap, lathering up my hands and, starting at her neck, gradually work my way down her body. When I reach her breasts, she sucks in a sharp breath, but I don't delay too long before moving across her flat stomach and down to her pussy. I kneel and she parts her legs instinctively, giving my hands access to her. I wash her carefully, paying close attention to her clit, then – just as her breathing is getting ragged – I move on down her thighs to her calves.

"Turn," I say. She obeys and I work my way back up, spending a little time on her perfect ass, before moving up to her back and shoulders.

She holds her hands out for the soap, clearly thinking that she's going to get to return the favor. I shake my head and quickly wash myself. The look in her eyes is pure bewilderment, but I keep mine focused on her, especially as I wash my engorged cock, stroking along the length of it with my soapy hands. Again, she sucks in a sharp breath and, then bites her bottom lip. Before I'm tempted to blow the whole morning's preparation, I move under the shower and wash off the soap.

"Hair?" I say.

She nods her head and I offer her my shampoo. She washes her own hair and I do mine and we rinse, before getting out. I grab a large towel from the shelf and wrap her in it, fastening it under her arms, before placing a smaller one around my hips.

"Can I have a small towel too?" she asks a little abruptly. "For my hair."

I hand her one, without comment. She's almost angry with frustration now. I don't want that and I know I'm going to have to do something with her… soon.

Back in the bedroom, my phone's ringing, and I go over and check the screen. It's Rob. I could ignore him, but there's a chance he'll come over. And he's got a key. I don't want any interruptions once we get started.

"Sorry," I say to Ali. "I'd better take this."

"It's okay."

She perches on the edge of the bed, the tension obvious in her shoulders. I definitely need to do something about that.

"Hi," I say into the phone.

"Where the hell have you been?" Rob asks. "I've called you three times already. I was just about to come over there."

Thank God I took the call. "What's wrong?" I ask him.

"I've been trying to get hold of Ali, but she's not picking up." He pauses. "Do you think she's okay?"

I smile. "Yeah," I reply. *She will be soon.*

"Only she normally picks up really quickly," he continues. *She's been kinda busy… with me.*

"Why did you need to get in touch with her?" I look up and notice that Ali has stood, pulled her hair free of the towel, and is now drying herself. She's being very suggestive about it too, keeping her eyes fixed on me, letting her fingers trail over her skin, taking her time around her breasts. I smile inwardly, but keep a straight face.

"Because we've had some amazing reviews online. I wondered if she'd seen them." Ali turns around, bending down to dry her legs, and I get an amazing view of her delectable ass. This won't do at all. She seems to think she can distract me and tempt me into giving her what she wants. All she's really doing is prolonging the moment – because I'm going to make her wait even longer now for trying to tease me.

"She hasn't seen them," I say, without thinking. *Fuck. Her distraction worked.*

"How do you know?" Rob asks.

"Because she's here, with me," I admit. There's no point in lying to him. Not now.

"Seriously?" He's shocked. "And you're not fighting?"

"No, we're not fighting." Ali stands now, looking over at me.

There's a pause. "What? So she came over for breakfast," he asks.

"No."

"She came for coffee?" Is he serious?

"No, Rob."

"You mean… she's been there all night?"

"Yes."

There's a moment's silence and then he chuckles. "You're a lucky son-of-a-bitch, Samuel Moreno. Don't fuck it up."

"I won't. If you'll just get off the fucking phone and let me get on with it."

He laughs out loud and I hang up.

"W—Who was that?" Ali asks.

"Rob."

"And you told him I spent the night here?"

"Yes. Why not? I'm okay with people knowing about us, aren't you?"

That caught her unawares and she stares at me, before replying, "There's an us?"

"Yes. Well, I think there is." I move closer to her. "Don't you?"

She nods slowly. "Yes. I just wasn't sure you did."

I take her hand and pull her down beside me on the bed. "Oh, I definitely do."

She smiles a sweet, sexy smile and I tuck my finger under her chin, raising her face to mine and kissing her gently.

"I want to try something with you," I whisper, breaking the kiss. "My way." Her eyes widen. "Would you like that?"

"Oh, yes please." Her enthusiasm is adorable.

"Stay where you are." She nods her head and I get up, pulling off my own towel, and go around to my side of the bed, opening the middle drawer. For the first time, I feel a little nervous, but I pick up what I need and close the drawer again, returning to her.

She looks up, focusing on my hands, and the black silky rope I'm holding, her eyes wider than I've seen them before.

"W—What's that for?" she asks.

"Do you want to find out?" I hold my breath, waiting for her answer.

She stares at me, her eyes locked with mine, then nods her head.

I kneel before her.

"Put your hands together, like you're praying," I instruct her. "Clasp your fingers as tightly as you can." She does exactly as I tell her. I adjust her arms, so they're close together and then, undo the rope and, clamping one end between her fingers, I start to bind her, coiling the rope around her. I can feel her eyes on me, watching my movements.

"It's soft," she says after a few minutes. I look into her eyes

"Yes. It's not meant to hurt you."

She nods, and I continue securing her, carefully wrapping the rope around her hands, and her wrists and a little way down her arms, before tying off the ends by her fingers and tucking them away neatly.

"How does it feel?" I ask her, getting to my feet again.

"Okay."

I put my hands on her bent elbows and lift her up, and she stands, bound in front of me, expectant, breathing hard, and maybe a little nervous.

"Don't be scared," I tell her. "I won't hurt you."

She swallows, staring up at me.

"Now…" I pause. "Are you ready?"

"Um… yes."

I wait for a moment, the anticipation almost killing me, and then whisper, "Kneel."

She looks at me, then her eyes drop to my straining erection. "Oh," she gasps.

"Kneel," I repeat, slightly louder.

She looks up into my eyes and I wonder if she's going to say 'no'. If she does, I won't force her to do anything. Because that's not how this works either – not with me, anyway. I'll release her and we'll talk, and probably do something her way instead. I'm not going to get mad, or end it just because she doesn't want to do this… but I really hope she does. I *really* hope she does.

She bites her bottom lip and her cheeks flush just slightly and then, very slowly, she drops to her knees. *Thank fuck for that.*

She tilts her head back and looks up at me, her hands bound in front of her. I'm so hard, my cock hurts and she looks so hot like that it's all I can do to hold back. I've dreamt of this for so long… I inch forward and rest my cock against her lips and she leans in and opens her mouth, trying to take me. *Oh no, baby.* I pull away from her again and wait, but she hasn't got the message and sidles forward on her knees, so I take a firm step back.

"That's not how it works," I tell her.

She smiles up at me. "But I'm hungry," she whispers.

I chuckle, despite my best efforts not to. "Yeah, I'd noticed."

I wait for a moment, before taking a pace forward and resting my cock on her lips again. This time, she doesn't try anything and I hold it steady. She looks up at me appealingly, but waits obediently for me to move. She's learning – she has to wait for me. I smile. "Good girl," I say, and give her a little more, letting her wrap her lips around the tip of my cock. She licks and sucks hungrily, and I pull back again, before giving her some more. She struggles to take me, but her enthusiasm is astonishing – enhanced by the wait, just like I knew it would be. She runs her tongue over the tip, while taking as much of my cock into her mouth as she can and moving her head back and forth with relish. This feels different to what I'd expected, but in a good way. It's better than I'd ever hoped or dreamed it would be, and seeing her like this is almost too much for me, and I'm just thinking I'll have to tell her to stop, when she does so herself, leaning back on her ankles and staring up at me.

"I don't get it," she says.

Okay, that's not meant to happen… but I have to make allowances. "What don't you get?" I ask her patiently.

"Why do my hands need to be tied?" she asks. "I'd happily do this anyway, and if I had the use of my hands, it might be more fun… for you." Her eyes darken seductively.

I grin down at her. "More fun?" I question, teasing. I know exactly what she means, but I want her to explain, to have to say what she's thinking.

"I can't take that much of you in my mouth," she clarifies, without a moment's hesitation. "You're too big. But if I could use my hands as well…" She leaves the sentence hanging.

My grin broadens. "Hmm. I see what you mean. The thing is…" I lean down so my face is level with hers, "that's not the point. This isn't about me."

She smirks. "Oh, really? It isn't?"

"No." I shake my head.

"Then I don't understand."

"Well, we can do what you're suggesting another time – when we're doing things your way."

"We can?" Her eyes sparkle and I fall in love with her, just a little bit more.

"Of course we can." I smile at her. "But right now… this is about you." She still looks skeptical. "Tell me, do you like sucking my cock? Does it turn you on?"

She nods her head. "Yes. Yes, it does."

"Turned on to the point where you'd like to finger your pussy at the same time?"

"Oh, God, yes…" Her voice drops a note or two.

"But you can't, can you?"

She stares at me for a moment, then moves her arms down. She can get her hands real close to her pussy, but the angle's all wrong. She tries again, but she can't make contact.

"No," she says, pouting up at me.

I laugh. "Frustrates the fuck out of you, doesn't it?" I whisper.

"Yes, it does," she breathes.

I straighten up, but she doesn't move. Instead she keeps leaning back, staring at me, still looking a little puzzled.

"Is this what you like?" she asks. "To frustrate me by denying me pleasure?"

"No," I reply immediately, crouching down in front of her so our faces are level again. "Not at all." I reach out and cup her face with one hand, gently rubbing my thumb across her lips. "In fact, it's just the opposite. By making you wait, by delaying the inevitable, when you do come, your orgasm will blow your mind. It's not about denying you anything, Ali. It's about giving you as much pleasure as you can handle from your own body."

I stand again. Her breasts are heaving as she struggles to breathe.

"Feeling even more turned on now?" I ask her.

"Yes, sir," she says, a coy smile on her lips.

"Don't call me 'sir'," I tell her, leaning down and kissing her gently. "That's not who I am." Not with her anyway. "I'm not your master, or your Dominant. I'm your lover, Ali. Just call me Sam."

"Yes, Sam." She smiles. God… Could I be any more in love with her?

I put my lips next to her ear. "This is what I like, baby," I whisper. "And this is what I want you to give me… your body. Complete control of your body."

As I straighten, she shudders, then she sighs loudly and I notice her thighs clench and unclench a couple of times. She's done this before and I swear to God, she's having an orgasm – just from my words. It's short, but I think it's quite intense… and it's really fucking hot. I've never been with anyone this responsive, or exciting. Ever.

Her eyes are wide and she's panting, partly with anticipation and partly from the thrill of what just happened to her body. I move closer and she captures my cock in her mouth, sucking me even more vigorously than before. She's good. She's really good. I reach behind her head, gathering her damp hair and holding it out of the way as she moves up and down my shaft, taking more and more of me with each stroke.

I pull back from her, releasing her hair and stepping away, just before I come, and she lets out a groan – like she's disappointed.

"You wanted my come?" I ask her.

She nods.

"Next time," I tease. "Next time we'll do it your way, and you can make me come." She grins. Then, with my hands on her elbows, I lift her to her feet and sit her back on the edge of the bed. "I told you, this isn't about me. Now, lie back," I tell her. She's earned this…

She lies down and I spread her legs wide, kneeling on the floor and leaning over. I can see how wet she is already, her beautiful shaved pussy lips swollen and glistening. I blow gently across her and she shudders, letting out a moan, and then I gently tease my tongue across her hardened clit. She bucks off the bed and I hold her down, leaning into her and biting gently on her nub.

"Oh… Yes!" she hisses. "That's so good."

I move down a little, swirling my tongue just inside her vagina, lapping up her creamy juices, before working my way back up to her clit. As I reach it, and flick my tongue across and around, she starts to tremble, her thighs quivering and she leans up, bringing her bound hands behind my head, screaming out her pleasure as she comes hard. I swallow down her sweet nectar, licking and sucking at her, until she starts to calm, her breathing harsh and ragged.

I glance up at her and see her eyes are closed, her breasts heaving as she gulps air into her lungs. She's muttering something and I strain to hear her words, making them out eventually.

"Thank you. Thank you. Thank you." Over and over, she repeats her gratitude. I'm a little overwhelmed by that, and her reaction, coupled with the satisfied smile on her face are my reward – for now, at least. I stand, staring down at her, just as she opens her eyes and starts to shimmy back up the bed, spreading her legs wider, inviting me to take her.

Oh dear… she still doesn't get it.

"What are you doing?" I tilt my head to one side.

"I want you," she says, lowering her eyes to my swollen cock.

I shake my head. "That's not how it works, Ali," I reply.

"How does it work then?"

I hesitate for a moment, wondering if she's really ready for the next step, because I know what I want that to be. I was gonna break all the rules; I was gonna wait a while, give her time to recover and get used to the idea of doing things my way before we did anything else, but looking down at her, so keen, so willing, I don't want to wait. And it's clear she doesn't either. I lean over and pull her up the bed, pushing the pillows to one side, so she's flat out on the mattress. She stares up at me as I kneel beside her, and I start to undo the ends of the rope.

"Um... Is it over?" she asks, looking worried, sounding scared. "Did I do something to make you angry?"

How could she even begin to think that? I smile down at her, trying to reassure her. "No, baby," I say softly. "Of course you didn't." I hold the loosened ends of rope in one hand and clasp her chin in the other, turning her face to mine. We lock eyes. "Are you sure you want more?"

"Yes," she whispers, nodding her head. "Yes please, Sam."

My smile turns to a wide grin and, using the rope, I pull her arms above her head, and tie her to the iron bedstead. She squeals loudly and I stop what I'm doing and lean down, my mouth right by her ear.

"Quiet," I tell her, and she hushes.

I finish tying the knot to bind her to my bed, and then move down, pulling her by her hips, so she's stretched, her back arched, her breasts proud. Fuck, she looks hot like that.

I kneel between her legs, and she raises her head, watching me as I palm my cock and gently stroke along its length until she's licking her lips in anticipation.

"This might hurt," I say quietly. "If it does, tell me. We'll stop and I'll change the position." I stare into her eyes. "Okay?"

She's so wired, I'm not sure she even heard that.

"Tell me you understood what I just said."

"If it hurts, I have to tell you," she whispers.

"Okay."

I lift her legs up onto my shoulders. I could take her like this, just kneeling with her lying before me, but I want more from her… much more.

"Remember, stop me if this hurts…"

I look down at her as she nods, and then I tip her back so her knees are almost touching her breasts and her feet are up close by her hands. I could tie her there too, bind her ankles to the bed, or her knees to her elbows – or even both – but she's new to this and, if it hurts her, I need to be able to free her quickly, so it's better not to complicate things. This time.

She's completely exposed to me and I lean over her, my hands up by her head, my cock poised by her entrance. This is going to be deep – really deep. I press into her and, in one move, I enter her – hard.

She screams, a guttural groaning howl, and I still, waiting and watching her face as she grows accustomed to the intrusion of my cock. Slowly a smile forms and then I start to move. With every stroke, I pull out of her completely – like I did last night. In this position, she's going to feel that deep, invasive penetration every time I enter her and, judging from the reaction I'm getting, she's loving every minute of it. Her moans are loud, throaty, so sexy I could almost come on the spot. Every time she feels me deep inside, she clamps onto me, like she never wants to let go. And she's looking straight into my eyes, like the connection is more than physical for her – just like it is for me. I'm joining us together, but it feels like so much more than that.

I have to support all of my weight. Bending her like this – especially when she's not used to it – could hurt her back and, pounding into her repeatedly, I'm soon on the verge of coming… but I'm not done yet. I want more from her. With every movement, I start to swivel my hips, just a little, and her moans become louder still. After a few more strokes, she opens her mouth and screams my name, in one long, unending cry of pleasure. Seeing that, hearing her ecstasy, and feeling her tighten around me, pushes me over the edge and, with one last deep thrust inside her, I explode, filling her, my whole body shaking with the fulfillment of finally finding someone who makes this feel as good as I've always believed it could be; someone who makes this about more than fucking, more than control… someone who makes it about love.

It takes her a while to calm, but I expected that, and pulling out of her, I kneel back up and lower her legs – I know she won't be capable of doing anything for a while. Then I lean over and gently untie her hands from the bed, moving them down and releasing them from the rope. She's exhausted and I lie beside her, pulling her into my arms. She nestles back, resting against me.

"That was so…" she mumbles, incoherently.

"Yeah, it was."

It really was. She was incredible. Each time with her seems to get just a little bit better.

"You're exhausted," I tell her. "Go to sleep."

"It's the middle of the morning."

"So? Go to sleep." She snuggles down and, within minutes, is fast asleep.

I lie with her for a while, enjoying her soft skin, her gentle breathing and the memory of her gorgeous body beneath mine, and then I slide out from under her and put on a pair of shorts, going through to the kitchen. She's going to be hungry when she wakes up, and I know the perfect cure for that…

"Sam?" I hear her calling and get up from the couch, where I've been reading a book, passing at least some of the two hours since she fell asleep on me.

"Yeah? I'm here." She appears from the corridor. Holy fuck. She's found one of my t-shirts and put it on… and I don't think anyone in the whole world has ever looked that sexy. I smile at her. "You look good," I say, going over to her and pulling her into my arms. I kiss her, deeply, my tongue claiming her mouth and exploring for a while. She moans into me, leaning against my chest, while I raise the t-shirt and cup her ass with one of my hands. "You feel good too." I smile down at her, breaking the kiss.

"You disappeared," she whispers, looking up into my eyes.

"I didn't go far." I clasp her chin with my other hand. "You were sleeping."

"And you got dressed…" She pouts at my clothes.

"Well, I had to make some lunch." I got dressed after I'd finished the preparation – in between watching her sleep for a while.

"Food?" she says, her eyes lighting up.

"Yeah. Food. I thought you might be hungry. You used up a lot of energy this morning."

"Hmm…" she sighs, like she's remembering what we did. It's kind of hard to forget.

"You okay?" I ask her. "You're not sore?"

"No." She gazes up at me. "Not yet…"

I hold my breath, before asking my next question: "Does that mean you want more?" She doesn't reply, but she doesn't look away either. "You've gotta tell me, Ali."

"Yes," she whispers, blushing. "I want more."

I let out my breath and smile. "Good." I wonder if she has any idea how relieved I am to hear that. "Let's have some lunch, and see what the afternoon brings, shall we?"

She grins and her eyes sparkle, but I'm not sure whether that's at the thought of food, or more sex. Maybe it's a little of both.

"What's for lunch?" she asks.

"I made pizza." I lead her into the kitchen, and sit her down at the island unit.

"Pizza?" She stares at me. "That's not on the menu."

"No. Pizza dough was one of the first things I learned to make with my mom."

"Your mum, not your dad?" I put the pizza in the oven.

"No. Mom taught us how to make the kind of things we liked to eat at home. Dad taught us how to cook professionally." I offer her a glass of wine, which she accepts, and takes a sip.

"What are we going to do this afternoon?" she asks, looking at me over the rim of her glass.

"Well…" I come and sit down beside her. "First, I think we should go back to your hotel…"

She turns to me, looking concerned – maybe even a little fearful. "Why?" she whispers.

"Because I want you to stay with me again tonight, and while I'm more than happy for you to wear my t-shirt today, you'll need some clothes to wear tomorrow."

"You want me to stay again?" She seems surprised, although I really don't know why. I guess I'm still not expressing myself very well.

"Yes. I want you to stay." I lean closer and take a breath. "Actually, I want you to stay every night. We could pack up all your things and bring them back here… if you're okay with that?"

"You want me to move in here?" She takes another sip of wine… well, it's more like a gulp, and I wonder if she doesn't like my idea.

"Yes," I reply simply.

"What about Rob and Ed?" she asks, putting down her glass and staring at me.

"What about them?"

She blushes. "I don't want them thinking I've moved in with you after just one night together."

"I don't give a fuck what Rob and Ed think – or anyone else for that matter." I raise my voice a little and she flinches. "Sorry." I reach over quickly, and pull her off of her seat and onto my lap. She's stiff in my arms. "Relax, Ali," I say. "I didn't mean to shout."

"I know." She leans into me. "You… you really want me to move in here? I know how much you value your space…" She leaves the sentence hanging and I'm tempted to tell her that my space means nothing, compared to her.

"You'll have to go home at some point, and I don't want to waste a moment of the time we've got together. I want you here, with me."

She twists in my arms and reaches up, caressing my cheek. "I want that too," she whispers.

"Then you'll move in?"

She nods. "Yes. But you've given me a lot to take on board in the last few hours," she says, smiling. "I still need to get my head around some of it."

"I'm sorry."

"Don't be sorry," she replies, moving closer and looking into my eyes. "I like what you're doing with me, what you're teaching me… I might just need to take a breath every so often."

"But you'll definitely stay here… with me?" I'm scared, and I don't really care if it shows.

"I'll stay," she says.

"Ali, we don't have to do things my way, if it makes you uncomfortable," I offer. And I mean it. As much as I need my lifestyle, I need her more.

"No. I like doing things your way," she clarifies. "It's just a bit new to me, that's all."

"I know. And you're spectacular."

"I think you'll find that's you," she says, softly.

I smile and tilt her face up, kissing her gently.

"This is so luxurious," Ali says, looking up at me from the deep bubble bath I've just run for her.

"It's a bath…"

She stares at me, like I'm missing something.

"It's very sweet of you," she says softly, holding out a dripping hand for me to take. I do, and then bring it to my lips, kissing her fingers. When I look up again, her eyes are fixed on me, with a gaze that makes my heart swell in my chest.

We've had a great afternoon. After lunch, we got dressed. Ali wore her dress from last night, and we went round to the hotel. She packed up her clothes and toiletries, while I ran to a shop down the road and picked up something I needed for this evening. I dropped it back at the apartment before returning to the hotel to collect Ali. I've kept it a secret from her, but I hope she likes it. Then we came home and had a coffee, before I decided we were wearing too many clothes. It didn't take long to get Ali undressed again, and we made love on the couch. Afterwards, we lay in each others arms for a while and then I came in here and ran her a bath. I knew her muscles would probably be aching after the last twenty-four hours, and a bath would help with that – especially as I've got no intention of letting up with her any time soon.

"Dinner in half an hour," I tell her, kissing her gently.

"You might have to wake me up," she calls as I go out into the bedroom and through to the living room.

I quickly prepare our evening meal, then once it's in the oven, I go back to the bedroom, making sure she can't see what I'm doing, and get the bed ready for later. I hope she likes what I've planned. I'm kinda nervous. It's the most romantic thing I've ever done and I'm not sure if it's too much.

I cut through the baking parchment parcel on Ali's plate, and then do mine.

"That smells divine," she says. She's wearing my bathrobe and she looks so adorable. It's huge on her, and she's rolled the sleeves up so she can use her hands.

"It's just chicken and some vegetables and herbs… oh, and garlic."

"Hmm…" She takes a sip of wine. "You make it sound so simple."

"Because it is."

She's obviously hungry and eats with enthusiasm, a smile on her lips the whole time.

"What are you doing tomorrow?" I ask her.

"I've got some things to go through with Rob," she explains. "I need to show him how to update the website and we've got to put up the photographs from the opening, " She has another sip of wine. "And then it's just making sure everything is going smoothly."

"And in the evening?" I ask.

She stops. "Oh… You'll be working," she says, her smile slipping.

"Yeah. How would you feel about working with me?"

She looks up at me. "Working with you?"

"In the evening, yeah. I know you've got your own work to do during the day, and I know you'll be tired, but I'd really like it if you'd come work with me in the kitchen during the evening – or at least come be with me. Please?"

She smiles again. "You want me to?"

"Yes. I sure don't want to spend the evening down there by myself, while you're up here."

"Neither do I. But I also don't want to get in your way..." She doesn't finish her sentence.

"I'm not gonna fight with you," I say quietly. "Those days are long gone."

"What do you want me to do... in the kitchen, I mean?"

"Whatever you want. I know you can cook. You can help Ed, or work in my area. It's up to you. Just be there with me..."

She nods her head. "As long as you're sure."

I reach out and take her hand in mine. "I'm sure."

We finish eating, still holding hands, because I don't want to let her go, and once we're done, I suggest that we take our wine to bed.

"I like the sound of that." Her voice is a soft whisper and I pick up my glass. "What about clearing away?" she asks.

"I'll do it in the morning." I pull her from her seat. "C'mon. I want you in bed."

She giggles and picks up her glass, following me down to the bedroom. I flick off the lights as we go, leaving the apartment in darkness.

In the bedroom, I've left the lamps on dim and I close the door behind us. We both put our wine down beside the bed and I turn, and pull the tie open on my bathrobe, revealing her perfect body. I can't help but look her up and down as I push it from her shoulders and let it fall to the floor. She's too beautiful not to admire.

I hold my breath as she pulls back the covers, hoping she'll like my surprise. When she sees what I've done, she murmurs my name, then turns to me.

"Rose petals?"

"You're like an English rose," I whisper. "It seemed appropriate."

"Where did you get them?" She picks up a few and holds them to her nose, breathing in their scent.

"While you were packing your things at the hotel, I ran down to the florists and picked up some roses and brought them back here – and then while you were in the bath, I pulled the petals off and put them in the bed." I'm waiting for her reaction. Is it too cheesy?

She places her hand on my cheek and steps closer. "This is the most beautiful thing anyone has ever done for me," she says.

"Better than the fish and chips?"

She pauses, like she can't make up her mind. "Just. But only just."

Then she leans up and kisses me so gently before climbing into bed and looking up at me. Within seconds, I've stripped out of my clothes and I join her. Without breaking eye contact for even a moment, I roll her onto her back, settling between her legs and I enter her real slowly, gazing down at her and showing her my love, even if I haven't spoken it yet. I will. I know I will. I'll tell her soon. I'll tell her I love her… with my whole heart.

"Anything you want to tell us?" Rob and Ed ambush us, as we come out of the door to the apartment. They're standing in the corridor that leads into the office and the kitchen, like they've been waiting for us to arrive. Rob's by the office door, leaning against the wall; Ed is opposite him, his back to the kitchen doorframe.

"No," I say, putting a protective arm around Ali.

"Sure?" Rob asks.

I glare at him. "No."

I feel Ali's arm come around behind me, her thumb resting inside the waistband of my jeans. My brothers stand, still watching us, like they can't quite believe what they're seeing. They're not gonna let this go.

"Okay," I say eventually, "Ali and I are… together." I look from Rob to Ed and back again. "Happy?" I say to him.

"Delirious, if it means you'll stop being a pain in the ass."

Ali sniggers quietly beside me.

"Oh, I'll still be a pain in the ass to you. But I'll treat Ali a helluva lot better from now on." I give her a squeeze and she rests her head on my shoulder.

Both Ed and Rob move forward at the same time, although Rob reaches us first, patting me once on the shoulder before he kisses Ali on both cheeks.

"Welcome to the family," he says, his eyes glinting.

"I think that's a bit premature," Ali says. "We've only been together for two days."

"Yeah, but I know how fast this guy moves." He looks up at me and I glare even harder. Did he really need to say that?

Ali glances at me, looking a little confused, but I don't want to explain Rob's comment right now.

"Some things are worth going after," I say to him, although I'm still looking at Ali, and she rewards me with the sweetest smile.

Ed steps forward, nudging Rob out of the way. "I'm really pleased for both of you," he says quietly.

"Thank you," Ali replies, seeming a little more shy now, but I think that's probably only because Ed's being serious, and she knows Rob was kidding.

"Just so you know," I say to Ed, "Ali's gonna be working in the kitchen tonight."

"Oh… okay." Ed looks at me, surprised.

Ali's phone rings and she pulls it from her back pocket. "Sorry, I need to take this," she says, leaning up and kissing my cheek before releasing herself from my hold and going down the corridor into the restaurant.

"In the kitchen?" Ed queries. "You're gonna have Ali working in the kitchen? Is that wise? You yelled at her the last time she was in there."

"Yeah… well, things change," I reply.

Rob moves right in front of me, looking up at my face, scrutinizing me. "Man, you've got it bad," he says eventually.

I look down at him for a long moment, then shrug my shoulders. "So what if I have?"

"Have you told Ali yet?" he asks.

"Told her what?"

"That you're in love with her…"

"No. And I'd rather do that myself, thanks. If you could just keep quiet about it. I really don't need her hearing that from you…"

He holds his hands up in surrender, nodding his head slowly. I think for once, I've shocked my brother into silence.

Chapter Thirteen

Ali

I'd forgotten how exhausting it is to work in a restaurant kitchen. And I only did an evening shift, not a whole day, like Sam. Once we've cleared away and cleaned down, it's all I can do to stay upright. Ed says goodnight – the last to leave – and Sam turns to me.

"Come here," he says and lifts me into his arms. I cling on to his neck and he carries me through the kitchen doors, flicking off the lights, and then turns and opens the door that leads up to his apartment.

"I can walk," I tell him.

"Really?" He looks down at me, smiling. "You look about ready to drop."

"I'd forgotten how tiring it is." I let my head rest on his chest as he climbs the stairs. "Where do you get the energy?"

"Years of practice," he says. "I've been doing this, pretty much non-stop, for over twelve years."

"I'm struggling after twelve hours…"

He opens the door at the top of the stairs and, without turning on the lights, carries me right through to the bedroom, depositing me on the bed.

"Can I get you a coffee?" he asks. "Or a glass of wine… or water?"

"I'm too tired to do anything."

"Anything?" He sits beside me, a sexy smirk forming on his face.

"Yes, anything." I lean into him. "I'm sorry."

"It's okay. It's my fault. I shouldn't have worked you so hard." He starts undoing the buttons on my blouse. "You did well tonight, though," he says. "You're good."

"Thank you."

"It was nice to have someone else in the kitchen – other than Ed – who I could just leave to get on with things and not have to check up on."

"You did keep checking on me though." I let him pull my blouse from my shoulders and he tosses it into the corner of the room.

"I wasn't really checking," he replies. "I just wanted an excuse to come over and see you… and touch you." He unclips my bra, pulling it off and throwing it over with my blouse. "Can you stand?" he asks.

"Yes." I get to my feet and he undoes my jeans, pulling them and my knickers down and holding my hand while I step out. "I need the bathroom," I tell him and he smiles, letting me go.

When I come back out, he's already in bed, and pulls the covers back so I can climb in next to him. I nestle down beside him, my head on his chest, his arms around me.

"I'm sorry I'm so tired," I tell him again.

"It's okay," he says softly. I snuggle down further. He's really comfortable to sleep on. "Did you have a good time?" he asks.

"I did." It's the truth.

"I wasn't too difficult to work with?"

"No." I say, smiling. "I like that you know what you want."

"You mean I'm bossy."

"Just a little. But it's nothing I can't handle."

"Hmm… I noticed." I think we both know we're not talking about cooking anymore.

"Tell me about your brothers," I say to change the subject.

"What about them?"

"Well, I get that Rob's a flirt… Is he also a player?"

He pauses for a moment. "Oh yeah," he says eventually. "Rob's a player. Well, at least, he was…" He seems thoughtful.

"What does that mean?"

"Oh, it's probably nothing."

I assume it's something private, something between the brothers that he doesn't want me to know.

He holds me tighter. "It's nothing secret," he says, reassuringly, like he's read my mind. "It's just that, at the opening, he seemed real keen on that photographer you hired."

I look up at him. "They were certainly flirting when I introduced them just before the first guests arrived, but Rob's good at that." I can't help but recall my initial encounter with him.

"I think there's more to it this time. Ed and I both noticed he was all over her."

"Isn't that all in a night's work for Rob?"

"This was different. *He* was different. He wasn't being a jackass like he normally is."

"You're mean to him."

"No more than he deserves."

"He cares about you," I tell him. "You and Ed."

He's suddenly serious. "Yeah, he does. We all care about each other. We're protective and loyal. We fall out sometimes, but that's just because we're brothers."

"And Ed?" I ask. "What's he really like?"

"Ed's not a player – or a flirt."

"I'd worked that out for myself. Does he have a girlfriend?"

"No. Not at the moment. He has done, over the years, but they've never worked out."

"Why?" I ask him.

"They were too demanding. They wanted him to give up his job. They felt it got in the way of their relationship."

"Well, knowing how awful a chef's hours are, I'm not surprised. That doesn't seem like an unreasonable request to me."

He leans back and looks at me. "No," he says, "not if you're serious about someone, I guess. But they weren't serious. And anyone could see they weren't right for him." He smiles at me. "I'm sure he'll meet the perfect girl one day."

"And if she wants him to give up his job, will you interfere?"

"No." His smile drops and he almost sounds offended. "I didn't interfere before. What makes you think I did?"

"Just the way you were talking. I'm sorry."

"It's okay. He has come to me for advice in the past," he admits. "But I've never given him a direct answer. I've let him work it out for himself. I'd never intrude in his life like that – or Rob's, for that matter."

"I'm sorry." I repeat, feeling guilty now. "I didn't mean—"

"Hey," he says, smiling again. "I don't blame you. I know I'm bossy, and controlling…" He smirks.

"Really?" I smile back at him. "I can't say I'd noticed."

"Then I'm obviously not trying hard enough," he whispers, and kisses me gently.

He turns us onto our sides so we're facing each other.

"Did you enjoy working with him?" he asks me.

"Yes." I spent about half of tonight's service working with Ed. "I've worked in a pastry section before, but I learnt a lot from Ed. He's very talented."

"Yeah, he is." Sam's gone quiet like he's remembering something. "Unfortunately, our dad knocked a lot of the confidence out of him," he murmurs. I wait… and wait, and eventually he starts speaking again. "Ed and Rob came into the kitchen a year after me," he continues, settling down into the pillows. "But Rob never really took it that seriously and went off to college. Ed, on the other hand… Ed was different. He was brilliant. He was better than me," Sam admits. "And I think our dad saw that. The problem was, Ed wasn't happy. He didn't enjoy it like I did, and he hated taking charge. Then, one day, the regular pastry guy went sick, and Dad asked Ed to take over."

"And Ed found his true vocation?" I guess.

Sam nods. "If I thought he was good in the main kitchen, that was nothing compared to how he was with pastry. He was a genius." He kisses my forehead a little randomly, which makes me smile. "When the regular guy came back, Ed asked Dad if he could stay on in the pastry section. Dad had never had much time for that side of cooking and wanted us both to follow in his footsteps. Having lost Rob to a business management course at college, he was determined to try and hold onto both of us – but especially Ed. He'd seen his talent and didn't want to let it go. There was a big fight. It went on for days and days. Rob was here at the time, on his summer break, and he and I backed Ed, and eventually Dad gave way… but he treated Ed like a pariah from then on. He'd never help him, or advise him. If he got anything wrong, Dad would show him up in front of the whole staff. It was ugly. Ed's self esteem took a nosedive, and to make it worse, from then on Dad nurtured me, built me up, praised everything I did, even if it wasn't that great. I used to argue with him about Ed, try and get him to see that his attitude was childish and hurtful, but he wouldn't budge. He's even more stubborn than me, which I know you probably find hard to believe, but the rows between the two of us were incendiary. Then he made things worse still by asking me to take over the main kitchen."

"How did that make it worse? Surely that gave you the opportunity to help Ed…"

"You'd have thought so, but dad wouldn't actually let go. He still supervised everything. Gave himself the title of 'executive chef' and drove us all insane."

"What happened?" I ask.

"He had a heart attack." Sam closes his eyes for a moment. "The doctors suggested a change of pace and mom and dad retired to Florida."

"And Ed?"

"It's taken a long time, but he's getting better. Much better. He still asks for advice sometimes, but I tend to just talk things through with him. He usually knows the answer anyway. He's just looking for confirmation. One day, he'll work out that he doesn't need to keep coming to me, or deferring to me, that his ideas work, that he's got what it takes. And then he might even realize he's the best of all of us."

"You know I can't possibly agree with that," I whisper, leaning up and kissing him.

"Only because you don't know him."

"Well, I know you. It sounds like you've spent a lot of years looking out for him."

"Only when he's needed it, and he'd do the same for me."

He smiles at me and I smile back. "Does Rob ever come to you for advice?"

He laughs. "Christ, no. And I'd never offer it either. I've been to him though…" His voice fades.

"Really?" I'm surprised.

"Well, that might have been putting it strongly. I didn't exactly *go* to him, but he made me listen."

"Rob? Rob made you do something?" I can't hide my astonishment.

"Yeah… When you ran out of the apartment, after I threw that pan at you, he… well, he sat me down and told me to stop being so mean to you and start treating you better."

I feel a lump forming in my throat and pull away from him, even though he hangs on. "You mean you didn't want to do that yourself? Rob had to persuade you?"

"No," he says quickly. "It wasn't like that. Rob knows what I'm like and he knew what I needed – namely someone like him telling me to stop being so dumb. I'd already realised it for myself – that's why I ran after you…"

"You did?"

"Yeah. When I realised how much I'd hurt you, I ran after you, but you'd disappeared. I was standing out the front, looking up at the restaurant, working out that you'd already made everything in my life so much better than it's ever been before, when Rob came out…"

"And persuaded you to be a human being?" I add.

He smiles. "Something like that."

We lie in silence for a while. "So, I've got Rob to thank, have I?" I ask him.

"No," he says. "You don't have to thank anyone. The reason I'm with you, is because of you, Ali." He leans down and kisses me, his lips brushing over mine really softly.

I look up into his eyes as he breaks the kiss.

"For identical twins, your brothers are not even remotely similar."

"They are in some ways," he says, leaning over me. "Like I said, we're all real loyal, and real protective of each other – and the people we care about."

I reach up and caress his cheek with my fingertips. "Hmm… I noticed."

He kisses me again. "Now," he whispers, "you need some sleep. I'm letting you off tonight, but tomorrow I want to try something with you."

"After work?"

"Yeah. After work."

"Not before?"

"I can't in the morning. Rob's got one of the suppliers coming in early. He wants me to meet him. And I won't have any spare time in the afternoon. Ed wants to see me about one of his recipes." He pushes a stray hair away from my face. "We'll have to wait until tomorrow night, I'm afraid… So, get some sleep."

He turns me onto my side, facing away from him and moves in behind me, his arousal pressing against me.

"You're sure you want to wait until tomorrow?" I ask, wriggling my behind into him.

"For what I wanna do? Yes," he replies, and I feel him move down slightly.

"What are you doing back there?" I ask.

"Just because I'm not going to make love to you tonight, doesn't mean I don't wanna be joined to you. Just lie still." He finds my entrance and pushes his erection into me. I gasp out my pleasure, pressing my behind further back into him. "Lie still," he repeats softly. "Nothing's gonna happen. I just want us to be connected." He slowly inches into me until we're completely joined, then he brings his arms tight around me. "Go to sleep, baby," he whispers in my ear.

"Now? Like this?"

"Yeah, like this. We're as close as we can be." His voice fades to silence, but then he takes a deep breath and whispers, "Dream of me. Please…"

Getting through today has been hard. Much harder than I expected, considering how good the last few days have been. I've spent a lot of it on my own, which has given me too much time to think. During most of the day I just wanted to go to Sam and hug him, but I don't know how he'd feel about that, which is odd. I ought to know how he'd feel about my reactions, but I don't. I ought to be able to gauge his, but I can't. This control thing of his has got my head in a spin. Since Sunday morning, we've done everything 'my way', as he puts it, but I get the feeling that whatever it is he wants to do tonight is going to be 'his way', and that's absolutely fine by me, except that I don't know what I'm meant to do. Or what I'm allowed to do, because when he's in that controlling mood, I get confused about how I'm supposed to behave.

By the end of the day, having spent the whole evening service watching him, but being too scared to even touch him, I've decided we need to talk. I know he wanted me to learn as we went along, but I need to understand the boundaries, and what he finds acceptable… and – more importantly – why.

"Can we talk?" I ask as soon as we get upstairs, not giving him a chance to distract me

"Sure. As long as we can get undressed at the same time." He leads me into the bedroom.

"What I mean is, can I ask you some questions?" He nods and I take a deep breath.

"What's wrong?" he asks, standing in front of me.

I look into his eyes. He's concerned, maybe even worried. "I'm just struggling with some of this. It's all very new to me."

"I know it is." He undoes my blouse, throwing it into the corner of the room, then removes my bra and tosses it over as well. My jeans and knickers follow suit and now I'm naked. Is this meant to help? He stares at me. "Tell me what you're struggling with," he says.

"I don't know what I'm allowed to do."

"*Allowed* to do?" he repeats.

"Yes. So many times today, I just wanted to come to you and have a hug, or a kiss, or just touch you, but… well, I wasn't sure if that was allowed."

"*Allowed*?" he says again, starting to undress. Once he's naked, he sits us both down on the bed and turns to face me. His expression is remorseful. "You think I want to control you that much?"

"I don't know. That's the problem. I know you wanted me to learn as we go along, but I don't know what I'm supposed to do, or how I'm supposed to behave."

"You're supposed to do whatever you want, and behave like yourself."

"And yet you want to control me?"

"No. I want to control your body, in certain situations." He sighs. "I sometimes want to control your body and your pleasures. I don't want to control your life… or you."

"So, you'd be okay with me coming into the kitchen downstairs and giving you a hug?"

He hesitates. "I don't know. I've never done anything like that before – not in front of other people."

"I gathered that from Rob and Ed's reactions to seeing us together."

He smiles. "Yeah. I think they were kinda shocked. But if that's what you need, Ali, if you need me to hug you, or kiss you, then maybe we can try a compromise?"

"Such as?"

"Such as you come and tell me, and we'll go someplace where we can be alone… at least until I get more used to how this works. A lot of this is new to me too. I'm learning as well."

"I know."

He looks down at me. "Something else is bothering you isn't it?"

"I'm just trying to understand. Can I go back to my questions?"

"You've got more questions?"

"Yes."

"Okay. Ask away." He seems slightly wary, but so am I. I've never been this embarrassed.

"Do you *need* to have this control over my body?" I ask quietly.

"Yes," he says after a moment's pause. "In certain circumstances."

"But how do I know when and what those circumstances are? How do I know which way you're going to want me and how I'm therefore supposed to behave?"

"I told you. I want you to behave like yourself."

"But… how do I know whether you're in a controlling mood, or not?"

He smiles. "It's probably safe to assume I'm always in a controlling mood, babe… but so far, I have tried to warn you in advance when I want to do things my way. I've given you time to get accustomed to the idea." It's true. He has. "And I can carry on doing that until you're more used to this, and can handle a little more spontaneity."

I hesitate before asking my next question. I don't want to talk about the past – his or mine – but…

"Has it always been like this? In the past, with previous partners?"

"No."

"You mean… you mean it's just with me?" I'm shocked.

"No. I mean the opposite. With one exception, all the women I've been with had the same preferences as me. They knew how this works. They liked doing things my way. All the time. We never did things… your way."

"One exception?" I picked up on that.

"Yeah. There was one woman… she tried to control me. It didn't work out."

I can imagine it didn't.

"So you wouldn't be happy for me to instigate things between us?"

"Things?"

"Sex…"

"Well, I guess if we were doing things your way, it might be okay. I've never really done that before, but we could try it, if you like."

"But I thought you said there was one woman who tried to control you… surely she must've…"

"She did. But not in the way you're meaning."

I'm not sure I understand, but at the same time, I really don't want any details about his past. He's told me more than enough already.

"So I could try instigating things if we were just sitting in the living room, or in the kitchen up here, say?"

He smiles. "Yeah. You could try."

I nod my head. "But if we were doing things your way…?"

"No." His reply is quick and abrupt. "My way is on my terms." He pauses, staring at me. "Is that a problem?" he asks, nervously.

I'm not sure how to answer that – not yet, anyway. I need to know more. "Does this controlling thing turn you on?" I ask him.

"Yes."

"But you get turned on doing things my way too?"

"With you, yes. Everything about you turns me on."

I smile at the compliment. "But that's only with me?"

"Yes. You're different. You're making me different…"

"Is that a good thing?"

"Yes. If I'm being honest, I really like doing things your way. It might be new to me, but it's good. Like I say, I'm still learning…" He leaves the sentence hanging. He's still looking nervous, even shy.

"I do appreciate that," I whisper. "I know this isn't usual for you either."

"That doesn't mean it isn't good. Really good."

I pause before putting my next question. I'm not even sure I want to ask it, but I need to know how far things might be allowed to go between us. "Could I try tying you up?" I ask.

His face falls. "No." He seems almost shocked by the idea. "No, I wouldn't like that. I'm sorry, but I couldn't give up that much control. Ever. Not even for you. Just the thought of it really scares me, Ali." Wow. He's being so open and honest – more so than I probably expected him to be.

"Are you a Dominant?" I whisper.

He hesitates for a moment. "No." He shakes his head. "I'm not *a* Dominant. I'm dominant. There's a difference."

"Yes. One's a noun and the other's an adjective."

He smiles again – which feels like a relief at the moment. "Yes, and one's a way of life, and the other's a sexual preference."

"So, which is it for you?"

"Before… before I met you, it was definitely a way of life." He pauses, letting me take that on board. "But now, it's just a sexual preference. I don't know what you're worried about, Ali, but I don't expect you to be submissive to me…"

"You don't?"

"No." He moves even closer so we're touching. "If you don't want to do things my way, we don't have to."

"Not ever?"

He stops and takes a breath.

"No… not if you don't want to." I wonder if he really means that; if that hesitation signified more than he'd like to admit. His eyes move from mine, to my lips and back again. "I thought you enjoyed what we did together, when I tied you?"

"I did…" my voice fades

"Then I don't understand…"

"I like the intensity of your way, but I wouldn't want that exclusively. I also like the romance and intimacy of my way too. I think I need to keep doing both. And I'm not sure how you feel about that. It… it just feels really complicated, Sam."

He brushes my cheek with the backs of his fingers so gently my breath catches. "I need both too," he says. "Well, I do with you, anyway." He pauses for a moment. "I was scared, before we got together, that I wouldn't be able to do things your way, that I wouldn't be able to relinquish control, but with you, I don't feel like I am. It just feels… natural. I feel like I've still got a lot to learn, but I'm enjoying the process. I'm loving the intimacy of your way, and the romance, although I've never done anything even vaguely romantic in my life, until I met you. I mean, do you honestly think I've ever put rose petals in a bed before?" There's a glint in his eye.

"No?" I give my answer in the form of a question.

"Damn right I haven't. I've never even given a woman flowers, let alone pulled them apart and put them in the bed. I had no idea what I was doing."

"Will you hurt me?" I whisper, scared to ask the question that's probably haunted me more than any other during my day of uncertainty.

"No. Of course I won't. I've told you I'll never hurt you, and I won't… in any way. I'm not into pain – sexual or otherwise. I just like control… that's all. And with you, it doesn't always have to be that way. I love doing things your way, baby. I really do, believe me."

He stares into my eyes.

"Apart from not being tied up, is there anything else you don't like?" I ask him.

"I've never liked women going on top," he replies after just a moment's hesitation.

"Why?"

"Because I feel like I'm relinquishing too much of myself in that position…" His voice fades.

I nod my head. "And is there anything else?"

"I can't think of anything, no." He pauses. "Can I ask you a question?"

"Yes."

"Are you happy with me?" The doubt in his voice is heartbreaking.

"Yes," I say quickly. Kneeling up and throwing my arms around his neck. "Yes. I'm sorry if I made you doubt that."

"You did, kinda."

"I didn't mean to. It's just hard to take all of this on board."

"Can't you just go with the flow?" he asks. "That's what I'm trying to do… I mean, you do enjoy what we're doing, don't you?" he clarifies again.

I nod my head and he pulls me onto his lap.

"Apart from confused, tell me how it makes you feel," he says.

I want to say 'loved', but I daren't. Just because I'm in love with him doesn't mean he feels the same. I can't look him in the eye, so I focus on his stubbled chin instead. "Wanted?" I say, again with more than a hint of insecurity.

"You are wanted."

I smile, and run my finger along his jawline. "You've given me pleasure like I've never felt before, Sam…"

"Look at me, Ali," he says, and I raise my eyes. His are filled with a breathtaking tenderness. "It's the same for me. You've shown me things I never thought I could have. I love your reactions, I love the way you make me feel, the things you do to me and how you respond to what

I'm doing to you. It's never been like this before – ever." He brushes his lips against mine, so gently. "Don't feel doubtful, or in any way negative about any of this, baby," he whispers. "I know a lot of what we're doing is new to you, and you've been amazing. Completely amazing." He kisses me again, harder this time and, as his tongue delves into my mouth, I moan softly. "You give me so much pleasure too. You really do," he mutters into my mouth, in between biting on my bottom lip.

I can feel my pussy tingling. I want him… badly.

I lean back. "You were okay with me asking all those questions?"

"Sure," he replies, tracing a line of kisses up to my ear. "I know I'm not good at expressing myself, but that's only because I've never done it before. That probably makes me seem like a closed book, but I'm not. Not to you, anyway. You can ask me anything. Anything at all…"

"I can?"

He nods, but even then I feel myself deflate. "What's wrong?" he asks.

"I can't ask you what I need to…"

"Why?"

I stare at him and tilt my head, hoping he'll understand. It takes a moment and then a slow smile crosses his lips. "You're feeling turned on?" he says.

I nod, just once. "Yes, but I'm not supposed to instigate anything."

He smirks. "But I said you could."

"Not if we're doing things your way," I explain. "And last night, you said…"

He thinks for a moment, then sits me back on the bed. "Oh yeah. I did, didn't I? Well, I'll let you off… just this once, being as you've evidently had a confusing day." Then he gets up, and goes around to the other side, bending down and retrieving something from the drawer which he holds behind his back as he comes back around to me, offering his hand. "Come with me," he says. My insides melt as I climb off the bed and take his hand. He keeps whatever it is he got from the drawer hidden behind his back as we go along the corridor, through the living room and into the kitchen. "You're feeling turned on," he says.

"So am I." That much is obvious from his erection. "And I've got a fantastic idea in mind for that."

I can feel the anticipation building. I've got no clue what he's planning, but I need him.

Without saying anything else, he stands me at one end of the butcher's block. "You really wanna do something my way?" he asks. "Even though you've been having doubts?"

"Yes," I breathe, and he smiles. I place my hand flat on his chest. "They weren't really doubts. I was just confused. I needed answers, that's all. I don't doubt you, Sam. Please don't think I do."

"Sure?"

"Yes, I'm sure."

He nods his head and all of a sudden, his demeanour changes, like a shadow passing over him. His eyes darken, his lips narrow and his jaw tightens. I feel my whole body tense and tingle in expectation. "Turn," he whispers.

I do as he says, facing away from him.

"Good girl. Now bend. Bend over." I obey, leaning right over the butcher's block, my feet just touching the floor. He moves in close behind me and, using his feet, nudges my legs further apart, before running his hands over my buttocks. I let out a soft moan, just as I feel him move away. He comes around to the front of the unit and, raising my head, I can see what he's holding in his hands. It looks like a pair of very wide leather handcuffs, with large gold buckles. He undoes them and places them by my head. "Put your arms out in front of you," he says.

I comply, moving my arms toward him. He takes my right hand and wraps one soft leather cuff around it, fastening it fairly tight, although it's padded, and comfortable. He then attaches a gold clip to the d-ring on the side, which he links through one of the hooks on the end of the table that he uses to hang his drying cloths. Then he does the same with the other hand, so I'm stretched out, face down along the length of the surface, shackled to it.

"I need you strapped down, but I won't tie your legs," he says. "Not this time. Just leave them where they are, unless I move them. Okay?"

I nod my head as he moves around behind me again. I can feel my heart beating fast and loud as he places the tip of his erection against my entrance.

"You're so wet," he mutters.

He holds his position, then leans over and whispers. "If anything I do hurts you, tell me and I'll stop. Okay?"

I nod.

"Tell me you understand," he says.

"I understand."

I wait, expecting to feel him push into me, but he doesn't. Instead, I feel a strange, warm, drizzling sensation, running down the length of my spine. I try to turn my head to see what he's doing, but I can't.

"Don't worry," he says softly. "It's just massage oil."

And he thought this would hurt me? The dripping stops and his hands rest on me for a moment, before he starts to spread the oil gently over my back, rubbing it into my skin. He works it up to my shoulders, kneading them with a light touch, then moves down my back to my waist, using his fingers to relax all the muscles. He's still got the tip of his cock in me as he works his hands lower. The sensations are disconcerting. I'm aroused and relaxed at the same time.

"Does it feel good?" he asks.

"Yes," I whisper. "I've never felt anything quite like it before."

"Oh, wait until I really get started," he murmurs. "I'm gonna show you pleasure like you never thought possible."

I sigh and he moves his hands lower still…

Sam

I massage over her hips and move further down to her beautiful ass. An involuntary groan leaves my lips as I rub the oil into her perfect, soft skin.

Her questions earlier had me rattled. They had me more than rattled. At one stage, I really thought she was gonna say she didn't want to be with me anymore; that she didn't like what we do together, that she couldn't handle it, and she wanted out… That's why I was so open with her. I knew if I wanted to keep hold of her, I had to let go of myself; I had to be honest, express myself better, let her know what she does to me. Maybe I should've told her I'm in love with her as well. I don't know… Like I said to her, I've never done this before, and the truth is, I don't have a fucking clue what I'm doing.

Well, that's not strictly true. I know exactly what I'm doing right this minute. I'm showing her just how good this can be.

She squirms back into me, trying to get more of my cock, and I smile. She can't see my face though, so it doesn't matter. I lean forward just a fraction and give her what she wants – well, an inch of what she wants, anyway – and she lets out a moan of satisfaction.

"Do you want more?" I ask her.

"Yes." Her reply is urgent, desperate. "Yes, I want more. Please give me more, Sam."

I pull out of her.

"No," she whimpers. "Please, Sam."

My smile broadens, and positioning myself carefully, I slam my cock into her.

"Fuck, yes!" she yells, and in that moment, she explodes, writhing on the block, arching into me as best she can. Jesus, that was fast. I pull out, and then plough back into her again, and she screams out her pleasure. I hold on as she shudders and shivers, her body twisting into the ecstasy of her orgasm. As she calms, I move back to massaging her butt, and she sighs out a long breath, relaxing just a little. I shift my feet, forcing hers even further apart. She came so hard, I can feel her juices dripping down between us, and I start to move inside her, slowly to begin with, but then I pick up the pace, until I'm pounding into her. I'm grateful that the island unit is bolted to the floor. If it wasn't, I'd have driven it across the kitchen by now.

She starts to moan and writhe again, and I feel a rippling deep inside her. She's gonna come again… real soon.

"Do you wanna try something new?" I'm not used to asking, but with Ali it's different. And after her questions, it feels important to make sure. "You can say no, if you want to."

"I'll do anything for you," she breathes. "Anything. Just please don't stop."

I trace my index finger gently down her oiled spine, starting between her shoulders and working lower and lower until I get to her butt cheeks, now spread apart. I keep going until my finger rests over her anus and I let it settle there, letting her know what I've got in mind.

"You sure?" I say.

"Yes," she groans. "Oh please, yes… I'm yours, Sam." Fuck, that sounds good. She's mine…

Keeping up the pace, I pull my finger away and she raises her ass slightly, impatient for the touch again. I smile and shake my head. She told me she wasn't very good at waiting – and she wasn't wrong. I spread my hand out, palm down, fingers splayed, just above her ass, and slip my lubricated thumb inside her tight bud. Instantly, she goes completely wild, trembling, bucking into me and screaming my name through the most extreme orgasm I've ever seen or felt. I can't take it and I let go inside her, filling her deeply. I keep going, my thumb still in place as she thrashes violently, my name a continuous cry on her lips.

The moment I know she's calming, I slowly pull out of her, and go around to unfasten the cuffs. She's completely spent, utterly exhausted and I raise her off the block, standing her up, and lift her into my arms, carrying her through to the bedroom and depositing her on the bed, pulling the comforter over her, before I go wash up.

When I return, she's already curled up asleep, half on my side of the bed, and I shift her slightly and climb in beside her, pulling her close and holding onto her.

She opens her eyes and looks up at me. "Thank you, Sam," she whispers.

"You've gotta stop thanking me," I say, kissing her forehead gently. "I'm the one who's grateful to you."

"But you're giving me so much," she says, slurring her words.

"No, you're the one who's doing all the giving."

She shrugs, like she doesn't understand and her eyes flutter closed again, as she murmurs. "Thank you, Sam," again under her breath.

When I wake up, she's still asleep, but she comes to within a few minutes and stares up at me.

"Good morning," she says, looking a little shy, maybe.

"Are you okay?" I ask her.

"Well, I'm not sore, if that's what you're asking."

"I wasn't, but I'm glad to hear it." I smile down at her. "How do you feel?"

"Um… Fine." She seems confused.

"Okay… I'll be more specific. How do you feel about what we did last night? You had a lot of questions yesterday; you made it clear you're having trouble coming to terms with some of the things we're doing and I know I introduced you to something quite different last night… So, how do you feel about it?"

She blushes, and lowers her eyes. This doesn't look good. I know she went kinda wild when she came, but that doesn't means she's gonna want to do it again. If she doesn't, that's fine.

"I liked it." Her voice is so quiet, I struggle to hear her.

"You liked it?" I'm surprised. I think it must show.

"Couldn't you tell?" She looks up at me again.

I smirk. "Well, if I'm being honest, I've never seen anyone come quite like that before… so yeah, I guess your enjoyment was pretty obvious."

"I'm not saying I want to do that all the time…"

"That's fine. Neither do I. I like variety."

She smiles. "Hmm. I noticed."

"Just every so often then…?"

"Well, maybe a bit more frequently than that," she murmurs.

She's full of surprises. Every time with her is different – and new. And so magically special.

It's Saturday again already, and I can't believe it's been a week since we got together. The last few days have been the best. We've had a lot of sex, but we've also talked. I've never talked this much in my life and I've made a point of communicating with Ali, so she doesn't feel confused or doubtful again. It seems to have helped and I feel like we're really 'together'. And I like that. I like that a lot.

Last night was ridiculously busy in the restaurant and we both just collapsed into bed when we got up here. We fell asleep in each other's arms, but the idea of doing more than sleeping was beyond either of us. All week, I've been mentally dancing around the thought that she'll be going home soon. It's something I've been trying to avoid thinking about, but we're going to have to face it. Sooner, rather than later.

I'm awake before Ali, but that's not unusual it seems, and I go and make us coffee. By the time I come back, she's sitting up in bed.

"Good morning," I say to her, handing her a cup.

"Hello." She seems a little subdued.

I climb in beside her, putting my coffee down on the nightstand.

"Can we talk?" I say quietly, turning to face her.

"Okay." Now she sounds worried.

"I don't want this to end." I can't think of another way of putting it. "I've never had anything like this in my life and I can't just let it finish. I know you've gotta go home, but I still want us to be together – somehow. So... can we try and work out a way for that to happen? Maybe we can arrange for you to come back over here again in a couple of weeks? Or I'll find a way to take some time off and come to you?" I've hardly paused for breath, and she's just staring at me, her mouth slightly open. Have I misread the whole thing? Was she just looking for a brief romance? Something to fill the time while she's over here? It hasn't felt like that... Surely it wasn't just about the sex for her, was it? "I—"

She leans over and puts her fingers on my lips, stopping me from speaking, and it's then that I notice the tears welling in her eyes.

"I want that too," she murmurs. There's a crack in her voice and I pull her hand away from my mouth and put my arms around her, holding her tight. "I want that so much, Sam. I can't bear the idea of going home and this just ending. I've been so scared you wouldn't want us to be together, but yes, if we can find a way to make this work, then there's nothing I want more."

I open my mouth to tell her I'm in love with her, and that there's no way I'm ever gonna let this end, when she leans up and kisses me. I smile to myself. I guess my first ever declaration of love is going to have to wait. Still, now I know we both want the same thing, that's fine. Tomorrow is our day off and we've got the whole of it to ourselves. As I move us down the bed, I think about maybe cooking her a meal in the evening… a romantic meal, with candles and everything. A meal during which I can tell her how I really feel about her. I want to make it special – for her.

"Shower with me?" she says, breaking the kiss, and I smirk. "What's wrong?" she asks. The irony isn't lost on me that I was thinking about creating a romantic dinner for the two of us and declaring my love for her… and Ali's thoughts were clearly running along more carnal lines. What a turn-around.

"Nothing," I say. "I'd love to shower with you."

I'm holding her in my arms, the water flowing between us, my hands clasping her ass, her legs wrapped around my hips, her arms around my neck and she's impaled on my cock.

"Harder, please… please, Sam," she whimpers.

I give her what she wants, moving her harder and faster up and down my shaft and she starts to groan loudly. She's gonna come – and so am I. I move my right hand slightly and insert just the tip of my middle finger into her tight anus, and within seconds, she flies apart in my arms, thrashing against me, and it's all I can do to hold onto her. She clamps tightly around me and I come deep and hard inside her, crying out her name. I lean back against the tiled wall as she calms, lifting her off of me and lowering her to the floor, but keeping hold of her, making sure her legs are steady.

"Oh God," she mutters, still clinging to me. "That was…"

"I know. It just gets better every time."

She looks up at me, smiling that sweet, sexy smile, puts her hands on my cheeks and pulls me down into a deep kiss.

When we get downstairs, Ali's got a few calls to make, so I give her a quick kiss by the office door and go into the kitchen. Ed's already busy – along with most of the regular staff and our two Saturday helpers.

"Is Ali with you?" Ed asks immediately, looking up from his section at the back of the room.

"She's in the office," I explain. "Why?"

"I've got something I want her to taste."

"Oh... well, I can go get her."

He nods and I go back out and across the corridor. Ali hasn't even opened her laptop yet.

"Ed wants you to try something," I tell her.

"Oh yes?" She looks up.

"Don't quote me, but I think he's finally perfected the gelato recipe he's been fretting over."

"The mango and raspberry one?"

"I guess."

She comes and joins me. I don't know why, but for some reason, this recipe has had him foxed. It's a variation on the new dairy-free idea he's come up with, but it's not on the menu yet because he didn't feel the balance was right. Over the last couple of evenings, Ali has been trying to work it out with him, when we've had the odd quiet moment.

"Okay... let's see if it's worked this time." I lead her into the kitchen and she goes straight down to Ed's section, while I grab a pan from the hook on the wall and turn to put it on the hob behind me. I'm stopped in my tracks when I notice Ed coming and meeting Ali halfway down the kitchen, a spoon in his hand.

"Try this," he says, holding it out. She leans forward and I'm mesmerized, watching as he puts the spoon in her mouth. I've seen them do this on a couple of occasions and, every time, it turns me on more and more. She closes her eyes as he removes the spoon and then... with the tip of her middle finger, she wipes a drip of gelato from her lip, dragging it slightly, and I'm immediately transported back to

Thursday night, when we decided to sit up after work and have a glass of wine together. Ali cuddled up next to me on the couch, her hand on my thigh. After a few minutes, she moved it up, so she was caressing my cock, through my jeans, and then, undoing them slowly, she knelt on the floor between my legs and took me in her mouth. I didn't worry in the least about her instigating things – we'd kind of agreed on that anyway, and besides, what she was doing felt too good to quibble over minor issues like that. Using her hands at the same time, it wasn't long before I knew I was going to come. I warned her, but she just took me deeper and I exploded in her mouth, holding the back of her head. It was exquisite… and afterwards, she used the tip of her middle finger to wipe a drip of my come from her lip. Once I'd got my breath back, I sat her up on the couch again and returned the favor, until she was screaming in ecstasy. But watching her now, repeating that action with her finger, I can't take my eyes from her and, as she looks up, our eyes meet and the pan slips from my hand, clattering loudly on the floor. Everyone jumps, which isn't surprising. It's rare for me to drop anything. I've been known to throw things, but not drop them.

Ali's so hot and she smiles, walking over slowly, her eyes fixed on mine.

Once she gets to me, she bends over and picks up the pan from the floor, putting it down beside me. "You're all fingers and thumbs, aren't you?" she says, her voice husky and filled with heat.

We both know exactly what she's referring to… my finger, and my thumb embedded in her ass while she came so hard. Twice.

She gives me the sexiest smile ever and turns, about to leave, but I grab her and pull her back into my arms. I don't care who's watching, I hold her head still and whisper in her ear, "I'll prove it later too. Fingers *and* thumbs. My way." She gasps and twists her head, so her mouth is beside my ear.

"Yes please," she breathes.

I almost choke, and to cover my reaction, pat her on the ass.

"Back to work." I say out loud.

"Yes, Sam," she replies, as demure as you please.

When she gets to the door, she turns back, looks over at Ed, who's standing with his mouth open, and says, "You've cracked it, Ed. The gelato is perfect." He smiles at her, and, with one last, long look at me, she leaves.

I'm aware that every eye in the kitchen is on me.

"Any reason why you guys are all standing around?" I ask, a little gruffly and everyone immediately finds something to do. I glance at Ed and he gives me a smile and a nod of his head, which I return, before getting on with preparing for the lunch service.

It takes me over half an hour to fully calm down though… I'm not sure how comfortable I feel about everyone seeing us together, but the thought of Ali and her responses has me more turned on than I can ever express. Now, all I can think about is how frustrated I feel. I want to take her upstairs right this minute, restrain her properly and show her exactly what I can do with my fingers and thumbs.

I'm just contemplating going over the hall and taking her up to the apartment, when Jane comes over.

"Sam…" I can tell from the tone of her voice that something's wrong.

"Yeah. What is it?"

"I think you'd better come and look at this."

And I know, without even seeing whatever's wrong, that my moment with Ali is going to have to wait.

Chapter Fourteen

Ali

"So, I'll get there around eleven, shall I?" Petra asks.

"That should be fine. I don't think it'll take more than a couple of hours."

"And you just want some photographs of the two chefs?"

"Well... I needed to talk to you about that. Can you take some more of Rob as well? I know you got some of him at the opening, but I'd like to have some where he's not..."

"Flirting?" she offers, tentatively.

I laugh. "I was going to say working, but yes, flirting covers it too."

"I can't believe he called me an angel when you introduced us at the opening," she says and even I can hear the doubt in her voice.

"Why not?" I ask. "I'm sure he meant it as a compliment." I'd actually thought they flirted well together, and he might have taken it further, if they hadn't been interrupted by the arrival of the night's first guests, but I don't say any of that.

"Yeah, and I'm equally convinced he says that to pretty much every woman he meets."

"Don't be so sure about that... and don't put yourself down." It's not my place to tell her that Sam thinks Rob might be interested. If he is, I'm sure she'll find out for herself soon enough.

I can almost hear her blushing, then she coughs. "Okay," she says quietly. "So, you need some shots done in the kitchen, and the remainder… around the restaurant?" She doesn't want to talk about Rob anymore. That's obvious.

"Mainly behind the bar, I think," I reply, respecting her wishes.

"That sounds fine. A couple of hours should still be plenty of time."

"Thanks for this, Petra."

"You're welcome. I'll see you tomorrow."

We end the call and I lean back in the chair, looking up at the ceiling.

What a morning…

After all the doubt and uncertainty I'd been feeling, having Sam tell me he wants our relationship to continue and develop, even though I've got to go home soon, was such a relief. I was so scared that I was committing so much of myself, both emotionally and physically for something that he saw as short term. But evidently not…

I wonder if maybe I should tell him I'm in love with him. I was tempted this morning, but then I decided to kiss him instead, and before I knew what was happening, I'd invited him to shower with me. I liked taking the lead like that. I think he did too… and as for what he did to me in the shower. That was spectacular. He's right, the sex really does seem to get better every time. I keep expecting it to disappoint, or at least reach a plateau, but it just seems to improve. What he does to me is mind-blowing… so much so, I can hardly think straight. I've got no idea why I'm like this around him, but I love it. I was never like this with Liam, but then we were never right for each other. It wasn't his fault – well, it was his fault that he cheated, obviously – but it wasn't his fault he couldn't really satisfy me. He just wasn't the right man. Sam is. Sam's the perfect man for me.

Now that I'm getting more used to him, one of the things I like most is the anticipation. He changes from sweet, sexy and romantic, to domineering and masterful almost in the blink of an eye. Both versions of him are just as satisfying, and I'm finding the alteration quite a powerful turn-on.

I lean forward again and try to focus on the page of figures that Rob's left me. He's attached a note, explaining that last week was the best the restaurant has had since the guys took over from their father. I'm really pleased for them. They've all worked so hard for this. And they still are...

I stare at my laptop screen for a while, but my concentration is completely shot to pieces. Every few seconds, an image of Sam doing something to me flits through my mind and I'm lost again. The way he held me in the restaurant kitchen just now was so special. To let everyone see that we're together like that was more than I ever expected from him and, if I'm being honest, I could do with another hug like that. Actually, I could do with spending some time with him, so I can tell him how I feel, and I wonder if I could go in to the kitchen and ask him if we can have an hour or so alone during his break this afternoon. I know it's not very romantic, but I really want him to know now, that I love being bound by him, and that I'm bound *to* him. Forever.

I make my decision and, am just getting up out of my seat, when my phone rings. I check the screen and see that it's Tess. She normally calls me in the afternoons – well, evenings for her – so I know something must be wrong and I answer immediately, sitting back down again.

"Tess? Are you okay?" I don't even bother with 'hello'.

"No," she mutters and I can hear her tears.

"What's wrong?" I lean forward, although I don't know what I expect that to achieve.

"I've just received an e-mail," she says, sniffing loudly.

"Who from?"

"James Alexander." He's the agent who manages our house in Dorset.

"Okay. What did he want?" She sniffs again and I can hear her sob. "Tess, tell me what he said."

"Hang on... I'll read it out to you," she says and there's a pause. "It's on my laptop," she explains, then she clears her throat. "Dear Miss Bishop," she begins. "I'm aware that your sister is currently working overseas, and ordinarily I wouldn't bother you, but I'm afraid this can't wait. I'm sorry to inform you that I have visited Waterside this morning and have discovered that your tenant, Mr Fletcher, and his partner, have vacated the property. He has not paid the outstanding rent which was due, and I regret to say that the house has been left in a..." She pauses and I hear her trying to calm herself. "In a state of disrepair. Perhaps you could contact me urgently with your instructions. I look forward to hearing from you. Best regards, James Alexander." She stops reading and goes quiet, although I can still hear the occasional sniffle.

I think about the beautiful house by the sea where Tess and I spent many happy childhood weekends and half-terms. Renting it out was a good idea of granny's and until recently we've had no problems at all. But the tenants Tess is talking about have only been in there for a few months and have been nothing but trouble. James has dealt with most of it, but then that's what he's paid for.

"Bloody hell," I say to fill the silence. "I half expected them to leave when we got James to issue the rent reminder, but I didn't expect them to do any damage."

"What shall I do?" Tess asks, her voice filled with uncertainty. "I—I don't know what to do, Ali."

I can hear the panic starting to rise in her voice and I know that really one of us should go down to the house to see what damage has been done and arrange to have it repaired. I can't ask that of Tess, especially not when she's only got a few weeks until her dissertation has to be handed in… I've got no choice; I'm going to have to go back and deal with it myself.

"Don't worry," I tell her, soothingly. "I'll come home."

"But… but the contract," she says, but, despite her words, I can hear the optimism in her voice.

"I'm sure they can do without me now," I reply. In terms of the work, they can. There's only really the photography shoot to deal with and I trust Petra to handle that herself. How Sam's going to react, I don't know… but we agreed to keep seeing each other this morning. I guess we'll just have to work it out a little sooner than we expected. "I'll check out the flights and text you the details," I explain. "In the meantime, send James a quick reply and tell him not to do anything about the house and I'll get down there as soon as I can… and then get on with your dissertation."

"Are you sure?" she asks.

"I'm positive." I smile as I'm speaking, hoping she'll hear that as well as my words.

"Thanks, Ali," she whispers.

"Don't thank me," I reply. "Just dry your tears and get back to work. With any luck, I'll be home tomorrow."

"I'm sorry to mess you around," she says.

"You're not messing me around." I reassure her.

We end the call and I feel better now that she's not crying. Tess has never been great at handling anything unexpected and I'm not sure that's ever going to change. I stand, putting my phone in my back pocket, and go out into the corridor. I can hear Rob laughing with the other waiting staff in the restaurant and am just about to cross into the kitchen when I hear a loud clattering and then Sam shouts, "For fuck's sake, Leo," at the top of his voice. "That's a whole fucking tray of salmon. What the fuck is wrong with you?"

Silence descends in the restaurant and I glance over at Rob, who rolls his eyes. I shrug and push on the kitchen door, entering Sam's equally silent domain.

Leo is crouched on the floor, picking up salmon fillets that have fallen from the tray he was obviously carrying, and dropped, and everyone else is trying to look busy, while Sam scowls.

"What?" he barks at me.

"Excuse me?" I stare at him, unable to believe he just spoke to me like that.

"Did you want something, or have you just come in here to admire the show?"

What on earth is the matter with him? "Sam… what's wrong?" It feels like I've stepped back in time, and the man in front of me is a stranger, compared to the man who was in bed with me this morning and who told me he didn't want 'us' to end. And who did those things to me in the shower…

"Everything's wrong. I'm having the morning from hell. So whatever you want to say, get it over with," he says, his voice maybe a little louder than before.

And there I was thinking how perfect our morning had been. To him, it seems, it's been 'hell'.

"D—do you know? I don't think I'll bother."

"Okay," he says, impatiently. "Then can I get on?" Who does he think he is?

"Yes. I'd hate to get in your way. Nothing I've got to say is that important – obviously. But if you'd like a piece of free advice, you might want to keep your voice down when telling off the kitchen staff. I think most of Hartford just heard you, and if the restaurant had been open, it wouldn't have looked good to your customers."

His face darkens and his eyes are almost black, and threatening.

"Finished?" he asks, sarcastically.

"Yes, thanks."

"Good." He steps forward and lowers his voice. "This is *my* kitchen, so don't ever come in here and speak to me like that again," he murmurs.

How dare he… "I tell you what…" I struggle to fight back my tears. "I'll make your day. I won't come in here at all. Ever again."

I turn to leave, but Sam grabs my arm, pulling me back.

"I'm sorry," he says, his face pale now, his eyes filled with nothing but fear. I don't care anymore though. He's gone too far. Again.

"Go to hell, Sam," I choke.

"Ali… please." I can hear the desperation in his voice. "Don't do this."

"Do what?"

"Whatever it is you're doing. My behaviour was inexcusable. I apologise."

As far as I'm concerned, his apology is too little, too late. "I thought we'd put all that behind us," I whisper.

"We have." He takes a step toward me, but I hold my hand up and he stops.

"Well, it doesn't bloody well feel like it to me."

"Ali?" I look up at his face and all I can see now is confusion, and uncertainty. "Let's go into the office and talk," he says.

"No, Sam. I don't want to talk to you at the moment."

"Why not?"

"Because I'm too bloody angry, that's why not. If I talk to you, I'm going to say something I think we'll both regret."

He swallows hard. "Okay," he whispers.

I step away from him and he lets me. We stare at each other for a moment, but I can't think what to say, so I say nothing and leave the room, going back across the hallway and into the office. I close the door and go over to the desk, flopping down in my chair just as my phone beeps. It's a message from Tess to say that she's emailed James, and thanking me again for going home. Without really thinking, I open my laptop, go to a browser and check the flights for this evening.

There's a flight at five-thirty, which means if I really hurry, I can get myself to the airport in time to catch it, and I'll get into London in the early hours of the morning. I wonder if I should wait, speak to Sam, catch a later flight, maybe even wait until tomorrow… but I know Tess needs me, and right now I'm so angry with Sam, I'm not sure why I'd bother to wait anyway. How could he? He wasn't supposed to be that man anymore, but I suppose people don't change… not really. Not unless they really want to. And I guess that means he doesn't want to; not enough, anyway. I brush away the tear that's just fallen onto my cheek and focus on the screen in front of me.

I book myself a ticket, then find a local taxi company and arrange for a cab to take me to the airport. Finally, I slam my laptop shut, then dump it in my bag and, picking up my handbag and my keys, I go straight upstairs to the apartment.

As soon as I get up here, I'm bombarded with memories; the fish and chips, lying with Sam on the couch, kissing for the first time, being shackled to his butcher's block… I put my bag and laptop down and go through to the bedroom. The memories are even stronger here. We've made love so many times now, but I can picture every moment. I can feel him inside me, I can feel the rope around my wrists, his arms around me, his lips on mine.

I shake my head and put my case on the bed, open it and methodically pack away my things, trying to forget what I'm leaving behind. I don't think it's forever, but after the way Sam just spoke to me, I'm not sure…

I don't know if we're over. I don't think we are, but I don't know anything at the moment, except that Tess needs me and Sam doesn't. And I have to go.

Once I'm packed, I carry my case down the stairs and through into the restaurant, which has just opened.

Rob's in the middle of seating a couple at a table and turns towards me as I approach him.

"I'm really sorry," I say quietly, steering him towards the back of the restaurant where it's quieter. "I've got to go."

"Go where?" He glances down at my bag and moves a little closer, presumably because I'm whispering.

"Home."

"Home?" He's shocked, understandably I guess. "Home, as in England?" I nod. "Is everything okay?"

"I've had a call from my sister, and there are some problems I need to go back to deal with," I explain.

"Your sister's not ill, or hurt, or anything?" His concern is touching, and now I feel like crying. *Dammit.*

"No, she's fine. I'm going to try and catch the early evening flight from Logan," I tell him.

"You're going that soon?"

"Yes. Tess needs me and I'm pretty much finished here. There's just the photography shoot tomorrow, and I'm sure Petra can handle that."

He smiles, I guess at the sound of Petra's name. "Is Sam taking you the airport?" he asks.

"No."

"Um… Is everything okay between the two of you?"

I shrug my shoulders. "If I'm being honest, I don't know. He just yelled at me…badly. Probably the worst ever." My voice cracks.

"Why?"

"Because I walked into the kitchen at the wrong moment… I think. We were fine this morning before work. Actually, we were better than fine."

"Then what happened?"

"I don't know. I only went in there to tell him I'm going home, but I never got the chance."

"You mean… he doesn't know?"

"No," I reply. I can feel my shoulders sag. "I thought all that was in the past, Rob… but I guess I was wrong."

"That's just Sam," he starts to say.

"Yes, but the thing is, we've been talking about the future, only I don't know if I want a future like that… where I'm always treading on eggshells, waiting for the next explosion."

"Are… are you breaking up with him?" he asks.

"I don't know what I'm doing, other than going home."

"Why don't you let me get him? You can talk it through before you go," he suggests.

"I can't talk to him right now."

"I'll stay with you. I won't let him hurt you," he offers.

I shake my head. "I can't," I repeat, trying hard not to cry.

"Then what am I supposed to tell him?" he asks.

I shrug again. "Tell him whatever you want, Rob… Only do me a favour and wait until the end of service before you tell him?"

"Are you kidding? He'll kill me."

I let out a long sigh. Rob has a point. I know that despite his offer to help, it's not fair to involve him in our quarrel. "Okay. Tell him if you must."

He looks at me, his eyes filled with sadness. "I'll only tell him if he asks," he says. "How's that?"

"Thanks."

He sighs. "Don't write him off, Ali. You're good for him… and he needs you."

"Maybe I don't need to be treated like that though."

He stares at me, then shakes his head right before he pulls me in for a quick hug. "He's a fucking idiot," he says, and lets me go. "How are you getting to the airport?" he asks.

He knows I relinquished the hire car once I'd been here for a few days, when it became clear I wasn't going to be using it.

"I booked a taxi."

"I'd have taken you," he says.

"I know you would. But you're working, and this is my problem, Rob."

Right on cue the cab driver comes in and asks for me and then carries my case out to his car. Rob hugs me again, and I wonder if I should go back and speak to Sam, but my anger hasn't waned in the slightest and, knowing him, he'd probably try and persuade me to stay, or tell me that Tess should grow up and handle the problem with the house all by herself… And then I really would yell at him, because he doesn't know Tess, or our background. And I don't need the hassle. And right now, I don't really need him either.

As the car pulls away, I wonder what Sam will do when he discovers I've gone without telling him. And for a brief moment, I pity Rob for having to tell him. I'm sure it won't be pretty.

Sam

What the fuck is wrong with me? I mean… what was I thinking?

Well, I clearly wasn't thinking, was I? Obviously, Leo dropping the tray of salmon was annoying, and it was about the fourth or fifth thing that had gone wrong since Ali left the kitchen earlier this morning. And it was one thing too many. I told her it had been the morning from hell and I wasn't kidding.

Yeah, I lose it a lot in the kitchen, but even by my standards, that was really losing it.

And to then take it out on Ali was inexcusable, just like I told her.

Like I said… what the fuck was I thinking?

"Are you okay?" Ed asks, coming over to me as Ali leaves.

"No."

"Wanna talk about it?"

"Not really." I want to talk to Ali – well, I want to apologize to Ali again, and preferably in private, so I can show her how sorry I really am – but she's just made it really clear I'm about the last person on earth she wants to talk to… and I didn't like the feeling I got in my chest when she said that. I didn't like it one bit.

Ed glances at the clock on the wall. "Leave her for a while. Let her calm down and talk to her later," he whispers. "Get the service over and done with and go find her… apologize to her and tell her how sorry you are."

"Yeah. I will." I'll also spend the whole of tomorrow making it up to her… and telling her how much I love her.

I know it's all an illusion, but that felt like the longest lunch service ever. Everything's gone smoothly, but I haven't been able to get my mind off of Ali and how she looked when she walked out of here a few hours ago… the pain in her eyes was self-evident. And what's worse is, I put it there. I need to talk to her and make it right again.

Ed's still clearing down his section, but I take off my white jacket, leaving it on the countertop and go through to the office to find Ali. The door's closed and I knock once and go in. It's empty. I guess she must be in the restaurant.

I close the door behind me and go through to the front of house.

"Rob, have you seen Ali?" I call out, noticing she's not in here either.

He's behind the bar and glances up, looking a little mad, although I don't know what about. Then he comes around and walks over to me.

"She's gone," he says gruffly.

My blood turns to ice.

"G—Gone where?" I stammer.

"Home."

"Home," I repeat. "You mean England?"

"Yeah."

I take a half-step away from him and grab the back of the nearest chair to steady myself. "And you knew about this?"

"She told me she was leaving, yeah, just before the cab came to take her to the airport."

"And you didn't fucking well come and get me?" I yell at him. He doesn't even flinch.

"No I didn't… and you've just demonstrated why."

"What are you talking about?" I shout, pulling my phone from my pocket. I need to talk to Ali, to find out what's going on, but before I can even call up her details, he grabs it from me. "What the fuck?"

"Just wait."

"Rob… give me back my fucking phone. Or, so help me God… I'm gonna hit you so damn hard."

He doesn't move, or blink. He just stares at me. "This is why she left," he says quietly.

"You're not making any damn sense." I hold out my hand. "Just give me the fucking phone."

He shakes his head. "No. Not until you calm down."

"How the hell am I supposed to calm down when the woman I love has just walked out on me… and I don't know why?"

"Don't you?" he asks. "Are you sure about that?" His eyes bore into mine. "She told me you yelled at her. Again."

I feel my world slowly grind to a halt. If I thought Ali being burned tore a hole in my chest, the idea that she's actually left me for good, because of something I did, rips me to shreds.

"She… she left because I yelled at her?" I manage to mutter.

"Kinda…" he says. "Sit down a minute and I'll explain."

"What's going on?" Ed calls from the back of the restaurant. "I heard shouting."

"Ali's left," Rob tells him.

"Left? As in gone home?"

"Yeah." He nods his head.

"Is this because Sam yelled at her?"

We all sit at one of the empty tables. "Not entirely," Rob says, "but at least you got that bit quicker than our brother."

"Why else did she go?" I ask. I need to know.

"She had a call from her sister," Rob explains, putting my phone on the table in front of him, but watching me carefully. "Evidently something's happened and Ali needed to go home."

"She didn't tell me," I say, staring at him.

"No. She tried, evidently, but you yelled at her."

I let my head fall into my hands, remembering the things we said to each other in the kitchen a few hours ago. "Shit..." I whisper. "I should've listened to her. She... she told me she had something to say, but I was impatient... rude. She changed her mind and said she wasn't going to bother telling me." I look up at them, then I let my head rock back and stare at the ceiling. "She's really left me."

I feel Rob's hand on my arm. "I'm not sure she has," he says softly, and I lean forward again, looking at him.

"What makes you say that?"

"Because I asked her if she was leaving you, and she said she didn't know what she was doing, except going home."

I feel a flare of hope deep inside my chest. "She said that?"

"Yeah. She also said she didn't much appreciate the way you'd spoken to her, and she didn't really want to face a future spent treading on eggshells... so don't get your hopes up." He shrugs.

"Can I have my phone now?" I ask him.

"Are you gonna be polite?" he replies.

"Yeah. I'm gonna be polite." I'm gonna be more than polite. I'll beg her to give me another chance, if that's what I have to do.

He pushes my phone toward me and I pick it up, look up her details and connect the call.

After five rings, I get her voicemail, but I wanna talk to her, not a recorded message, so I hang up.

"She's not answering?" Ed asks. I shake my head and go to my message app.

— Where are you? We need to talk. S x

Her reply is instant.

— I'm at the airport, waiting for my flight. Why do we need to talk, Sam? A

No kiss. She's mad at me. And she's hurt.

— Miss the flight, please. Wait for me. I'll come find you. I'm not explaining why we need to talk in a text. I'll tell you when I see you. S x

She responds straight away again.

— ***No. I can't miss my flight. I have to get home. A***

— ***I'll leave now. I won't hold you up for long. Just don't get on that flight. S***

— ***Stop telling me what to do, Sam. You don't own me. A***

"Fucking hell," I whisper, trying to calm down.

— ***Sorry. Please wait for me. There are things I need to say to you. S x***

— ***Maybe I don't want to hear them. Maybe I don't want to be shouted at anymore, Sam. A***

— ***I'm not gonna shout. I promise. I just wanna talk to you. Please wait for me. S xx***

I want to add 'I love you', but I can't tell her that for the first time by text.

— ***No, Sam. A***

I let out a sigh.

— ***How many ways do you want me to say sorry? S x***

— ***As many ways as you like. The problem is, you have to mean it. A***

— ***I do. Please, Ali. Just wait for me. S x***

— ***I can't. Tess needs me. I'm sorry, my phone battery is almost dead, so I'm turning it off. A***

She can't. I won't let her…

— ***Don't you dare turn your phone off. S***

I wait a couple of minutes, but there's no reply, so I call her number and it goes straight to voicemail.

"She's turned her damn phone off."

I look up at my two brothers, who are staring at me expectantly, and I know what I've gotta do.

"Sorry," I say to them both. "I know you don't need this, but I've gotta go after her."

I check my watch. I have no idea if there's another flight tonight, but I don't want to sit around here talking about it. I want to go; even if I have to wait at the airport overnight and catch the first flight out tomorrow.

"Now?" Rob queries.

"Yeah. Right now."

"Whoa, hold on a second." He leans forward. "You can't just take off." I'm surprised. I expected Ed to object, not Rob. "We've only just reopened. All the recipes are new. You created them. In case you've forgotten, you're the head chef around here. Why can't you call her later, when she gets home, apologize, talk it over and then go and see her in a couple of weeks when everything here is more settled?"

"Because we've got things we need to talk through." Starting with a massive apology from me. "And none of what we need to say can be said over the fucking phone."

Ed puts his hands on the table. "We'll cope," he says. Ed's usually more of a worrier than a coper, and the look in his eyes tells me nothing's changed – he's still worried, but I can also see his concern for me. "Go," he continues. "We'll manage. You've written down all the recipes, and the sous-chefs know them pretty well by now. I—I guess we can take the specials off the menu while you're away, and tomorrow's Sunday, so I've got all day to get some practice in." He's forgotten about tonight's service, but it would be counterproductive of me to remind him at this stage.

"We've got the photographer coming in tomorrow," Rob says.

"So? She can photograph me cooking, can't she?" Ed replies.

"And what about Sam?"

"I'm sure she won't mind coming back to take his pictures another time." Ed's got an answer for everything.

"I'll be on the end of the phone, if you need me," I tell him. "Even if it's the middle of the night over there. You can just call me." I sigh. "And I won't be gone for long… probably a few days at most. If I can't work it out with Ali by then, I'll be back." I don't want to think about that though. I can't.

Ed and I both look at Rob, and eventually he shrugs his shoulders. "Okay," he huffs. "I guess I'm outvoted." He gets up and goes over to the bar, reaching underneath and pulling out his laptop.

"What are you doing?" I ask him.

"Two things..." he says, tapping on the keyboard. "First I'm gonna book you on the next flight..."

"And?"

"And then I'm gonna look up Ali's address in London. I've got it on her emails. I'm guessing you don't want to wander the streets looking for her."

I smile over at him. "Thanks," I say quietly.

"And then I'd better drive you to the airport. I'll ask Jasmine if she can cover for me until I get back... but Ed's gonna be needed in the kitchen."

"Oh... God, yeah." Ed pales. "It's Saturday night..."

"You'll be fine." I put my hand on his shoulder and squeeze. "Just stay calm, think through the orders and work methodically. You've spent years watching dad and me. You can do this. And call me if you need me."

"You'll ace it," Rob adds, and Ed nods.

I look from him, to Rob and back again. "Thanks, guys," I whisper. "And I'm sorry to do this to you."

"Just make it up with her," Ed replies. "She's good for you."

"Yeah... she is." I'm not gonna argue with him on that one. "I'd better pack... fast." I start toward the back of the restaurant.

"Ready?" Rob says as I come back downstairs. It was hard not to notice that Ali had taken everything with her, except her scent, and my memories, that is. The apartment felt empty without her, and I feel lost.

Rob's got his jacket on, and his keys in his hand. Ed's standing beside him.

"Yeah."

Ed steps forward. "Try and bring Ali back home," he says. "You're a much nicer person when you're with her."

"Thanks."

"No... I mean..." He stumbles over his insults.

"I get what you mean," I tell him. "And I agree with you. Ali makes me a better person. I know that. I can't guarantee I can bring her back though. England is her home, and she has to think about her sister, too. I can't just uproot her from her life."

"Try," he says. "Bring the sister back as well, if you have to."

I laugh. "What do you want me to do? Kidnap them?"

"If necessary, yes." He smirks. "Ali didn't just make you a better person. She helped all of us." He looks around at the restaurant. "Look at this place. We'd never have done this without her."

"I know."

Rob jingles his car keys. "We need to go," he says. "Have you got everything you need?"

"Yeah, I think so."

"Passport?" he asks.

"Yeah."

"Cuffs? Restraints?"

I start and flip my head around toward him. *What do they know?*

Rob's smirking, so I guess he knows everything, and in the grand scheme of contemplating a life without Ali, I wonder if it matters. "Well," he says, "you were talking about kidnapping her… so…"

"Ha fucking ha. Just take me to the airport and stop being a smart-ass."

I say goodbye to Ed, reiterating that he can call me anytime, but that I know he'll be okay, and Rob grabs my bag as we head out the door.

We've been on the freeway for about twenty minutes before Rob breaks the silence in fairly typical fashion.

"Why are you always such a fucking idiot?" he says gruffly.

"It's genetic." I keep looking out through the windshield, but I can feel his glare.

"I'd never have done what you've done, if that's what you're suggesting."

"I'm not suggesting anything. But one day, you're gonna fall in love, and then you'll work out it's not as easy as you think."

"Yeah, I get that, but why couldn't you just be grateful for what you had? Why did you have to fuck it up?"

"I was grateful. I will be grateful… if she'll forgive me and let me have another chance," I tell him. I can't think about the alternative.

"So why did you yell at her?"

"Because I was having a shitty morning, that's all."

"And that's a good enough reason to hurt the woman you love, is it?"

"No," I tell him. "But like I say, one day, you'll find out that love isn't as easy as you seem to think it is."

"I'm not saying it's easy," he replies, reasonably. "I'm just saying you've gotta stop hurting her, or one day you'll push her too far, and she won't come back, Sam, that's all. Is that a risk you're willing to take?"

I don't reply. I don't need to.

The fact that I'm about to fly three thousand miles to apologize is all the answer we both need.

Chapter Fifteen

Ali

Tess puts a cup of coffee in front of me.

"Thanks," I say, looking up at her.

"You look awful."

"Well, I've been up for..." I glance at my watch, but it's still on American time. "I don't know how long I've been up for actually. Too long, anyway."

I didn't sleep on the flight. I took off at five-thirty pm local time, and landed at five am London time. Except I'd just about got used to American time, so to me it felt like midnight when we touched down. Still, I don't think that was the reason for my wakefulness. I couldn't have slept, even if I'd been in the most comfortable bed in the whole world, in total silence, with nothing to disturb me. And I wasn't. I was flying economy class, with a young mother sitting beside me, accompanied by a child, who clearly would have rather been pretty much anywhere else other than on that aircraft. I knew how he felt. Being awake through the long flight just gave me time to think... which was probably the last thing I needed. It gave me time to remember Sam's words, his harshness, the expression on his face as he spoke to me. It gave me time to think about a future like that, and to decide that's not what I want, no matter how much I love him. Unfortunately, it also gave me time to remember the better moments... all the things he did and said, the fish and chips, the rose petals in the bed, the way he looked at me, whispering in my ear, his fingers and thumbs, his heartfelt pleas that we could keep seeing each other… being bound by him, and tied to him…

"Are you okay?" Tess asks, breaking into my thoughts.

"No." She sits on the sofa beside me, but now I can't bring myself to look at her.

"Do you want to talk about it?" she asks.

"Not yet." I take a sip of coffee. "Tell me about the cottage."

She reaches forward to the coffee table, for her laptop. "The agent came back, after I told him to do nothing, like you said."

"And?"

"He said he'd checked out the address the tenants had left for forwarding their mail." She pauses, then adds, "It's false."

"A false address?" I can't believe what I'm hearing. "Didn't James check these people out before renting the place to them?"

"I asked him that and he said he did."

"Yeah. I bet he did." I flop back onto the couch and stare at the ceiling. "So, we've got no way of going after them for the rent they owe, or for whatever damage it is they've done?"

"No. Evidently not."

"And do we know how bad the damage is?"

"No. James wasn't exactly forthcoming about that."

"Great." I'm guessing it's quite bad then, but I don't say that to Tess.

"Sorry." Tess's expression is apologetic, full of self-reproach.

"It's not your fault." I sit forward again and put my arm around her, giving her a squeeze. She smiles across at me and, without warning, I burst into tears. Uncontrollable, wracking tears.

"Oh… Ali," she says, throwing her arms around me. "What's wrong?"

She sounds worried, which is understandable. I never fall apart – not in front of Tess. Not even when Liam did what he did. I might have cried silent tears in my room, but I never showed my heartache to Tess. I'm the brave one. Until now, that is.

"I'm fed up, that's all," I say eventually, sitting back and trying to sound stronger than I feel. "I'm fed up with there always having to be another hurdle to jump… and I'm really fed up with men."

"What does that mean?"

I look up through my tears and see her staring back at me, and I know I have to explain.

"I met someone," I say quietly, sniffing.

She passes me a tissue from the box on the table and I wipe my nose. "Someone in America, I presume?" she says.

"Yes. He was one of the owners of the restaurant." I might have been talking to or texting with Tess every day, but I haven't mentioned anything to her about Sam, not since our early conversations.

"Which one?" she asks, surprised by my admission.

"Sam."

"Wasn't he the one who was horrible to you?"

I nod, the irony of her using the past tense not being lost on me. "Yes."

"But you went out with him?"

"Not exactly. He… he stopped being horrible and we got along a lot better. And… well, we didn't do much actual going out."

She blushes. "Oh… I see."

"I'm sorry I didn't tell you about him," I say, "it's just I wasn't sure where our relationship was going, until yesterday morning."

"And? Where is it going?"

"Well, yesterday morning, when we woke up, I thought it had a future. He asked me if we could keep seeing each other, long term. We both realised it wouldn't be easy, what with me living here and him living there and us both having commitments, but he said we could work it out somehow…" I let my voice fade.

"But?" she asks. "I'm sensing a but…"

"There is. After you called yesterday, I went through to the kitchen, where he was working, and he was… he was absolutely foul to me."

"Why? Because you had to come home early?"

I look at her. "No. It had nothing to do with that. I don't know why he did it, other than someone had dropped a tray of salmon on the floor."

"That wasn't your fault though, was it?"

"No."

"Then I don't understand..."

"Neither do I," I say wearily. "Everything was so perfect... and then it wasn't."

"And you loved him?"

"No. I *love* him." I swallow down more tears. "I don't think Sam's someone you forget in a hurry. If you can forget him at all. He's... he's different."

"In what way?"

I turn away. "It's hard to explain. We... we did things... I did things I've never done before. I let him do things to me I've never even thought of doing with a man before – really intimate things. I—I let him do so much..." I start crying uncontrollably again.

"And you still love him?" Tess whispers.

"Oh God, yes."

"Is that why you let him do those things to you?" she asks. I could almost laugh at her beautiful innocence.

"No, sweetheart," I reply quietly. "That's not how love works. I let him do those things to me because I wanted him to. I enjoyed it, and I loved being with him as well as loving him. I loved him so much, Tess. I still do. I don't think I'll ever stop loving him."

"Do you think he loved you?"

"I suppose I thought he might, yes..." I sit back again and Tess copies me. "Neither of us had actually said anything, but he seemed to care about me." I look across at her.

"Did you speak to him? Ask him why he'd been so horrible again?" she asks.

"No. I was too angry with him. Part of me still is, although I think I'd like to ask him now. I'd like to know what I did to make him like that, and why he thought it was okay to speak to me in the way he did. But I didn't talk to him yesterday because I knew if I did, I'd have ended it with him... and I didn't want to."

"So you're still together?" she asks.

I turn to face her. "I have no idea."

"Why don't you call him?" she asks.

"Because it's the middle of the night over there."

"Well, call him later then."

I shrug. "I'll charge my phone first, and see if he calls me again."

"Again? You mean he's called already?"

"Yes. He called at the airport, but I didn't take the call. And then he sent me several text messages."

"Saying what?" she asks.

"Telling me to wait for him, that we needed to talk."

"That sounds romantic," she says, smiling.

That sums up Tess. Romantic to the core. "Well, it would've done, if he hadn't been so dictatorial. He even sent one telling me not to dare turn my phone off, even though the battery was almost dead and I wanted to hang onto the little bit of life it had, in case of emergencies."

"Oh…"

"Yeah… oh."

"Maybe he was upset," she suggests.

"Maybe he was… but he still owes me an apology."

"Well, if you called him, he could apologise."

"No. He's going to have to call me."

She shakes her head. "That's a bit childish, Ali," she says quietly.

"I know. But I'm feeling childish. He needs to apologise for what he did."

I glance at the clock. It's ten-thirty in the morning… which means it's five-thirty in Hartford and I imagine Sam lying in bed. I wonder how he slept without me… except I don't want to think about that. I don't want to think about him assuming I'll go running back to him, with my tail between my legs, apologising for whatever it is he thinks I did wrong… because that's not going to happen.

"I need a shower," I say, getting up decisively.

"Okay. I'll put your washing in the machine," Tess offers, standing and taking my bag through to the utility room.

"And then I should probably eat something, before I think about driving down to Dorset," I reply. "Although I have no idea what meal it should be."

"Maybe have brunch?" she calls.

"Yeah…" My voice fades as I recall Sam's scrambled eggs, his pancakes, and the French toast he used to make, that we sat together and ate at his kitchen island, usually naked. I close my bedroom door and go through to my bathroom, stripping off my clothes and walking into the shower.

I take my time. The water feels warm and healing… but it can't heal my aching heart.

Sam

I check my watch just as the cab pulls up. It's a few minutes after twelve noon. I feel like I've been awake for days – but then I guess I have, really. I didn't sleep on the flight over here. I couldn't. All I could think about was Ali and how badly I treated her yesterday, how sorry I am for that, and what she must be thinking of me. The thought that she's flown three thousand miles to get away from me has got me more than scared.

"Here you go, mate," the driver says, turning around to me.

I glance up at the building he's parked in front of and suck in a breath.

"Are you sure?" I ask him.

"This is Berresford House," he says. "Why? Is there a problem?"

"It's just not what I expected, that's all." I climb out of the cab and stand by his window to pay him.

"Better or worse than you thought?" he asks.

"Just different," I reply.

He nods and, when I tell him to keep the change, thanks me profusely, before driving away.

I look up at the building. I knew Ali lived in an apartment in North London, and that was all I knew. I didn't expect anything this luxurious. It's all smoked and frosted glass and chrome, with huge balconies and a large doorway right in front of me. I check my phone, where Rob stored the address. It's definitely Berresford House, and the name over the door, etched into the glass confirms that. I shrug and climb up the six steps, pushing the door open and entering into an opulent reception area, with a marble tiled floor. There's a white leather couch off to one side and ahead of me is a curved desk, with a middle-aged man sitting behind it. He's wearing a smart suit and I feel really under-dressed in jeans and a t-shirt, my leather jacket slung over my arm and my bag in my hand. He smiles over at me.

"Can I help you, sir?" he says. His voice is calm and polite, as though he greets people who look like me every day.

"Um… I don't know," I reply. "I'm not sure I've got the right place."

"Well, why don't you tell me who you're looking for and I'll tell you if you're right or not."

I go over to his desk. "I'm trying to find Alison Bishop," I say.

"Then you're in the right place," he says, smiling again and picking up a telephone that's lying on the desk. "I'll just let her know you're here. What name shall I give?"

I hadn't expected this.

"Um…" I lean over, resting on my elbows. "The thing is, I've just come over from the States, and it's a surprise visit. Do you think you could just skip the announcement and let me go on up there?"

I've got a feeling that if this guy lets Ali know I'm here, she may just tell him to remove me from the premises, and then I'll never get to see her.

He hesitates for a moment, then smiles again. "I see," he says, with a twinkle in his eye. "I'm sure we can arrange that." He gets up from behind the desk. "This way, sir," he adds, reaching into his pants pocket for a key that's attached to his belt hook. He's walking over to the elevators, and I follow. He puts the key into a lock between the two elevators and turns it clockwise, pressing the button above at the same time. The doors open immediately and he stands to one side, letting me enter. "You need the fifth floor," he says. "Apartment fifty-two." I glance at the number pad beside the doors, as the man coughs gently. I look back to him. "Good luck, sir," he says, like he somehow knows I fucked up.

*

I exit the elevator and follow the sign for apartments fifty through fifty-three, to my right, passing through a heavy door. I don't have any trouble finding number fifty-two, and I stand outside for a moment, just gathering my thoughts. I need to get this right, because I'm fairly damn sure that, if I don't, Ali will throw me out on my ear and I won't get another chance.

I press the doorbell, which I can hear just quietly ringing inside, and wait.

The door opens, just a fraction and I find myself looking down at a woman I assume to be Ali's sister. She's shorter than Ali, at I'd guess maybe five feet five or six. She's got darker blonde hair and incredibly clear delicate skin. Facially, I can see a few similarities between Tess and her sister. They have the same shape mouth and nose but Tess's eyes are a darker blue and right now, they're really large in her face. She looks like a deer caught in the headlamps of an oncoming truck – which I guess makes me the truck. Overall, the impression I get is that she's fragile… beautiful, but fragile.

"Yes?" she says, her voice barely audible. "Can I help you?"

"I'm looking for Ali," I reply. "Ali Bishop."

"Who is it?" I hear Ali's voice from behind her, and then the door opens a little wider and I see her. She's wearing jeans and a t-shirt. Her hair's damp, so I guess she's just showered, and she's carrying a piece of toast, which is now poised a couple of inches from her open mouth.

"Sam?" she says.

"Yeah."

"What are you doing here?"

"Looking for you."

She swallows, evidently lost for words.

"Would you like to come in?" Tess offers, standing to one side.

"Thanks," I reply, and enter their apartment and, once again, I catch my breath as I look around the hallway, which is probably as big as my living room back home. I had no idea Ali came from this kind of money.

"Um… come on through," Tess says, being as Ali seems to have lost her voice.

Tess leads the way, followed by Ali, and then me, into a living room that defies belief. It's huge. But it's odd. In a space like this, in a building like this, I'd have expected to see modern, angular furniture, instead of which, set against one wall, there's a large, cosy-looking couch in a soft cream color. Placed either side are two matching chairs, which are covered in a dark blue fabric. Over the back of the couch is a patchwork quilt, and I can just imagine Ali curled up with that spread across her legs, reading a book, ideally with her head resting in my lap. On the floor is a sheepskin rug, with a low coffee table set on top. It's a homely enclave in this vast space. The room bends around into an L-shape and, as we go further in, I can see this area is set up as a study – presumably it's where Ali works. The whole of the far wall is made of glass, looking out across London, and there are two enormous bookcases, overflowing with books.

"This is incredible," I say, without really thinking, then turning and looking at Ali, who's still staring at me. I can't take my eyes from her.

"Thanks," Tess replies. "Can I get you a coffee?"

"Thank you. That would be great."

Tess goes back out into the hallway and – I guess – the kitchen, and Ali and I are left alone.

She stares for a moment longer, before blinking and seeming to come back to her senses. There are two plates on the coffee table, with what looks like the remains of bacon and scrambled eggs, and Ali deposits her half-eaten piece of toast on one of them, before going to pick them both up.

"I'll just clear these away," she murmurs.

"No. Leave them."

She glares at me. "Stop it," she says.

"Stop what?"

"Telling me what to do, Sam. You did it earlier. You even did it by text… telling me not to dare to turn my phone off. I'm not yours. You don't own me."

I dump my bag and jacket on the floor where I'm standing and walk over to her, coming to a stop right in front of her and looking down into her eyes. "Did I ever say I owned you?" I ask.

"No. But you keep acting like you do… barking out instructions."

"Then I apologize," I murmur and take a final step toward her. "I'm sorry, Ali." Her eyes widen. "Although you're wrong about one thing."

"Oh? What's that?"

I'm close enough that I can put my mouth by her ear, so I do, and I whisper, "You are mine."

She shudders, and then lets out a moan, and I want to hold her so much, it's all I can do not to take her in my arms. I don't though, because we've still got so much to talk about, and getting physical – which we will if I so much as touch her – isn't gonna help.

Right at that moment, Tess comes back in, carrying a tray with three cups of coffee set out on it. She lays it on the table. "Let me clear these plates," she says, picking them up and taking them through to the kitchen. Ali glances at me, like she's daring me to say something. I don't. I've learned my lesson. Tess comes back into the room again and we all sit down, Ali and I on the couch and Tess on one of the chairs, and an awkward silence ensues.

"You've got a beautiful apartment," I say, desperate to find something to fill the gap.

"It was our father's," Ali replies, and I nod. She's never spoken to me about her family, other than to tell me about Tess, and I wait to see if she's going to say anything else. She doesn't.

"Who's the reader?" I ask, nodding toward the bookcases.

"They're mainly Tess's," Ali says.

"You're at university, aren't you?" I ask Tess, because I'm not getting anywhere with Ali, it seems.

"Yes," she replies, staring at Ali, who looks uncomfortable. This isn't going how I'd thought it would at all. I'd thought I'd be able to sit with Ali, apologize to her, explain what an idiot I'd been and we'd make up. These difficult silences aren't like us at all, not the 'us' I've gotten used to, anyway.

"I'd better drink this and think about going," Ali says, picking up the cup nearest to her.

"Um… going where?" I ask, leaning forward in my seat.

"I've got to go to our house in Dorset."

"You have another house?"

"Yes." This is something else I didn't know, and I'm starting to wonder if I should make a list. "It belonged to our parents."

I notice the past tense, but don't say anything, although I guess their parents must be dead, and I remember Ali telling me that Tess once lived with their grandmother.

"And you need to go there now?" I ask.

"Yes. I suppose I should explain," Ali continues and takes a sip of coffee, looking at me over the rim of the cup. "We have a house in Dorset," she says. "And we rent it out."

"Okay. Um… where's Dorset?" It feels like it would be useful to know that.

"It's in the West Country," she says, like that's meant to help. "Our house is on the outskirts of a small seaside village." She sips her coffee again. "Anyway, Tess was contacted yesterday by the agent who looks after it for us and he told her the tenants had disappeared, without paying the last three months' rent, and that they'd done some damage to the property." Her voice cracks as she finishes the sentence. "Tess and I both love the house," she explains. "And Tess was really upset when she got the message, so she called me."

"In the US?"

"Yes." Ali looks at me. "And I agreed to come back here to deal with it."

"And that's what you came into the kitchen to tell me?"

She nods her head, but doesn't say a word.

"Only I bit your head off."

She shrugs and swallows the last of her coffee. "And now I really should get going. It's a three hour drive… I'm tired, and I need to get there before dark."

She goes to stand, but I pull her back down again. "And this can't wait until tomorrow?" *Until we've had a chance to work things out?*

"No. I just explained. I need to get down there to see what damage has been done."

"In that case, I'm coming with you," I reply. We need to talk still, and besides, I didn't come all this way for a cup of coffee.

"You're what?"

"I'm coming with you," I repeat. "Ali, I've just flown three thousand miles to talk to you. If you're going to Dorset, then I'm coming with you… because I'm sure as hell not going home yet." *Not without you.*

Her mouth drops open and, for a moment, she doesn't say a word.

"Would you like me to help you pack?" Tess offers, and I glance at her and see she's smiling. She seems to be on my side and something tells me I'm gonna like Tess. Ali turns to her.

"No, thanks," she says slowly. "I did it after my shower."

She looks back at me again. "Well, I guess if we're going, we'd better go."

It's a small victory, but after the last twenty-four hours, it still feels like a victory.

Chapter Sixteen

Ali

I've had the windscreen wipers on for the last hour, and there's still at least thirty minutes until we get to the house. So far, we've barely spoken, other than for Sam to comment that he likes my car, which is a BMW X5. I think the silence is mainly because we're both so tired, we're worried we might say the wrong thing and I don't think either of us wants to do that. Neither of us has the energy for any more fighting.

He insisted on carrying our bags down to the garage and loading them onto the back seat, together with our jackets, and then he stood, leaning against the car, while I said goodbye to Tess. She needs the time and space to get her dissertation finished, and it's best if I deal with the damage at the house by myself. If it's bad and Tess sees it, she'll be devastated. As much as I know she needs me, she's better off staying in London.

Even though I keep looking across at him, and I'm aware of him looking at me pretty much all the time, I still can't believe Sam's here, if I'm being honest. He came after me. He flew all this way… for me? For us? I also can't believe how good he looks, despite the tiredness. He still gets to me, just like he always did. Just his whispered words are enough to spark off every nerve in my body, which just goes to show, nothing's changed. It also makes me glad, in a way, that we didn't go into the office and talk yesterday lunchtime, because I know I was too angry to talk sensibly, and I probably would have ended it with him… and I don't want to end it. I really don't. I can't see a way forward right now, and I might feel like I'm floundering in an emotional no man's land, but I don't want us to end.

"Is it much further?" he asks, breaking into my thoughts.

"No. About half an hour, or just under," I tell him, pulling off the dual carriageway. "That's if the traffic isn't too bad."

"We can stop, if you want," he suggests. "You must be getting tired by now."

He's suggested this a few times, and we did stop for coffee twice. "I'm okay," I reply.

"You know, I'd drive if I could."

"Yes, I do. But like I said last time you suggested it, you're not insured."

"Then maybe we should put me on your insurance," he suggests, twisting in his seat slightly, so he's facing me.

"Are you planning on staying that long?" I ask him.

"I'm not planning any of this," he replies. "But it doesn't matter how long I stay this time around. If you're here, I'm definitely gonna be coming back." I glance over at him and see he's smiling. It's really hard not to smile back.

It's early evening when we pull up outside the cottage and, even though the rain has now stopped, I can see from the outside that this isn't going to be good.

"Oh God," I murmur, getting down from the car. Two of the upstairs windows have been smashed and the curtains are soaking and billowing in the wind. "What the hell was James Alexander thinking?"

"Who's James Alexander?" Sam asks, coming around the car and standing next to me, looking up at the house.

"He's the agent, the guy who's supposed to look after this place for us."

"Oh. Can I say he's not going a very good job?"

"Yes, you can. Not that it helps."

"Sorry," he replies.

I lock the car and start up the garden path. "I know Tess told him to do nothing about the house until I got here, but the least he should've done is to secure the place, not just leave it open to the elements like this."

Sam looks around. "I'm surprised no-one noticed and called the cops. Are any of these houses occupied?" he asks. There are two other houses in the lane and they're both in darkness.

I point to the one opposite, which is considerably larger than Waterside. "That's a holiday let," I tell him. "But I guess it's not occupied this week."

"And the other house?" He nods towards Beatrice Evans's house, which is next door to ours.

"The lady who lives there usually goes to Spain to see her son at this time of year," I explain.

"And people don't come down to the beach?" he asks.

"No. It's a private beach, and I'm sure you noticed how the entrance to the lane isn't exactly easy to spot."

He nods and I put the key in the lock, turning it and pushing the door open.

"Jeez," Sam says, and we both put our hands across our mouths and noses. "What's that smell?"

"I have no idea… but I think we're going to find out." We go inside and I close the door behind us, even though it just makes the smell more intense.

I flick on the light switch, but nothing happens. "No power?" he asks.

"There should be."

He turns on the torch on his phone, and shines it up at the light fitting in the middle of the room. "You've probably got power," he says, "but the assholes broke the fitting."

"Marvellous."

We tread gingerly between the broken furniture, torn books and smashed pictures that litter the floor.

"Oh dear God," I whisper, and spotting the remains of a photograph my mother took of the beach at low tide, I burst into tears.

Before I even have time to bend down and pick it up, Sam's arms come around me and he pulls me into a hug, holding me tight and letting me cry against his chest.

"It'll be okay," he murmurs into my hair. "It'll be okay."

As I calm, I look up at him. "How can it be okay?" I ask him. "How can it? Look what they've done..."

"I know," he says, and holds me to him again.

After a while, I pull away, but he keeps hold of my hand and I don't stop him. It's good to feel the reassurance of him in the middle of all this turmoil. "I suppose we'd better take a look at the rest of the place," I say, although I'd much rather just go back out to the car and cry.

"Okay," he replies. "Just watch your step."

He helps me through the mess and down the steps into the kitchen, and once again, I start to cry. The kitchen was always my mother's pride and joy, and it's been destroyed. Even in the near darkness I can see the cupboard doors are hanging off, the crockery and glasses are broken on the floor. There's food lying around in various stages of decay and the smell is even worse in here. I can feel myself retching.

"We need to open a window," Sam says. "I know it's blowing a gale, but we need to get rid of this smell."

He lets go of my hand and goes over to the sink, leaning over and opening the window. The wind blows in, catching my hair and, for a moment, I sense the smell of the sea, before the stench of something decaying overwhelms me again.

"I'm not sure it's helping," I tell him.

"No. We need to come back here in daylight, to see what's causing it." He takes my hand again. "Do you want to go upstairs?" he asks, sounding almost fearful.

"I suppose we have to."

He leads the way up the stairs and we find the three bedrooms in a similar state to the living room. The two at the back are a mess, but the one at the front – the master bedroom – is so much worse. Because this is where the two windows are broken, the room is wet and cold, the wind whistling in through the spaces where the glass should be. I shiver and look around. The bed frame has been smashed and, judging from the smell, I dread to think what's been done on the mattress. I go through to the bathroom. The damage in here is less – thankfully. The only thing I can see that's immediately wrong is that the shower head is hanging loose. At least they didn't smash the glass screen, or the toilet and basin.

"How could they do this?" I ask.

"I don't have an answer to that," Sam replies from behind me and I turn to him.

"I know I don't have the right to ask this," I say softly, "but do you think you could hold me again."

He walks over and pulls me into his arms. "You do have the right to ask," he whispers. "You'll always have the right. And I'll always hold you."

We stand like that for ages, until eventually, the cold gets the better of me and I lean back in his arms, looking up at him.

"I'd better see if I can get hold of an emergency glazier," I suggest, and I pull my phone from my pocket. Tess has sent a message, asking if we've arrived and I tap out a quick reply, telling her that we have, we're fine and I'll call her tomorrow about the house. I can't face telling her tonight. Then I go onto the internet and find the number for a local glazier – one who offers an emergency service. It's going to cost a lot of money for him to come out at this time on a Sunday, but I don't care, and besides, I can't leave the house like this in a storm. I dial the number and wait. A man answers eventually, sounding harassed and I explain the situation.

"There's not a chance today," he says. Judging from the noise, it sounds like he's struggling with something.

"But I've got no glass in the two windows," I explain again.

He sighs. "I'm sorry," he says, more kindly, having clearly sensed I'm close to tears. "It's these winds. I'm snowed under. I'll be able to get to you tomorrow lunchtime."

"Tomorrow lunchtime?" I repeat. "What do I do in the meantime?"

"Have you got any cardboard?" he asks.

"Maybe. I'm not sure."

"Well, see if you can find some… or a bin liner. Tape that over the window on the inside. It'll keep the worst of the weather out for the time being."

"Okay. Thank you."

"I'll be with you tomorrow," he says, sounding a little more reassuring.

I put my phone in my pocket and stare at Sam.

"No dice?" he says.

I shake my head. "He's snowed under because of the storm," I explain. "I guess it's to be expected."

"What did he suggest you do about that?" He points to the broken windows.

"He said to tape some cardboard over them."

"Do you have cardboard?" he asks.

"There might be some in the cupboard under the stairs," I say and we start walking downstairs and back into he kitchen, where I open the cupboard. Sure enough, there are two collapsed cardboard boxes, which I think we can cut to size, together with some packaging tape.

"Now we just need to find the scissors," I say, handing the boxes to Sam. He takes them and looks around the kitchen.

"Where are they normally?" he asks.

"Somewhere in here." I wave my hand around.

He leans the boxes up agains the wall. "Let me look," he says. "There's broken glass everywhere."

"I can find them," I reply, childishly defiant. It's my house – mine and Tess's – and I feel like someone's invaded it, stolen it from us. I want to reclaim it, for her and for me, and I want to do that by myself.

"Let me do it," he says adamantly, and with hindsight, I'm too tired to argue with him over something so petty, so I let him rummage carefully through the debris that's spread out on the kitchen floor. It doesn't take him long to find the scissors, with the aid of his torch, and then we go back upstairs. Luckily, the tape, although old, is still quite sticky and, once Sam's cut the cardboard to size, I put several layers of tape down each side of and we stick it up, in the hope it'll hold against the weather.

Once we've finished, I turn and look around the room. There's no way anyone's going to be sleeping here for the foreseeable future. I look up at Sam and, once more, burst into tears.

Sam

I pull her into my arms again and hold onto her. This has gotta be soul destroying. This place belonged to her parents and, just from the expressions on her face and Tess's when they talk about it, I can tell it means a lot, so to see it like this must be awful. She's sobbing into me again, her tears soaking through my t-shirt and onto my chest.

"Ali?" I whisper, stroking her hair.

She leans back a little and looks up at me. "Yes?"

"Let's go back to the hotel on the main road," I suggest.

"We can't. There's too much to do here."

"None of which we can do in the dark," I reason.

"You go back, if you want," she says, with that same slightly childish pout she had earlier.

"Ali, we're both exhausted. We need to eat, and to sleep and we can't do either of those things here. And then tomorrow, we'll come back together and look at this place in daylight."

"You don't have to do anything, Sam. This isn't your problem. And besides, do you actually think it's gonna look any better in daylight?"

I ignore her first comment. "No." I think it's gonna look a damn sight worse. "But we can't do anything in the dark, baby." She sucks in a breath and leans into me again, sobbing. Is that because I just called her 'baby'? I'm not sure… and I'm not sure about her reaction either, but I can't think about that yet. "C'mon," I say. We need to get out of here. And we really need to talk.

I pull back and take her hand, leading her carefully down the stairs and back into the kitchen, where I close the window. It really stinks in here, but we'll deal with that tomorrow too. She follows me up the few stairs, into the living room, and we pick our way through the debris and to the front door, which I open and let her pass through. I pull it closed and am about to walk away, when Ali puts the key in the lock. I want to tell her there's no point, that the cardboard we've put over the windows hardly poses a barrier to any would-be burglar. But I don't. She's not in the mood for that.

"Do you want me to drive?" I offer as we walk back up the path toward her car.

"You're not insured," she replies, repeating her earlier reason for not letting me take the wheel.

"I'll promise not to hit anything."

She shakes her head. "It's fine. We're only going ten minutes up the road."

She unlocks the car, but I get to the door before her and hold it open for her while she climbs in. "Thank you," she murmurs, as I close it again. I go around to the passenger side and climb in beside her.

She looks beat. "Let me help you," I say quietly, turning to face her.

"I am."

"Really?"

She turns too, and now we're looking directly at each other. "Please. I'm too tired to fight, Sam."

"I'm not gonna fight. I just wanna help."

"And I'm letting you help."

"This is your idea of letting me help?" She sighs and goes to put the key in the ignition. "In that case, why does it feel like you're keeping me at arm's length? We need to talk, Ali," I say.

"Make your mind up, Sam," she replies, angrily. "A minute ago, we needed to go to the hotel to get something to eat, and to sleep… and now you want to talk?"

"Yeah. I do."

She sighs. "Okay… talk."

"What's changed?" I ask her.

"You mean apart from discovering that the house Tess and I love has been destroyed?"

"I mean what's changed between us?"

She looks out of the windshield and I think she's biting her lip. I reach up and flick on the interior light. She's not gonna hide from me. "Everything," she murmurs.

"What? What does that mean?" Fear creeps through me, like a plague.

She turns back to face me and my heart stops. Her eyes are filled with pain and tears and I know it's got nothing to do with her house… which means it's to do with us, and I know that pain and tears aren't good in this situation. "It means you scared me yesterday…" she whispers. "I didn't think you were capable of being that man anymore. Not with me, anyway."

"I'm not."

"Yes you are, Sam. The way you spoke to me, when you told me not to come into your kitchen and talk to you like that… I thought we could say anything to each other… anywhere." Her voice fades.

"I know. And we can. I'm sorry. I got it so wrong yesterday. Please forgive me."

"Until the next time?" she asks, a tear dropping onto her cheek.

"No. There won't be a next time." I reach over and wipe the tear away with my thumb, and she lets me.

"That's easy to say."

"It's easy to mean too. I can't lose you, Ali." I lean toward her. "Please… please don't end it."

"I don't want to," she says. "I really don't. I want to be with you so much." Another tear falls, followed by a third. "But I can't live my life waiting for the next explosion."

I let out a long breath. "There are always gonna be explosions with me, baby," I say, cupping her cheek with my hand. "I'm that kinda guy…"

"Exactly… so you can't promise—"

"You didn't let me finish," I interrupt her. "I was gonna say that I promise you I won't explode at you again."

"How can you make that promise, Sam?" she asks. "How can you be certain you won't?"

"Because I've had a taste of what losing you feels like, and I can't let it happen again. I can't live without you, Ali. I love you."

Chapter Seventeen

Ali

I can't help the small gasp that escapes my mouth. Did he just say 'love'?

I stare across at him, confused beyond belief.

"Why are you saying this?" I ask him.

"Because it's true," he says quietly, his hand still cupped around my face. "I'm in love with you, Ali. I've known for ages, but I'm completely useless at expressing myself. And I was scared you didn't feel the same way, but I'd decided yesterday morning that I was gonna tell you, and to hell with the consequences. I'd planned a romantic dinner in the apartment for tonight, and I was gonna tell you exactly how I feel about you."

I feel his arms come around me and he lifts me onto his lap, holding me against his chest, and despite the fact we've still got a lot of things to talk about and work out, and that my house and my heart are both still wrecked, I really feel like I'm home again.

After a short while, he leans down, his eyes locked with mine.

"May I?" he asks.

"May you what?"

"Kiss you." He doesn't wait for answer, but brushes his lips across mine. Like a bolt of electricity coursing through me, my body comes to life. I open up to him and his tongue moves against mine, urgent and demanding as ever. I've missed this – even if it has been less than forty-eight hours. I need him so much, I'm breathless in an instant and run my hands up behind his head, holding him in place as he deepens the kiss, groaning loudly into him.

He breaks the kiss eventually, sucking my lower lip into his mouth.

"I love you, Ali" he whispers.

"I love you, Sam." I look up at him.

He leans back, staring at me. "You do?" He's surprised?

"Yes."

He grins, pulling me closer again. "Since when?"

"I'd suspected it for a while, but I knew for sure after you first made love to me."

He chuckles. "There I was being trying to be romantic," he says, "and you just wanted my body."

"Pretty much, yeah."

He kisses me again, his tongue delving deep inside my mouth, claiming me, making me his again.

"Does it bother you?" I ask him, teasing.

"What?"

"That I just want your body."

"Hell, no." He laughs and kisses me once more.

"I was going to tell you too," I admit, once he breaks the kiss. I'm being more serious now.

"When?"

"Saturday. Yesterday? I've lost track of the days now." I lean my head on his shoulder. "I'm so tired."

"I know you are." He kisses the top of my head. "Why didn't you tell me?" he asks.

"Tess called. And I came into the kitchen to tell you about her call, and that I was going to have to leave, and that we needed to talk… because I wanted to tell you how I feel about you…"

"And I yelled at you… because I'm an idiot."

"You did scare me Sam," I whisper.

"I know. And I'm sorry." He leans back and raises my face to his. "If I tell you I'm sorry every day for the rest of my life, will you forgive me?"

"You don't have to do that. I know you're sorry."

"And do you forgive me?"

"I'll try." He raises an eyebrow. "I'm going to take a while to forget what you said, Sam."

"I know." He looks so contrite.

"It's okay," I whisper, leaning back into him. "I may still be a little confused, and wary, but I do love you."

"I love you too, baby."

I take a breath. "You need to understand the consequences of what you do, and what you say. You made me feel like my world was falling apart, Sam."

"I'm sorry, baby," he says.

"I don't want to feel like that again."

"You won't. I won't ever make you feel like that again."

"Good. I didn't like it." I lean up and kiss him. "Can we go to the hotel now?" I ask him and he smiles.

"Yeah. Although I still think you should let me drive," he says, even as he's putting me back in the driver's seat

"Like I said, you're not insured." I start the engine and execute a perfect three-point turn.

"Then we're getting me insured," he reiterates. "Aside from the fact that you're exhausted. I hate being driven."

"Really?" I say, glancing across at him. "I'd never have guessed."

Sam

Despite my words, I have to say, Ali's a very good driver and my concern about her driving had a lot more to do with her tiredness than any worries about her ability behind the wheel.

"I liked your sister," I say as we get to the end of the lane and she turns out onto the main road. I want to make conversation with her, but I also want her to stay awake, even though it's just a short journey.

A smile forms on her lips. "I think she liked you too. She certainly seemed very willing to help out."

"Yeah. I noticed."

Ali shakes her head. "I can't believe she offered to pack my bags for me."

I chuckle. "She wasn't exactly subtle."

"Well, I suppose she knew how I feel about you, so…" she falls silent and bites her lip.

"So?" I prompt.

"Sorry."

"Why are you sorry?"

She glances at me. "Because I told her I love you before I told you."

I reach over and put my hand on her thigh, giving her a light squeeze. "It's okay… I kinda told Rob and Ed too."

"You did?" She flips her head round to me, then swerves the car and I grab the steering wheel.

"Are you okay?" I ask, letting go again and putting my hand back on her leg.

"Yes… I'm just shocked, that's all. I wouldn't have thought you'd be the type to discuss your feelings with your brothers."

"I'm not. They guessed. I just confirmed it. I've never been in love before, and I think they noticed there was something different this time."

She nods her head. "That makes a lot more sense than you sitting down and having a heart-to-heart with them."

"Yeah… that's probably not my style. Certainly not with Rob, anyway."

"It's a shame it took us so long to get there ourselves," she whispers, just as she pulls off the roundabout and into the hotel parking lot.

"We got there in the end, baby. That's what matters." She parks up fairly near the door, and turns off the engine, and for a moment we both just look at each other.

"I guess we'd better go in," she says eventually. "If we want to eat before going to bed."

I'm not sure I do. Right now, I'd rather just take her to bed and forget the last forty-eight hours ever happened, but I guess food is probably a good idea.

"Okay," I reply and I lean over and give her a quick kiss, before getting out and going around to her side. She's already opened the door, but I help her down and then grab the bags from the back seat. Ali leads the way in and goes straight over to the reception desk. A middle-aged woman is standing behind it and looks up, smiling at us.

"Good evening," she says, with an accent I've never heard before.

"Can we have a room, please?" Ali says.

"Certainly. Just the one?" She looks at me, then back at Ali.

"Yes," I say quickly.

"Double or twin?" she asks.

"Double," I reply again.

Ali turns to me and raises an eyebrow. I smile at her and after a moment, she smiles back. The woman taps a few keys on her computer.

"I'll need a credit or debit card," the woman says, looking to me, then back at Ali.

I drop the bags and reach for my wallet, but Ali gets there first, handing over a card.

"Seriously?" I look down at her.

"Yes." She looks like she wants to laugh and, although I'm not happy, I'd rather see that than her tears.

"You know they don't charge the card until we leave, right?" I say to her. "I can always switch it with one of mine…"

She shrugs. "If it matters that much to you," she murmurs.

"Yeah. It does."

The woman behind the desk is still holding Ali's card, looking from her to me.

"Take his," Ali says to her, and I reach into my back pocket, giving the woman my credit card. She gives Ali back hers and she shakes her head, replacing it in her purse.

"Thank you," I murmur, leaning down and kissing her cheek.

When I glance up again, I notice the woman is tapping on her keyboard once more, but she's smiling to herself.

"Shall I book the room in this name?" she asks, waving the card at us.

"Why not?" Ali says, looking up at me. I half expect her to be angry again, but there's a glint in her eye. "I'd hate to emasculate my boyfriend any more than I have already," she adds.

I almost choke and cover it by coughing, which makes her laugh.

"Are you alright?" she asks.

"Yeah," I manage to say eventually.

The woman – still smiling to herself – turns and offers Ali a key, which she accepts.

"Would you like dinner?" she asks.

"Yes please," Ali replies. I'm still clearing my throat and can't speak properly yet.

"You'll need to be quick," the woman says. "As it's Sunday, we stop serving at eight-thirty."

"Okay. We'll drop the bags and come straight back down."

We climb the stairs to the next floor and Ali leads the way along the corridor to the room, opening the door and letting me pass through with the bags, which I dump beside the bed.

"Am I in trouble?" she asks, her lips twisting into a smile.

"No. And I'm certainly not gonna yell at you, if that's what you're thinking. I told you I wouldn't and I meant it. But you called me your boyfriend, so of course you're not in trouble."

"Well, we are sharing a room. What else was I going to call you?"

Disappointment overwhelms me. "So, that was just for the receptionist's benefit?"

She moves closer, and rests her hand on my chest. "No, not entirely," she says.

I can actually feel my heart expand and pull her into my arms, holding her close.

"We really have to go straight back down?" I ask her, running my fingertips gently down her cheek.

"Well yes, if we want to eat."

"I'm not sure I do want to eat… not food, anyway."

She looks up at me. "Hmm. Maybe we should have got separate rooms after all," she says.

I place my feet either side of hers, staring down into her eyes. "Like hell we should." I clasp her chin in my hand, and kiss her really hard, taking what I need from her and giving her everything I think she needs in return. And I know I've got it right, because within seconds, her breathing changes. She's panting, moaning and arching her back into me, her breasts pushing against my chest. I grind my hips into her, letting her feel my erection, and she groans louder still. "You still want separate rooms?" I whisper, breaking the kiss.

"No." She looks into my eyes. "But I'm not sure I can just go straight back to where we were yesterday morning."

"Okay. I understand that. But I still want to sleep with you, Ali. I want to hold you in my arms. I want to wake up beside you and, whenever you're ready, I want to make love to you again." She sucks in a breath and bites her bottom lip. "Stop that," I tell her.

"What?"

"Being so fucking sexy."

"But I'm not doing anything," she whispers.

"Yeah, you are."

"Well, I'm not doing anything intentionally."

"I know. That's what's so fucking sexy." She giggles. "C'mon," I say, and I grab her hand, pulling her from the room.

The menu is – as Ali would put it – dull, but we're both too tired to care, and order the steak. It seems safe.

While we're waiting, and sipping on a glass of average red wine, we both make comments – none of which are too favorable – about the decor, and what we'd do to make it better. I like her ideas; they're stylish, like her. Once we've exhausted that topic, and had a few laughs, I bring up the subject of her apartment in London. "It was bigger than I expected," I tell her, after having explained how I got her address from Rob. "So…it belonged to your father?" I'm digging… well, actually I'm mining. But that's because today I discovered how little I know about her, and how much more I want to know.

She lets her eyes drop to her wine glass, twirling it in her fingers. "Yes, it did." She goes quiet for a moment, then adds, "Our parents are dead," her voice a barely audible whisper.

"I'm sorry."

She looks up again. "It was a long time ago." She looks like she's about to say more when the waitress bring over our food. She flutters her eyelashes at me a few times and takes way too long putting my plate down in front of me, but I ignore her and she leaves again. I glance down at the dishes in front of us.

"Don't be a chef," Ali pleads.

"I'll do my best."

It's a struggle, but I manage to make it through the mediocre meal without actually criticizing anything, although every time I look up at Ali, I can tell she's trying hard not to laugh.

We've almost finished when her phone buzzes. She's put it beside her on the table and she presses a button, looking at her messages.

"Is it Tess?" I ask her.

"No. It's Rob." She picks up the phone, intrigued.

"Rob?" I'm intrigued too now. "What does he want?"

"Um… Petra's contact details."

"Petra? The photographer?"

"Yes." Ali looks up at me. "You thought he was interested in her, didn't you?"

"Yeah, both Ed and I did. Why?"

"Well, she should have finished the shoot hours ago and I'm sure if there was a problem she'd have called me – or Rob would. I'm wondering if he's asking for her details for some other reason."

"Like the fact that he's interested, you mean?" I reply, smiling over at her.

She hesitates, twisting her phone in her hands. "The thing is," she says quietly, leaning closer, "Petra's really nice, and… well, Rob's a bit of a flirt."

"That's putting it mildly," I interject.

"It's just… I mean, I don't know her that well, but I don't think she'd be into one night stands. And that's pretty much what Rob does, isn't it?"

"Yeah. It's all Rob does."

"I don't want him to hurt her, Sam," she murmurs. "But what do I say to him…?"

"Hang on," I say and reach into my back pocket, pulling out my own phone. I type out a quick message to my brother.

— Ali can't ask you this, but are you fooling around with Petra, or are you actually serious for once? S

"What have you done?" Ali asks me as I put my phone down on the table.

"I've just asked him whether he's planning on messing her around."

"What? Just like that?"

"Yeah. That's kind of how we speak to each other. Rob and I, anyway. It's kinda different with Ed. He's a bit more… sensitive."

My phone beeps and I pick it up, reading his reply:

— I'm serious this time. She's different. R

"Well, I'll be…"

"What?" Ali asks.

"He's serious about her," I reply, looking up.

"So you think it's okay to give him her details?"

"Yeah."

She taps on her screen a few times, before replacing it on the table again. "Done," she says.

We both sit back, but neither of us continues to eat. I think we've both had enough now, although I'm not sure whether that's because the food is so average, or because we're so tired. Within a couple of minutes, our phones beep again, almost simultaneously.

I pick up mine and glance down at the screen. His message is a little longer this time.

— Thanks for persuading your girlfriend to help me out. And sorry I tried to stop you from going after Ali. Why didn't you tell me it was like this? R

I smile at his use of the word 'girlfriend', but I don't bother to reply; I think he'll probably be busy himself.

I glance up at Ali, and my breath catches in my throat. She's gone white.

"What's wrong?" I ask her.

She raises her eyes to mine and I see the tears welling there.

"Ali? What's wrong?"

"I don't know, Sam," she says, really quietly. "You tell me."

She hands me her phone and gets up, walking quickly away from the table. I stare at her for a second, and then look down at her phone in my hand, and for the umpteenth time in the last two days, I feel like my life's disintegrating. The message is from Rob.

— Thanks Ali. You're obviously with Sam, and I'm glad the two of you caught up, and presumably made up. I'm sure he's told you about his disastrous first marriage… I'm absolutely certain his second one will be better ;) Take care of each other, and see you soon. Rob x

I don't even hesitate. I grab my phone and run out of the restaurant and up the stairs.

Chapter Eighteen

Ali

I walk as quickly as I can out of the restaurant, and then I run.

And I don't stop running until I get to our room. The problem is, I'm shaking so much, I can't get the key into the lock.

"Let me." Sam's voice echoes through my body just as his hand comes down over mine and he turns the key and opens the door.

I go inside and then turn to face him, just as he's closing the door again. "You were married?" I ask, walking backwards and feeling behind me for the bed, then sitting down on it.

"Yes," he says simply.

"And when were you going to tell me this?"

He shrugs. "I don't know. I've just been enjoying being with you so much…"

"Were you ever going to tell me?" I interrupt. "Or are you another liar?"

He looks confused. "Of course I was going to tell you. It's just not something I like talking about."

I feel myself shiver. "Why? Are you still in love with her?"

He chuckles but there's no humour in it. "Hell no. I never was."

I want to laugh, but I can't. "Well, that's ridiculous. You married her, so you must've been."

"Not necessarily." He steps further into the room.

"Stay where you are," I snap, and he does, although is eyes are wary. "How do you end up married to someone you're not in love with… you, of all people?"

He sighs. "I'm exhausted, Ali. If I'm gonna tell this story, can I at least sit down?" He nods towards the chair by the window.

"Yes."

He walks over slowly and sits down, and I twist on the bed and face him, my legs tucked up underneath me.

He looks over to me, his eyes filled with such confusion, but beneath that, there's an underlying honesty and I know whatever he's going to tell me, it's going to be the truth, and it's going to be hard for him. "I met Amber when I was twenty-six and she was twenty, although I didn't know that at the time. I thought she was older."

"You didn't bother to ask how old she was?"

"I didn't bother to ask her name to start with."

"What does that mean?"

He swallows hard. "You really wanna know?"

"Yes."

"It means I had sex with her within ten minutes of meeting her, and a couple of times after that, without even knowing her name, Ali." I can't hold in my gasp and he looks away, focusing on the fireplace. "I'm not proud of the way I behaved, but I wasn't her first," he adds, his voice a distant whisper, "and in my defence, she instigated it." He sighs. "She was good at instigating things."

And he let her? Sam let her instigate things? She must've been special. My eyes fill with tears at that thought.

He focuses on me again, his head tilting to one side. "Don't cry," he murmurs.

"How can I not?"

"Because you don't understand."

"Then explain it," I tell him.

"You want me to?" he asks.

"I need you to, Sam."

He nods his head slowly, then thinks before he starts speaking. "My relationship with Amber wasn't normal right from the beginning. Even by my standards, it wasn't normal. It consisted of two things – fighting and…" He pauses.

"And what?"

"Fucking," he says and I suck in a breath. "The two were pretty much always connected," he continues. "It was how she operated."

"Is that why you argued with me so much at the beginning?" I ask, although I can barely hear my own voice now.

He gets up and comes over to the bed, sitting on the edge and twisting to face me.

"No, Ali. No. Not at all. I was confused by you. I didn't understand my reactions… my emotions. I wanted you from the very first time I saw you. I was just being a stubborn ass. It's one of my stronger character traits, in case you haven't noticed. I like getting my own way; I didn't like the fact that Rob had brought you in without consulting me and Ed first, and I resented you – especially when it transpired you were so damned good at everything. Hell, you even cook better than me."

"No I don't," I mutter.

"Yeah, you do. I just didn't want to admit it." He takes a deep breath. "I was scared of how I was reacting to you, of how I felt about you. I got it so wrong with you before we got together. I never meant the things I said to you and I never, ever meant to hurt you. Being with you was so different to being with Amber. I wasn't fighting you in the same way at all. If anything, my battles with you were battles against myself, and you were the collateral damage. I'll always regret that."

I stare at him for a moment, trying to take on board everything he's saying, while still remembering he's been married, and that he neglected to tell me.

"So, you used to fight? You and… Amber?"

"Yes. She used to start fights with me."

"Why?"

"Because it always led to us having sex," he whispers sheepishly.

"Always?"

He nods his head.

"And you let her do that? You let her instigate things like that, knowing where it would lead?"

He shrugs. "It wasn't really a question of letting her. She wasn't that kind of person."

I shake my head. "I'm sorry," I murmur. "I'm just struggling with the concept of you giving anyone that much control."

"Believe me, I struggled with it too. Remember? I told you there was one woman who tried to control me?"

"That was Amber?"

"Yes. I also told you… it didn't work out."

"But if she was like that from the beginning, why did you marry her?"

"It was a mistake. We were young, stupid, impulsive. It was all way too fast… It was just about sex."

"Good sex, presumably," I murmur, curling in on myself a little, because I don't want to hear his answer. I don't want to hear how good she was.

"I guess it was," he murmurs and I feel the pain take root in my chest. "At the beginning at least, although she wasn't right for me in all kinds of ways. But whether it was good or not, it was nothing compared to you." I look up at him. He's staring at me, with so much love in his eyes it takes my breath away. "You're so different; you're different in *every* way… I'm in love with you, Ali. And no matter what mistakes I made with her, I never loved her… I got that bit right."

"And yet, you still married her," I whisper. I can't get my head around that fact. "You don't seem the marrying kind in the first place, but to marry someone who didn't fit in with your… your way of doing things, it just feels all wrong."

"It was all wrong." He looks down at his hands. "But I think I saw her as a challenge," he admits.

"In what way?"

"I thought I could… change her," he says.

I stare at him. Is that what he wants from me? Does he want to change me too… to make me become more accommodating of his ways? I've told him already that I like doing things his way, but I don't think I could do it all the time. I'm just not built that way. I thought he understood…

"Why?" I ask him. "People don't change; not in that way."

"Yeah. I know they don't." He seems sad.

"I'm sorry, Sam, but I still don't understand."

"What don't you understand?"

"Any of it. You say you didn't love her—"

"I didn't," he interrupts.

"You say she was just a challenge, and it was a mistake," I continue, ignoring his interruption. "But what I don't understand is why someone like you would propose in the first place… to someone you knew was wrong for you."

"I can't explain it, other than to tell you what I already have."

"So, you went down on one knee and proposed… on a whim?"

"No, Ali. It wasn't like that."

"Then how was it?"

"We were in bed. It was at a um… critical moment. I wasn't thinking straight."

I can't reply for a minute. "You could've changed your mind, backed down…"

"You might have noticed, I'm not a 'backing down' kind of guy, any more than I'm a 'getting down on one knee' kind of guy," he says, attempting a smile.

I can't return it. "No. No, you're not." I sigh.

"If it's any consolation, Rob and Ed thought I was making a huge mistake too," he reasons. "They tried real hard to talk me out of it. Rob especially. He was adamant I was being an idiot, and I should dump her. I didn't listen, of course. Not because I was madly in love with her or anything like that, but because I'm a stubborn asshole." He pauses. "We've never talked about it, but it wouldn't surprise me to learn that Amber tried something with him too."

I stare at him. "Excuse me? What do you mean?"

"Amber cheated, Ali. She had an affair with her boss."

I move a little closer to him. "So you didn't split up because she wouldn't adapt to your lifestyle?" For some reason, that makes me feel more optimistic about our future – assuming we still have one.

He shakes his head. "No, of course not. I wasn't remotely happy with her, but I'd have stuck with it and tried to see it through. We made vows. I intended to stick to them. She didn't."

"So you divorced her?"

"Yes. I packed her bags once I found out about the affair. She threw a nice parting shot that he was better in bed than me, and that was it. As far as I was concerned, we were through. I filed for a divorce the next day. My parents didn't disguise their disappointment in me. They still don't. They wanted me to try again with her."

"They liked her?" I ask.

"No. Not particularly. They just don't believe in divorce."

"Even when you're unhappy?"

"They don't think there's anything that can't be saved, if you try hard enough."

"And you?" I ask him.

"It wasn't worth trying. I had nothing with her that was worth saving." He twists a little further around and moves closer to me. "I kind of went into hibernation after that… But you woke me up again, Ali," he says gently. " You brought me back to life. I thought I'd lost that part of myself forever, until I saw you."

"Is it just about sex for us too then? It's just a physical attraction?"

"No. I mean obviously I'm attracted to you, but it's about love, not sex." He sighs and runs his fingers through his hair. "I thought you got that. I told you over and over how different you are. Maybe not in so many words, but you knew I'd never kissed anyone before you, never had a date, never just sat and talked. I'd never made any real effort at all. If I'd come across anyone else crying over being homesick, I'd have told them to pull themselves together, not tried to make them feel better." I smile, because I can't help remembering the fish and chips. "If anyone in the kitchen had burnt their hands, I'd have thrown them the first aid kit and left them to get on with it. I sure as hell wouldn't have sat freezing my own hands off for nearly an hour. I was an inconsiderate, selfish son-of-a-bitch. I was used to doing things my way, Ali. But you made me change." He kneels up on the bed and crawls over to me, so we're inches apart. "When you left Rosa's on Saturday lunchtime, for a little while, I faced the awful reality of life without you. I didn't like it. I couldn't imagine waking up and you not being by my side. I couldn't imagine going to sleep and not having you in my arms.

I couldn't imagine never kissing you, or holding you again. Or never seeing your smile, or hearing your voice, or kissing away your tears. And none of that has anything to do with sex, Ali. It's just about you. I have to be with you. I can't lose you…" His voice cracks on the last two words and I close the gap, leaning into him.

Sam

I pull her close, holding her.

"You're mine," I whisper into her ear and she shudders against me, letting out a long sigh. I know exactly what that means, but I'm not gonna react. She's not ready yet.

She leans back and looks up into my eyes. "Tell me she's in the past," she whispers and I can feel her fear, even if it is completely unfounded. I guess I need to work on that…

"She's in the past, baby. I promise, you're everything I want."

"Sure?"

"Absolutely positive. Don't ever doubt that."

She nods her head slowly. "Sorry I ran out on you," she says.

"Which time?" I ask, smiling down at her.

"Downstairs," she clarifies. "It was just such a shock, reading it like that."

"I know. I'm probably gonna kill Rob."

"It's not his fault."

"No. It's mine. I should've told you before now. I was just so happy. I didn't want to spoil it by talking about my ex."

"Talking about something in the past doesn't mean we can't still be happy now, does it?" she asks, sounding doubtful.

"No. No, of course it doesn't," I reassure her. "It was just a timing thing… honestly."

"You weren't hiding anything from me?" She's still uncertain about that?

"I'm not hiding anything from you, Ali. I promise."

"Okay," she whispers, lowering her head.

I lean down to kiss her, but she pulls back. "It's nearly eleven o'clock," she says. "We really should get to bed…" She breaks away from me and shifts to the other side of the bed, getting to her feet. I'm guessing she wants to sleep, rather than make love and I have to respect that, even though I want her more than I ever have.

"Do you wanna go to the bathroom first?" I suggest.

She nods her head and, before I can say anything else, disappears through the door in the corner of the room, closing it behind her. I put our bags on the ottoman at the end of the bed and unzip mine. I can hear her brushing her teeth and water running and, within a few minutes, she's back out.

"Your turn," she says, a little too brightly. Something's still clearly wrong, but I can't push her, so I just go into the bathroom, closing the door behind me.

This is so surreal. Back home, she was never like this. We were always able to talk. Hell, she spent an entire evening after work telling me about her worries over my lifestyle, and she didn't hold back. And there was none of this getting undressed separately, either. She was never ashamed of her nakedness, or mine. The things she did with me, and to me – and the things she let me do to her – left me in no doubt that she was comfortable with her body. Now though, she seems embarrassed, shy even. I'm gonna have to work this out with her, but not tonight.

I give her what I think is long enough to get undressed and into bed before coming back out into the bedroom. She's already in bed, with the comforter pulled up to her chin. *Christ… since when, Ali?* I undress quickly, down to my shorts, and sit on the edge of the bed, turning to face her.

"Are you okay with me sleeping with you?" I ask her. That's not a sentence that's ever left my lips before, and I hope it never does again. "If not, I can sleep on the floor."

She doesn't reply, but pulls back the covers on my side, while holding hers in place.

I guess that's something. I stand and pull off my shorts, my erection obvious, and she sucks in a breath as I climb into the bed beside her and pull up the covers again.

I look over to her. "Can I hold you?" I ask her.

Again, she doesn't say a word, but she moves over toward me and I put my arm around her, pulling her close. She's not wearing anything, which kind of surprises me. After the way she's just been behaving, I'd have expected her to have put on a t-shirt, or some pajamas. She rests her head on my chest and her arm comes across my stomach, just lying there. I pull her closer, knowing she's already asleep.

I lie still, holding her, feeling her soft skin against mine, wondering how so much can change in so little time. Just yesterday morning, we lay in my bed at home, naked and wrapped up in each other, talking through how we were going to keep our relationship going with an ocean between us, both entirely certain that we could, and then she invited me into the shower, with spectacular consequences. And now? Although she's in my arms, we may as well be on a different continents.

I wonder if hearing my story has made her nervous. I wonder if she thinks I'll expect her to change, like I did Amber, and maybe want to be more controlling, want to do things 'my way' all the time. That's not going to happen. It's never going to happen. I don't want to change a single hair on Ali's head. She's perfect, exactly as she is. The only thing that needs to change in our relationship is me. I need to be more tolerant, less demanding, *less* controlling… a lot less 'Sam'. I can't be that guy anymore. I can't risk losing her again. I've gotta change and be better… be the kind of guy she wants. There can't be any more 'my way', because from now on, it's about her. Always. And if that's what it takes to keep her happy, to keep her with me, then I'll do it. I'll give up everything for her, including myself.

When I wake, it's not quite light. I check my watch, which I kept on, and see that it's six am. I still feel tired, but I guess that's not surprising, my body clock is all over the place and so is Ali's, I imagine. Her legs are entwined around mine, our bodies fused. I'm still bone hard, but I think I might have been all night. I shift slightly, moving my hand down her back and she wakes.

"Hello," I say and lean down to kiss her.

She pulls away again, just like last night, only this time, she pushes against my chest too.

"What's wrong?" I ask. We need to get to the bottom of this. Now.

"I had a dream," she says, staring at a point over my shoulder, vaguely in the direction of the window.

"Okay. Wanna tell me about it?"

She looks at me now. "You got back together with your ex-wife," she says simply.

"That's not a dream, babe. That's a fucking nightmare. And it's never happening. Ever."

"Sam," she continues, seriously, "be completely honest with me. Do you still have any feelings for her."

"I'm always honest with you, and no, I don't. I never did. I never loved Amber."

She sighs and I know we need to talk this through, because she's not telling me everything.

"What's worrying you?" I ask her.

"If we get back together..." she says and I feel my blood turn to ice. She told me she loved me; she called me her boyfriend, we just spent the night together – even if we didn't make love – and yet us being together is still an 'if'? "... our relationship is going to be long-distance. I'm scared you'll get bored waiting around for me, that you'll find someone else. Maybe someone who's better at this lifestyle of yours than I am."

"Okay," I say, making an effort to stay calm and not sound too much like the man I'm trying not to be. "Firstly, us getting back together is not an 'if'." I need to get that straight. "We never broke up, not as far as I'm concerned, so we don't need to get back together. Secondly, you're my life, so my *lifestyle* is irrelevant." I'm not ready to tell her yet that my 'lifestyle' is a thing of the past. She'll find out soon enough. "And, like I told you yesterday, our relationship isn't just about sex," I continue, "so if I can't be with you for whatever reason, then I'll just wait until I can. I love you, Ali. And falling in love with you had nothing to do with sex, nothing whatsoever."

"It didn't?"

"No. I was attracted to you from the moment I first saw you, but think I realized I was falling for you when you were crying into your fish and chips in the apartment that Sunday evening, and I knew for sure when you were crying over your burned hands."

"So it's got everything to do with me crying then," she says, the corners of her lips twitching up into a smile.

"Yeah, and the fact that I wanted you not to."

"But I must've looked horrendous – both times."

"Which also shows you that falling in love with you had nothing to do with how you think you look. To me, you looked beautiful. But it was never about that. It was about how you made me feel. Seeing you in pain hurt me – and I mean *really* hurt me. I'd never experienced anything like that before in my life. And then being with you, talking to you, watching you, holding you… well it made me feel alive, Ali, for the first time in my life." I pull her closer again and she lets me. "No matter what you dream about," I tell her, "I'm not gonna leave you. Ever." She brings her hands up and rests them on my arms, clinging to me. "Can I ask you something?" I say eventually.

"Yes," she murmurs into my chest.

"Can you tell me who it was that hurt you?"

She stiffens, but I keep hold of her. "Who said anyone hurt me?"

"You did," I reply and she raises her eyebrows. "Last night, when I chased you up here, you asked if I was 'another liar'. I didn't query it at the time, because I didn't want you to think I was trying to deflect the conversation away from talking about Amber, but I'm guessing someone – some guy – lied to you, and hurt you. My question is, why don't you want me to know about it?"

She sighs. "Because I was stupid. Because I let him use me, and I was too dumb to see what he was doing."

"What was he doing?" I ask.

"Living a double life," she replies. I wonder what that means and I wait for her continue. "His name was Liam," she says eventually. "I thought he was the man I was meant to be with. He kind of swept me off my feet. He was romantic, charming, sweet and very loving." I'm not sure I like the sound of this, but I bite my tongue… "He made me think I was the only woman in the world." She sighs and closes her eyes. "He was good at gestures," she adds.

"What happened?" I'd prefer to cut to the chase, I think, rather than hearing any more about Mr Perfect.

"He came to see me one day, just over a year ago, and told me he'd been seeing someone else."

"He cheated?" Dumb son-of-a-bitch.

"Well, not exactly. Not like Amber. He'd been seeing this woman – Fiona – for pretty much the whole time we'd been together. He lived with me and Tess for part of the week, and told me that he had to travel on business the rest of the time, but he was actually living with Fiona for those days. It meant we never saw him at weekends, because those were her days."

"And he told you about this?"

"He had no choice. He got Fiona pregnant, and decided to propose to her. He told me he thought it was the decent thing to do."

"Decent?" I can't hide my surprise at the guy's idea of appropriate behavior.

"Evidently, yes."

"He hurt you," I murmur. I don't like the way that makes me feel. The realization that she loved the guy enough to let him hurt her makes me feel less important, somehow. Let's face it, all Amber did to me was bruise my ego…

"Yes, but after I met you, I understood it better."

"You did?" What's she saying?

"Yes. I realized then that I'd never loved him. Not really." She pauses, looking up at me. "And I love you so much, Sam." Her voice cracks a little with emotion.

I smile at her, feeling like, in bearing our souls about the past, we're finally getting somewhere at last. "Good." I move us both down the bed a little. "I'll never ever betray you, Ali. I hate the idea that you flew three thousand miles to get away from me, and I don't want you to ever do that again. Whatever happens, if I fuck up in the future for any reason, you've gotta promise me you'll talk to me, not run from me."

She doesn't reply, but I'm not sure she can. Instead she nods her head and I hold her real close, feeling her body along the length of mine as she lets out a soft sigh. I know we've still got things to talk through; there's a lot I still don't know about her, and I need to reassure her that I don't expect anything from her, and that I certainly don't want her to change, but that can all wait for now. At the moment, I just need to kiss her.

Chapter Nineteen

Ali

He leans down and kisses me gently, just tentatively to start with, but it doesn't take him a moment to build it to something a lot more passionate, and soon we're rolling around, touching each other, breathing hard, whispering 'I love you' between kisses. It's intense and wonderful. We've never done anything like this before, and I really like it.

He rolls onto his back, with me on top, kissing me hard, holding my head with one hand, the other resting on my behind, and then he leans back into the pillow, pulling away from me.

"Take me," he mutters.

I look down at him. He can't mean that… "Sorry?"

"Take me, Ali."

I sit up slightly and stare into his eyes. "You don't mean that, Sam. You know you don't. You already told me you hate it when women go on top."

"Take me," he repeats.

We lock eyes and I can see he really does mean this. I suppose it's maybe his way of saying we're different. *I'm* different. I hope so.

I sit up completely, moving down his body, and straddle his hips. He places his hands on my waist and lifts me over his erection, which seems even bigger than usual to me. Then he lowers me down and I feel that familiar stretch. I close my eyes and let my head rock back as he slides me down his length, filling me entirely. The sensation is breathtaking. Once he's completely inside me, he lets me go, resting his hands on my thighs.

"Take me," he says once more and I look back at him. His eyes are still fixed on me, focused on my face as I start to move. He closes his eyes for a moment, and I wonder if he's finding this too difficult, but nonetheless I keep moving up and down the length of his shaft, and when he opens them again, the look he gives me is so hot. He reaches forward and takes my nipples between the thumb and forefinger of each hand, and pinches. I squeal as a bolt of pleasure shoots straight down between my legs.

"Oh, God… that's good," I manage to say between clenched teeth.

"More?" He smiles up at me.

"Yes, more." I nod my head, riding him just a little harder.

He pinches again and I throw my head back, moaning in ecstasy. Then, keeping his left hand on my breast, he moves his right downward, and starts rubbing over my clitoris with his thumb.

"Come for me," he murmurs softly, pinching my nipple once more. "Let me feel you come, baby."

The sensations, combined with his words are too much, and my body obeys his command, tipping over the edge, the waves of pleasure washing over and over me while I grind my hips onto him, taking him as deep as I can.

Before I've even calmed, and without pulling out of me, he flips us over, so I'm on my back and he's between my legs. Then, leaning up and looking down at me, with just a second's pause, he begins to move, really fast, hard and deep. I bring my legs up higher, wrapping them around his waist.

He groans loudly and looks down at me. "You're gonna make me come if you keep that up," he whispers.

"Good." I feel another orgasm building already. "Me too."

His eyes sparkle into mine. "I wanna watch you come again," he murmurs, swivelling his hips into me so his cock rubs against the front wall of my vagina. After just a few more strokes of that, I'm gone. I cry out his name as the first wave hits me and he leans down and kisses me, swallowing my screams as he stills inside me, shuddering out his orgasm.

We sit opposite each other at breakfast. "We mustn't forget, the glazier is coming at lunchtime," I remind him.

"When's lunchtime over here?" he asks.

"Well, I guess anytime between twelve and two."

He checks his watch. It's nearly nine o'clock. We were the last guests down to breakfast, but that's because we had a shower together, and Sam made love to me again, raising my leg over his arm and entering me hard. It was quick and spectacular. When we sat down at our table, a few people stared at us and I whispered to Sam that maybe they'd heard us upstairs. We weren't exactly being quiet and I felt embarrassed. He said he didn't care. Well, he actually said he didn't give a fuck, but that's because Sam swears – a lot.

"Okay," he says. "We'll finish up here, get back to the house, and have a look around. And wait for the glazier to come. The windows need to be fixed."

"Yes, they do. I can't believe the agent left them like that."

"I think we maybe need to have a talk with your agent," he says.

"I think I need to consider what I'm going to do with the house," I muse, more to myself than to him. "I'll have to speak to Tess… but…"

"But what?" I look up at him, and feel tears pricking behind my eyes. He reaches over and takes my hand in his. "What's wrong?" he asks softly.

"It's difficult to explain. But I'm not sure I even want to keep the house any longer."

He sighs. "That's a big decision to make," he says. "Why not see how you feel after a few days? I think you're probably still in shock."

I know he's right, but after the damage that was done, I'm not sure I need the aggravation of continuing to lease it out.

"Either way," he continues, "I think you should fire your agent."

"I'm going to. Stupid bloody man."

He smirks. "I was gonna offer to help, or do it for you. But I think you can manage fine all by yourself."

"Um... Yes, I think I can."

"Well, just don't be too nice to him."

"Nice? You think I'm going to be nice to him, after what he did? Why would I? Tess loves the cottage even more than I do."

"So this is about her?" he asks.

"Yes... and about our parents." I can't help the crack in my voice.

He stares at me. "Are you finished?" he asks, looking at my plate. I've eaten everything except the grilled tomato, but that's because I hate grilled tomatoes.

"Yes."

"Okay. Let's get out of here."

He takes my hand and we walk out of the restaurant and through the reception.

"Are you checking out today?" The woman behind the desk is different to the one who was there last night, who seemed amused at me making fun of Sam. This one is younger and very pretty and, as we turn towards her, her eyes widen noticeably, raking up and down Sam's body, and she licks her lips. The woman should try taking lessons in subtlety, and I glance up at Sam but he doesn't seem to be paying her any attention, or if he is, he's hiding it well. She's nearly as bad as the waitress who served us last night, although he didn't seem to notice her either, to be fair.

"No," he says, putting his arm around me and pulling me over to the desk. "I think we're gonna need to stay on for a bit longer." He looks down at me. "We're not gonna be able to sleep at the house, are we?"

"No, I suppose not."

"Do you know how many nights you'll be staying," the receptionist gushes, leaning forward unnecessarily to reveal too much cleavage.

"Not really," Sam replies.

"Can we just take it on a day-by-day basis?" I ask.

"Certainly," she replies, but doesn't look at me. "Do you want to book for dinner tonight?"

"No," Sam says quickly, squeezing my shoulder, then adds a belated, "thank you."

She stares at him, looking a little disappointed, but we don't need to hang around here any longer and I roll out of his embrace and take his hand, pulling him away and out of the door to the car park. As he helps me into the driver's seat, he leans over and kisses me, looking into my eyes.

"Still blue," he says cryptically.

He smirks and shuts the door, going around to the passenger side and climbing in beside me.

"What did that mean?" I ask, looking over to him.

"Your eyes." He says, as I start the car.

"My eyes?"

He doesn't reply.

"Are you suggesting I'm jealous?" I ask when the penny finally drops, just as I'm pulling out of the car park.

"Maybe," he smirks again.

I feel a little humiliated and I focus on driving, embarrassed that he's seen through me so easily. We get around the roundabout and onto the main road that leads back to the village when he reaches over and puts his hand on my thigh.

"Stop it," he says.

"Stop what?"

"Overthinking."

"I'm not."

"Yeah, you are."

"No, I'm not. I'm just annoyed that you saw through me so easily."

He laughs. "It wasn't hard, baby," he says. "You practically dragged me out of there. And she wasn't being entirely subtle."

"No, she wasn't. And neither was the waitress last night…"

"Doesn't mean I was interested, Ali." His voice has softened. He's not making fun of me anymore. He lets out a sigh. "Do you wanna find somewhere else to stay?" he suggests.

"No."

"Sure?"

I glance at him. "What would be the point? I'm sure all the other hotels will have a pretty receptionist, or waitress, or even a chamber maid too."

"Stop the car," he says, all of a sudden.

"I can't stop here."

"Yes you can. Stop the fucking car. Now," he barks.

I check the mirrors, make sure there's nothing behind me and pull over. "What?" I ask him, putting the car into 'park'. "What's wrong?"

He turns to me. "Listen," he says sharply. "I'm not interested in anyone but you, okay?"

I look over at him, tears forming in my eyes. "Sorry," I whisper.

"Don't be sorry." He sighs. "Look, I know the last couple of days have been hard for you. I know a lot of that is down to me. I treated you badly and I made you scared, and I'm sorry. On top of that, I've given you a lot of information about my past, and I know it might have been hard to hear, but I need you to accept that, no matter what's gone before, I've never loved anyone else. I'm never going to love anyone else… and I will never hurt you. Ever again. I love you too much to risk losing you. Please, just try and trust me…" He leans over and kisses me quickly. "And remember I'm yours, just as much as you're mine."

I turn to him, not really sure what to say.

"You'd better drive," he says, grinning. "We're not meant to stop here, remember?"

"You're impossible," I reply, putting the car in gear again.

"It's one of my better traits," he says, squeezing my thigh.

The sun's come out and, when we get to the cottage, Sam helps me out of the car and we go inside.

"Fuck," he murmurs under his breath. "It looks so much worse in daylight." I don't reply. Tears are forming in my eyes again and he comes over and hugs me. "We can work this out," he says a little louder.

"How?" I look up at him.

He glances around. "Well, it's gonna take some doing, but… nothing's impossible."

"Except you," I reply and he winks at me.

He pulls away and takes my hand, leading me down the steps and into the kitchen.

"The smell…" he says, covering his nose with his free hand.

"God. It's even worse today."

He lets go of me and wanders over to the fridge. "The assholes left the refrigerator door open, and turned it off."

He reaches in and pulls out something green and slimy on a plate.

"What was it?"

"Raw chicken? Maybe?" He puts the offensive article down on the work surface and looks around. "This isn't as bad as it looks," he says. "I think we could probably get this clean in a day. We'll need to get some more cooking equipment, crockery and glassware."

"You're assuming I'm not going to sell the place."

He walks over. "Even if you are, we still need to cook, and eat off of something while we're fixing up the rest of the house. There's a limit to how many meals I'm willing to eat in that hotel. Why the hell do you think I ducked out of dinner tonight?"

"There's a pub in the next village," I point out.

"Even so. It'd be nicer to eat here, don't you think?"

"You're really serious, aren't you?"

"Yeah. Of course I am." He grins.

"You think we can eat here tonight?"

"I think we can have a damn good try."

I turn and take a look around. He's right. Although it looks bad and smells worse, most of the damage is superficial. The cupboard doors will need re-hanging, but that's not hard, and I'll need to get a new table and chairs and new china and glassware – as Sam said. I think he might be being optimistic with his estimate of a day, but I suppose if we make a start…

"Okay," I say.

He takes my hand, looks down at me and just whispers, "Good girl."

By two o'clock, I'm amazed at the change in the kitchen. We've deliberately ignored the other rooms, knowing that if we get waylaid, the kitchen will be held up, so even when we have to wade through broken furniture to let the glazier in, we don't get tempted to start clearing things up.

The glazier has been and gone in under and hour, and charged me a fortune for the privilege. Still, at least the house is secure and I feel like I can turn the heating back on again, which is good, because it's really cold and damp in here.

Sam's re-hung all the cupboard doors and I've swept up all the debris from the floor and cleaned it thoroughly along with all the work surfaces, and the tiled walls. He was very brave and took on the task of cleaning out the fridge. I offered him rubber gloves, but he gave me a look that told me 'real men' don't need them. We've left it turned off with the door open for now, to try and get rid of the residual smell. If it hasn't gone in a couple of days, I'll buy a new one. If we're going to stay here, we'll need a functioning fridge. The oven still works, so all we need to do is get hold of a table and chairs and some cooking equipment – oh, and food.

"We're going to need to drive into Bridport," I tell him.

"How far away is that?" He checks his watch.

"About a ten minute drive?"

"Oh… okay." He smiles. "I thought you were going to say it was an hour away."

"No." I laugh. "You have to remember this is quite a small island. Things tend to be quite close together."

He laughs too and takes my hand, leading me out of the house.

"It's actually worth locking now," he says, as I turn the key.

"Yes, it is." I lean up and give him a quick kiss. "Thank you for all your help."

"We're not done yet," he replies. "But it's a start."

Luckily, I know Bridport fairly well, and we find a cookware store, where I pick up enough china and glasses, cups and cutlery for Sam and I to survive. He chooses some good, but not too expensive pans, and we take our first purchases back to the car.

Then we're faced with the ordeal of buying a table and chairs.

Ideally, I'd prefer to buy something antique, that suits the house better – something like my parents would have chosen – but that's not very likely in the time we've got available, so I steer us in the direction of a shop that sells soulless flat-packed furniture. I suppose it doesn't matter. It won't be for long, and it's convenient.

"Whoa," Sam says, dragging me to a stop. "Look at that."

"What?"

"There's an antique market on this week… down there. Look." He points to the sign, tied to a lamppost. "Wanna go take a look?"

"I doubt they'll have anything. Those kind of markets are usually just filled with old bits of china."

"Come on," he says. "What have we got to lose? It's not even four o'clock yet. We'll have a quick look around and if there's nothing there, we'll go on to this other place."

"Okay." He pulls me down the narrow lane, following the signs. "How did you know I'd prefer an antique?" I ask him. I hadn't mentioned it to him.

"Call it a lucky guess." He smiles down at me, then admits, "I noticed the furniture in your apartment in London. It didn't fit with the building at all. Your desk looks like it's older than pretty much anything I own."

"How did you know it was my desk? It could've been Tess's." I point out.

"It just seemed like your kind of space." He's still looking at me as we walk. "While we're on the subject of Tess, can I ask you something?"

"Yes." I look up at him.

"I know you came home because of her call, not just because I was an idiot and yelled at you, but why couldn't Tess handle things herself? Why did she have to summon you back here?"

"She didn't summon me," I snap, defensively.

"Don't bite my head off," he says. "I'm just asking a question."

"Sorry."

"And don't say sorry." He sighs. "You're really hard to get information out of, you know that?"

"What does that mean?" I stop walking and look up into his eyes.

"C'mon, Ali… I had to basically drag it out of you that you'd had a boyfriend before me… I mean, I obviously already knew there'd been someone, but I still don't know if he's the only one."

I glare at him. "Does it matter?"

"No, but..."

"Well, he was – the only one, that is. And, right back at you, Sam. Would you have told me about Amber, if Rob hadn't said something?"

"Probably."

"And I'd probably have told you about Liam. We just hadn't got there yet, had we?"

"And Tess? And your parents?" he says, softening his voice.

"What about my parents?" I mumble through the tears that are threatening to fall already. "I told you they're dead."

"And there's more to it than that," he whispers, moving closer. "I know there is."

"Yes, there is. But I'm not going to talk to you about it in the middle of Bridport."

He pulls me into his arms. "Okay," he says, softly. "I'm sorry."

We start to walk again. "What brought that on?" I ask him.

"I—I realised, when I got to your place in London, how little I know about you, that's all."

"Such as?"

"Such as your background. I didn't realise your family had the kind of money you've obviously got."

"What difference does that make?"

"None."

"Then what does it matter?"

He shrugs. "I guess it just would have been nice to know."

I cough slightly. "Can I point out you know I'm twenty-eight, that I had one boyfriend before you, that I run my own business, that I used to be a chef, that I've got a little sister who lives with me, that our parents are no longer with us, that I live in London and have a house in Dorset, and that I'm reasonably well-off. That's a lot more than you knew about Amber – and you proposed to her."

He stops again. "I'm sorry," he says. "I'm being an idiot, aren't I?"

I reach up and touch his face. "No, you're not. But we're just starting out, Sam. We only had a week together. Of course we don't know much about each other. I don't know a lot about you either. These things take time..."

He stares at me, his eyes darkening, and then starts walking again.

After a couple of minutes, I look up at him. "What did you mean when you said you already knew there had been someone in my past?"

He stops again and turns towards me. "There was one real big clue," he whispers. I look up at him and shrug my shoulders. "I wasn't your first…"

"Oh… Sorry."

He tilts his head to one side. "Why are you sorry?"

"I don't know. I just… I wish you had been."

"So do I," he says, smiling, and then he pulls me into a hug. "Don't regret the things you can't change, baby," he murmurs.

"No… I'm serious. I wish you had been. Sex with Liam was absolutely lousy," I tell him and he laughs really loudly.

"Okay," he says eventually, "well, that's good to know." He moves closer and cups my face in his hands, suddenly serious. "Listen… I'm not gonna say I'm sorry that Liam was disappointing, but in all honesty, it really doesn't matter. I'm not interested in how many guys you've slept with, or what you have or haven't done with them. I asked about the guy who hurt you because I thought it might have had some bearing on what I'd done to you. That's all. I wanted to learn from it – preferably so I don't fuck up again. The only thing I care about is us, Ali. I'm only interested in what *we* do together, now and in the future. The past is the past, and the only reason I want to know anything about it, is because I want to understand you. Period."

I look up into his eyes and see the truth of what he's saying, right before he leans down and kisses me.

The antique market is just at the end of the lane and, although it's quite late in the day, it's still busy. We try and make our way around as fast as we can, aware that the shops will be closing fairly soon and we need to find a table somewhere before we go back to the house. Sam keeps hold of my hand the whole time, his thumb caressing my knuckles. I think he feels guilty for his earlier outburst, but I do understand how he feels. I feel the same. We need time to get to know each other. The problem is, we live too far apart to have that time, and I think that's just dawned on him too.

"Over there," he says all of a sudden and drags me off to the left. "Look."

He pulls me to a stop and we look down at a small rectangular table. It's antique pine and has four matching chairs. "What do you think?" he asks.

"I think it's perfect." I smile up at him and he smiles back and calls over the stall holder, a man probably in his mid-forties, with a pleasant face.

"Can we take this?" he asks.

"Certainly, sir," the man says, with a broad west country accent.

"How much is it?" I ask. There's no point in blowing money, just because I prefer antiques.

"Normally, it'd be seven-fifty," he says. "But for you…" he pauses, looking at me appraisingly. "Let's call it six hundred."

Sam looks down at me, raising an eyebrow.

"Do you take cards?" I ask the man.

He smiles. "I certainly do."

We arranged that the man would keep the furniture while we went back for the car, and drove it to the entrance of the antiques market, where Sam and I loaded everything into the back. It's not the first time I've been relieved I bought such a big car.

On the way home, we stopped at the out of town supermarket and picked up what we wanted for dinner. Sam chose – he said he's cooking. He also paid.

"You bought everything else," he murmured as he put his card into the chip and pin device.

"Because it's my house," I replied.

"Even so."

Back at the house, he set up the table and chairs while I unpacked everything else and then he started cooking. Sam's making me his mother's bolognese, which I feel is a bit of an honour, really. He says the meat sauce takes a couple of hours to cook, but that's fine, it's still early.

In the meantime, once he's put it on to simmer, we sit at the table with a glass each of Chianti.

"We need to talk," Sam says, taking my hand.

"This sounds ominous." I smile across at him.

He doesn't smile back and I feel a cold chill pass over me, before he takes a deep breath and continues, "When we were in bed on Saturday morning, talking about the future, I thought we could do the whole long distance relationship thing, with me coming over here every so often, and you coming to the States for visits… but I've realised now that we can't. Neither of us is cut out for that kind of life. We live too far apart to make this work." I guess at least he got to the point quickly, rather than dragging it out.

"Are you breaking up with me?" I just about manage to croak out the words. After everything we've been through in the last couple of days, it's too much.

"Of course I'm not. Far from it." He lets go of my hand and gets up coming around to my side of the table and sitting beside me, turning my chair, so we're facing each other. "I want to be with you all the time. I want to take care of you and give you the security I know you need."

"That's going to be hard, Sam. You live in America and I live here. We've both got commitments; family, businesses. I can't just leave Tess."

"I know. I understand that. I may have only met her very briefly, but I noticed she seems fragile."

"Tess has had a hard life, Sam. She needs me."

"I kinda got that too. The fact that you came rushing back here was a huge clue, although I still don't understand why. You dodged answering that question"

"Yes, because we were in public, and I can't talk about it in public." I take a breath and a large gulp of wine. "It's to do with our parents," I say, staring at the grain on the surface of the table.

"Do you want to tell me now?" he asks.

"It's hard for me to tell, but you won't understand either of us, or the way we behave, if I don't."

"Okay." He places his finger under my chin and raises my face to his. "Let me see you," he says.

I sigh, staring at his face. His eyes are so full of love, it's somehow easier to start talking. "There was a fire," I say simply. "At our house… thirteen years ago. I wasn't there. I was away with a friend at the time, but Tess and our parents were there. A neighbour raised the alarm, and my dad managed to get to Tess and lower her down out of the window, before dropping her to Mr Bowen."

"Mr Bowen?" he queries.

"The neighbour." He nods his head. "Dad told Tess he was going back for our mother and he'd be with her soon, and he went back to find mum." I feel Sam's hand tighten around mine.

"He didn't make it?" he guesses.

I shake my head.

"Neither of them did. Tess had nightmares for years afterwards. Well, she still does from time to time. She didn't talk for two years. She just drifted through life."

"And you both lived with your grandmother?" he asks.

"Yes. How did you know that?"

"You told me Tess lived with her, I just assumed…"

I nod. "She was an incredible woman."

"Was?"

"Yes. She died too… about eighteen months ago." I swallow down the lump in my throat. "That hit Tess really hard too. They were very close."

"And you?" he asks.

"She meant the world to me as well, but I moved out of granny's house after three years. Tess was there a lot longer. She was only eight when we moved in with her. Granny had a huge place in her life. It's thanks to granny that we're financially secure. She took care of all of that when Mum and Dad died."

He nods his head.

"Tess has a fear of being abandoned, or even just being left on her own," I explain. "She's wary of getting attached to people – in her experience, they have a habit of leaving her. She was really fond of Liam, and look what he did. That's what I hate him for the most. He let her get attached; he encouraged it, knowing he had Fiona in the background the whole time..." I pause, staring at him. "I had to think really hard about taking the contract with you and your brothers," I continue. "Tess persuaded me to go, and that she'd be okay, but then she was on the phone to me every day, either calling or texting. I knew she was lonely. That's why I found it so difficult on that Sunday, when she sent her message about getting a take-away and watching a box-set. I knew she was telling me she was finding it hard. I knew I should be here, with her." He keeps his eyes fixed on mine. "I'm sorry, Sam, but I can't leave her. Everyone else has and I can't. I can't do that to her."

He leans back, just a little, taking a deep breath. "I understand," he says, and I feel my heart start to shatter. He's going to tell me we're over... this has all been for nothing. A tear drops onto my cheek. "Don't cry," he whispers, leaning forward and kissing it away. "I'm so sorry about what happened to your parents. I can't imagine how terrible that was for both of you, and I know, in the same situation, I'd wanna stay with my brothers too. So, I do understand exactly how you feel."

I nod. There's no way around this. He needs to be in America and I need to be here; it doesn't matter how much we need to be with each other. It can't work.

"I want you to come back to the States with me," he says.

"Sam... I've just explained."

He puts his finger on my lips, silencing me.

"And I want Tess to come too. I'll take care of both of you. And I'll never let you down. Either of you."

Sam

She stares at me, long and hard.

"Sam, this isn't even practical," she murmurs, lowering her head again.

"Why not?"

"Well, to start with, Tess has to finish university."

"Okay. How long does she have to go?"

"She has to hand her dissertation in at the end of the month."

"Well, that's okay then." I reply. "That's over three weeks away. It's gonna take us that long to fix this place up. We're gonna have to repaint the living room and the bedrooms, and get the shower fixed and the carpets cleaned, or relaid… and buy at least *some* new furniture."

"Sam, you can't stay here until the end of the month."

"Who says I can't?"

"Ed and Rob, I should imagine," she says, smiling half-heartedly.

"Leave them to me."

She stares at me again, like she's struggling to take in my suggestion.

"I can't just move to America."

"Yeah, you can." I grin at her, encouragingly.

"No I can't. For a start, I don't have a reason to move there, and I'm fairly sure they don't just let you move there on a whim."

"No, they don't. But there are certain conditions in which they'll let you move…"

"Such as?"

"If you've got a job to go to," I tease.

"Which I haven't," she replies.

I lean closer to her "Or if you're getting married to a US citizen," I say softly.

"But I'm not…" she stops and stares. "Wait… Are you proposing?"

"Yeah. I am."

"But… but we've already established that we don't really know each other, Sam. We said that just this afternoon. We need time to get to know each other better."

"Yeah, time which we're not gonna have unless you come back with me, and the only easy way to do that is to marry me."

"You don't think you might be repeating past mistakes?" she asks. "You said you rushed into things with Amber, remember?"

"Yeah, but this is nothing like that. I didn't love her, for one thing, and I love you so much I don't even wanna think about living without you, let alone having an ocean between us. When you ran from me in Hartford, and I contemplated trying to live without you, it scared me to death. All I could think about was how I was gonna win you back, because I knew I had to. I don't wanna make comparisons between you and Amber, or anyone else from my past, but I sure as hell wouldn't have abandoned Ed and Rob just a week after re-opening, and flown three thousand miles for anyone but you." She's staring at me, wide-eyed and open mouthed. "I know it's quick," I add, "but that doesn't make it wrong."

"What about Tess?" she asks, after a short, slightly scary pause. "You can't marry her too."

I laugh. "No, I can't."

"And she might not want to come."

"There is that possibility, I suppose. Does she have a boyfriend, or anyone else she'd want to stay here for?"

Ali shakes her head. "No, she's never had a boyfriend."

"Really?" I'm surprised. Tess is very beautiful.

"Well, I think that's partly my fault," Ali replies, looking down at our hands in her lap.

"Why?"

"I—I kind of built our father up as a romantic hero, and I don't think there's a man alive who could hope to compete," she says softly, tears welling in her eyes again. This is tough for her. "Our parents were found together," she explains slowly, taking a deep breath, "in their bedroom, in each other's arms. Both of them had succumbed to smoke inhalation, but our mother died first, and the authorities queried the fact that dad didn't seem to have tried to rescue her. They were just lying in bed together, you see, like they were asleep. I didn't query it though. Not once. I've always believed he knew Mum was dead when he dropped Tess out of that window; that he'd decided he couldn't go on without her and had chosen to lie down and die with her, rather than go through life on his own." She swallows hard and another tear falls onto her cheek. I wipe it away with my thumb this time. "Believing that made it easier to accept him leaving us, but I think that story has made Tess even more of a romantic than me. I think she's looking for something that doesn't exist. She's looking for a man who would give up everything for her – even his life, if necessary."

"What about you?" I ask.

"What about me?"

"What are you looking for?"

She gives me a slight smile. "I was always a romantic, I suppose, but Liam took the gloss off of that. He was good at the gestures, to the point where I didn't even mind that the sex wasn't great..." She smiles at me. "But then he betrayed us both. The way he managed to lead a double life so easily was astounding. I never suspected a thing. His betrayal was absolute. I gave up on romance and looking for things that don't exist after that."

She looks so sad, it's more than I can handle, and I reach across and pull her onto my lap. She comes willingly and nestles into my arms.

"I want you to listen real carefully," I say, keeping my voice as calm and purposeful as I can. "We're gonna spend the next few weeks fixing this place up, and then I want to take you home with me. You *and* Tess." I struggle for a moment to choke down my emotions, before continuing, "And then I want to spend the rest of my life with you, proving that romance does exist, most often where you least expect it. And if the need ever arises, I promise, I *will* lie down and die with you, Ali." I hear her sob and she brings her arms around my neck. "I will make sure you're safe – both of you. Always. And I'll never let anyone hurt either of you." I raise her face to mine, tears streaking down her beautiful cheeks. "All you've gotta do is say yes."

Epilogue

Ali

"He wants you to move to America with him?" I can hear the doubt, the confusion and the hurt in Tess's voice. Once I'd finished crying on Sam last night, I told him I couldn't give him an answer right away. He said he was okay with that. I felt I should be saying yes though, because I've never wanted anything more than I want him. He was offering me the world, and more. He was proving to me that dreams really do come true. But he was also asking me to move across an ocean with him, and to take my little sister too. I had to think it through. And talk to Tess.

But I decided not to do it right away. I wanted a few hours to get used to the idea myself – not of marrying Sam, but of emigrating – so I waited until after dinner tonight, and now I'm in the living room, sitting on the floor, talking to Tess, and I've left Sam in the kitchen talking to his brothers on Skype, to break the news that he's going to be staying here until the end of the month. I don't want him to hear our conversation. His is going to be hard enough, but mine…

"He wants *us* to move to America with him. He wants me to marry him."

"I—I can't live in America." She sounds like she's about to cry.

"It's not as bad as you think," I tell her. "And Sam's brothers are lovely."

"I'm not saying you shouldn't go," she replies. "And I'm not saying you shouldn't marry him. I think you should."

"You do?"

"Yes. I know I didn't see him for very long, but I liked him. I think you suit each other. He obviously loves you… let's face it, he flew across an ocean to win you back. And you love him, Ali. I know you do."

"I can't go without you, Tess."

"Yes, you can."

"No." I'm firm and she sighs.

"This is too much, Ali. You're making me responsible for your future."

"I'm not leaving you," I say again.

"And he can't live here?" she suggests.

"I doubt it." It's not something we've talked about. "I can start my business again over there," I explain. "But I doubt Sam could afford to set up his own restaurant here, and I can't imagine he'd want to without his brothers. They're a team. I also can't see him working for someone else."

"No," she says quietly, like she's thinking. "If I agreed," she continues after a moment, "what would I do for a living?"

"Probably something similar to whatever you were going to do here once you've graduated."

"And if I can't find work?" she says. "Won't the authorities kick me out?"

"Sam says they'll give you a job in the restaurant, if it means you can stay."

The line goes silent.

"I need to think about it, Ali."

"I know. It's a big ask."

"It is."

"Listen to me," I say, seriously. "If you really don't want to go, then you have to say so. I'm sure Sam and I can work something else out." I'm not; not really, but I can't tell Tess that.

"Let me think about it," she says.

I go back in to Sam, who's finished his call, and tell him Tess's response, half expecting him to get mad that things aren't going his way. He's leaning against the work surface and I go over and stand in front of him. He puts his arms around me.

"Okay," he says quietly, surprising me a little. "At least she didn't dismiss the idea altogether."

"No." I look up at him. "Did you speak to Ed and Rob."

"Yeah." He smirks and shakes his head.

"What?"

"They've said they'll cope, but I don't think they're very happy with me."

"I can't imagine they're too happy with me either," I reply.

"Why not?"

"It's me that's keeping you here, isn't it?"

"Yeah. But they know how important you are to me. They told me before I even left the States that I should bring you home again."

"They did?"

He smiles. "Yeah. I think their lives are a lot easier when you're around," he says.

Although I've never thought of them in this way before, I suddenly realise that Rob and Ed are exactly what I'd wish for if I had brothers of my own, and I miss them both, but knowing that isn't making this any easier. "What do we do if Tess really doesn't want to come?"

"We'll find a way around it," he says, sounding more confident than I feel.

"Like what?"

He pulls me closer. "I don't know. But we'll work it out. I'm not giving you up."

He leans down and kisses me and, as his tongue finds mine, despite my fear that we can't make this happen, I try to believe him. I really do.

We've quickly settled into a routine. We've been sleeping at the hotel, and having breakfast there, then we spend the rest of the day at the house, and Sam cooks for us in the evenings.

By the end of the first week, we've nearly completed the master bedroom and bathroom, which we decided to do first so we can move in here and give up the hotel room. The bed was delivered today, so we're going to check out this afternoon, and will spend tonight here.

Although I still haven't given him an answer, Sam's been amazing. He's been attentive, kind, considerate. He's held me when I've cried – which I've done quite a lot, usually over small things, like a broken picture, or torn book. He's been practical too, getting on with jobs around the house without me even having to suggest them to him.

He's also been really affectionate, kissing me at every opportunity, and each night, when we've got back to the hotel, he's run me a bath, and afterwards, we've made love. It's always been 'my way', as Sam used to put it, and although he's still definitely in charge, there's been no sign of the dominant personality that was so visible in Hartford. Part of me is missing him, but I don't know where he's gone, or how to get him back.

I've spoken to Tess every day, but we haven't really talked about the decisions that we both need to make. I know she's got to finish her dissertation and I'm wary of pre-occupying her too much with other thoughts, although I'm sure she thinks about it a lot. I know I do. I think about it all the time. I think about saying yes, because that's what I want to do… more than anything.

"I guess we should go and check out of the hotel," I call out to Sam as I climb up the stairs. He's in the bathroom, putting a new cabinet on the wall.

"Sure," he replies. "Just give me five minutes."

I sit down on the closed toilet seat. "This looks so much better."

"Well, they didn't do much damage in here. Not as much as elsewhere."

"Thank you for all your help." It's something I say pretty much every day, but I am grateful to him, and he didn't have to do it.

"You don't have to keep thanking me, Ali," he replies, tightening the screw into the wall.

"Well, I kind of do. You've done so much."

"I'd do more for you, if you'd let me." He turns and stares down at me, and smirks.

"What's funny?"

"Having this conversation while you're sitting on the toilet."

"The lid's closed," I reply.

"Even so, it's weird."

He puts down the screwdriver on the back of the basin and comes over, standing in front of me and pulling me to my feet. "That's better," he says, leaning down and kissing me. "Let me, Ali, please," he whispers. "Let me care for you."

I can't answer him yet, so instead I put my arms around his neck and hold onto him.

Sleeping at the house has made things much easier, although now we've got a bed, we're tempted to make more use of it, even when we're supposed to be working. Over the last few days, Sam's come up behind me quite regularly, when I've been painting and suggested a 'quick break'. He's hard to resist, although he still isn't the same man he was before. I'm not sure how to bring up the subject. Apart from anything else, I know I'm not meant to instigate things, but waiting for him to get back to normal is killing me. I want to do things his way again. I need to feel that intense side of him again; to know we're back where we belong.

After a hard day's decorating, we're in the kitchen together and I'm watching Sam preparing our dinner. He's tying up a piece of pork that he's stuffed with herbs and garlic. Seeing him working on the knots so expertly reminds me of how he used to bind me and I wonder if this might be my opportunity to say something. I stare at him, trying to work out how to start the conversation and, once he's finished, he turns to look at me. I guess my look must give me away, because he comes over slowly and stands in front of me. His eyes are dark and I wonder if he's going to suggest something, or order me to do something and I've already resolved that I'll do it, whatever it is, when he leans down and murmurs, "Stop it."

"Stop what?" I look up at him.

"Thinking about that."

"How do you know what I was thinking?"

"I just do." He pauses. "And I'm sorry, but I can't."

"Oh." I feel deflated, and he moves away.

It's only later in bed, when he's making love to me really gently and slowly that I wonder whether he meant he can't do things his way, because he hasn't got the necessary 'equipment' – as it were. I'm not exactly overflowing with supplies of silky rope or cuffs, and I wonder whether he's finding that as frustrating as I am. It makes sense that he wouldn't start something he couldn't finish – well it does to me anyway.

The next morning, while he's painting upstairs in the guest room, I go online and – for the first time in my life – search for 'silky bondage rope'. Some of the results are scary. Others are funny, but I find a place where I can purchase rope that looks identical to the stuff Sam used on me. It's not black, it's purple, but I doubt the colour matters very much. They offer express delivery, which means it'll be here tomorrow morning. As I confirm the order, I can feel myself tingling already with anticipation.

The post arrives late, but I manage to get to the door before Sam and take the parcel from the postman. Part of me thinks we should wait until tonight, but to hell with it, I'm so wired, I need this now. The problem is, how to instigate it, without actually instigating it.

He's painting again and I go upstairs, and put the parcel in the bedroom before going to find him in the spare room. I can't help admiring the view. He's wearing one of his tight t-shirts and his muscles ripple every time he moves. I go over to him and put my arms around his waist. He stills and I rest my head on his back.

"Feel like a quick break?" I say to him, mirroring his suggestions.

I can feel his shoulders shake. He's laughing, or trying not to.

"Sure." He turns around. "Let me just get rid of this." He holds up the paintbrush, before putting it down on top of the tin of pale yellow paint, and taking my hand. "C'mon then… lead the way."

That's a suggestion that's too good to turn down. Maybe I can guide him to doing what I want and what I think we both need. I lead him from the guest bedroom, into the master, and over to the bed, where I sit down, looking up at him.

"I bought you something," I say quietly.

"You did?"

"Yes." I hand him the parcel. "Open it," I whisper.

"Okay." He tears off the top of the package, peering inside and pulling out the purple rope. When he looks back at me, I'm holding my hands out to him, clasped together, like I'm praying.

"Ali?" he says.

I stare up at him. "I know I'm not supposed to ask, or instigate, but I need you."

He sits down beside me.

"You've got me," he says.

"I need all of you."

"You've got all of me." He sighs and puts the rope down beside him, taking my still clasped hands in his. "I'm sorry," he murmurs. "I thought you understood… I can't do this."

"You… you can't?"

"No."

"Why not?" What have I done? Why doesn't he want this anymore? I try to pull my hands away from him, but he holds on tight.

"Don't," he says. "Don't pull away from me."

I try to relax a little. "Why, Sam?" I ask. "Why can't you do this?"

"I know you had doubts about us… about me, and about this." He nods towards the rope. "When I told you about Amber…"

"Yes, I did."

He sighs. "And I know you were scared that I wanted you to be the same as all the others… to be some kind of submissive, all the time."

"How did you know?" I ask him.

"I just did. And I was right, wasn't I?"

"When you first told me about her, and how you wanted to change her, yes. I thought you wanted that of me too. But then…"

"But then what?" he asks.

"But then you asked me to take you. At the hotel."

"And?" he prompts.

"And I realised how different that makes me."

"You are different. I keep telling you that."

"I know, but you letting me take you like that… I know it was a big step for you."

He closes his eyes for a moment. "I'm not sure you do, but I needed to prove a point to you. I needed to show you how different you are, because I knew my words weren't working."

"And you showing me convinced me."

He shakes his head. "I still can't," he repeats.

"You can." He looks at me. "There's something else, isn't there?" I ask him. "What is it?"

"You want romance, Ali. Now I've heard the story of your parents, and your father, I understand that… And I want to give you that. I want that more than ever."

"And you do. You are romantic, Sam."

"This isn't." He glances down at the rope again.

I smile at him. "It can be. It's certainly intimate."

"Not always it isn't. It can tip over into… something else." He turns away slightly, evidently thinking, probably about something in his past, and I free one of my hands, then reach over and place it gently on his cheek.

"Whatever you're thinking about, or remembering, forget it. It's intimate for *us*," I tell him. "I fell in love with all of you; the romantic side of you, *and* the dominant. I need both. I need all of you, Sam. Please…"

He focuses back on me, his confusion obvious. "Need?" he says.

"Yes. Need." I twist around, kneeling beside him. "I don't think you realise how much you gave me, or how much it meant to me," I say quietly. "It was all so new, but it was so good, so rewarding."

"It wasn't *all* new, Ali. You'd had sex before."

"Not like that I hadn't."

"Okay, I get that it wasn't great with Liam, but you'd still done most of the things we did, just without the ropes and the cuffs," he says.

I take a breath. I can see I'm going to have to spell this out. "No I hadn't," I murmur quietly and his eyes widen. "That first time, for example, when you bound my wrists, I'd never done that before."

"I know. I know you'd never been tied."

"That's not what I mean." I look at him, hoping he'll understand without me having to say the words myself.

"You… you mean you'd never performed oral sex on a guy before?"

I nod my head and I know I'm blushing.

He smiles and leans closer. "Well, you're really fucking good at it," he says. He looks away, staring at a blank space on the newly painted wall. "It was a first for me too," he whispers.

"I'm sorry?"

"No-one had ever done that to me either."

"While being tied up like that, you mean?" I ask, uncertain what he's saying.

"No. No-one had ever done it at all."

"Are you serious?"

"Yes." He turns to look at me and I can see the honesty in his eyes.

"But… but you're so experienced."

His shoulders drop. "Yeah. Not something I'm really wanting to shout about right now, but yeah."

"And no-one's ever done that before?" I can't hide my surprise.

"No. Remember me?" He points a finger at his chest and whispers simply, "Home run." His eyes fix on mine and I recall our baseball conversation.

"Oh. And you never wanted to get another woman to do what I did?"

"Not particularly, no. Oral sex is really intimate. I wasn't into intimacy."

"Then why me?"

He leans closer. "Because I did want to be intimate with you. And besides, there's something about your lips," he whispers, and I shiver.

"There is?"

"Oh yeah." A smile touches the corners of his mouth. "Do you remember when we were eating the fish and chips in the apartment, and you were saying how good the chips were?"

"Yes. And you agreed… except… you weren't talking about the chips."

"That's right." His smile widens. "I'd been thinking about how sexy you looked. The way you touched your lips had me so hard, all I could think about was how they'd feel around my cock. And then when you said you were gonna beg me to tell you what I was thinking, I knew exactly what I wanted to do with you. I knew, if I ever got the chance to try anything with you – my way – it'd be to tie you and get you to suck me."

"Did the experience live up to expectations?" I tease.

"It surpassed expectations."

I smile. It's nice to know. But then another conversation crosses my mind. "I remember, our very first time together – my way – when you did that to me," I say nervously.

"You mean when I licked you?" he clarifies, because I'm too embarrassed to say the words.

"Yes. You told me you'd done it before. Surely that was intimate, wasn't it?"

"No. It was with Amber. It only happened once. On her terms, not mine, and it definitely wasn't intimate…" His voice fades.

"But it was with me?"

"It *is* with you. You taste amazing, Ali."

"You showed me a side of myself I never knew existed, Sam. I want that back." I edge closer, putting my hands back together, clasping them tight and holding them out to him. "Please," I whisper.

He turns and looks at me, still seemingly doubtful and hesitant, and I let my arms fall again.

"It's okay," I mutter, trying and probably failing to hide my disappointment. "We can just make love."

He grabs me. "No, wait," he says and I feel the hope spike inside me. "Can we try something new?"

"Yes." I nod enthusiastically. Sam's idea of 'new' has never disappointed me before.

"Okay." He lets go of me again and whips his t-shirt over his head, before kneeling up in front of me, so we're facing each other on the bed, then he gives me the rope, and puts his hands together, holding them out to me.

He wants me to tie him? No. That's too much. I remember what he said about how this would make him feel and I know he's never given himself like this to anyone. I don't think I can do this. I stare at his clasped hands, then up at him. His eyes are burning into me. "No, Sam," I mutter. "I can't."

"Yeah, you can. I want this."

"Do you? You really want me to tie you up?"

"Yeah. I need to."

I hesitate, but his expression is so sincere, I know I'm going to have to try. I uncoil the rope and straighten it out, trying to remember what he did. I recall he put one end between my fingers, so I do that and then I start wrapping the cord around his wrists, over and over, until I'm left with just enough to tie it. It doesn't look like it did when Sam tied me. It looks loose, messy and uneven. I look up into his eyes.

"What do I do now?" I ask him.

He smiles. "That's up to you, baby," he says. "You're in charge."

I sit back on my ankles. "I don't know what I'm supposed to do though."

His smile widens. "You're not very good at this, are you?" he murmurs.

"No, of course I'm not."

He shakes his head and moves his elbows out, twisting his wrists and freeing himself easily.

"Oh," I say quietly, staring down at the coiled rope now lying on the bed between us.

"Well, I think the first thing I need to teach you is how to tie a better knot."

"I'd rather you just tied me up in one," I reply, looking up into his eyes.

He picks up the rope, and gets up, standing above me.

"Oh, baby," he says, his voice low and a little firmer. "You *know* that's not how it works."

I smile up at him and catch the glint in his eyes, just before he leans down and puts his mouth next to my ear. "Stand up, and turn around," he orders, and I can feel myself shaking, partly with anticipation and partly with relief that he's back.

Even before we'd finished the work on the house, I'd already decided that the best thing was probably going to be to sell it. I spoke to Tess and she reluctantly agreed. We obviously couldn't trust the agent, and the whole experience had left us with a bitter taste in our mouths. As much as we didn't want to part with one of the last links to our parents, the idea of going through that again was too much for either of us.

So, once everything was completed, I put in a call to a local estate agent, who came and valued the house and I signed the documents to put it on the market.

Now he's gone and we've got the house to ourselves again, I turn to Sam and fall into his arms, sobbing my heart out. I don't want to do this. I really don't. We love this house and parting with it is going to break my heart – Tess's too.

"It'll be okay," Sam says gently when I finally calm down. He doesn't need me to explain what's wrong. He understands without words. "I'll be here for you. No matter what. I'll always be here for you."

I look up into his eyes and I know, no matter what decision I make, he will be.

Sam

Asking Ali to marry me was simple, because I can't let her go. I've known that for a while now – well, since she left, and I faced the thought of a future without her. Of course, back then I had no idea about her bond with her sister or the reasons behind it. Finding out about that, about what happened and how it affected her and Tess changed a lot – well it did for me, anyway. It made me realize how much she's done by herself, how much she needs someone she can really depend on… someone who'll put her first, who'll put her sister first, someone who won't ever let her down. Someone who'll lie down and die with her. It also made me realize how much I wanna be that someone.

I want to take care of both of them. Always. I just need Ali to say yes.

Ali's put the house up for sale and all the renovations are completed. It's been hard work, but worth it. The place looks really good, and the valuation was way above anything I expected. She still hasn't given me an answer though, and I'm trying real hard not to press her for one, even though I told Rob and Ed that I'd only be gone until the end of the month, which is Saturday… so just a couple of days away.

They weren't exactly happy with me when I called them. It was understandable. I'd told them I'd only be a few days, and suddenly I was telling them I'd be a few weeks instead, and leaving them to run the restaurant without me. Once I'd explained the situation, they agreed they'd cope – somehow. I can completely see their point. It's hard work, and Ed certainly didn't sign up for that. I told them that I've asked Ali to come back with me, but that it's dependent on Tess's decision, and they seemed much more sympathetic after that.

Ed's called a few times since, asking questions, but I think he's just looking for reassurance. He's told me that Rob's helping out in the kitchen, so I dread to think what's going on. I haven't got the heart to tell them that if Ali doesn't give me an answer by the weekend, which is when I've said I'll go home, I'm gonna stay on here until she does. I know it's a huge ask for her and Tess, and if they need more time, they can have it, but I'm not going home without an answer. Actually, I'm not going home without them…

It's kinda hard having our future in someone else's hands, and I'd like to know what Ali's decision would be if we took Tess out of the equation, but I'm not gonna ask her, because I'm fairly sure she'd think I was suggesting that as a possibility, and I'm not. I know they come as a package. Even so, I'd like to know what Ali feels about my proposal. I'd like to know if she'd say yes if it was just the two of us.

I didn't expect it to be this hard. The waiting is killing me; so is the uncertainty. But I've decided that if Tess says no, I'm not gonna give up. I'll just have to think again, and I'm working on that already…

The other thing I didn't expect was the turn of events a few days ago. Ali came and asked me if I wanted to take a 'quick break', which has become another way of us saying 'let's go to bed for a while'. I wasn't about to turn her down; it was the first time she'd instigated anything between us since I got here, and I was pleased she felt she could. To me, it showed me she felt relaxed enough around me to make the first move again. I liked that.

What I didn't anticipate was that she'd somehow gotten hold of some rope – in a fairly garish purple – and that she was gonna offer herself to be bound. I wasn't ready for that at all. Seeing her like that, meek and submissive, confirmed all my thoughts and fears about my lifestyle and made me realize I was right to try and leave that side of myself behind. She told me she thinks it's intimate, but it wasn't always like that. There have been times – especially with Amber – when the lines have gotten blurred, and for a moment, I was haunted by an image of me pinning my ex against the wall by her throat. That's the kind of thing that can happen when you're in that situation, and don't have complete control. Ali has no idea what it can really be like – and I've got no intention that she should ever find out. On top of that, hearing her story, about her father sacrificing himself threw my life into stark relief, and I knew I wanted to give her the romance she craves. The way I do things doesn't fit with that, not in my view, anyway. In any case, I was really getting to like vanilla… I'd managed to let her take me. I did it to prove a point, to show her she's different, but to my surprise, I actually enjoyed it. That was because it was Ali, of course, but having my hands free to play with her, and watching her come apart on me was beautiful. We've done that a few times since and, like everything with her, it just keeps getting better. I really wasn't sure I wanted to go back to the darker flavor of my past.

What shocked me was that Ali said she needed that controlling, dominant side of me. She needed what we had before. I still wasn't convinced, but she looked so disappointed, so I offered myself to her. I'm not going to deny it was hard doing that; the idea of relinquishing all control absolutely terrified me, but I wanted to do it. I wanted to show her that I'll give up everything for her – and I mean *everything*.

She did a God-awful job of tying me up, and she had no idea what she was gonna do with me once she'd bound me. It made me see that she's not cut out to take control. But the look in her eyes, and her obvious need for what I can give her turned me on. It was like flicking a switch and I knew I needed it too. But not my way. Not entirely. I can't do that any more… this had to be *our* way. It took a couple of seconds to free myself and once she worked out that I was back, she obeyed my instruction to stand and turn around without hesitation. Her eagerness made me smile, although I didn't let her see that. Instead, I pulled off her t-shirt and took off her bra, then bound her hands behind her back before I turned her around and knelt her down on the floor, slowly undoing my jeans and lowering them and my trunks to the floor, so she could suck me. Despite the obvious temptation, I didn't come in her mouth. Instead, I stood her up, released her hands, and re-tied her to the corner post of the bed. By that stage she was shaking with anticipation, unsure what I was gonna do next, so I took my time removing her jeans and panties, prolonging the wait, and then finally, I bent her over, told her to hold on tight, and slammed my cock into her soaking pussy, fucking her real hard, while she begged for more. Just to spite her, I slowed the pace, and she moaned out her frustration, which made me smile again. While teasing her with my cock, I leant over, whispering in her ear that I'd forgive her for begging, and for instigating things, just this once, but in future, she needed to remember that my way really does mean *my* way. Of course, it doesn't, not anymore. It means *our* way, but just hearing me say that made her come really hard, so I think we can keep calling it 'my' way, if that's what she likes. I exploded inside her after just a couple more strokes and then untied her and lay her down on the bed. She kept murmuring 'thank you', over and over, just like she did back home. I lay beside her, rubbing her shoulders, and told her to never thank me again.

"But I'm grateful," she said, looking up at me.

"Don't be grateful. You give me so much."

I wanted to ask her to give me the one thing I really need from her. I wanted to ask her to say yes to being mine forever. I didn't.

This morning, we woke at roughly the same time and I held her in my arms. We kissed for a while and then she looked up at me, seemingly confused.

"Why haven't you done that thing to me again?" she asked.

"What thing?" I had no idea what she was talking about.

"That *thing*..." she said, with emphasis.

"Ali, I don't know what you mean."

She flushed bright red. "With your fingers and thumbs."

That was when I got it. "You mean this..." I reached around behind her and ran my index finger over her puckered anus.

"Oh God... yes," she whimpered, shuddering slightly. "That..."

I smiled down at her. "I've thought about it over the last couple of days," I told her, honestly, because since I tied her to the bed, and had her bent over in front of me, so temptingly, I have been contemplating it. "But I'd like to try something else with you... Something a little different."

"There?" she asked, her eyes widening.

"Yeah... there."

"With your fingers and thumbs?"

"Not necessarily..."

She gasped. "I can't take *that*," she said, leaning back and looking up at me. "Not there." And I knew she was thinking about my cock.

"I'm not suggesting that." *Not yet, anyway*.

She looked confused.

"Then I don't understand," she murmured, clearly intrigued.

"I know you don't."

She nestled into me.

"You know I like trying new things," she whispered. "So why don't you... just try...?"

"Because I don't have everything I need."

She looked up again, her brow furrowed in confusion. "What does that mean?"

"You'll just have to come home with me and find out."

"Tease," she said and tried to pull away from me.

I wasn't having that and grabbed hold of her, rolling her onto her back and pinning her there. "I left in a hurry," I explained. "Packing restraints wasn't a priority."

"Restraints?" she breathed.

"Yeah. Restraints."

"You mean like those cuffs you used on me?"

"Similar to those, but different."

She looks confused. "But surely a rope is a restraint, isn't it? We've got a rope..."

I laughed loudly. "Yeah, it is, but it's not the kind of restraint I need for what I've got in mind."

"Why?"

"God, I love your inquisitiveness," I said, prolonging her agony a little longer.

"Stop teasing and explain."

"Yes, ma'am." I leant in closer. "What I've got in mind is gonna be real intense. There's a chance you might find it too much." She sucked in a breath. "And that means I might need to be able to release you quickly. I can't do that with a rope... Well, I can, but I'd have to cut it and I'm not gonna risk taking anything sharp near you at a time like that."

"You've done this before?" she asked, breathless, her eyes wide.

"No."

"Why not?"

"Because it's too intimate..."

That was a fairly big clue, but I'm not sure she picked it up. She studied me for a moment. "Then how do you know it'll be intense?"

I leant down and put my mouth beside her ear and whispered. "Because I know you. I know how you respond, and what I've got in mind is so much... more."

"Oh God," she shuddered into me and I knew exactly how her body had reacted... just to my words.

We don't really have anything to stay here for now. The house is ready, it's gone up for sale – there's even a sign outside to prove it, and in theory, I'm due to go home the day after tomorrow. We decide to have one last night here, and then go back to London in the morning, which will give me Friday afternoon and Saturday morning in London before potentially flying back home… or not.

Not long after lunch, I prepare our evening meal, which is Spezzatino di manzo, an Italian beef stew. It's another of my mom's recipes, which I've adapted a little over the years. It's one of those dishes that can cook quite happily for hours and actually tastes better the longer you leave it. Ali's been talking to Tess for over half an hour, but that's not unusual at the moment. Tess is due to hand in her dissertation tomorrow and I think she's nervous. Ali's been offering her reassurance over the last few days.

She comes out to the kitchen just as I'm putting the stew into the oven.

"Finished?" I ask her.

She nods, looking pensive. I'm not sure if that's good or bad, but I've been doing a lot of thinking myself over the last day or so and I need to talk to her.

"Can we go for a walk on the beach?" I ask.

"Okay." She looks out the window. The weather's quite sunny, even if it's not warm. "I'll go and get my coat."

"Can you bring mine too?" I ask her, going to the front door to find our boots.

"Sure."

Once we're dressed up for the weather, we leave the house, locking the door, and walk down to the beach. We've only been down here twice since I got here. We've been busy with the house, and the weather hasn't been that great; I think we've only had two days where it hasn't rained. I hold Ali's hand, rubbing her knuckles with my thumb as we walk.

"I've been thinking," I say to her, staring out to sea. It's quite calm today – which is the opposite to how I feel. My insides are churning.

"And?" she prompts.

"I've been thinking back over our time together," I pause, but don't give her a chance to say anything. "And I need to ask you a question." She nods her head. "Do you remember when we first talked about the refurbishment to the restaurant, you asked where we're from, and we told you..."

"Positano," she whispers.

"Yeah. Do you remember your reaction?"

"Do you?"

"Of course. You got upset."

"I didn't think you cared enough to notice."

"Well, that's where you were wrong," I tell her. "I cared, even then." She looks up at me, like she doesn't quite believe me. "I was just completely shit at showing it," I explain. "The thing is, you never really explained why Positano meant so much to you."

"Yes I did. I told you I'd gone there with my parents."

"Yeah, but I've been to quite a few places with my parents, and none of them would produce that effect."

"Oh, I see," she says, stopping and turning to me. "It was the timing. That was our last holiday together. We went there in the May half term, which is right at the end of the month, and they died at the end of June."

I pull her close. "Your memories must be bittersweet."

"No. They're all good. I can't remember a single bad thing about Positano. Not one. That's how I was able to do what I did in the restaurant. It was cathartic for me too."

"I wondered," I tell her. "It occurred to me when I saw the photographs that you'd put a lot of us into it, but a lot of yourself too."

"Yes. I've never done that before."

I move a little closer. "It's almost like you belong there..."

She pulls back, looking down at my chest.

"Sorry," I say quickly, and we start walking again. "I'd like to take you back there one day."

"The restaurant?" she queries.

"No. Positano. I'd like to see it through your eyes."

"I'd like that too," she whispers, then stops again. "I need—"

"Please," I interrupt, putting my fingers over her lips to stop her speaking. I've got a bad feeling about what she's gonna say. "Please, just let me finish what I'm trying to say first. Then I'll listen to whatever you want."

She pauses, then nods her head.

"I've spent a lot of time over the last couple of days picturing the restaurant," I say, looking into her eyes. "That's why I just asked that question. I wanted to understand the connection better. I've tried imagining myself back there without you, and I can't do it." She goes to speak again, but I put my forefinger on her lips. "Please, Ali." She nods again and I take a breath before continuing, "I love that place, especially after everything you did to it. I love my brothers too, more than I'd ever tell them. But I'm gonna give it all up and move here to be with you, if that's what you need me to do." She gasps and tears well in her eyes. "I've got absolutely no idea how I'm gonna make it work. Ed will be devastated and I'll probably need to go back and explain it to him in person. I'll have sit down with him and Rob and see if they can buy me out. I'm not sure they can, and if not, I'll just have to find a job." That thought doesn't inspire me at all, but I don't say that out loud. "I'm not losing you, Ali. So, I've decided I'm gonna move here…"

Tears are falling down her cheeks now. "You… you haven't said anything to Rob and Ed yet, have you?" she asks.

"No."

"Thank God for that," she says.

"Like I said, I think it's something I need to do in person. Ed's kinda insecure. I'm not sure how he'll feel about the three of us splitting… Wait a second… What do you mean 'thank God for that'?" I ask, realizing what she just said.

"Thank you," she says.

"For what?" None of this is making much sense now, and the tears are still falling. I've gotta admit, I'm real confused.

"For saying all of that. For being willing to give up so much for me… for us."

"I'd give up everything for you."

"I know. But you don't have to."

"I don't?" Is she saying what I think she's saying?

"I've spoken to Tess," she says. "We had a really long talk. I know she's been preoccupied with her dissertation, and she probably needed more time to decide about the future, but you don't have any more time. I told her that I—I have to be with you. I can't give you up."

"Seriously?" I'm shaking. I think I must be in shock.

"Yes."

"And Tess?" I ask, because I know it's a big deal.

"She said she's scared of living in America, but she's more scared of being by herself, so she's agreed to come with me – with us." I can see the relief in her face.

"So, you're saying yes to marrying me?"

She nods her head, smiling.

"Wait… wait," I say. "If we're gonna do this, we're doing it properly."

I drop down onto one knee, looking up at her, and she gasps and puts her hands to her mouth.

"Say you'll marry me, Ali. Say yes. And say it out loud."

"Yes," she whispers through her tears.

I stand and pick her up, swinging her around in my arms, and she squeals in my ear.

"God, I love you," I yell at the top of my voice.

"I love you too," she whispers.

I lower her to the ground, holding onto her. "You'll really marry me?"

"Yes. I want to marry you, I want to live with you, in America. I want everything you're offering me – all of it."

I grin at her. "It's all yours. I'm all yours," I murmur and I lean down and kiss her.

"I thought you weren't a 'getting down on one knee' kind of guy," she says, when I finally break the kiss.

"And I keep telling you, you're different. You make me different." I kiss her again, then I take her hand and we carry on walking. "Why is Tess scared?" I ask after a couple of minutes of staring into her eyes and taking in that Ali is really going to be mine forever.

"It's new to her. She's not good with change. She didn't like moving to London, but she did it because of her Uni course, and because I was there. This is a huge step for her. It's a whole other country..." Her voice fades and I appreciate the enormity of what they're both doing.

"Well, we'll make her part of the family," I tell her.

"The family?"

"Yeah. We'll take care of her, but so will Rob and Ed."

"Rob?" She scoffs. "Rob will flirt with her."

"No. He's in love now, don't forget. She'll be quite safe with him."

"Oh yes. Petra... I'd forgotten. I wonder how that's going?"

"Knowing Rob, he's fucked up somehow."

"You haven't asked him?"

"No. He'll talk to me if he needs to. Anyway, I've spoken to Ed most of the time. I know Rob's helping out in the kitchen, and I guess Jasmine's maybe stepped up in the restaurant." I shrug. "To be honest, I've got no idea how they're managing."

"We need to get back there, don't we?" she says.

"Yeah. How quickly do you think we can do it?" Now I know we're going, I'm impatient to get home.

"You could leave at the weekend, as you planned and we can follow afterwards..." she suggests.

"No way." I stop and pull her into my arms. "We're going together. All of us."

She leans up and kisses me, then sighs. "Well, if we go back to London tomorrow, I guess we can close up the flat in a couple of days, sort out a visa for Tess and leave... maybe Tuesday or Wednesday? I don't think we can do it any quicker."

"Quicker? I half expected you to say a couple of weeks," I say, smiling down at her.

"There's really not that much to do," she explains. "We'll have to pack, but most of our things will need to be shipped."

"Will you sell the apartment too?"

"Yes. Tess and I talked that over. I'm going to leave it with my father's solicitor to deal with."

"You're cutting all ties?" I don't know why, but I'm surprised.

"Yes. You and I are getting married, remember? You belong in America. I belong with you."

"Yeah… you do. And Tess?"

"She's decided she belongs with me."

"You won't need to be separated, Ali." I say to reassure her. "She can live at the apartment with us, and we'll involve her in everything."

"Everything?" she smirks.

"Okay, not everything, but as much as we can."

"What about our honeymoon?" she asks. "I assume we'll have one…"

"Of course we will." I'm already planning it.

"And that will mean leaving her on her own, in Hartford." She bites her lip doubtfully.

"She can come with us, if you want."

"Um… no," she says, smiling. "Our honeymoon is for us."

"Okay, well, I'll make sure that Rob and Ed look after her then. It'll only be for a couple of weeks."

She nods her head, then turns toward me, taking my hands in hers and looking up at me.

"And you'll pack properly?" she asks.

"Pack properly?" I don't understand.

"Yes. You said there was something 'new' that you wanted to try with me but you didn't pack the right equipment…" her voice fades and her cheeks flush.

"If you think I'm waiting until our honeymoon for that, you're very much mistaken," I whisper. "That's happening on our first night back home."

"Oh… God, yes," she murmurs.

I lift her into my arms and turn back toward the house. "Don't worry about a thing, baby," I whisper into her ear, feeling her shudder in my arms. "From now on, I'm gonna make sure I've always got everything I need to give you everything you could ever want."

The End

Keep reading for an excerpt from Suzie Peters' forthcoming book
Play Games With Me
Part Two in the Recipes for Romance Series.

Available to purchase from September 7th 2018

Play Games With Me

Recipes for Romance: Book Two

by

Suzie Peters

Chapter One

Petra

I check my watch. It's five-thirty. I'm due at Rosa's in fifteen minutes and I really don't want to be late. I close the front door and pull my camera bag firmly onto my shoulder, setting off down the street. The walk should only take ten minutes, so I'm sure I'll be fine.

I clench and unclench my fists a few times as I walk. I'm excited and nervous at the same time. I'm excited because I love this kind of work. I love taking candid pictures, catching an atmosphere, creating something a little different. I'm nervous because I've never met the three owners of the restaurant, and I'm not great with strangers. I never have been. Still, I know at least one person who's gonna be there: Ali.

She's the one who commissioned me to take these photographs. She might not own the place, but she's been refurbishing it for the owners and, when I met up with her a couple of weeks ago to discuss her requirements, we got along really well. We were meant to just have a brief discussion over coffee at her hotel, but that turned into dinner and drinks. She's lovely – really lovely. She was upset, partly because she was feeling homesick for London, and also because she was having a hard time with one of the owners… a guy called Sam, who's the head chef, and who was being a bit of a jerk, from what she told me. That made me kinda nervous about meeting him, but when we spoke on the phone last week to finalize our arrangements, she sounded a lot more cheerful. She was a little coy about what was going on, but it wouldn't surprise me in the least if they've fallen for each other. I've got no idea what he's like, but she's beautiful. Any guy would be mad not to want her.

I'm sure I'll find out all about it later – assuming we get the chance to talk. Or maybe I'll just get to watch them together and work it out for myself, while I'm busy blending into the background. It's what I do best, usually in the hope that no-one will notice me. Not that many people do these days. Adrian saw to that. *Damn...* I haven't thought about him for ages and there he is, just when I need him the least – invading my head, making me feel insecure and self-conscious. Great.

I suppose it was inevitable I'd think about him tonight. He used to take me to Rosa's quite a lot – at least twice a week. That was years ago though, when it was run by a husband and wife – the parents of the current owners, so Ali informs me. They've evidently retired to Florida and left the restaurant to their sons, who've now renovated it, with Ali's expert guidance, and are re-opening tonight – an event for which I've been commissioned to take promotional photographs. I remember I used to talk to Rosa Moreno most times we went there. She ran the restaurant itself, while her husband worked in the kitchen. I was aware she had sons, because she always talked about them with such pride, but I thought there were only two – who were training to be chefs with their father.

Adrian loved this place – and so did I. The decor might have been dated but the food was always great. That's one of the reasons we ate there so often; until Adrian's accusations got too much. There are only so many times you can take being accused of sleeping with a guy, just because he's glanced up from his veal parmigiana and happens to have looked in your direction.

I'd thought at the time that, if we ate out less, I might lose some of the weight I'd been piling on, but Adrian insisted on doing the shopping, and the cooking... and my weight kept creeping up. In the end I worked out what he was doing. He was fattening me up. He was making me less attractive to other men. The problem was, that still didn't stop him from accusing me of sleeping with every man who came into my life: clients, models – especially models – repairmen, even the pizza delivery guy. His jealousy was oppressive. It was too oppressive.

The restaurant's just up ahead now and I slow down to catch my breath. I try and walk as much as I can these days, just to get some exercise. I don't like going to the gym, and I'm really not good with routine, but I know I need to do something to keep fit – well, to get fit in the first place, to be honest. I've managed to lose some of the weight in the four years since Adrian left, but I'm still not the size six I used to be before I met him. I'm stuck at a size ten.

I'm starting to regret my high-heeled boots now, and how I'm going to get through the next few hours in them is another matter, but as I stand and look at the exterior of the restaurant, I forget all about the discomfort. It's beautiful. Before, it was all dark wood and slightly garish lettering. Now, the paintwork is dark gray, the windows are plain glass – so you can see inside to the subtly lit interior – and there are two trimmed bay trees either side of the door. It's understated and refined. I like it a lot.

I take a deep breath, and reach inside my open-necked blouse for the necklace I wear every single day, clutching the silver letter 'A' between my thumb and forefinger and pressing it against my lips. "Wish me luck, baby," I whisper, then let it drop back down and check I'm not showing too much cleavage before I push on the door and let myself in.

I stand just inside and take in the changes. It looks so different. All the dark wood has gone. The tables are covered with white linen cloths and surrounded by gray leather high-backed chairs. The walls are painted white and dotted with beautiful framed pictures. From here, I can't tell exactly what they're all of, but the ones I can see are really lovely. The back wall is the most noticeable feature: a large photograph of a magical-looking cliff-side town at night covers the entire expanse, but it's been broken up by white vertical lines. It's a truly stunning effect.

"Petra." Ali appears from a corridor at the back of the restaurant. "I'm so sorry. I should have been here to meet you." She comes toward me, making her way between the tables. She's as beautiful as her surroundings. She's got very light blonde hair, which I know is long and curly, but tonight she's wearing it in a loose up-do, and rather than the jeans that she wore at our meeting, she's got on a really stylish deep red dress, which shows off her slim figure. Ordinarily, she'd be the kind of woman I'd love to hate – because she's just so perfect – except I think it's impossible to hate Ali. She's way too nice.

"It's fine." I step forward and she hugs me. "I've just been admiring your handiwork. It's remarkable."

She blushes. "Oh… thank you."

"I can't believe how different it looks."

"Of course. I forgot, you used to come here, didn't you?"

"In a previous life, yes. It's so much better now."

Her blush deepens and she checks her watch – either because she's embarrassed by my compliments, or because she's concerned that time's moving on and the first guests are probably due to arrive soon.

"I could do with getting some light readings," I say to her. "Do you mind if I dump my bag behind the bar and just wander a little?"

"Feel free." She steps out of the way so I can move further into the restaurant. "I really need to get on anyway. I've got to find Rob. He's in the office, giving the waiting staff a last-minute pep-talk, but he should be out here by now…"

"You carry on," I say. "Just ignore me."

"I'd never do that," she says, moving toward the corridor again.

"Ah, but that's the whole point," I remark. "If I'm visible, I'm not doing my job properly."

"If you need anything, just let me know," she calls over her shoulder, before disappearing again.

I can hear voices coming from the back of the restaurant – the kitchens I guess, and I wonder, just for a moment, how nervous they all are. Still, I've got my own nerves to deal with. I go over to the bar, the front of which is covered by what appears to be a huge sheet of perspex, with a soft white light behind it. It's another nice feature that Ali's added. I open my camera bag, retrieve my Canon, put on the zoom lens and stow the bag in the corner – out of the way, hopefully – and I take a look around. The lighting is quite subtle in here and it's gonna be a challenge to get the kind of shots I know they want, but I'm always ready for a challenge.

Under the bar are some matches and I grab a box and go to one of the tables in the back corner of the restaurant and light the candle in the centre, stowing the matches in my jacket pocket. I want to take a few micro images of the table setting. They'll be useful for Ali anyway, but they'll also help me to get the camera settings right.

I'm staring through the view finder when I hear the sound of murmuring voices and am aware of a group of people coming into the restaurant from the corridor. They head straight for the bar, seemingly unaware of me, and I ignore them and carry on with what I'm doing.

"I don't know what you mean. I'd never do such a thing." I hear a deep male, kinda sexy-sounding voice, coming from the corridor, but continue taking my shots. I've gotta try and get this right before the guests arrive.

"Yes you would – and we both know it," Ali replies, laughing. "Just try and behave, for one night. Please?"

"Okay. I'll try."

I'm currently crouched on the floor, a few feet from the table, focusing on trying to get the depth of field right. I check the image I've just taken on the screen at the back of the camera. It's not quite right and I make a couple of adjustments and try again, conscious now that someone is standing right beside me.

"Two seconds," I say, assuming I must be in their way.

"No problem." That's Ali's voice, so I take the shot and look up at her. "I was just going to introduce you to Rob," she adds, and moves to one side, just as I'm getting to my feet to be faced by a pair of dark, smoldering eyes. At this precise moment, I'm grateful that I always wear my camera strapped around my neck, because I've just dropped it, and I'm fairly sure my mouth's fallen open as well… and my tongue's probably hanging out too. God, I hope not. That would be so embarrassing. Oh Lord… He's gorgeous. Utterly and completely gorgeous. He's tall – very tall – with short, dark hair that's spiked on top, light stubble, a square jaw and full lips. He's wearing a black shirt that shows he's got very broad shoulders, muscular arms, and a perfectly formed chest.

I don't know how long we've been standing here while I study him, but I really should say something. I'm saved the trouble by him taking a slight step forward.

"Hi," he says and I recognize the deep sexy voice I heard a few moments ago. Dear God. He's the complete package. Tall, dark, handsome, sexy… total fantasy material. Except this isn't a fantasy. He's real, and he's standing right in front of me.

"Hello." I whisper and manage to hold out my hand. He takes it and, not taking his eyes from mine, he raises it to his lips, kissing my fingers. My legs turn to jelly, my stomach flips, and I grab hold of the nearest chair to steady myself. Did he really just do that?

"Rob, this is Petra Miller," Ali says, and I'm grateful to her for saying something, being as my vocal chords seem to have temporarily malfunctioned.

"Petra," he murmurs, still holding my hand. My name on his lips sounds like stardust falling from the sky. He focuses for a moment on my mouth, then my eyes and then my hair, before smiling. "You look like an angel," he says.

I stare at him. An angel… me? Oh. I get it now. He's flirting, and I can't help but smirk. "An angel in torn jeans and a leather jacket?" I counter.

"Yeah," he says, looking a little quizzical.

"Well," I reply, pulling my hand away, "I hope you like your angels with attitude."

He smirks himself and his eyes light up, and maybe widen, just a fraction, before he moves a little closer. "Oh, yeah. That's my favorite kind of angel," he whispers.

Rob

"Has everyone got it?" I ask, looking around the collected faces before me in my office. They all nod, but I wish they'd look a little more convinced. "Sure?" I say. Again they nod. "If you have any problems, come find me or Ali. I'd rather you asked than kept quiet." We've been retraining the restaurant staff for the last few days, and I'm fairly sure they know what they're doing, but they seem nervous. I guess that's understandable. They know my brothers and I have a lot riding on this. We've spent a lot of money on the refurbishment, and now the opening is here, we're all feeling pretty anxious – although I'm trying real hard not to let it show.

There's a quiet knock on the door, it opens and Ali steps inside.

"Rob?" she says quietly. Everyone turns to look at her. "Have you seen the time?"

I check my watch. "Shit." Where did that last half hour go? "Okay, everyone. Let's get out there."

Ali stands to one side and lets the others pass, waiting for me.

"Okay?" she asks, stopping me by the doorway.

"Yeah," I whisper. "I didn't realize time had run away with me quite that much, but we're about as ready as we're ever gonna be."

"Calm down," she says, encouragingly. "Everything will be just fine. I promise."

She must sense my nerves.

"Yeah. I know. You've done all this before, haven't you?"

"Just once or twice. But I do understand that it's harder for you. It's your restaurant. Well, yours, and Sam's and Ed's."

"How are they?" I ask, nodding toward the kitchen doors opposite.

"I've got no idea. I haven't been in there."

"Probably for the best," I reply, smiling.

We start down the corridor toward the restaurant. The six wait staff are all gathered by the bar, chatting among themselves. I deliberately chose our most experienced employees for tonight. We can't afford to get this wrong.

Ali stops me just as we get to the end of the corridor.

"Do you think there's any chance you could avoid flirting too much tonight?" she asks, a smile lighting up her face. It's at times like this I really understand why my big brother Sam is so in love with her. He may not have done very much about it yet, but I completely understand his feelings. She's beautiful… really beautiful. And if he ever does get around to getting it right with her, and she even half returns his feelings, he's gonna be one lucky son-of-a-bitch.

"I don't know what you mean," I reply, grinning back at her. "I'd never do such a thing." We both know I flirted like mad with her when she first came here all those weeks ago, before we employed her to refurbish the place and she wanted to see us without us putting on a show for her. Man did I put on a show… and lived to regret it when she revealed her true identity. She took it well though, and we've become friends.

"Yes you would – and we both know it," Ali replies, laughing at me now. "Just try and behave, for one night. Please?"

"Okay. I'll try." I fake a pout and we go out into the restaurant.

She grabs my arm and lowers her voice. "We've just got time for me to introduce you Petra," she whispers. This is the photographer she told us all about, the one who's gonna be taking some publicity shots for us tonight. "She looks busy, but…" Ali leads me over to the back corner of the restaurant between the tables. Crouched down on the floor I can see someone with a thick mane of dark hair, her shoulders encased in a black leather jacket. She's got a camera held to her face, so that's pretty much all I can see. Ali stops a couple of feet away from her and waits.

"Two seconds." I can just about hear Petra's voice and I'm reminded of how sexy she sounded on the phone when she called a while back to speak to Ali.

"No problem," Ali replies. "I was just going to introduce you to Rob."

Petra finishes up and, moving the camera away from her face, she gets to her feet. My mouth dries and my chest feels like someone dropped a lead weight onto it. How the fuck am I supposed to breathe now? She's perfect. She's completely perfect. Okay, so she's maybe a little tall, but who cares? Other than that, she's perfect. I guess she's around five foot eleven, but I'm six-two, so that's fine. And she's curvy, which his great because I'm really not that keen on skinny women. She's also perfectly proportioned. Her full, large breasts are straining slightly against her white blouse, making it gape slightly between the buttons. I can see a tantalizing hint of white lace beneath just before her camera drops from her hands and covers the view. Letting my eyes roam downwards, I take in her rounded hips and the ripped jeans that encase her shapely thighs, as well as the sexy high heeled black boots. I guess I can revise my earlier perspective. Take the heels off – although I'd really rather not – and she'd be around five foot seven – which makes her exactly what I thought she was already: perfect.

I manage to raise my eyes back to her face again. She's got light olive, absolutely flawless skin, and sparkling gray eyes, and her lips are full, slightly pouting, and really kissable.

I'm suddenly aware that I've been standing here staring at her and that I really should say something before I stumble over my own tongue.

"Hi." I mutter, moving slightly closer to her. Is that really the best I can do?

"Hello," she whispers and the sound of her voice reverberates straight to my cock. She holds out her hand but I don't want to just shake with her, and I remember something my dad used to do to my mom, which always used to make her smile. I take her hand in mine and, while keeping my eyes fixed on hers, I raise it to my lips and very gently kiss her fingers. The contact is electrifying – like nothing else I've ever felt before. Weirdly, she grabs hold of the back of the chair beside her, staring at me, but unlike my mom, she doesn't smile. I'm not sure that was the reaction I was looking for.

"Rob, this is Petra Miller," Ali says, bringing me back to my senses – well kind of.

"Petra," I murmur, still holding her hand. Her name suits her. It's exotic and erotic – and there's something about her that exudes both of those qualities.

I gaze at her lips, wishing I could lean forward and kiss them, then move my attention to her sparkling eyes, and then her hair, which flows in shiny black ringlets over and around her shoulders. It's wild, untamed and long enough to hang below her breasts. She's standing right beneath one of the down lighters and it gives her a kind of glow – a kind of angelic aura. "You look like an angel," I say quietly, voicing my thoughts.

She stares at me for a moment, looking a little confused, and then a slight smirk appears on her face. "An angel in torn jeans and a leather jacket?" she replies. I wonder if she thinks I'm flirting. I'm not. I'm being serious. Sappy, yeah… but serious.

"Yeah," I say. I hope she gets it. I hope she understands that, to me, she's an angel. A perfect angel.

Her smirk becomes a smile, but she pulls her hand away from mine. "Well, I hope you like your angels with attitude."

My cock hardens to steel, and I can't help but smirk myself, before I move just a fraction closer to her. "Oh, yeah," I whisper. "That's my favorite kind of angel."

Her smile widens, her mouth opens and I catch sight of her tongue. Fuck, she's hot.

"Rob," Ali says, interrupting the steamy direction my thoughts having been traveling since the moment I first set eyes on Petra.

I reluctantly turn toward her. "Yeah?"

"Customers."

Fuck.

"Go do your job," she urges, pushing me toward the front of the restaurant.

"I'm going." I quickly turn back to Petra. "See you later?" I say to her. She nods, just once, and that's all I need… for now.

I always knew tonight was gonna be busy, but it's surpassed even my expectations. We're about three hours in, and it's been crazy. I've already taken bookings for the next six weeks or so, and I've had to set up a cancellation list, which is a first for us. I've hardly had two seconds to look at Petra, let alone talk to her, but I'm aware of her all the time. And that's weird, because she's kind of invisible. She real unobtrusive, melting into the background, like she belongs here, and I really like that idea.

At around nine-thirty, I realize she hasn't had anything to drink all evening and, while I'm behind the bar, covering for Greg so he can take a quick break, I manage to attract her attention and call her over.

"Red or white?" I say simply.

"Sorry?" she replies.

"Wine… red or white. You haven't had anything to drink all night."

"Oh. Um… just water, thanks. I need a completely clear head."

"Okay. Water it is." I grab a highball, fill it with ice, add a couple of slices of lime, and a couple of sprigs of fresh mint, and pour over the San Pellegrino, handing it across to her.

"Thank you," she says, giving me a beautiful smile.

"You're welcome."

"It's going well," she says, taking a small sip.

"Yeah, it is."

All of a sudden, a guy near the back of the restaurant starts clapping and I glance over Petra's shoulder to see what's going on, a smile spreading across my lips. Sam and Ed are standing by the entrance to the corridor that leads to the kitchen, looking – frankly – embarrassed, as the whole restaurant explodes into spontaneous applause.

"What's going on?" Petra says, leaning forward.

I look back at her, glimpsing her sublime cleavage, and it's all I can do not to groan – loudly.

"My brothers," I reply, nodding toward them. She turns, then looks back at me again.

"They're the chefs, right?"

"Yeah. They never normally come out here, but I guess Ali talked them into it. I know she was gonna try." She told me about this earlier today. I warned her she probably wouldn't get them to agree, but I guess she's more persuasive than I thought… especially with Sam.

Slowly, everyone starts to settle down again, resuming their seats, although I notice a couple of people go over and shake Sam and Ed by the hand. It's a nice touch and I'm pleased for them. I always make sure to pass on the praise we get from customers, but it's good for them to see the appreciation for their food first hand.

Sam and Ed return to the kitchen just as Greg comes back from his break and I go around the other side of the bar.

"I'd better get back to work," Petra says. She looks a little flushed, but I guess it's warm in here.

"Oh… okay." I'd been hoping we'd have a few minutes to talk, but that's okay… it can wait until the end of the evening.

"Thanks for the drink."

"Just let Greg know if you want anything else," I tell her. "Or find me."

"Okay."

She gives me another smile and moves further back into the restaurant. I lean against the bar and watch her as she passes between the tables, her hips swaying gently. Looking at that perfect ass in those tight jeans, I think I'd give away my share in this place for one night with her. Except I already know one night won't be enough. One lifetime won't be enough. I'm still staring at her, thinking about what that means to a guy who's always specialized in one night stands, when the sound of the front door opening brings me back to reality. I can think that through later. Right now, it's time to work…

I turn and switch on the smile, to be faced by four women.

"Good evening, ladies," I say.

One of them steps forward – well, to be more precise, she elbows her way forward, flashing her teeth and cleavage in my direction. "We've booked a table," she simpers. She's pretty, tall, blonde, stacked. Apart from the hair color, I'd say she'd normally be my type… until about three hours ago, that is.

"Okay. What name?" I ask.

"Barnes. Alexa Barnes."

I scan my iPad, find their reservation and look up again. "Great. If you'd like to follow me?"

As I turn, I notice Ali standing at the entrance to the corridor. She raises an eyebrow, a slight smirk on her face and I smile back at her before she disappears again. I know what she's thinking. I don't blame her, but I've got no intention of flirting… not with anyone but Petra, anyway. Since meeting her, I'm just not interested in anyone else; it's like every other woman has just faded into insignificance.

I guide the four women through to table eleven, which is at the rear of the restaurant, help them to their seats, and hand out their menus.

"Ria will be looking after you this evening," I tell them and go to move away.

The one called Alexa reaches out and grabs my arm. "You mean we won't be getting your personal attention," she says.

"Of course you will." What else can I say? "If you need anything, just let me know." I pull my arm away as gently as I can.

"Anything at all?" She looks up at me through her thick eyelashes.

I don't reply this time. Instead, I just give her a smile. Ordinarily, I would have probably told her she could have anything she wanted – and I'd have meant it. Now I just want to tell her I'm not interested and I'm not available. I can't do that politely, so the smile seems like a good compromise.

We're officially closed now, but the table of four women are taking their time over coffee, as are a couple of other diners. Petra's been busy all evening and we haven't had any further chance to talk. As it's gotten quieter in here, I've noticed her taking a few shots of the pictures on the wall… the ones of Positano. She keeps stopping and looking at them, like she's intrigued. I'd like to go over and explain what they are – that our parents are from there and that Ali went out of her way to source the images – but I can't, not until I'm officially off duty anyway. Right now, she's sitting at the bar, talking to Ali, while the rest of us are clearing down tables, although I'm slowly letting the wait staff go, as the place gets quieter. Eventually, there's just me, Ria, Ali and Petra left.

Finally, Alexa Barnes asks for their check and, trying not to noticeably heave a sigh of relief, I take it over myself. Ria's dealing with the other couple, who are just paying too. When Alexa Barnes hands me her credit card, she slips a piece of paper into my hand at the same time. I don't react. I just slide it into my pocket and process her payment, returning her card to her. I show them to the door and, as we pass the bar, she puts her hand on my arm again, pulling me back slightly. "Call me," she whispers. Again, I don't make any response.

"I hope you all had a great evening," I say, loud enough for her friends to hear.

"We did," one of the others replies, turning around. "It's really lovely in here now."

"Thank you," I reply, ushering them out the door, more than relieved to see the back of them.

I go back inside, looking forward to having a few minutes to talk to Petra, and maybe taking the chance to persuade her to stay and share a drink with us.

"Rob?" Ria calls me from the back of the restaurant.

"Yeah."

"I've got a problem."

So much for a few minutes with Petra… I go over and Ria explains that her iPad hasn't recorded any of the drinks that were ordered by the couple she's attending to. They've been honest enough to point out that their check is wrong, and they're quite right – there are no drinks charged. I take Ria's iPad and go back through the order and, sure enough, there's nothing showing. The couple assure me they both had a cocktail before eating, then shared a bottle of Pinot Grigio, and the guy had a Jack Daniels with his coffee. I hope to God neither of them is driving…

"It's fine," I tell them. "It's on the house. It's our mistake."

"Seriously?" the guy says, clearly surprised.

"Of course." I smile at him.

"But that's gotta be seventy bucks," he replies.

"Like I say… it's on the house." It hasn't actually cost us seventy bucks, but he's about right with what we would have charged him.

"Well, thanks," he says, holding out his hand to me as he gets to his feet.

I shake hands with the guy and give Ria back her iPad at the same time.

"Our pleasure, sir." I hold his wife's chair while she gets up. "Would you like me to get you a cab?" It seems wise to offer, in the circumstances.

"No, it's fine. We only live a block away. We're gonna walk."

Thank fuck for that…

Ria shows them out while I finish clearing their table.

"Is that coming out of my salary?" she asks, walking back to me. She sounds really worried.

"No." I turn to face her. "You know that's not how we operate, Ria. It was a mistake, that's all."

"I'm sure I recorded it," she adds, although she doesn't sound that convinced.

"Is there a problem?" Ali comes over.

"I'm not sure." I hand her Ria's iPad and explain what's happened.

"Did anyone else have a problem tonight?" Ali asks.

"No," I reply.

"Okay. Well, we'll see if it happens again and, if not we'll just have to assume it's a glitch."

What she means is we'll just have to assume Ria got it wrong, but she's too kind to say that.

"I'm sorry," Ria says.

"It's fine." I put my hand on her shoulder. "It's a few drinks. Nobody died. Besides, they're gonna tell all their friends what nice guys we are. It'll probably do us good in the long run."

She smiles, just lightly, although I know she'll feel bad about it.

"Go on… you get off home," I say. "You've done really well tonight."

"Are you sure?"

She'd dead on her feet. "Yeah. I'm sure. I'll see you on Monday."

I think we're all real glad that tomorrow's Sunday and we've got a policy of closing on Sundays. It's something our dad started when he first opened the restaurant thirty years ago. He was always real strict about the hours he was prepared to work. He decided to open for lunch, then close again at three and have a couple of hours off, before the evening session. And on Sundays, he chose to remain closed all day. Even when all our competitors started to stay open all day, seven days a week, he resisted. Dad wanted to have at least one day he could spend with his family, and although we don't always do much family stuff anymore, it's nice to have one day to ourselves.

Ria pulls off her black apron and makes her way toward the corridor, to go out through the back door in the kitchen, just as I turn and find that the rest of the place is empty, other than Ali, who's still standing right in front of me. Petra has gone already.

... to be continued

Printed in Dunstable, United Kingdom

77803346R00191